THE ORIGINS OF FAITH

Israel does not have, and never did have, a divine right to the land of Palestine

Best wishes

Mike Kelley

'During times of universal deceit,

telling the truth becomes a revolutionary act.'
George Orwell

'Those who can make you believe in absurdities

can make you commit atrocities.'

Voltaire

'From the beginning men used God to justify the unjustifiable.'

Salman Rushdie, *The Satanic Verses*

ISBN: 978-1-291-77292-0

Typeset in 12 Garamond

Mike Kelley (Publisher)

50 Beech Avenue

Alfreton

Derbyshire, DE55 7EW

England

mgkelley@hotmail.com

Ordering Information:
Special discounts are available on quantity purchases by corporations, associations, educators, and others. For details, contact the publisher at the above listed address.

Acknowledgements

I would like to thank David Ratner without whose help this book would never have been completed.

Thank you for your patience, guidance and your use of the editor's red pen…

Dedication

To my lovely wife Valerie

London - England

Bending down to retrieve his paper programme, which had fallen to the floor, Jacques Gendron only half heard the cry of, 'Allah Akbar'. (God is great) The cry meant nothing to him, so did not register.

First there was a blinding flash, followed quickly by a deafening raw, knocking Jacques to the floor between the rows of seats and stunning him. Dazed and unsure of what had happened he just lay there for a few moments. There was a pregnant silence; graphically broken by piercing screams all around.

'Mary', mumbled Jacques. 'Mary', he repeated, but there was no answer from his wife. He was wet! Why was he wet? He just could not understand what had happened, nor register his thoughts, his head was buzzing and his ears hurt. He struggled to comprehend why he was wet, as though that was his priority. 'Mary', he said again. It took a lot of effort for him to do so, but with a heave he pulled her toward him, turning her around at the same time to face him. As he did so Jacques mouth opened in a silent scream. He could not comprehend what he was looking at; his beautiful wife Mary had no face! There was no skin, just a mess of blood and flesh, blood was all over him, one of her eyes had disappeared; the other hung there lifeless on her cheek, dangling on sinews; her beautiful hair, so immaculate just moments before, had been torn off. Jacques senselessly reached to pick up a handful of her hair, experiencing for the first time a terrible pain in his shoulder. Some unknown objects had penetrated his left shoulder ripping large gashes into his flesh.

People began climbing over him and his stricken wife, in their attempts to rushed towards the exits. Jacques tried vainly to project her, but people in their panic just did not know what they were doing. Screams of fear and agony rent the air, while Jacques tried unsuccessfully to haul himself up. As he did so, there was another cry above the din of, 'Allah Akbar', which came from the vicinity of the exits, toward which the frenzied people were heading.

Jacques remembered nothing of what happened next.

A day later he lay in a hospital bed, still trying to comprehend what had happened. As he lay there he was almost in a dreamlike state; his physical pain dulled by the drugs administered to him, but not his mental pain. 'My beautiful wife,' he thought to himself, lying there whilst trying to recollect the events of that dreadful day. A day which had started so well. He recalled Mary's joy and how her face had beamed with happiness as they walked briskly together, with her clutching hold of his arm. She had been to the hair dresser that morning and her long blond hair looked resplendent, bouncing off her shoulders as she walked. He wistfully went back in his mind and recalled thinking how contented he was seeing her bubbling with excited joy. It was hard for him to bring back this recent memory.

He remember how she had said, 'Thank you my darling, I'm so glad you found time to bring me here. You know how I love these occasions,' and how she had cocked her head to one side giving him, the man whom she adored, a beautiful beaming smile.

Jacques was an executive for an international oil company, and as such he led a very busy life. He travelled the world, looking after the many needs and demands required of his position. His lean stature and slim face, in normal times, concealed a hard and determined character required of such a man skilled in trouble-shooting for the vast petro-chemical industry. In rare times of anger his piercing blue eyes could cut right through those who opposed him. As always, that fateful morning he had set out with a purpose in his stride; smartly dressed and clean shaven with the wife he deeply loved by his side.

It was hard for him to come to terms with the fact that his wife Mary was now dead. He just did not want to, and no he could not, accept this. He tried to find some comfort by going over in his mind those last precious hours together.

Mary had been born in London, England, but after she married Jacques, the love of her life, she had taken his nationality as a Canadian citizen. They had made their home in Calgary, the capital city of the state of Alberta; an area of truly outstanding breath-taking grandeur. It was a modern city that Mary soon began to call home. Although she had been very happy in Calgary, occasionally she still pined for her home town of London. Whenever she could she would persuade Jacques to take time out from his busy schedule allowing her to return to her roots. That terrible day, was just such a day.

Jacques recalled her saying how much London had changed since she had been a girl there. So many people had moved into that city; people who were from so many different ethnic backgrounds to that of her own. In spite of London's dramatic racial changes, from that of its traditional culture, she still missed much of London's vibrant life.

It was to appease this feeling within her that Jacques had arranged a special day for her. He smiled when he thought of how she had been just like a little girl at Christmas time, putting her head on his shoulder pulling him closer to her in a one arm loving embrace, whilst striding out together. They had made their way toward the stadium of White Hart Lane, the home of London's Tottenham Hotspur Football Club. 'Spurs'; as everybody called this team. There had been many occasions when they would participate in friendly banter about the name of this sport; should it be called 'Football', as Mary called it, along with most of the world, or should it be called 'Soccer'? For Jacques, and those from North America, it was always Soccer, but for Mary it had to be Football: but for both of them it didn't really matter.

The weather had been dark and grey, with an impenetrable layer of cloud giving a solid covering; which was typical for a November day in London. Even so, it had not dampened the atmosphere for Mary. She had been excited and happy at the thought of watching her favourite team. That day Spurs were to play against one of the most successful teams in the world of football; namely of Manchester United.

In some considerable discomfort Jacques lay on his hospital bed looking up at the ceiling of his private room, while reflecting on Mary's constant chatter during that day. She was in full voice as they had walked toward the stadium; full of the plans she was making for Christmas. Then, as these images of joy came to his mind, tears flooded his eyes.

It had never ceased to amaze Jacques, just how popular was this game of soccer; many times as he had travelled the world outside of North America, he found it truly was a worldwide sport. Wherever he went in the world it was there; from the Middle East to the Far East, even in the smallest villages of Africa. On one occasion he had been somewhat taken aback when coming across rough goalposts erected in the middle of nowhere, in deepest Yemen. 'Amazing', he thought, 'even here where there are no visitors or international contacts, yet they still play this game of soccer.'

More than anything else, he knew how his wife had loved this sport, even though the low scoring levels was something he himself did not always understand. He was more used to the high scoring games common in North America, such as basketball and ice hockey. 'The irresistible force against the immovable object,' had been one of Mary's many attempts to explain this game to him, but he had never really grasped that idea. Still, he had been happy that morning as they walked together towards the stadium, because she was happy, and that had been enough for him; he had adored her.

Across from the entrance to the stadium, had stood a programme seller, a man with a large scarf denoting the colours of Spurs was wrapped several times around his neck. 'Programme Sir?' he had asked. Buying the programme had been a matter-of-fact gesture, which Jacques had not given much thought to at the time. Then after he had paid for this programme they both entered the turnstile and climbed the steps into the ground.

'Just look how many are here,' Jacques remembered saying as he looked at the number of people within the stadium in amazement. 'There are tens of thousands here. And to think this is repeated in every city in Britain,' he had muttered to Mary, whilst thinking of all the money involved in this truly international game; but then thought, 'I better not bring this subject up just now. After all I just want her to enjoy the occasion.'

He remembered looking for their seats which were situated on the far side of the ground directly opposite the player's entrance. It was so cold in the spectator's stands as they settled down, and those hard plastic seats did not make him feel any warmer. Still, it was reasonable seat with a fine view of the playing area. Groups of fans from different sections of the crowd were chanting; but Jacques could seldom tell what they saying, yet the chanting seemed to be all in good humour.

Lying now on his hospital bed, he tried to think what her last words to him were. 'It should be a good game', she had said as she studied their recently purchased programme, page by page, eagerly devouring every word.

Jacques remembered glancing over towards her open programme, 'Just look at all those player's names they must have come from all over the world to play here,' he had said.

'Yes they have,' agreed Mary. 'This is why this league is so popular; they attract the best players of the world. Look', she exclaimed as she had peered intently down the tunnel entrance on the far side of the ground. 'They are getting ready to come out.'

He always found it odd, that there was none of the razzmatazz associated with most North American games, no marching bands and no cheer-leaders: for one thing it was too cold and wet for such girls. Still it had been an intense, exciting atmosphere. Then the welcoming roar erupted from the crowd, as the first glimpse of the emerging teams were seen by the expectant fans. Almost in unison, those assembled for the anticipated spectacle, had risen to their feet. 'Except for me', recalled Jacques. 'I had been in no particular rush to stand up, I had just made myself so comfortable sitting down. I remember smiling at her as I looked up to her standing with the rest. She was jumping up and down with excitement, and clapping her hands at the same time.' Jacques smiled to himself as he reflected on those last few moments, it had made him feel good to see her so happy: her beautiful eyes shining - then he began to cry again.

'It was that programme which saved me. God how I wish I had died with her,' his thoughts were now running away, and felt strangely guilty to be still alive, as the terror of those last moments flooded his mind. 'I remember slowly and methodically starting to rise to my feet,' he recalled to himself, 'I had decided that I should also stand up with her, for I could no longer see the spectacle if I had remained seated. Then, just as I stood up, I had to bend down again to retrieve the paper programme which had slipped off Mary's lap and onto the floor. As I bent down they killed my beautiful wife.' Jacques slid down further into the bed, in an attempt to hide his sobs.

****

London - England

Adnan Al Saqqaff was satisfied with his work. His young face, largely hidden by a long ragged full black beard, was grim, but determined. The room he was in, located above a fast-food take-away shop, was small and unkempt, discarded pieces of paper strewn around. Taking his time, his piercing dark eyes slowly looked at the seven men who stared at him with expressionless faces, each of whom were anticipating Adnan's words. Adnan made eye contact with each one as he looked intently into their expectant eyes.

'Mahmoud Daoud and Ali Saleh are true martyrs of Islam,' he began. 'They will be receiving their rewards in heaven now. They are the most fortunate of people, for they stand now in front of the full glory of Allah, and his holy prophet Mohammed - peace be upon him.'

'Peace be upon him,' they all repeated.

'Think of those rewards my brothers. Rewards which only God in his wisdom can give, rewards the like of which we cannot even begin to imagine. Our brothers will be receiving those rewards now. How we wish we could be with them. Your chance will come, for this is only the beginning.' Adnan paused whilst gathering his thoughts, his intense gaze and dominant personality demanded attention.

We are surrounded by infidels, who will not bow to Allah. Their life style shows contempt for the teachings of the Prophet. Look how they allow their women to dress! They flaunt their sexuality walking around the streets in tight fitting clothes, revealing their bodies and inviting a man's eyes to sin. They strut their bodies causing wilfully causing God fearing men to sin. These Westerners have sex like donkeys; they fill their bodies with alcohol and pay no attention to the only true God.' Adnan's voice went up an octave, 'So they should not be surprised that we, God's warriors, will wreak God's vengeance upon them. Yes we will terrorise them!'

Mumbled agreements came for the assembled seven.

Adnan had been born in England, where he studied hard to become a chemist. His Pakistani parents had found it difficult to settle into their new life after arriving in England. They were now in a strange country where they felt their own culture had little in common with the practices, behaviour and beliefs of the indigenous British. It was for the hope of a better life that his father had moved his family from Pakistan. The wages and living conditions were so much better for him in England; and although this new country was so very different to his own, his father had continued to run a strict religious household. His father's religious zeal had moulded Adnan's views on life, but his deeply held Jihadist beliefs had been instilled into him during his time in Yemen and Somalia. As a student he became incensed at what he considered to be Britain and America's attacks on Islam, resulting in him constantly letting his feelings be known and heard in his local mosque. As a result he had been approached by radical members of his congregation to consider a way he could give vent to his pent up feelings.

It had been so easy for him to get to both Yemen and Somalia. First he had taken a flight from London to Dubai, then a second flight onward to Yemen's capital, the ancient walled city of Sana'a. After the fall of Ali Saleh, the former President of Yemen, Al-Qaeda had managed to build an almost independent autonomous state within Southern Yemen. These religious extremists played on the resentment still felt in Southern Yemen for their defeat and subjugation by the Northern forces of Ali Saleh back in 1994. The radical Aden-Abyan-Islamic-Army had merged with Al-Qaeda and now they fermented terrorist actions and guerrilla warfare against the North. Adnan was welcomed by them with open arms. His hosts quickly moved away from Sana'a to the homeland of Al-Qaeda in the South. They were keen to embrace someone who could work for them deep inside the territory of the hated West. Yemen for a long time had a justified reputation of producing fighters for foreign wars, and Adnan was another such fighter, a fighter with good western connections. However, Yemen was only his first destination.

After staying in Sana'a for a several months undergoing further indoctrination and Jihadist training, arrangements were made for him to sail on a traditional Arabic wooden dhow across the Gulf of Aden, from Aden to Somalia. There he stayed for almost a year. His training in both these countries had been intense, undergoing the rigors required of all those who wished to become skilled in the disciplines of Jihadist warfare. His hosts in Somalia were Al-Shabab, another militant Islamic cell of Al-Qaeda. As had been the case in Yemen, they trained their Islamic fundamentalist recruits well, delighting in the prospect of terror such well trained activist could bring on their unsuspecting hosts. Now Adnan was carrying out, what he considered to be, his divine mission of terror against the hated enemies of Islam.

'The only thing which is good in this world is faith in Allah.' Adnan looked upward with a glazed look in his eyes as he said this. 'This is Allah's earth, Allah created it, Allah gave everything to them', referring to unbelievers. 'If they choose to disdain the work of Allah, then they must reap the violent consequences. We have done a great service to Allah this week, but we will do more; much, much more. All enemies of Islam will be called to account, and we are the tools God uses.' There was silence in the room, as they gave Adnan their rapt attention, along with their deep admiration. 'Look how they not only tolerate homosexuals, but encourage such godless men. They allow those godless sinners to walk the streets. Such an abomination deserves God's punishment by stoning to death. Sharia Law demands death for their unnatural wanton actions of their evil sin.'

They nodded and murmured their agreement, as Adnan continued, 'When Allah is followed and Sharia Law is the law of this land those who steal will suffer the just punishment of amputation. And any who speak against Islam will be beheaded. Islam will rule the world. Disbelievers are the firewood of hell. Allah Akbar.'

'Allah Akbar,' was the instant response.

Adnan continued this rhetoric for which he had become well known among the believers, 'Do they really think that a bunch of filthy retarded kuffars (unbelievers) are going to stop us from doing God's will? Do they really think such idiots can stop the fastest growing religion on earth from spreading? All those British and American troops who have invaded Muslim lands will continue to be slaughtered and by God's will they will continue to return home in body-bags.' A cheer went up from those listening. 'It will continue this way until they withdraw from Muslim lands. Until then,' Adnan's voice rose again, 'they must be prepared for things to get much worse, for them in their own lands. Inshallah (God willing) all the filthy scum invading Muslim countries will burn in hell. A hell we will make for them. Amen.'

'Amen, amen, amen,' repeated the group.

The noise of the traffic outside did not distract Adnan, he was in full swing now, 'Just a small bomb of only two pounds can do a lot of damage, especially if shrapnel of nuts or nails is taped to it. Just by putting one in the middle of a busy street we could hit maybe fifty or sixty unbelieving kuffars. Seven or eight bombs in different places, all set to go off at the same time,' Adnan paused, then smiled, 'boom, boom, boom everywhere, non-believing kuffars will wet themselves.'

A muted chuckle came from the others. 'However', Adnan snapped, 'we are not going to do that. I am not content to simply play around the edges; we must hit them much harder than that. We have a generous benefactor from Saudi Arabia, who is keen to support our needs with his money. Among other things, we will use his money to set up an Islamic Learning Centre here in London; it will be a beautiful cover for us.'

A stifled scream came from an adjoining room. Adnan smiled. 'Sounds like Nasser is using his whore well,' Adnan could see eager looks on the faces of the men in the room. 'No doubt he is stubbing out another cigarette on her tits again.' They all laughed. 'These white bitches never learn; they still think they can flaunt their wares and dress provocatively and no one will touch them.' Adnan slapped his fist into his open hand, 'Well now they are dealing with *real* men, not some pacified Westerner.' He spat the last two words out.

It was clear just how much the men crammed into this small room stood in awe of Adnan. To them he was a man of action, a man who fought unbelievers in the name of Allah, a man who had undergone the strict and brutal training of a Jihadist warrior, a man they could all look up to.

Just then the door to an adjacent room opened to reveal Nasser Mohammed, a fat middle aged man with a short ragged beard, who was belatedly still struggling to fasten his jeans over the folds of his enormous belly as he entered the room. Turning around he reached back into the room and dragged out a naked, terrified sixteen year-old girl.

Thrusting her so hard to the centre of the assembled men, she fell on her knees. Whimpering she kept her eyes down, looking at the floor, she had learnt not to look them in the eye. Nasser snarled, 'I've been teaching her to say her name,' he grinned, showing his yellow teeth as he spoke. He turned and kicked her on the thigh, 'What's your name?' he asked. When she did not answer, he slapped her across the face, bent down and pushed his face close to hers, 'I said tell them your name.'

'F...fuck...f...face,' she stammered.

'Again, so all can hear you,' ordered Nasser

'Fuckface,' she replied.

Spittle ran down the corner of Nasser's mouth in sexual excitement, 'Now go and crawl over to Adnan, and show him how you can take his manhood all the way down that little throat of yours.'

Adnan liked this. He always enjoyed it when he could humiliate a white kuffar bitch in this way. He slowly unzipped his jeans, while the others looked on in excited anticipation, eagerly waiting their turn.

'Note this well,' said Adnan to Nasser, who was now the eighth man intent on hearing what Adnan had to say. 'Sexual slavery of non-Muslim women is a practice which is in accord with Islamic law and within the parameters of Islamic morality. It is lawful for us to have sexual slaves: let no one tell you otherwise. When a Muslim nation is at war with a Christian nation, or any nation which has not the religion of Islam, it is lawful to take their women, to do with as we wish. We are at war with them; therefore there must be prisoners of war.' Adnan held the back of the girls head as he thrust his penis deep into her mouth, almost chocking her.

Unlike the other men in that room, Nasser had been born in Pakistan. He had entered England after having had an arranged marriage to Salma, a British born girl of Pakistani parents. Salma had never known happiness since that day when her father had taken her to Pakistan for a holiday! At the tender age of fourteen she little realised her strict Islamic father had no intention of giving her a holiday; instead he had been more interested in a marriage for her that he had arranged. This was a marriage which had brought her father good financial gains, the fact Nasser was thirty years older than Salma did not register with him as anything unusual, or unfair.

Forced to stay in Pakistan until Salma was old enough to legally be a wife in Britain, she had suffered constant abuse from her husband. Then he had used her as a passport to enter into England, where he had joined with Adnan's group in their shared hatred of the West.

All the men became aroused at the spectacle before them. It was not long before Adnan had become sufficiently aroused to ejaculate into his victim's mouth.

'I'll go and get the other two,' said one of the other men, opening the door to leave. 'They are all white-trash, worthless whores. We will use them well.' By now all the men in that room were in a state of primitive sexual arousal, anticipating the delights which they would partake of that evening.

****

London - England

For several days Jacques had lay on the hospital bed, his life shattered. Through medication the pain of his body was beginning to ease, but not the pain of his mind. He had loved Mary so very much. He could not think of a life without her; he lay there with tears still in his eyes, sweating at the terrible thought of never being able to see her again and playing over and over, that dreadful image of Mary's face. Christmas was only three weeks away now and all he wanted to do was to leave this London hospital and return to his home town of Calgary; as quickly as he could. He wanted to see his parents and gather what comfort he could from his family during this his time of deep grief. They had wanted to fly over and see him, but he told them to wait as he would soon be able to fly back to them in Calgary. His company had been very good to him; indeed they always were. They had provided him with the best private medical care, but his wounds were slower to heal than he had first thought. Wounds were one thing and his broken heart was another, but it was his seething anger toward the perpetrators of his current predicament which filled his body the most. He could not think of his life without Mary, and could not come to terms with this fact; laying there he felt depressed and low, sweating at the terrible thought of never being able to see his wife again.

Small metal particles from the bomb, which had killed Mary and so many others, had penetrated Jacques' body with great force. The power of the explosion had ripped open a large deep gash on his left shoulder. Not only this but he had also required an operation; a large incision through the abdominal wall to gain access into his abdominal cavity; a laparotomy they called it. This incision was to investigate the cause of his disorders resulting from the bomb. He also had multiple lacerations and burns, but these had not been too major, so now he was beginning to recover and eager to be on his way home, back to Canada, in time for Christmas, even though the thought of Christmas now had a hollow ring about it. In one way he felt guilty to be alive. A strange feeling; why was he alive, when his beloved Mary was not? They had told him he was lucky, because fragments of bone from the second suicide bomber had penetrated many other victims and these fragments had apparently tested positive for hepatitis-B virus and HIV. His doctor had told him that this hepatitis-B virus is transmitted by exposure to infectious blood or body fluids, and that it is fifty to one-hundred times more infectious than the HIV virus. 'At least I do not have that to deal with', he thought somberly.

'How can people do such things?' he repeatedly asked himself, as he lay there still looking up at the ceiling. 'Just what is it that drives men to commit such horrors; and all in the name of their god? What drives a man to become a suicide bomber? Why is there such violence in those people? Is there no justice; or shall I have to seek that myself?' These questions flowed repeatedly through his mind; whilst feeling an unquenchable and intense anger toward those who had committed this atrocity, bringing so much suffering to his own door, and forever changing his life. Over and over again he kept asking these same unanswered questions, 'What is it in religion that drives people to commit such crimes?' He began to contemplate religious violence in the past; such as the Crusades, the many Protestant and Catholic massacres which had taken place in Europe. Even today the remnants of this interdenominational war were still being felt in Northern Ireland. Then there was the persecution of the early Christians, the Arab/Israeli conflicts, the Islamic conflicts between Sunni and Shea, the Muslim/Hindu massacres during the Partition of India and now his own suffering at the hands of religious extremists. Hatred toward those who had brought him so much sadness and the loss of his wife gave vent to a vile feeling of revulsion toward them. So-much-so that he even toyed with the idea of paying for hit-squads who would go looking for such Muslim extremists to kill them; but he was not a violent man at heart, just a man temporarily bereft of reason.

'Do you want something to read?' a voice broke through these, his darkest innermost thoughts, as he lay on his bed. An elderly gentleman had quietly approached his bedside, pushing a trolley full of newspapers, magazines and a few old, well read books. 'Would you like something to read?' he repeated.

Jacques shook himself away from the dark thoughts searing through his mind, 'Yes, thank you, I could do with something to pass the time. I am not used to being so inactive.' Jacques forced a smile and reached out onto the trolley. There were only a few old books and none took his eye especially. Then, after hesitating a moment or two, he took hold of one dog-eared book, *'The God Delusion'* by Richard Dawkins. 'I'll take this one please and also that newspaper,' Pointing to an edition of *'The Sunday Observer,'* heavy with many supplements, typical of the Sunday newspapers in Britain.

There was always so much to read in these Sunday papers. Normally he would not have had the time to read them in detail, but now it was different, totally different. He had far more time on his hands than he really wanted. Slowly he started to thumb through the book, which was not easy with the pain in his shoulder. Not being sure which to read first, he was about to discard the book in favour of the newspaper, when his eyes focused on a paragraph within the book. The words jumped out of the page to him. In his current state of mind the words he saw hit home immediately. He read it quickly, paused and then read it again, this time more slowly.

> *'The God of the Old Testament is arguably the most unpleasant character in all fiction: jealous and proud of it; a petty, unjust unforgiving control-freak; vindictive, bloodthirsty ethnic cleanser; a misogynistic, homophobic, racist, infanticidal, genocidal, filicidal, pestilential, megalomaniacal, sadomasochistic, capriciously malevolent bully.'*

Jacques eyes widened as he read the next sentence.

> *'Those of us schooled from infancy in his (God's) ways can become desensitised to their horror.'*

'That's it, that's exactly it,' he thought. 'Those, so schooled can and do, become desensitised to the horrors they commit.' He read the paragraph again. 'This must be what drives men to carry out such atrocities, in the name of their god. Of course they must be deluded to commit such horrendous acts,' he reasoned. Putting the book down, he was determined to read it in detail later.

Turning to the newspaper he started to read. His eye was drawn to an article entitled, '*Egypt's Influence on the Bible, and Beyond*', by someone called Doctor Robert Boucher. It was a long article so Jacques settled down to read it thoroughly.

Within the article he read stunning phrases, such as:

> *'People have been killed for revealing unwelcome facts about religion, and in some places of the world, they still are. Ever since the first monotheistic religions (belief in one god) started in ancient Egypt they have been the*

cause of much of the world's violence. In fact all monotheistic religions are inherently violent. So when they come up against each other, whether it is Judaism, Christianity or Islam, there will inevitably be conflict. From the very beginning of monotheistic religions, when such believers first left Egypt they have been aggressive toward others. These Egyptian emigrants were commanded by God not leave alive anything that breathes within the countries they encountered. (Deuteronomy 20:10-17) This theme of violence has continued ever since, so it must not be wondered at, as to why there is so much conflict in the world.'

Jacques pondered over these words, *'Egyptian emigrants'*, this was an unusual turn of phrase he had not come across before in this context. Reading onward, the article gave many examples of Biblical utterances from the time of Moses, when God instructed his followers to commit acts that today we would call genocide. Such as:

'One only has to look at Moses when he ordered the murder of three thousand golden calf worshipers (Exodus 32: 27, 29) or when God found favour with a man called Jephthah for killing his own daughter as a sacrifice to the Lord. (Judges 11: 29, 39) One can only imagine the newspaper headlines today, "Religious Fanatic Sacrifices Virgin Daughter". How many know that a human sacrifice was approved by God in this instance?'

Jacques was stunned, and repeated in his mind the earlier phrase he had read, *'... desensitised to the horrors they commit.'* Reading on he saw how many practices in today's religions find their origins in Ancient Egypt; such as:

'Egyptian rituals and religious depictions far preceded and predated any religious concepts of today. Thus most, if not all modern religious practices have

derived from those very early teachings. For example; you cannot simply say that the word "Amen" means "so-be-it" for there is no linguistic translation for Amen, because it is a name and not a word. The use of the word **Amen** *is first found in Egypt, for* ***Amen-Ra*** *was the name of their Sun God. The pyramid texts (Possibly the oldest known religious texts in the world) said their followers must repeat the name of their God whenever they said a prayer, so they concluded by saying his name – Amen-Ra. And around four thousand years later, they are still saying it! One example is a piece of graffiti which has been found, in the Egyptian district of Qurna, tucked away in the tomb of a priest. It is a prayer and concludes by saying, "Oh Amen, great lord, found by those who seek him, drive away our fear. Fill our hearts with joy, for joy is for those who see you. Amen!'"*

'The name of Amen-Ra, sometimes also written as Amun-Ra, and the name of this god was incorporated into the names of several pharaohs and leading nobles, such as **Amen-***hotep,* **Amen-***ophis ,* **Amen-***emhat,* **Amen-***mose who was the son of a pharaoh, and of cause even the famous King Tut, Tutankh-***amen.** *(Which can also be spelt as Tutankh-***amun***) So to this day people are still invoking the name of the Egyptian god Amen-Ra, a god who was given such titles as, "The Hidden One", "King of the Gods", "The Sun God",* ***"T****he Sky God", "The Ultimate God - hidden in the sky".'*

Jacques felt dazed by what he was reading. 'My wife died at the hands of religious bigots', he thought to himself, 'Just how deluded are they? Could it be we have all been subjected to a *"God Delusion"*, as Richard Dawkins states in his book? I need to know more about this.' At the end of Dr. Boucher's article it mentioned he was a consultant Egyptologist and Honorary

Research Fellow of the University of York, scheduled to deliver a lecture on the subject of this article in a few days time at King's College, London. Jacques mused to himself, 'They said I should be discharged soon, I really would like to attend this lecture before I fly back to Canada.'

****

Derby - England

'Death to those who insult Islam,' shouted Adnan through a megaphone. 'Sharia Law, the law for Britain,' he boomed. Adnan was dressed in traditional Arab style attire, with a white and black chequered head band wrapped around his head and face, showing only his penetrating black eyes. He stood at the front of a crowd of around one-hundred, all of whom were screaming abuse toward a much larger hostile group nearby, who in turn were carrying English and Union Jack flags. By his side stood his plump friend Nasser Mohammed. Nasser was carrying a placard above his head on which was written, *'Jesus is Allah's Slave'*. Adnan's orchestrated group were attempting to force the local authorities to grant a planning application to convert a historic old church into a mosque. The application, currently undergoing a planning consideration in the midland city of Derby, was not popular with the majority of the city's inhabitants. Due to revelations of the repeated sexual abuse of underage girls and children, by groups of Muslim men, the population in general did not trust a culture they found to be so threatening. Therefore the local governing council was nervous about the granting permission for another mosque.

Others around Adnan and Nasser were holding large placards, waving them aloft, containing slogans, such as *'Islam will take over the world'*, *'We demand more Mosques'*, *'Sharia Law for Britain'* and *'Death to those who insult Islam'*.

The spearhead of the opposition to this proposed new mosque was the 'English Defence League'; often referred to as the EDL. A group, whose mission in life is to oppose all Islamic fundamentalism and the spread of this alien culture within England. They were particularly opposed to such things as converting an old church into a mosque, something they earnestly sought to block. Their perception, that militant Islam as a threat to British society, was not, they felt, being taken seriously enough by British authorities. This perception led to them forming their own action group against Islamic fanatics.

'E-E-EDL, E-E-EDL,' was the constant chant from the midst of the mainly young English, who genuinely believed Islam was disrespecting the culture of their homeland. The people who formed the backbone of the English Defence League had become horrified upon seeing many city centres of Britain transformed into Muslim strongholds, and populated by a people they viewed as aliens; a people they believed were deceived into following the primitive laws of the seventh-century Dark Ages. They had been formed into an organisation when aghast at seeing radial Muslims spitting and insulting British soldiers returning from Afghanistan. They were equally revolted at seeing radical Muslims burning the *poppy*, a symbol of the British dead in two world wars; and the many smaller wars since.

'E-E-EDL, E-E-EDL', they continued without letup.

Frustrated at not being allowed to march through a prominent Islamic area in the city, the EDL had commandeered the Old Market Square in the centre of the city, where the massed ranks of police had managed to contain them into one section of that large open square. It was difficult to keep these two opposing sides apart, and the police, dressed in their florescent yellow jackets, struggled to form a human barrier between the two vociferous opposing sides.

Adnan had earlier demanded to lead his protestors in a provocative march through the town and away from the residential Islamic area into the main centre of the city, a move which had frustrated the EDL even more, for they were being forced to stay in one small section, and not allowed to march as they wished.

A nervous news correspondent, a woman in her mid-twenties, tried several times to interview Adnan for her local radio and television stations, but she was finding it difficult. Seeing her attempts to talk to Adnan, a Muslim woman taking part taking part in the demonstration, dressed all in a black burka and displaying only her eyes, shouted into the face of this would-be interviewer, 'Who are you trying to attract to sleep with you tonight?'

Unable to comprehend the meaning of this intended insult she responded defensively, 'What do you mean by that?'

'Look at you! You are dressed only to attract men who will sleep with you,' was this uncalled for slur.

Considering her modest dress and uncovered hair, the news correspondent opened her mouth to respond, then thought better of it, realising that any answer would have been fruitless to such a narrow closed mind as displayed by this protesting woman. Instead she thrust the microphone directly toward Adnan again and asked, 'Why do you want to convert the church of Saint Michael into a mosque?'

Adnan felt contemptuous loathing for this woman from the media and wondered why she dared to even to speak him. 'That church has been empty for a very long time; no one goes to worship there any longer.' Pulling his headband tighter across his face, his eyes glared into hers, 'The followers of Islam pray to Allah five times a day. We will have no trouble filling this new mosque. Once it is a mosque it will not lie empty, it will be full of those who bend the knee to Allah.' Then shouting for everyone to hear above the increasing noise of the crowd he yelled. 'Allah Akbar'.

The Muslims again took up the cry and chanted, 'Allah Akbar, Allah Akbar'. Speeches ensued by more than a dozen Imams in a mixture of Arabic, Urdu and English, urging Muslims to honour the name of the Prophet and not back down in the face of the Councils reluctance to act. Chants of 'Allah Akbar' continued and also, 'Mohammed is the Prophet of God'.

When the EDL heard this chanted call they took up a counter chant themselves, 'Mohammed was a paedophile, Mohammed was a paedophile, Mohammed was a paedophile.' This chant referred to their prejudice view of the Islamic faith, and in particular to the six-year old girl Aisha, who the Koran says, Mohammed took as a bride at that tender age, and recorded that he consummated that marriage when the girl was just nine-years of age. And so they continued to chant, 'Mohammed was a paedophile.'

This chant infuriated Adnan and those around him, so-much-so that a red midst descended over his eyes. He pushed his way forward through the surging crowd, aided by Nasser, to confront that woman from the media again. She was followed everywhere by her cameraman. Startled by this forceful, aggressive approach from Adnan, she backed away from him, but before she realised it Adnan and Nasser had forced their way forward again. This time Adnan's anger was on full display.

He looked straight into the camera, seizing this opportunity to use the media to preach his hatred. 'Listen to those sons of Satan; they will all burn in hell. Hell will take them all soon. Sharia Law will have such people killed.' Then he yelled at the top of his voice, 'God will punish them for their blasphemy.'

It was plain the woman did not know what to do, for she had never confronted such hatred before. Other support crew from her news media now stepped forward in an effort to try and extract her from this fracas. Yet Adnan and Nasser still followed the would-be interviewer.

Nasser shouted further abuse into the continuously running camera, 'All homosexuals should be stoned to death, any thief should have amputations for stealing, and all who speak against Islam will be beheaded.'

Seeing that more cameras were being trained on him, Adnan belatedly realised he was drawing too much attention to himself. He turned and nodded to Nasser and the pair suddenly sank back into the crowd, falling to the rear of the melee. In his bitter determination, Adnan vowed he would make the people of Derby pay dearly for their insult to the Prophet.

As he spoke he trembled with rage, 'I will make sure they burn in hell for this insult,' he yelled at the top of his voice. A shout immediately repeated by Nasser as they both slipped away from the scene.

****

London - England

Christmas was fast approaching as Jacques walked slowly along London's Thames Embankment, toward King's College. It was dark and drizzling with rain, the Christmas lights reflected a colourful pattern onto the wet road, and the faint sounds of Christmas jingles hung in the air. Jacques needed to walk with the aid of a stick, his pace slowed considerably from his bold stride before the bomb blast, which had changed all that. Some of the physical pain was still with him, a nagging discomfort from his wounds. He could not understand why it was, but he felt a little nervous about tonight: was it because he could feel himself being pulled into something he was unsure of, or something he was unsure he wanted to venture into?

In spite of his somewhat painful pace, Jacques arrived early at the venue. Technicians were still setting up the speaker's laptop and projection equipment. He gathered that the gentlemen fussing around must be Doctor Boucher. Short in stature and rather over weight, with long thin strands of blond hair pulled over his balding crown. Clean shaven, and with rather crumpled clothes, he sported large dark rimmed glasses which seemed to sit oddly on his round face. Gradually the hall began to fill with people. Jacques could see the majority were students, no doubt eager to be getting away soon for their Christmas holidays; but there were also a significant number of other people there as well.

Eventually Doctor Boucher was satisfied that everything was ready and started his lecture:

'It will soon be Christmas during which time Christians around the world will celebrate the birth of Jesus Christ. This child is commonly depicted in his mother's arms.'

An image was projected of a stone statue of a mother holding her baby child. At the back of the mother's head was a circular, halo type disc. 'This however, is not Mary, but the Egyptian goddess Isis holding her baby son, Horus. Horus was a god, made king while on earth, similar to Jesus who many call "Christ the King". Mother and child worship did not start with Roman Christianity; it is far older than that.' So saying he superimposed another picture over the original, this time it was a picture of Mary painted during the Renaissance. 'Notice, not only the similarity between these two images, but also the disc displayed behind each of the women. In the former it was the sun disc, in the second it is called a halo. The halo is a relic of the sun discs, which had been frequently depicted in ancient

Egyptian artwork. Not only that, but look at the similarity of the names and titles given to these two women. Isis was called "The Mother of the Gods" Mary is called "The Mother of God". An even more striking similarity is that both women are said to have conceived their child without male impregnation.'

He paused and then added, 'Incidentally, Isis is said to have hidden her baby Horus in the bulrushes, away from those who wanted to kill him.' Then, throwing his arms wide open, as if to encompass the whole audience, asked, 'Where have we heard that before?'

A muted ripple of stifled laughter lifted up from the audience.

Pointing to another of his computer images depicting the biblical Mary, he stated, 'If you Google "Queen of Heaven", you will get hundreds of images of the Virgin Mary. Mary is often given this title "The Queen of Heaven", yet a long time before her birth, the Bible in Jeremiah 7:18, condemns the Israelites for taking offerings of cakes and wine to "The Queen of Heaven", showing this was an ancient goddess even then, during the time of ancient Israel.'

'The divine Mother and Child are common and abundant in ancient Egyptian artwork. For example, this was created in the sixth century B. C.' He now projected an image onto the screen, which depicted another statue of Isis holding her son Horus. 'This statue is now in the Turin Museum. It was such a statue which clearly inspired the fifteen century painter Masaccio, in this, his presentation of The Virgin and Child.' Again he superimposed one image on that of the other. 'We can easily find one, or several, such ancient Egyptian statues in museums throughout the world.'

These images made it clear what Doctor Boucher was saying, namely that the worship of Mary as Queen of Heaven, goes a long way back before the time of Mary, to that of ancient Egypt.

'Not only that, but there is also a link even in their names, for the full name of Isis, is "Isis-Meri". The Egyptian word "Meri" meaning, "the beloved", which served, as a title for this goddess. I do not have to elaborate, you can draw your own conclusions from this.' He did not dwell on this particular subject, so smiling he just left it hanging in the air.

'Let us briefly look at the husband of the goddess Isis, namely Osiris. There we find yet another parallel with Christianity, for according to the legend the god Osiris was killed and his body chopped up. This legend goes on to say that Isis collected these body parts and reassembled them. The gods were so impressed by the devotion of Isis that they resurrected Osiris back to life.' Bob paused, walked away from the rostrum, and then throwing his arms up in the air, exclaimed, 'In other words a god was killed; then rose from the dead.' An audible gasp could be heard from the audience. 'This was the ancient Egyptian belief.'

Then walking back to the rostrum, he looked quizzically around at his audience, knowing the links they were making. 'The pharaohs of Egypt associated themselves with Osiris in death, believing that, as Osiris rose from the dead, so they would do also. They believed if they were in union with Osiris they would inherit eternal life through a process of imitative redemption. The pharaohs were convinced they would imitate this god Osiris and that they themselves would rise from the dead.'

Jacques, along with many others, was furiously making notes, listening intently to this lecture.

Doctor Boucher continued on for some time, explaining as he did the origins of many Christian and some Islamic beliefs. Explaining further how the cross, the last judgement, holy water and the priesthood, all had their origins in the religion of Ancient Egypt.

Yet it was his final remarks which were to shock the audience the most, 'The link between ancient Egypt and subsequent Christian and Islamic beliefs are truly fascinating and clear to see for all scholars of this subject. However the studies I am currently researching have even greater poignancy. I am presently researching evidence which will show, once concluded, that Israel does not have, and never did have, a divine right to inherit Palestine as their Promised Land. With the help of modern archaeological findings I hope to prove this before much longer, but that will have to be the subject of another lecture!' And with that he walked away from the stage, neither waiting for questions, nor giving this final statement further explanation.

The lights went up and a buzz of excited chatter echoed all around. Jacques just sat there, his head swimming with bewildering thoughts, unsure what to do next.

After a short while most of those in attendance had already left, leaving Jacques still sitting there, struggling with the pains wracking his body. Slowly he stood up and leaning heavily on his stick he headed for the small side door which Doctor Boucher had previously gone through. As he entered he found himself in a corridor, where he saw several other doors inside. Jacques was unsure which one to try. While pondering on this another door opened and out stepped Doctor Boucher himself.

'Are you alright?' he asked, aware Jacques was struggling to walk.

'As well as can be expected,' replied Jacques, 'considering the circumstances.'

The exertion of getting to the venue and attending the lecture had been a little too much for Jacques and he started to sway a little.

'Here, come and sit down a moment, you don't look too good old boy.' And with that he took Jacques by the arm and led him into an office lounge. 'Let me get you some water,' he said, after sitting Jacques down in an easy-chair.

'I'll be alright in a moment,' said Jacques thankful for this help.

'Have you had an accident?' asked Doctor Boucher, looking at the facial bruising still evident on Jacques face.

'No, I was one of the victims of the recent bomb outrage at White Hart Lane. My name is Jacques Gendron.'

'Good god! You poor fellow, Mister Gendron', his compassion was genuine.

'I was fascinated by your talk tonight. There are so many questions I have, and you seem to have a lot of answers. You see I also read your article in the *Sunday Observer* which prompted me to attend tonight. I am glad I came, but the exertion has been a little more than I expected.'

Jacques was talking fast and a little excitedly. It was not long before he told the whole story, glad to be able to unburden himself, even to someone he hardly knew. Doctor Boucher sat there passively, as his kind and gentle nature taking over. He gave Jacques his genuine rapt attention, realising this man needed someone to talk to about his recent ordeal.

'Why are Muslims so violent?' asked Jacques. 'What makes them do such terrible things?' An unchecked tear welled up in Jacques's eye.

Bob bent forward in his seat, clasping his hands in front of him, 'I have found there is a powerful link between religious belief and brutality. The history of Islam has been especially one of violence from its very beginning; although they would say otherwise. A lot of their beliefs are similar to, or have come from, the teaching of Moses, and he was a violent sort of chap.' Looking at the sadness in Jacques eyes, he said, 'Fancy a drink? You look like you could do with a brandy.'

'No, not a brandy due to my medication, but I'd love a beer,' a relaxed smile returned to Jacques sullen face.

'Come on I know just the place,' he said, while helping Jacques to stand up and gather himself together. 'What is your name again, young man?'

'Jacques, Doctor Boucher,' he replied.

Doctor Boucher held out his hand for Jacques to take and said, 'Just call me Bob. OK?'

Twenty minutes later they were in the comfort of a traditional English pub, where a real log fire gave off a homely warm glow. Both men held a pint of beer.

'I am writing a book about the origins of Islam,' confided Bob. 'It is a subject one has to be careful with as I could well finish up with a Fatwa against me, similar to that on Salman Rushdie.' Bob said, shrugging his shoulders.

'Could be dangerous though,' observed Jacques correctly. 'It is a religion which seems to breed violence and is very intolerant towards any kind of criticism.'

'That's what they rely on. Fear! The same as the Christian church did for a long time. Fortunately those days are now gone as regards Christianity; but not so with Islam. They still try to stifle any who question them. They believe their Muslim righteousness entitles them to commit acts of violence. So I seek to enlighten the darkness which has permeated their religion since its inception.'

'It's true though that Christians have also engaged in a great deal of violence throughout their history, so both religions may be the same with regard to the violence they perpetrate, or used to,' suggested Jacques.

'Hmm!' responded Bob. 'That is not strictly true. You see, Christians who have engaged in violence, are betraying the explicit teachings and examples of their founder Jesus Christ. On the other hand, Muslims who take it upon themselves to destroy their alleged enemies, in the name of God, can rightly claim to be following the commands of their God in the Koran and imitating

Mohammed as their role model. And that, old boy, is the major difference.'

'How very true,' accepted Jacques. 'I have never thought of that before.'

'You see,' continued Bob, warming to his theme, 'the Koran says, *"Those who follow Mohammad are merciful to believers but harsh to unbelievers"*, (Sura 48 vs 29) which is in stark contrast to Jesus' injunction in the Sermon on the Mount, when he said, *"Love your enemies and pray for those who persecute you"*. (Matthew 5:44) This is the fundamental difference between these two religions,' explained Bob.

'So this is certainly a major difference between the two,' said Jacques.

'Yes indeed. You see,' he continued on his theme of Islam, 'when my new book is published it will show evidence from the known historical records that the early Arab conquests of the Middle East were not religious conquests at all. Yet today Islam claims that they were, but I can show they were in fact conquests of aggression, simply to seize other lands. These invasions caused great devastation to those conquered regions. Furthermore my book will show that Islam as we know it simply did not exist at the time of these initial Arab conquests. In fact, archaeological findings completely contradict the traditional picture of Islam.' Bob sank back relaxing more in his chair, comforted by the warm glow from the fire.

'Well that is certain to cause some dissention if you intend to publish all that,' Jacques was beginning to feel a little concerned for his new found friend. 'Aren't you worried for your safety?'

Bob just shrugged his shoulders, 'I intend to show that non-Muslim chroniclers, writing during the time of those early Arabian conquests, made no mention whatsoever of either the Koran, nor Islam, or even of Muslims; and they hardly ever mentioned Mohammad at all. I have found that contemporary non-Muslim sources of the seventh century do not corroborate the story as laid out in the Koran. Islam has surprisingly shaky historical foundations.'

Jacques sipped his beer, savouring the taste. 'Well, it's their violence which concerns me the most,' repeated Jacques. 'I would not like to see you go through what I am going through.'

'Thank you for that,' said Bob in appreciation. 'I have to speak out though, for they seem to be filling the world with wild-eyed crazed fanatics. Those who are able must do what they can to check them. To quote the old saying, *"All it needs for evil to triumph is for good people to do nothing"*. Some of the things I have found will help to provide that check. For example, the earliest biographical material about Mohammad dates from at least one-hundred and twenty-five years after his death. As I said, it was more than sixty years before the Arabian conquerors even mentioned Mohammed, or the Koran, or even the word Islam. Yet Muslims today say those Arab invasions were motivated by their need to spread the word of Mohammed to others. They firmly believe that is why they set out on their conquests. Baloney, complete baloney,' stated Bob rather forcefully. 'Historical evidence says otherwise.'

Lowering his voice, Jacques said, 'Well I wish you well with your project. When are you thinking of publishing all this?'

Bob simply ignored Jacques question, he was being carried away by the subject he loved, 'I will show evidence that the Koran was constructed from existing material, including that of Christian texts. The fact is that Arabian leaders fashioned Islam for their own political reasons later and not the other way around.'

Jacques responded, 'Well Judaism and Christianity have been subject to searching scrutiny and interpretation for more than two centuries now, whilst Islam has never received this same treatment on any significant scale, people are killed if they do.'

Jacques could empathise with Bob's earnest convictions, and had taken a liking to his new found friend.

'Exactly right, old boy; and I will do my bit to change that. One might suspect that the main reason why so many Muslims often tend to react with extreme aggression against anyone questioning their religion is because it was built on very shaky foundations and could collapse if it is subjected to close academic scrutiny. Let me give you an example of that. Modern scholars have questioned whether Mecca, as an important trading city and center of pilgrimage, truly existed by the year 600 A.D., as is claimed by Islamic sources today. Its location makes no sense, if it was supposed to be located on the trade routes between the Indian Ocean and Mediterranean Europe, it's in the wrong place for that. No non-Muslim historian mentions it in any of their accounts concerning trade during the sixth or seventh centuries. Given the centrality of Mecca in their traditional Islamic beliefs, this casts the entire canonical story of the origins of Islam into doubt. Not a single source outside Arabia mentions Mecca before the Arabian conquests.'

Bob pulled out his iPad and brought up a map of Saudi Arabia, to illustrate his point. 'Mecca was allegedly the centre of Arabian trading routes before Mohammad's time. Such a great ancient city would surely have received a mention in ancient history. Mecca is certainly not on the natural overland trade routes, it is a barren valley. This would put into question the need for Muslims to make their pilgrimage to Mecca. For you see, archaeologists have found that many early mosques did not even point to Mecca, as all modern mosques do. And this my friend is the reason why so many ancient mosques in Saudi Arabia and elsewhere have been forcefully destroyed, so the focus on Mecca is not distracted from.'

Bob stood up with two empty glasses in his hands. 'Now would you like another beer?'

'Why not?' said Jacques grinning. He was now succumbing to the warm atmosphere and his pleasant company, and glad to be in the company of his new found friend.

****

South London - England

Nasser Mohammed's wife Salma, hated the very presence of her pot-belly, violent and uncouth husband. Since the age of fourteen, when she had been taken to Pakistan for her marriage to him, a marriage arranged by her father, she had led a miserable life, seldom able to leave the confines of her own house. She was a small and delicate girl, and although she was still in her late teens she had experienced nothing but sexual, verbal and physical violence since the day of that marriage.

Kept as a virtual prisoner in her own home, no one outside knew her, even when Nasser's many friends came to call she was hurried to another room, out of their way and out of sight. On the odd occasions she was allowed to go outside of their house, Nasser was always with her and he insisted she was covered in a full black burka garment, with only her eyes showing. So, for the rest of the world, Salma had ceased to exist.

Since Nasser had started to see more and more of Adnan Al Saqqaff he had been going out for ever longer periods. Salma was glad of that, even though when occasionally she had been in the presence of that man, he made her skin crawl. She could sense the pent up fury, which was never far from the surface within Adnan. Seeing Nasser becoming so engrossed with Al Saqqaff was a mixed blessing for her; it meant Nasser was away more and more, giving her time on her own, but when returned he was always more violent and often had the smell of a woman on him. Sometimes he would stand at the window of their bedroom looking at the children going to school and repeating loudly how all those girls down in the street below were all god forsaken whores.

This weekend Nasser had gone away again with Al Saqqaff on some demonstration somewhere, so she felt a little freer and had even dared to venture outside; visiting shops or just walking around. Not only that but she had not worn her burka , which gave her a feeling of rebellious, almost sinful, freedom. Even though the constant abuse she suffered had made her ever more timid and nervous of people, something inside her had stirred. Her heart was beating rapidly as she walked to a large supermarket. It was here where she could sit in the quiet corner of the cafe within the market spending an hour to sip a cup of coffee. By any standards it was innocent enough yet she had been so indoctrinated, she could not help but feel guilty. Why should she feel guilty? She pondered this as she sipped her coffee. The last time she had done this, a young man similar to her own age had smiled at her and her heart raced. Would he be there this time? She knew it would not matter if he was, for there was nothing she could do, so tied up in an aura of fear which permeated her waking life.

****

Calgary - Canada

It had been two days before Christmas when Jacques had returned to Calgary. He had begun to feel a little better and more able to travel. Spending Christmas with his family had been a hard time for him. Everyone wanted to help, but there was so little they could do. He still felt empty inside, his heart aching for the loss of his wife. His parents had done all they could to help him; but inwardly he was glad when this period of religious celebration and family reunion was over. After the holiday he returned to his Company's Head Office in a high-rise tower block in down-town Calgary. Everyone there could see the fire had gone out of Jacques blue eyes, but they did what they could to make him feel welcome; perhaps too much, for Jacques over-reacted to some of the exaggerated concern over his misfortune. His colleagues advised him to take a longer break and come back when he was fully recovered and ready for work.

Standing at the window of his office, Brian the Vice-president confided, 'We could do with your help Jacques, if you feel up to it.' He spoke with a forced almost plastic smile on his face, hoping that Jacques would agree. 'It's this business in the Sudan,' he went on. 'As you know we are seeking to get a partnership with several other oil companies in a new oil project in that country. Quite frankly Jacques it's difficult. It's a volatile country; as they all are where the oil is found, but this one has special challenges, and it's risky. I know you never shy away from a challenge, but it may be what you need after your recent bereavement.'

Jacques nodded, this appealed to him and he felt brighter for a moment. 'I like the sound of that Brian. Count me in.'

'Good man. I knew you would. Take your time, say a couple of weeks,' both men laughed at this small, but truthful joke. 'Then come back and we'll discuss it.' Brian picked up his iPad and stood up. 'Now excuse me Jacques I have to look at the problems we are having in Yemen; so I'll see you next week. Take a trip up to the Rockies, it will help your recovery.' And with that he strode out of the long plush office, an office befitting the Vice President of a major oil company, happy that Jacques was back in business.

'Yes I will,' thought Jacques to himself, deciding there and then he would head north out of Calgary toward the ski slopes of Banff and Lake Louise. As always at this time of year there was plenty of snow around, even if he would not be able to ski this time, due to his injuries. Having travelled to many parts of the world, Jacques felt considerable contentment in the thought that this, his own home state of Alberta, is one of the most beautiful places on earth that he had seen; even though it had the accompanying sub-zero temperatures of a Canadian winter.

The majestic scenery helped him to relax a little as he drove north from Calgary, along the Trans-Canada Highway. A few hours later he looked out from his bedroom window in the large French style Chateau, which was perfectly situated at the end of the lake at the breathtaking beauty of Lake Louise, a true winter wonderland. The snow covered mountains and forests forming a dramatic backdrop to ice covered lake. A lake which in the summer was a vivid translucent green.

As he gazed out at the wonderful scene before him, a moment of depression came over him again. 'What is the point of going on, when there is no going back?' he thought. 'Mary loved the beauty of this place and the skiing.' The melancholy music he had played in his car while driving north, had not helped his state of mind, now tears once again began to stream down his face as the impact of his bereavement closed in depressing his very soul.

Reaching for his laptop he decided it was time to do a little research on Doctor Robert Boucher. Bob's lecture and their subsequent conversation had had a profound effect on Jacques, yet much of what had been said still troubled him: as did the 'delusion' prospects from Richard Dawkins' book. In his book Dawkins had shown that virtually the whole Christian story had been borrowed from religions already in existence in ancient times, religions from around the Mediterranean area. He had searched the web and found Dawkins had been correct when he said there is an endemic violence within the Law of Moses, to which Judaism, Christianity and Islam state their beliefs stem from. Also, during this casual research he found such inhuman statements set out in the Law of Moses. A law within which was the requirement for the death penalty for seemingly common things, such as adultery and homosexuality, or even for ludicrous things, such as the gathering of sticks on the Sabbath and even for cheeking your parents.

As expected, he soon found that Bob Boucher had his own website, which he read enthusiastically. Locating an Email address he decided to write a personal letter to Bob. Writing carefully, Jacques told Bob he was beginning to feel a lot better and how much he had enjoyed his company in London. He thanked him again for that pleasant evening in London then informed him about his new assignment in Sudan, adding he would be flying out to Khartoum soon. In conclusion he asked if he could provide more information regarding his final tantalising statement at the lecture, concerning the land of Israel.

Satisfied with the message, he was just about to close his laptop and go for a meal, when a 'ting' indicated there was already a reply to his Email. It was an elated note from Bob, 'Wonderful! I will be in Egypt for the next several months researching the project you referred to. Love to meet up with you again, can you travel to Sudan via Cairo?'

'Great!' thought Jacques and wrote straight back, *'This is a pleasant surprise. Yes, I will be able to travel to Cairo or even Luxor on my way to Sudan. We can meet up again there.'*

Jacques felt uplifted. It wasn't long before they arranged to meet together in Cairo; Jacques adding the rider, *'Let us hope things are quite there,'* in reference to the recent Arab Spring Revolution, which was still causing some unrest in the streets of Cairo.

****

Calgary - Canada

After a few days of rest at Lake Louise, Jacques returned to Calgary. And as expected, had still not been well enough to ski on the slopes there, and anyway he now wanted to get on with his new assignment in Sudan. Was it just a whim, or a rash thought? he could not be sure, but for whatever reason Jacques on impulse had made a phone call to the giant Baitun Nurew Mosque, not only a new building in Calgary, but the largest mosque in the whole of Canada. It was a building of immense size and looked as if it had been bodily transported from Saudi Arabia; having the appearance of an alien structure. He did not understand why he had suddenly decided to make a phone call to this mosque, but he had. He asked if he might meet with a religious leader there, an Imam or Mullah, he wasn't sure which, nor did he know what the difference was, anyway.

The request had been readily granted and so now Jacques sat in a small room facing a refined elderly gentleman with a neatly clipped full grey beard, his rimless glasses seemed to emphasis his good education. Abu-Bakr Kahn was dressed in a long dark grey robe covering his whole body and wore a small white turban on his head. Jacques had said nothing about the bomb outrage in London, only that he wanted to know what were the differences and similarities between Christians and Muslims.

'Thank you for agreeing to see me,' began Jacques. 'As I said on the phone, I would like to know how Christianity differs from your religion and how they are the same; indeed if there are any things which are similar.' Jacques couldn't help himself, but a seething anger toward this man, a man he had never met before, writhed like a wild thing inside of him. All he could think of was that this man, unknowingly, represented the religion Jacques personally held responsible for the death of his beloved wife. A calm exterior belied these inner feelings.

'I should ask you why you want to know this?' smiled Abu-Bakr. 'But you can tell me when you are ready.' Folding his arms he sat upright. 'There are many similarities that Islam and Christianity have in common. A great leader once said, "The difference between us is as thin as a line drawn in the sand."'

'Huh!' interjected Jacques. 'That just makes the wars, animosity and in some cases, sheer hatred, all the more difficult to understand.'

Still smiling Abu-Bakr, put his hands on the desk in front of him as a gesture of concern, continued, 'Sadly that is true. Yet the Koran makes frequent reference to Jesus and the Virgin Mary, they are cited more times than in the New Testament. The Koran clearly states that the people of the scripture, the Jews and Christians, are far closer to Islam and Muslims than all other religions.'

'Are you saying you or the Koran accepts Jesus Christ?' queried Jacques.

'We accept Jesus as a prophet of Allah. However, Muslims believe that Islam supersedes Judaism and Christianity and that the Koran is the final and complete Word of God. Whereas Jesus was a prophet of his time, Mohammad is the last of the prophets and his teachings replaced, or improved upon, those of Jesus. Muslims consider Abraham, Mohammad, Moses, and Jesus as prophets and messengers sent by God. However, these prophets were human beings, not divine, and should not be worshiped either directly or indirectly. Islam says Jesus was a holy man, but no more than that, he was not God, nor was he the Son of God.'

'To be honest,' said Jacques, I am not so much interested in such spiritual values; but I am interested in the violence perpetrated by Islam.'

Abu-Bakr looked shocked, 'Islam is a religion of peace,' he defended. 'Why do you say otherwise?'

'Because you only have to watch the news or read a newspaper and you will see Islamic violence around the world in one form or another. Besides, I have been the victim of such violence,' said Jacques raising his voice somewhat.

'I am sorry to hear that, may I ask how?'

'My wife was killed at the recent suicide bombings in London and I was injured.' Jacques face had hardened as he gritted his teeth saying the words.

'Oh! So that is why you are here,' acknowledged Abu-Bakr, looking crest fallen.

'You say Islam is a religion of peace, yet there is more violence carried out in that name than any other religion,' Jacques eyes widened as he began to sound belligerent.

'Really?' questioned Abu-Bakr. 'What about the Crusades, the Inquisition, the burning of heretics, or more recently Northern Ireland?'

'True,' conceded Jacques. 'I was thinking more of the current wave of violence carried out in the name of Islam, I am interested in today's violence not so much yesterdays.'

'Well, unfortunately we sometimes cannot understand one without the other,' was Abu-Bakr's logical retort. 'The fact is we want to spread Islam through love and dialogue instead of using force. We love peace and want to conquer the world through love and dialogue. There is no space for terrorism, militancy or extremism in Islam and those involved in such activities cannot even claim to be Muslims.'

'Well that is good to hear. So then, how do you explain all the acts of terror and the actions of Jihadists?' Something about what had just been said unsettled Jacques a little, but he could not put his finger on it. Was Abu-Bakr just saying this because he was living in the West, in a Christian country? Would what he was saying now, be repeated or agreed with, in Pakistan or Saudi Arabia? Jacques was unsure, but felt the answer would be negative.

'We have to look at the world situation to understand Jihad,' continued Abu-Bakr; but this time in a more sombre tone. 'Many in the media talk about Jihad without understanding its meaning within Islam. Living a good Muslim life; praying ritually five times a day; keeping the hard fast of Ramadan; going on the pilgrimage to Mecca; rearing one's offspring in the fear of Allah: all this is a Jihad. The early Muslims also had a Jihad when they had to strive in battle against attacks by their enemies. The Koran states clearly the circumstances in which an Islamic state may resort to war. These are: When there is a grave and sudden threat to our religion; when Muslims are subjected to oppression; when Muslims are forced out of their land; when political entities commit deliberate breaches of treaties and pacts.'

Abu-Bakr gave a sigh, 'You see there are many Muslims who feel they are under attack, and that their land has been taken away from them. Ever since the British took Palestine away from us and gave it to Israel, that was the start of the modern troubles. The British promised the Arabs freedom to rule their own countries, all over the Middle East. They said, if we supported them against the Turks and the Ottoman Empire during the First World War they would give Arabs control of the lands taken away from those Ottoman Turks. So we fought for them and won; then they broke their treaty with us and divided our land up between Britain and France for themselves.'

'So this is the origins of Jihad?' asked Jacques.

'Unfortunately, yes,' replied Abu-Bakr with a look of sadness in his face. 'The Arabs had hoped, with their faith in the British promises, that a new Arab state would include all the Arab lands stretching from Aleppo in northern Syria to Aden in southern Yemen. Instead, after the Arabs had helped defeat the Ottoman Empire, which at the time was an ally of Germany. Britain and France then ignored their promise and officiated over their complete seizure of the Middle East. The territories of Arabia, Iraq, Syria, Lebanon and Palestine all fell into European hands. The French and British drew the borders of the modern Middle East, and the League of Nations sanctioned their domination of the region. The French took Syria, Lebanon, Algeria and Morocco and the British, took control of, or continued to hold, Palestine, Egypt, Sudan, Iraq, the small Emirate States of the Arabian Gulf and Aden in southern Yemen. This encroachment has prompted much bloody violence ever since.'

'So how will this violence end?' asked Jacques, taken aback by this revelation.

'As you know, these former colonial powers no longer control these countries; they have long since departed from them. Although they still are at the forefront of several wars there,' said the cleric raising his eyebrows. 'About the time Britain was set to leave Palestine, unfortunately the United Nations General Assembly, under the strong influence of Britain, adopted a resolution recommending the adoption and implementation of a plan to resolve the Arab–Jewish conflict by partitioning Palestine into two states, one Arab and one Jewish: in other words they gave away the Arab land of Palestine to Israel. A legacy the world is still in turmoil over. Now of course, where Britain left off, America has carried on with its unflinching support for Israel.'

There was a prolonged pause why both contemplated what had been said.

Eventually Abu-Bakr continued, 'This is why, those you call Islamic Fundamentalists, wage a war against the West.'

'If it was a war just against the West, that would be one thing, but it is not just against the West; is it? They also bomb and kill each other,' Jacques voice went up an octave. 'Just look at the conflicts between Sunni and Shea, Muslims against Hindus, Muslims targeting and killing Christians.' Jacques inner anger was now becoming apparent. He now started to shout, 'So regardless of the cause, the fact is Muslims kill innocents because of perceived misdeeds done to them a long time ago. There are more acts of violence and civil disruption committed in the name of Islam than any other religion on earth.'

'No! We do not condone such actions,' retorted Abu-Bakr. 'Islam is a religion of peace.'

Jacques voice was now trembling, 'So why don't you speak out more against all these terrorist actions taking place? If Islam is a religion of peace, its leaders should surely condemn such actions. Yet I don't hear you! Your voice for peace is silent on the world stage and Muslims continue to kill innocent peoples all around the world.' As he said this Jacques thumped his fist on the table, and said, 'Your silence is deafening.'

The cleric paused and stood up, to indicate this interview was over. He could see there was not much point in continuing further with this conversation. 'There are many who believe that the continued foreign policies of the brother nations, American and Britain, has oppressed, killed, or otherwise harmed Muslims throughout the Middle East; it can be condensed into the phrase, "They hate us for who we are, not what we do." Good day Mister Gendron.'

Driving home Jacques had many thoughts whirling around his head, but one phrase in particular, which the cleric had said repeated itself over and over in his mind, *'They want to conquer the world through love and dialogue.'* Jacques pondered over this, reflecting, 'You cannot conquer anyone without the use of force; extreme force!'

****

Cairo - Egypt

After the bitter cold of Canada and the wet damp climate of England, it was good to get away from the winter of the north. As always the sun shone brightly in Cairo. Jacques took a taxi from the Marriott Hotel, on the river island of Zamalek in central Cairo, to the famous museum of that city. Since the revolution, called the Arab Spring and the subsequent overthrow of the political party called the Muslim Brotherhood, tourists had been slow to return to Egypt and things were still not back to their pre-revolution days. Tension and unease hung in the air.

Jacques had spoken several times on the phone to Bob and both were keen to meet up once again. Bob said he was ready to provide answers to some of the questions Jacques had been seeking. In a strange way, this pursuit Jacques had embarked upon was helping him come to terms with the loss of his wife; yet he could not really understand why nor how.

Jacques smiled when he saw Bob in the distance, for in spite of his diminutive stature, Bob stood out above the others who were milling around the entrance to the museum. He was wearing a beige coloured two-piece suit, over an open necked white shirt. On his head he sported a broad brimmed straw hat with a dark coloured band around it; yet it was his large dark rimmed glasses which gave him a look which belonged to another age.

'Bob,' shouted Jacques with a beaming smile as he reached out to shake his hand. 'It is so good to see you again.'

'Likewise old boy,' was the now familiar reply. 'Glad you could get. Did you have a good journey?'

'Quite nice actually, I was able to sleep for several hours. I'm fully rested now.' Jacques, in his tee-shirt and blue jeans felt a little underdressed by the side of Bob.

'I think I can answer some of your questions today, and maybe also give you a few more to ponder over!' The instant warmth between to two was genuine.

Both men paid their entrance fee and passed through the portico. Beyond this entrance, a broad stone pathway led across this famous and beautifully kept garden, with numerous Egyptian artefacts placed carefully around it. The pathway divided around a large square Lilly-pond which was in full flower; two reclining sphinxes guarded either side of the entranceway, while a little way behind were two large statues of Egyptian gods, striding out, each sporting an animal head. The dark pink stonework of the museum contrasted sharply with the sprawling concrete structures around it. Both men took a seat on a low retaining wall surrounding the ornate pond. It was a most pleasant setting for this prime palace to Egyptian history.

'In actual fact,' said Bob, 'I have so much on at the moment it is good to be able to take this opportunity for a break. As you know my work on the origins of Islam is soon to be published and I don't want to be in the Middle East when that happens. It may provoke demonstrations and such things can quickly get out of hand in these countries.'

Jacques agreed, 'You would be foolish to take such a risk.'

'Also old chap, I am now working on the origins of Israel: fascinating stuff, truly fascinating. You told me you are particularly interested in the violence apparently inherent in monotheistic religions.' Bob suddenly checked himself, looking more serious, 'I am sorry Jacques, I should have asked first how you are feeling? It is easy for me to get carried away. I must say you look a lot better than when we last met.'

'Thank you,' replied Jacques. 'I am still not right, but getting better by the day. It is not so much my physical injuries, but missing Mary which hurts me the most. My life feels so hollow now without her. It seems there is a big space in my life, which she used to fill.'

Bob sympathised, 'There is far too much violence carried out in the name of religion, our history and that of the world, is written in the blood of slain innocents. Even Abraham was prepared to kill his own son; and if that horrifies people like me today, then why didn't it horrify God?' Bob took out his handkerchief to wipe the sweat from his forehead. 'Then there is Moses. A more violent person you would not wish to meet.'

'Yes I have read some of your comments on this before,' acknowledged Jacques.

'Under Moses the Israelites slaughtered men, women, children, cattle, sheep, donkeys, in fact anything that breathed. Utter Destruction. Multiple cities and their populations were completely annihilated by Moses. His people massacred the inhabitants of sixty different cities in total. Yet the Bible repeatedly sanctions this, which can only be called the genocide of the original native inhabitants of those lands; lands the Israelites wanted to take for themselves.'

It was beginning to get too hot in the sun, so Bob stood up and nodded to Jacques to follow him. 'This way,' he said.

Walking into the main entrance of the museum Bob continued with his spiel, 'The Bible advocated similar genocide for the adherents of all other religions, just in case they converted Israelites to their pagan beliefs. This becomes very clear when we consider the way Moses and the God of the Bible dealt with some of those indigenous nations, such as the Moabites and Midianites. The Israelites were told to slaughter all Midianite males, including their male children and all adult Midianite women.'

Both men stopped and looked up, inside the building, while their eyes adjusted to the darker interior. The large, spacious interior was filled with thousands of historical treasures all carefully laid out before them. At the far end stood a huge stone statue of a pharaoh and his queen dominating their surrounds and giving the appearance of a royal court. Pillars and sweeping Romanesque arches supported a perimeter balcony and with many other hidden rooms leading off from there.

Clearly not wishing to dwell on any exhibit in particular, Bob continued talking, 'And if that was not bad enough, Moses said God had commanded that the young girls of those tribes be tested for virginity and if they were virgins they could be given to their captors as sex-slaves.' He turned to Jacques and looked him in the eye, 'Not many vicars preach that from their pulpits do they old boy!'

'That would be classed as war crimes today,' said Jacques only half seriously. 'From what you are saying it would seem violence was inherent from the start.' Jacques was only subconsciously aware that they were walking along the ground floor of the museum toward the far side of the building. This was one of the most important museums in the world, if not *the* most important; and yet they were not taking any time to look at all those massed ranks of famous exhibits. This frustrated Jacques a little.

Eventually Bob stopped. He turned to face Jacques, who was one step behind him, then cocking his head backwards, both men turned to look up at a large stone statue which towered above and in front of them. Lifting his straw hat from his head,

Bob pointed his hat toward this exhibit, 'What do you know about this fellow?'

'Wow!' exclaimed Jacques. 'How odd!' He looked up transfixed. He was staring at the unusual sculptured features of this image in front of him. 'It's a man, I think! A pharaoh, I guess, because he is wearing the head dress of a pharaoh; he has a man's misshapen head yet with a very feminine looking body. He has a pharaoh's beard, but with incredible female thighs and hips.' Then looking closer Jacques observed, 'He may even have breasts, but they are partly covered by his crossed arms. And his head is not normal; it's unnaturally long, as are his ears. His head is surely not of the correct proportions. Who was he?'

Bob had suddenly become very serious in front of this statue, 'History is shaped by individuals, unique personalities, not by social processes. This is one of those men. A true giant of a man, yet unfortunately he is hardly known today, outside of the academic world.'

'That is a very profound statement Bob, one I should remember', said Jacques smiling quizzically.

'Even more than that,' Bob pulled himself up to his full diminutive height, 'for I truly believe this was the man who has had more influence on the world than any other person who has ever lived throughout history.'

'Wha!' Jacques jaw dropped open. 'You will have to explain that to me Bob, You've lost me.'

Almost triumphantly Bob outstretched his arm, his finger pointing upward toward this strange stone face before them, 'This is Amenhoteb IV,' he said as a bold statement. 'Later he changed his name to Akhenaten. He was the first man in recorded history to believe in one god; the very first monotheist that we know of. And now the majority of the world follows monotheistic religions. Before there were Jews, Christians, or Muslims,' Bob paused for emphasis, 'there was this man.'

'My god!' uttered Jacques in exclamation, failing to see the witticism of his remark. 'I've never heard of him before.'

'No Jacques, unfortunately most people haven't. They just accept what they are told without asking too many questions. And if you are a Muslim, you are not even allowed to ask any question which might possibly challenge your beliefs. This is of cause how it used to be with Roman Catholics. How many died of torture because they dared to ask inquiring questions? Untold thousands.'

'The first man to believe in one god,' repeated Jacques. 'This is amazing. How did all this come about? Who was his god?'

'Taking your last point first, his god was the Aten. It is spelt A-t-e-n but pronounced as *Are-Ten*: hence his name Akhhen-*aten*, which means, "The Living Spirit of Aten". The name he was given at birth Amen-hoteb meant "Amen is Satisfied", but after a religious awakening he changed it to Akhen*aten*. Aten in many ways was a god of the sun, but official Egyptian language avoided calling the Aten a god, giving this solar deity a status above that of mere gods. Aten was *the* god, being above all others in every way. In fact the worship of all other gods was banned under Akhen*aten's* reign. The king himself formed the only link between this god Aten and the ordinary people; not unlike the medieval popes and bishops did in Europe. He ordered the eradication of all of Egypt's traditional gods, sending royal officials to chisel out and destroy every reference to Amen-Ra and the names of other deities on tombs and temple walls. He insisted the people should be instructed that the Aten was the only one true god. In addition to this religious censorship, Akhen*aten* decreed that he, as pharaoh, was the only priest needed for the worship of the Aten, effectively eliminating the necessity for the priests of Amen-Ra and all the other many gods of Egypt.'

Bob smiled at the transfixed look on Jacques' face, as he stood there looking up with his mouth open. Then Bob continued, 'Because this idea of one god was so revolutionary, after this pharaoh's death they branded him as a heretic, and even to this day he is often called, "The Heretic Pharaoh".'

'So this man was the first to believe there was only one god, but he thought that this god was the sun?' quizzed Jacques.

'That's the nub of it, but it's not quite that simple. The Aten was seen as the invisible source of energy from the sun, of which the visible manifestation of Aten was the solar disk. All creation was thought to emanate from this god and to exist within that god. Unusually for that time this god Aten was never depicted in human form at all, but only as rays of light extending from the sun's disk. This had never been done before. Nowhere else in the ancient world had a god been depicted not having a human nor animal form. Don't you find that truly amazing? The only god in the ancient world not depicted in any form at all; other than the unseen rays of the sun.'

Bob was now in full swing on his favourite topic, 'The Aten was first identified as a divine form in its own right in a small inscription proclaiming the victories achieved by Thutmosis IV, during his reign, sometime around 1395 B.C. You see Thutmosis IV was the grandfather of Akhen*aten*. The son of Thutmosis IV was Amenhoteb III who continued their royal association with this new solar deity. So we have the grandfather and father of Akhen*aten* as Aten worshipers: but then the grandson, Akhen*aten* took things a step further and imposed the worship of this one god Aten on the whole country. He declared the worship of Aten to be the state religion.'

'That must have caused considerable upheaval,' suggested Jacques.

'You bet it did,' said Bob shaking his head slowly and pursing his lips. 'Now this is where your personal interest comes into play. You see up until then Egypt was tolerant of the worship of all kinds of gods, but this new worship was not tolerant at all; far from it. Akhen*aten* banned the worship of all other gods, which caused mayhem. Hundreds of priests were disbanded and their temples closed down. It was not unlike the Dissolution of the Monasteries carried out in England under King Henry VIII. This rift with the past was the first demonstration of a monotheistic religions aggression toward other all religions.'

Bob patted the side of the statue with his hand. 'It is here, with this man, that intolerant violence toward other religions can be traced. Can you image the anger and confusion this would cause, not only among the general population, but especially among the priests, who were now not only all out of a job, but they had lost their influence over the people and their prestige as well. Whenever any ruler throughout history has said, his is the only correct religion and all the others are wrong, it has always caused trouble. Catholics were banned from worshiping in England at one time, as were Protestants in France. The outcome has always been the same; intolerance and violence. History has done this many times and is still doing so, constantly repeating religious violence. It must have been just the same back then; those who did not want to convert to this new religion either had to suppress their pent-up anger, or displayed it in expressions of violence.'

'So you are saying the violence inherent in monotheistic religions has its origins with this man and the followers of the god Aten?' Jacques wrinkled his forehead. 'That seems a big pill to swallow.'

'What makes a man great?' asked Bob. Then proceeded to answer his own question. 'When the man dies he has changed things.'

Whilst they had been speaking these things, the two men had started to wander around the museum, still without looking at any further exhibits, until that is, they climbed the stairs to where most of the tourists headed for first. Jacques knew immediately where they were now standing. They were looking into the glass case containing perhaps the most famous artwork in the world; the solid gold death mask of Tutankhamen.

'Well I know this is King Tut,' said Jacques. 'Everyone knows that.'

'Yes, but did you know his original name was Tutankh-aten, "The Living Image of Aten"?'

'No!' Jacques was stunned for a moment. 'So he also must have worshiped the god Aten as well.'

'Indeed he did, for he was the son of Akhenaten, so he was schooled in the worship of Aten. However, he was only nine when his father died, therefore his father's religious revolution and fearsome devotion to this one god could not carry on. At this time there was a powerful general called Horemheb, and he along with other powerful lords and disenfranchised priests made sure the boy king would return the country back to the old religious ways. It is clear a great deal of pressure, if not force, made this boy-king return to the multi-god worship of their ancestors. When this happened the young king had to change his name from Tutankh-aten to Tutankh-amen "The Living Image of Amen-Ra": which, if you remember my talk in London, can also be spelt as Tutankh-amun.'

'Yes of course I remember I am not likely to forget where that word *amen* came from.'

'In hieroglyphs, the name Tutankh-*amen* was typically written *Amen*-tut-ankh, because of a scribal custom which placed a divine name at the beginning of a phrase to show appropriate reverence.'

'So I presume the worship of this one god did not last long?' reasoned Jacques.

'Yes that is so. You see Akhenaten only reigned for around eighteen years, yet during that time he managed to accomplish quite a lot towards his religious beliefs. There were many who followed him,' then Bob wagged his finger in a mischievous way, 'but there were a lot more who did not wish to follow him.'

Bob was now bending forward looking at the golden guilt throne of Tutankamen. He pointed to the beautifully painted sculpture on the upright back of this chair, 'Look at this; an image of the young king with his wife, basking in the sun rays of the god Aten. So it would seem he still held on to his father's beliefs, even though during his reign the supremacy of Amen-Ra was restored, and the ban on his worship lifted; so the priesthood were back in business, and their prestige restored.'

Jacques was so full of questions; this was proving to be a most revealing day. 'Tell me why is Akhenaten's image so, so...so disfigured?' He didn't quite know how to put it, for he had never seen such a statue before.

'The short answer is we don't really know. There is a great deal of study and discussion about it. I can surmise a couple of things. Some say Akhenaten was the first pharaoh to have images and paintings made of himself and his family, as they actually looked. You see many of the pharaohs had themselves depicted with bulging muscles, perfect features and striding out to get things done; as giants among men. Then, when you look at his statue you see it was not so with Akhenaten. If realism was the way they depicted things, then his wife Nefertiti was surely one of the most beautiful women who ever lived, you will find her image everywhere in Egypt today, it is her image which is the best selling image to tourists today. Although it is possible Nefertiti also may have had a deformed elongated head: their daughters' certainly did. We have many artefacts which show his daughters also had deformed heads. So we can only assume the pharaoh had himself depicted as he really was.' Bob smiled at this. 'So this period not only had a major change in religion, it also had a major change in art as well. During this brief time art depicted things as they really were; scholars refer to this art as the

Amarna Period, and are genuinely have deep respect of this art form. "Warts and all", as Cromwell once said.'

'As regards *why* he looked the way he did, there are all sorts of conjecture. The most recently suggested possibility for Akhenaten's deformity is a genetic disorder known as Marfan's Syndrome. Skeletal abnormalities in Marfan's patients are a long face, an unusually tall stature, a short upper body in comparison to the lower body and overgrown ribs. One of the most distinctive characteristics of Marfan's Syndrome is unusually long arms, fingers, and toes.'

Bob was now heading back down the large staircase, with Jacques listening intently to his every word, 'His mummy has never been found, and until we do, if ever we do, for it may have been destroyed, we will never know for sure.'

Back now on the ground floor, Bob walked over to a very large slab of black granite towering above them both, and situated with a recess of the main hall. The stone was covered in hieroglyphic writing. Pointing to it, Bob said, 'This is the Merneptak Stele.'

Whilst Jacques was looking upward to its large size, Bob crouched down and beckoned to Jacques to do the same. 'Merneptak, or Merne for short, was a pharaoh and son of the mighty Ramesses II. The work on this stone is dated to around 1208 B.C., give or take a few years.'

'What's a stele?' asked Jacques.

'Sorry I forgot this is not your trade,' laughed Bob. 'A stele is an upright stone or slab with an inscribed or sculptured surface, used as a monument or as a commemorative tablet of some special event or occasion.'

'OK, so why do you find this interesting?' asked Jacques.

'On this stele is the earliest record of the word "Israel". It has a very interesting inscription.' Bob was now becoming somewhat intense, 'It lists all the countries which Merne had conquered or subjugated; many of them are listed including Canaan and Ashkelon. For example this text reads here, *"Canaan is plundered with every evil way. Ashkelon is conquered and brought away captive, Gezer seized, Yanoam made nonexistent."* Then it goes on the say, *"Israel is wasted, bare of seed."'*

Both men stood up to stretch their legs. 'It is not just what it has to say, but the way it is said,' stated Bob.'

'What do you mean?' asked Jacques.

'The hieroglyph for Israel describes them as "a people", whilst all the others are described as "lands". So this means that Israel wasn't a kingdom yet when this was written. In other words they are referred to as an ethnic group rather than an organised state. The word used is that for "foreign people", not that for a "country". This sign was typically used by the Egyptians to signify nomadic tribes without a fixed city-state, thus implying that Israel was a semi-nomadic or rural population at the time this stele was created.'

'So what?' inquired Jacques.

'So,' responded Bob, a little irritated by Jacques apparent flippancy. 'So it means that by 1208 B.C. Israel was not yet a kingdom. They were either still wandering or just beginning to settle into the land of Palestine which was then called Canaan: either that or they were at the period the Bible refers to as the "Judges". You see, the chronology of the Exodus story is essentially religious rather than of a historical nature. This inscription helps us in narrowing that period down considerably. Assuming they were in the wilderness wandering for forty years, then the start of the Exodus would be at least forty years before this inscribe date, which would bring us to 1248 BC. We maybe could add ten years for their initial conquests and settlements which would take us to approximately 1258 BC, for the possible year of the Expulsion, commonly called, "The Exodus."'

'Wow!' exclaimed Jacques. 'I see now why you say this is so important. This gives a historical context to the Exodus. Why then did you call it the "Expulsion"?'

'That, my dear fellow, is what I am currently working on. You remember what my final comment was when I delivered my lecture in London?'

Jacques spoke in a whisper, not wishing to draw attention to what he said, 'I am hardly likely to forget that. It has played on my mind ever since I heard you. How did you put it, "Israel does not have, and never did have, a divine right to the land of Palestine". That is very emotive language.'

'Indeed and I don't wish to discuss this further where we could be overheard. But what I will say, is this: most people think, because of the time frame I have just given you, that the Israelites left Egypt during the reign of the pharaoh Ramesses II, who was ruling during that time period.'

'The most famous pharaoh of them all,' stated Jacques.

'Yes indeed. He is also known as Ramesses-the-Great, ruling from 1297 to 1213 BC. This would fit in with the timescale I have just shown you of 1248 BC as a possible date for the Exodus. And like most people this is what I also believed, until quite recently.' Bob wagged his forefinger in the air and gave a knowing look. 'However, it always puzzled me that there are no recorded plagues of Egypt during that time; nor anything similar, such as natural disasters.'

'So what changed your mind, and when do you think all this took place then?' Jacques' curiosity was burning.

Bob looked deadly serious, as they walked out of the museum back into the strong sunlight. He removed his hat and wiped the sweat from his forehead. 'I am sorry; I'm not really ready to discuss the finer details of this just yet Jacques. A lot of it is confidential and very controversial, so I'd rather wait until I have more evidence. I'll just say I have discovered something which would put the expulsion of the Israelites back to the time of either King Tut or his father Akhenaten; at least one-hundred and fifteen years before the Merneptak Stele was made. One thing I can say now, is that in the Bible the name of the pharaoh is not mentioned, he is just referred to as "The Pharaoh"; which is very strange. You see other foreign kings are frequently mentioned by name in the Bible. Kings, such as Cyrus, Sennacherib, Darius, Artaxerxes, Nebuchadnezzar and Belshazzar; to name but a few. They are all named. So why is there no mention of the king of Egypt's name? I believe the answer is that Akhenaten was classed as a heretic, and his son King Tut would likewise be tainted. The name of Akhenaten was erased from all records and public buildings, so in effect he was the king whose name must not be mentioned. This is speculative of course, but my main reasons for saying the Expulsion was in the days of King Tut is not speculative; but that will have to wait for another time.'

'I understand,' said Jacques; not wishing to let this little disappointment spoil such a wonderful day.

They now wandered back to the main entrance of the museum. 'This has been fascinating Bob, thank you for a splendid time in the museum. You have answered many of my questions; except for that last one, on the timing of the Expulsion, as you call it.' Jacques smiled at this.

It was obvious Bob wanted to depart, so Jacques reached out to shake Bob's hand.

Bob took Jacques hand but held on to it for longer than normal, 'Look Jacques, I'll be honest with you. One of the reasons I was happy to meet with you again today is that I was hoping you could do something for me. You see I want to travel to Sudan soon, but it is such a difficult country to get into and there are so many strings to pull. If you can help me get there maybe I will be in a better position to explain things further to you.'

'I am sure I can do that for you Bob, but on one condition,' Jacques grinned.

'What's that old boy?'

'You take me on one of your field trips there.'

'That my dear fellow will be a great pleasure,' Bob turned and walked across the garden toward the entrance. 'Now, why don't you go back into the museum old chap, and take a look around at all the wonderful stuff they have here. I have to get things ready to publish my findings on the prophet Mohammed!'

Jacques appreciated what Bob had taught him, 'Thank you for a fascinating tour. You have given me a lot to think about.' The two men shook hands, 'I'll see you in Sudan then.'

And with that Bob walked away leaving Jacques standing there with his head buzzing over all the new things he had learnt from the man he had come to like and respect.

****

Khartoum - Sudan

Passing through the airport of Khartoum had not been a pleasant experience for Jacques. The airport was dark, dusty and gloomy, with too many official checks, and a long period waiting for baggage. Whilst standing at the baggage reclaim belt, wondering if it would ever start to move, a Sudanese man with a beaming smile greeted him. He had been sent by Jacques's Company to meet him in order to help ease his passage through the nightmare of Third World airport officialdom; a situation he had found endemic in many similar countries which choose to isolate themselves from the rest of the world.

In the city of Khartoum the traffic was chaotic, the roads had many potholes and once off the main roads they were no more than dirt tracks. In fact dirt and grime seemed to be the norm in this city, a far cry from the cleanliness of Jacques's home in Canada. Yet it was the friendliness of the Sudanese people that he found to be the most pleasing. These friendly people seemed to be a contradiction to the chaotic politics which were the ruin of this country; politics which had the Sudan engaged in almost constant warfare, ever since the British left there in 1956. Jacques's Company was seeking to become a partner in the oilfields there, which were yet again being fought over by rival native factions. It was this troublesome situation that was the reason for Jacques visit. He was authorised to help with the ongoing negotiations at government level, to try, in some way, to resolve this messy situation. He well knew it would be a difficult, if not an impossible task. However, Jacques had been well briefed and had been given many influential contacts to help him achieve his goal.

There had been such a long history of hatred, distrust and downright oppression between North and South Sudan, that he knew this was almost a 'Mission Impossible'. Even so, somehow he had to try, after all that was his job and he was good at it. There were many places in the world were oil had been discovered in politically unstable areas and this was one of them. Jacques often found the oilfields to be in the centre of, or the cause of, many conflicts in the world; even so, this one was different. In Sudan there was a racial and religious divide within the country, which literary had ripped the country in two; a situation he knew was fraught with potential dangers. The divide was mainly between the South, who are racially black Africa and largely Christian; whereas the North are Arabic and mostly Muslims. The two had never got on well together and often these cultures and religions clashed violently. Here was a country which clearly demonstrated that a Muslim majority could not rule peacefully over a large Christian minority.

After years of hard fighting between the North and South which caused over two and a half million deaths, the South of Sudan had eventually managed to break away from the North and form their own independent country in the year 2011. By this secession, South Sudan became Africa's first new nation since 1993; yet their efforts to become independent had a major problem. This problem was that on the north-south border there was oil, right in the middle of the racial and religious divide of Sudan. Large amounts of their oil reserves were in the land-locked South, but the pipeline taking this expensive commodity out, traversed through the northern lands up to Sudan's only sea port, Port Sudan. It was a recipe for trouble, and trouble flared constantly. To break away from the North the South had fought long and hard, yet even as they broke away fighting flared up in and around the oilfields.

It was a depressing situation. Jacques well knew it would be an uphill struggle to keep the interests of his Company protected by trying to preserve their risky investment in this volatile land. The only thing Jacques could work on was that some form of settlement was in the interests of all concerned. Yet neither side seemed to want to move away from their entrenched positions.

After several days of fruitless talks Jacques spirits were lifted when he received an Email from Bob asking if he could join him on a trip he wanted to take to an ancient Sudanese site: a trip Bob said he would find very interesting. He also asked if he had been to the National Museum of Sudan yet? He recommended that he should do so, stating it was not far from the Hilton Hotel where Bob had booked to stay, by the banks of the river Nile. Jacques replied to his Email saying he would visit this museum before they met up again.

Three days later Jacques arrived at the Hilton Hotel, a modern building situated on a rise overlooking the River Nile. There were not many good hotels in Khartoum, but Bob had chosen this as one of the better ones and arranged to meet with Jacques therein order to take him on the trip he had promised while they were in Egypt. It was early morning, just before the sun rose, when Jacques arrived. Bob had told him they would have a long drive ahead of them, so to make sure their journey could be covered in one day, he requested this early start.

Upon seeing Bob, Jacques was rather taken aback, because he was not alone. By his side was a very attractive olive skinned, dark eyed woman. By any standard she was a stunning beauty.

'This is Mary McIntire,' said Bob after greeting Jacques. 'She is my assistant and a very helpful one too.'

Jacques's response did not come out as naturally as he intended it to. Somehow hearing the name of 'Mary' again brought images flashing through his mind. Images of an equally beautiful face; horribly disfigured. 'Nice to meet you Mary,' was all he could immediately muster.

Mary gave Jacques a broad warm smile showing her perfectly formed white teeth. Being the daughter of an English father and a Coptic Christian mother from Egypt, she had been brought up and educated in England. She had been horrified at the way Coptic Christians had been so badly persecuted in Egypt, especially after the revolutions which had brought to power, firstly the Muslim Brotherhood, then yet another military coup. During this period of upheaval Muslim violence against Christians had increased considerably, as religious fundamentalism became more pronounced within Egypt.

'Nice to meet you also, Jacques.' Her eyes flashed as she spoke. 'I have been looking forward to this day for some time,' she stated.

'Well I am not sure what to expect, nor where we are going!' exclaimed Jacques with a slight mocking tone directed towards Bob.

'That's typical of Bob, Jacques.' Then in a mock scolding she retorted, 'Fancy not telling Jacques where we are going.'

Bob completely ignored this chastisement, accepting it as a matter of course. 'Thank you for helping me to get the visa I needed Jacques,' he said. Then scoffing added, 'You would not believe this place, it has been even harder for us to obtain a travel permit for today's trip, than it was to get visas to get into this place.' Then shrugging his shoulders added, 'But, after a lot of hassle we finally have one. This is such a restrictive country, that even if you get a visa to enter this place, it does not allow you to travel freely around the country.'

Jacques was only half listening; he was transfixed by the presence of Mary and the delightful omnipresent of the eastern perfume she wore. Around her head was a loose head-scarf only partially concealing her shining black hair, worn as an obvious token to the sensibilities of this country. Her dark eyes flashed as she glanced toward Jacques. Around her neck a discreet gold cross, displayed her beliefs. Her long sleeved white blouse was set off, by a black waistcoat, beautifully embroidered with gold thread. Her long navy-blue skirt went right down to her ankles.

'So you work with Bob?' asked Jacques tentatively, unsure why he found it necessary to repeat what Bob had already said.

Her smile was intoxicating, 'Yes,' she replied. 'I have done so for some time now. I am really looking forward to today, I have been waiting to see this place for a long time.'

'Maybe someone will tell me what this place is, you both seem to so be excited about?' Jacques was beginning to get just a little frustrated.

'All in good time old boy,' said Bob as all three began to walk to the hotel's car park.

Mary loved her work with Bob and relished the opportunity to be able to help him further with his research work.

As they set off in a Land-Cruiser, Jacques asked a little more forcefully, 'So will someone tell me where we are heading then?'

'Merowe,' was Bob's reply.

Recognising the name Jacques asked, 'That's where the new dam is; are we going to the dam then?'

'No we are not, not that bloody dam,' was Bob's curt and unexpected reply.

'Don't be so rude Bob,' interjected Mary. 'Probably Jacques does not know the story.'

'Sorry Jacques, it is just that not only do we have an oppressive regime here, the Chinese have taken over in a big way in this country. That blasted dam has been built by the Chinese right across the remains of sub-Saharan Africa's earliest urban civilisation.' Bob was clearly upset at the thought of this.

'It is so very sad,' added Mary. 'I feel this is yet another atrocity, against the African people. Nubia is a treasure-house of artefacts that attest to the ancient greatness of this country. Now much of it has been inundated, causing irreparable harm to this noble heritage. Neither the Chinese, nor the Sudanese government, care one jot for the historical heritage of Sudan. That dam has now submerged immeasurable archaeological treasures in its reservoir. It cost one-point eight billion dollars and was funded mainly by the Chinese. It is one of the world's most destructive hydropower projects there is; would you believe it is ten kilometres long. Archaeologists have had to work frantically hard to record and to move just a few of the objects, but the world was not interested so the funding was grossly inadequate.' The irritation in Mary's voice was clear

Jacques could see that Mary was no ordinary woman. She was well educated and obviously had a strong conviction for her work. Her presence was a factor in the uplift Jacques was feeling as they drove along. He had not felt this way for some time.

In a philosophical tone, Jacques let his own feeling be known, 'I can well understand your feelings. In my own work I have come to believe that the Chinese may be in the process of colonising Sudan. They have not only built the main oil pipeline, which takes my Company's share of the oil out from the south, but they have also built hundreds of miles of new roads, and now you say they have also built this dam. I predict they are not going to let anything get in the way of their massive investments; so there is a danger that if things do get out of hand here, they will almost certainly move Chinese troops in to protect their interests and investments and the world will be able to do nothing about it, except to wring their hands.' Jacques thought for a moment, then continued, 'Just as the British did in India all those years ago. It was in order to protect British trade there that they moved their troops in, which resulted in the colonisation of India. I fear the Chinese will do the same here.'

'You may well be right Jacques,' Bob's natural smile had gone.

'So if it's not the dam, what are we going to see in Merowe?' asked Jacques yet again. Bob was still pondering on what Jacques had said about China for a moment, then responded. 'The place we are going to in Merowe has survived the vandalism of the area. You will find there are more than forty pyramids there.'

Seeing the look of surprise on Jacques face Mary stepped in immediately. 'Yes but they are much smaller than the pyramids of Egypt; yet still impressive nevertheless.' Mary's eyes seemed to glow at the prospect. 'You see there was a time when Sudan once ruled Egypt, during the time of the Black Pharaohs. This part of Sudan was part of the Nubian Kushite Empire. This is an area of history which has been so overlooked and yet in many ways it is just as important as that of Egypt. Nubian culture was at its height between the eighth and third century B.C.'

'Did you get to see Sudan's National Museum?' asked Bob.

'Yes I did,' answered Jacques. 'The museum has not been very well looked after though, but interesting nevertheless. I had not expected to see so many artefacts with an Egyptian connection here in Sudan. Those two huge colossal statutes of pharaohs standing outside were truly amazing.'

'Yes they were statues of Natakamai a later black Nubian pharaoh of Kush, made around 1 B.C. to 20 A.D., when Egypt was ruled by Rome. Yet before Rome ruled Egypt there was a time when the most powerful of the Nubian Kushite kings ruled the whole of not only Egypt but Sudan as well, serving as pharaohs of both countries. They even referred to northern Sudan as Upper Egypt. The greatest of these southern black pharaohs was Taharqa who ruled from 690 to 664 B.C., this was at the time when the Assyrians were coming out of Iraq to eventually conquer Egypt.'

Before that,' added Bob, 'Egypt appointed a viceroy to govern Kush......' Bob's words tailed off. Something on the road ahead of them, made their conversation suddenly dwindle. 'What have we got here?' Bob looked concerned as traffic was being halted for a road block.

'It will be a travel permit check,' replied Jacques. 'They are common throughout this country.'

Two scruffy officials carrying assault rifles approached the car. It was impossible to know if they were police or military. They barked an order in Arabic, which only Mary understood.

'Travel documents gentlemen,' she informed her companions.

The officials looked intently at the documents then closely at the faces of the passengers within the vehicle. They then walked away carrying all their passports and travel permits with them.

Several discussions took place with a number of other armed men, who were now also looking at these documents.

The original two returned to the party, 'No, you go back,' ordered one of them, in broken English.

Mary spoke in Arabic to them. There were some loud and forceful words exchanged between them. 'They won't let me pass,' said Mary. 'They don't like to see a woman in a car who is not related to the men she is with. I am so sorry.' She was downcast, but resilient.

'Hang on a minute,' Jacques took out his mobile phone and began making a call. After a moment or two he handed the phone to the officer. Shouted words could faintly be heard coming from the phone.

The officer look annoyed and embarrassed at the same time. He gruffly handed the phone back, then snapped, 'You go,' he said waving his arm in a gesture of anger.

'How did you do that?' asked Bob, as they set off once again along the road.

'That was the Minister of the Interior,' beamed Jacques. 'It helps to have good contacts in these places.'

'Good job we had you along old boy,' beamed Bob. 'Shouldn't like to tackle those fellows on my own.'

After a short while along their journey, Jacques returned to their former conversation, 'You were speaking about the black pharaohs ruling all of Egypt, I would have thought they were all either black or dark skinned.' This was an honest enquiry from Jacques.

Bob thought carefully for his words, 'Where we are going to was a powerbase of the Nubian black pharaohs and they did in the later years rule all of Egypt. They seemed to have flourished from the Twenty-first to Twenty-fifth Dynasty, around 740 B.C. Piye and Taharqa being two of the most notable pharaohs of this

Nubian rule. However, the Nubians were forced to retreat back south into Sudan or Kush when the Assyrians conquered Egypt.'

'So that was the period of the black pharaohs,' added Mary. 'Frustratingly it is no longer "politically correct" in our modern society to say this, but there is overwhelming evidence to show that the early pharaohs were white.'

Jacques raised his eyebrows, 'Now that does surprise me,' he said. 'What evidence is there of that?'

Bob took up the answer to this question, 'The statues and portraits of kings, queens and nobles show certain pharaohs and nobles as white. Some from around 2,800 B.C. are depicted with white skin and blue eyes. The famous bust of Queen Nefertiti is clearly that of a white woman, around 1,350 B.C. King Tut's great-grandfather had blond hair, Ramesses II had red hair and white features; his nose, face shape excreta. King Tut's DNA has a close correlation with modern Western Europeans. The white Egyptians left many references to the black population in Nubia as being distinct from themselves, and at one point their writings recorded a law that forbade blacks from entering their country at all.'

Mary took up this theme, 'You see this is a hot potato to the modern mind, for there are many pro-black historians who have attempted to distort the historical records by claiming that the Ancient Egyptian civilisation was black in racial origin. However the evidence shows it was only in the later years of Egypt's history that the black, Semitic and white merged into a racially divergent nation.'

'I'll do some research on this myself,' said Jacques.

'Please do,' said Bob. 'You will find what we have said to be true; even if it is not politically correct.' And with that he smiled, adding, 'Another hour and we should be there.'

****

London to Derby - England

'It won't work!' retorted Adnan emphatically.

Driving north along the congested motorway was always a trying time for Adnan, but more so when he was constantly being distracted by what he considered to be a futile argument. Trying to explain to an excited Nasser Mohammed why his ill conceived plan would not, and could not, work was wearing to Adnan's active brain. Both were returning to Derby for the first time since the demonstration there, when they had clashed with the EDL. To start their journey Adnan had first driven to Nasser's home in South London, where they had tea before they headed north. The tea had been served by Nasser's wife Salma who appeared to be more nervous than normal to Adnan; but he just put this down Nasser being overzealous with his delicate young wife.

During their journey north Nasser had bombarded Adnan with questions and situations from the moment they had set off together in the car. Nasser was convinced he had a good plan of action, a plan to poison the water supply of the city of Derby. To Nasser it all seemed very plausible, but not so to Adnan. In places their vehicle slowed to a crawl, and sometimes a complete stop, which irritated Adnan even more. Adnan had plans for Derby, and saw himself as being the instrument in bringing God's vengeance against that place. Plans which he was trying to carefully formulate and mull over in his mind; plans he could not yet discuss. Now Nasser's scatterbrained ideas were stopping him from thinking these ideas through clearly.

'Why not?' screeched Nasser in exasperation. 'We could make a massive political and religious statement by this; we could kill or make sick thousands. It will have far more impact than a few bombs placed here are there.'

'Look Nasser, just listen for a moment', said Adnan who was on the verge of losing his temper. Wrestling with his own feelings Adnan realised that Nasser's enthusiasm for their beliefs could be put to good use, so his calm outward facade belied his inner feelings. Struggling with these thoughts Adnan continued, 'The first requirement is to deliver a lethal dose of a poison, which means we need to deliver at least twenty-five to fifty times the lethal dose per person to each household.'

Still not really listening to Adnan's reasoning Nasser continued on, 'We could use arsenic or cyanide, because both are soluble in water and can be lethal. Sodium cyanide is relatively plentiful and accessible, because of its use in the mining and metal industries. It is an odourless white salt, stable and highly soluble in water.'

Adnan gritted his teeth, 'Yes Nasser, I know all this: I am a chemist. Whether we use cyanide, arsenic or strychnine, if we are going to poison a city we would need something like twenty tons of the stuff. Now just think of that for a moment, that will be twenty one-ton pickup trucks! Then we have to get the poison into the water system. If we dump it into a reservoir it will first pass through a purification plant. There the water would be tested and the poison discovered, and even if it was not discovered very little would get through the purification process.'

Nasser was not going to be put off that easily, 'Then don't put it into the reservoir, but put it into the water after it leaves the water treatment plant.'

There was a brief silence while Adnan tried yet again to compose himself. 'You are not thinking this through Nasser.' Dim-whit was what he really thought. 'Even if we could find a way to get twenty tons of poison into the water supply after it leaves the treatment plant, the outflow pipes are under pressure, that's how they move the water along the pipes. So if we dig down into them and cut a hole with the intention of shovelling the poison in, the water will simply gush into the sky; then the repairmen will arrive. And then what?' he snapped. 'Use your brain.'

Nasser went quiet, brooding and sulking as he realised his plan had not been well thought through.

'I have other plans for Derby,' said Adnan, breaking the brief silence. Then, looking at the crest fallen Nasser, he added, 'Derby City Council have rejected our attempt to convert their old church into a mosque. So, I intend to give them all such a taste of God's anger that they will never forget it.'

The pair remained silent for a while. 'My plans will require our Derby brothers to tighten up their parameters considerably.' Adnan was now thinking out loud, working out the plans he had for Derby. 'I presume they have Christian girls serving their needs in Derby?', he questioned.

Nasser smiled, thinking of the many pleasures those girls, both willing and unwilling, had brought to him. 'Yes they do, they have some real beauties. After the demonstration there I stayed on for a few days to sample their delights,' he said giving a slavering laugh. 'But they are all stupid. All we have to do to these kuffar bitches is to say we love them. Then fuck them a few times, give them drugs and alcohol, tell them we need them to fuck our brothers; and they do.' Nasser burst out laughing again, becoming sexually aroused by his own inner thoughts. 'It's so easy. They have no morals they just let themselves be used. And we do, again and again.'

'I agree', said Adnan, 'all western women are whores. Even the female news readers on TV have short skirts so you can look up their legs. They are all the same. So we are right to use them as the spoils of holy war. However while this operation is on, which I am planning for Derby, you must have no contact with those whores in Derby.'

Nasser looked bewildered, disappointed and crestfallen. 'Why not? What do they have to do with the plans you are making?'

'How old are the youngest? Adnan asked.

'How young do you want them?' said Nasser half jokingly, but as a serious statement.

'That's my point,' said Adnan emphatically. 'You are missing sensible reasoning again Nasser. They could bring attention to us we do not want. I am sure some will be under sixteen and if the police or social workers come looking for them it could compromise my whole operation.'

Again Nasser saw the sense in Adnan's logic; but retorted, 'That could be difficult. These bitches have come to rely on our brothers for drugs and things; besides they have nowhere else to go. If we just turn them out they will go to the authorities to find somewhere to live.'

'Good point,' acknowledged Adnan, who went quiet while thinking of an solution. 'In that case take them all up to our brothers in Bradford. Let them entertain them for a while, well away from Derby. At least until this operation is all over.'

Adnan at last felt he could now relax a little, as they entered the city of Derby.

****

Merowe - Sudan

The journey had been long, but the constant enlightening conversations had made it pass quickly. Now, after parking their vehicle it was heavy going, tramping up the hot, soft sand surrounding the pyramid site of Merowe. With the hot wind biting into their faces the three companions trudged up the steep climb to the where the crude entrance gate to this historic site lay. A dusty and dark shop formed an integral part of the entrance, with an old man and two children trying to sell what little they had in the way of souvenirs. Further away, another man lackadaisically beckoned the party to come over to his reclining camel, just in case they, the only visitors of the day, wanted to take a ride on the beast. Ignoring the prospect of a camel ride, they passed on through the entrance gate. At first Jacques could see very little, other than a number of ruined manmade structures sticking out above the sand dunes. But gradually, as they climbed up the hillside, with the sand over their ankles, the vista began to slowly open up before them. Finally as they rounded the top of the sand dune Jacques realised why his friends had brought him here. There before them were the mysterious beacons of a long lost age.

Jacques was mesmerised. He had never seen anything quite like what had now emerged before him. Mouth open and initially speechless he just stood looking at this vista; an archaeologist's and historian's paradise was spread out in front of him. Dozens of pyramids stretched for a mile or more, most were half buried in sand. They were much smaller and with steeper angled sides than those of the more famous pyramids of Egypt; but it was still clear to see that what they were looking at here was from an Egyptian culture. Many of the pyramids had their tops missing and were in various states of decay. It was apparent that some kind of ill-conceived attempt to rebuild a number of them had taken place at sometime, for the stone they had used did not match that of the original. It gave the site a patchwork appearance. In front of each pyramid there was what passed for an entrance, looking something like a gated chapel. This entrance was attached to, and formed an integral part of, the main structure.

'Why isn't this place better known?' questioned Jacques, when he finally found words to speak. Then checking himself he gave a broad grin, 'Treat that as a rhetorical question Bob. I know the answer.' Then he elaborated, 'This country has a dictatorship, with a restrictive, oppressive government. I guess they don't really encourage tourists. In fact the President of this country, Omar Bashir, has been accused by the International Criminal Court of genocide, war crimes and crimes against humanity, among other things. They have even issued an arrest warrant for him. I should know, for I've been trying to deal with his government, and believe me it is not easy.'

'That's true,' responded Mary. 'It is so sad. This is one of several places in the Sudan which could become a major tourist attraction with the right kind of investment and a less restrictive government in control. Just look at how neglected it is.'

'Tourism is one thing,' lamented Bob, 'but what this place needs is major investment for serious archaeological excavation and study. It's criminal letting it deteriorate like this. This place looks very much like the Sphinx must have looked when Napoleon first arrived in Egypt; uncared for and mostly buried in sand. It has had some archaeological work, but nowhere near enough. I believe there is more buried here than we can possibly see without serious excavation.'

'It's an eerie and otherworldly sight, as if we have stepped into a movie,' commented Jacques, still a little dazed at the sight before him. 'Tell me why are the tops missing from most of the pyramids? It looks deliberate?'

'Hole in one old boy,' responded Bob. 'It was indeed deliberate. Some Italian guy in the nineteenth century thought there must be gold inside these structures, so he simply dynamited the tops off them: such a sacrilege.' Bob shook his head in despair to think that anyone could treat historical monuments of world value, so disgracefully.

'How old are these pyramids?' asked Jacques as he gazed in continued wonder.

'They were built between 800 B.C. and 300 A.D., a much later period than the Egyptian pyramids,' was Bob's precise reply. Then shaking his head sadly lamented, 'You say about no tourists being here, but many have actually struggled to make this long journey here, only to find when they arrived that they cannot get in unless they have a permit from Khartoum, more than two-hundred kilometres away! And of course no one saw fit to tell them that while they were in Khartoum. That would really get you depressed, would it not?' he hissed sarcastically. 'Such is the crass stupidity of a centralised dictatorship.'

Mary scanned the horizon gazing around, holding her hand above her eyes to shield them from the glare of the sun, 'Bob told me there are close to two hundred pyramids around this relatively small area of Sudan, they are the ancient burial site of the Nubian Kingdom sometimes known as the Kingdom of Kush.'

Bob wiped the sweat off his brow, and put his large heavy rucksack containing their food and his equipment down on the ground. 'As you see Jacques, these Pyramids are smaller than their Egyptian cousins but equally impressive due to their number, there are more than forty kings, queens and other important individuals around this site. You see Egypt was a Nubian state, a colony even, for one hundred years, until the Assyrians invaded Egypt from the North-East. The Kushites then retreated back to their homeland of Nubia, where their kingdom remained strong for a millennium.'

Bob picked up his bag, and the three comrades walked casually over towards one of the larger pyramids, entering the small chapel like entrance. Once inside about ten feet away was a solid stone wall. 'As you can see this is a false entrance to the tomb,' said Bob. Then, pointing to what Mary was doing, said. 'Look at this.'

Mary was photographing the faded carvings on the inside walls of this false entrance to the tomb. Looking up Mary said, 'Here is the Egyptian god Amen-Ra along with Anubis the god of the dead; which was always depicted as a jackal.' She carefully took several photos of this ancient artwork. 'You see Anubis is standing by the side of Amen-Ra. Over here is a Nubian female pharaoh, with her captives cowering before her, bound together in rope bonds: this is Queen Amenitore of the first century A.D. Most of these carvings are faded and difficult to see clearly.' Mary was clearly frustrated at the neglect of this site. 'There has been little or no attempt to protect them from the elements. They have simply been left to the wind-blown sand to wear them away. It is so sad.'

They continued on for a while looking intently at more of the ancient artwork carved into the stone, as the three walked on together around the upper part of the site, slowly trying to absorb this vast site which lay before them. After a period of wandering and wondering just what could be lying hidden beneath the many banks of sand, they decided to sit in a shaded part, where a gentle wind blew. After their long journey the lunches provided by the hotel were unpacked and eaten with relish.

Queen Amenitore of the first century A.D. Most of these carvings are faded and difficult to see clearly.' noted Jacques.

'Yes,' agreed Mary. 'Only ardent travellers and archaeologists get here.'

'The worship of the one-god Aten came to Sudan,' said Bob suddenly. 'It spread this far south. Not long ago, in the year 2003, a Swiss archaeological team excavating near the ancient city of Pnubs in Kerma, part of northern Sudan, found stone blocks which had been used for the flooring of a later temple. These blocks had older carvings and painted decorations underneath them, yet they had been placed face down and deliberately hidden from the public view; pressed into the dirt of the ground. They had been obviously taken from earlier structures. Some of these stones actually displayed the sun rays of the Aten and even his name was there as a hieroglyphic cartouche. These many fragments had been cut up for reuse; presumably when the worship of the old gods was restored.'

'So Aten worship was widespread,' said Jacques.

'Yes, this new form of worship spread throughout the whole Egyptian Kingdom, either by force, or by genuine commitment,' commented Mary as she delicately tucked into a delicious chicken leg. 'I think we must accept that in many places this new religion would have been imposed by force; and as such it would be very unpopular indeed. Bob and I are convinced these revolutionary teachings were either taken up by Moses, or he already had them from his birth. Whichever it was there are so many similarities between the beliefs of Akhenaten and those of Moses that the more you examine them the more you realise they are virtually the same.'

Jacques said nothing, but listened in rapt attention, realising there was more to be said.

'The origins of the Jews are of great political importance to our world,' Bob had lost his natural smile as he continued. 'Most of the terrorist actions in the world today, stem from the controversy surrounding the existence of Israel. Through religious beliefs we have been handed down a series of myths and legends about a promise from God to give Palestine, as the promised land, or Canaan as it was then, to the followers of Moses. At this time the God of Moses, the God of the Old Testament was called Yahweh; sometimes wrongly translated as Jehovah.'

'So this is what you were referring to during your lecture in London', said Jacques in realisation.

Before Bob could respond, Mary interjected, 'We have been researching this for a long time now Jacques. We will soon be ready to publish our findings. It is very exciting.'

'And controversial,' stated Jacques.

'Indeed,' agreed Bob. 'As Mary has said, when you look more closely into it you can see how the beliefs of the heretic pharaoh Akhenaten are similar, if not the same as, the teachings of Moses.'

Jacques nodded his head in agreement, 'I agree it does seem to be more than a mere coincidence that the first two monotheistic religions known in world history, had their start so close together in both time and location.'

'Well obviously it cannot just be just a coincidence,' said Mary. 'There is much more to this than a causal connection between the worship of Aten and the worship of Yahweh of the Hebrews. When Bob publishes his findings the world will know Israel did not have a divine right to the land of Palestine. Show Jacques what we have found Bob.'

Bob took his iPad out of his rucksack and opened it up. 'Look at this,' he said. 'The Jewish creed says: "*Schema Yisrael Adonai Elohenu Adonai Echod*", which in English means *"Hear, 0 Israel, the Lord thy God is one God"*. That word "*Adonai*" is important. The last two letters *"ai"* of the word is a Hebrew pronoun meaning *"my"* or *"mine"* which signifies possession. The first part *"Adon"* was correctly noted way back in the 1930's by Sigmund Freud, as the Hebrew word for Aten.'

'That's incredible,' gasped Jacques.

'You see,' continued Bob, the Egyptian *"t"* becomes *"d"* in Hebrew, and *"e"* becomes an *"o"*, so *"Adon"* is the Hebrew equivalent of the Egyptian word *"Aten"*. Thus Adon and Aten are the same.'

Pointing to the screen Mary added, 'Therefore this sentence from the Jewish creed should be translated as, *'Hear O Israel, our*

God Aten is the only God". And we have many archaeological finds and inscriptions which has Akhenaten saying, *"The Aten is the only God"*.'

'I'm stunned', said Jacques. 'This is truly amazing. It is becoming clear to me how the first two monotheistic religions both came from the same source.'

Bob looked up from his iPad, 'What I have found is that those who followed the beliefs of Akhenaten were hated by those who wished to keep to the ways of the old gods. So when Akhenaten died the priestly class wanted to rid Egypt of these troublesome heretical religious fanatics. The Aten worshipers had opposed the traditional religious and social order, and hence the very authority of those priests and thereby the need for them to even exist. The priesthood of Amen had been the most powerful body in the country. These priests, and many of the population, therefore wanted to drive the Aten worshipers out of Egypt.'

'I see,' said Jacques with a realisation of clarity. 'So that would be the Expulsion you referred to in Cairo.'

'Exactly,' responded Bob. 'You see the evidence is that those who left Egypt were not just Hebrews but Egyptians as well. In fact we have evidence to show they were mostly Egyptians who had taken up this new belief in one-god. It has been argued by some that they were all Egyptians.'

'Even Moses was an Egyptian,' explained Mary. Her lovely eyes blazed with clear and determined intent as she continued. 'The Bible itself says he was brought up in the royal household as a prince, and the name Moses is clearly Egyptian. Even in the Bible at Exodus 2:19 you will find that Moses is called an Egyptian. We find the name Moses is used many times as part of an Egyptian common name. It comes from the Egyptian word "mose" meaning *"is born"* or *"son of"*; such as in the names of Amen-mose, meaning *"born of Amen"*, or Ramoses meaning *"son of Ra"*, or in Thuth-mose *"son of Thoth"*.' Then girlishly smiling she added, 'How many women have said, they had *found* a child, or had a *divine visit,* by way of explaining an unexpected or unwanted birth!'

Bob started to search for something on his iPad, then without looking up said, 'We can go to several unconnected ancient Greek and Roman historians who wrote of a time when a renegade Egyptian priest "*led an army of lepers*" against the pharaoh who finally expelled them from Egypt. There is a great deal of evidence to show the Exodus was an Expulsion of unwanted people. The use of the word *"leper"* here would be a derogative term for a hated group; similarly to the way Germans were called *"bosh"* during the First World War. '

'So they left Egypt and went out to conquer new lands for them to live in,' said Jacques seeing how all this fitted into a pattern.

'Yes Jacques,' agreed Bob. Then turning to Mary he asked, 'And what do conquerors do to justify their conquests Mary?'

Mary smiled eager to continue, 'Conquers will do all they can to justify their aggression and conquests. They will write a self-righteous, colourful account to glorify and justify their actions, and often re-write the facts to suit their own aims. They have all done this throughout history. Let's just take one example: William-the-Conqueror told so many lies to justify his invasion of England in 1066 that these lies were taught in schools as facts, right up until late in the twentieth century. The Israelites were no different; they told stories to justify their invasion and their cruel treatment of those indigenous inhabitants. Stories still believed by many today.'

Bob puffed out his cheeks, 'Fabricated stories very loosely based on real events. The people who tell such stories are called Spin Doctors in today's political circles.'

'I have a few of them in my Company as well,' laughed Jacques.

Mary had not finished, 'For example, the numbers of people involved in the Exodus according to the Bible and Torah simply could not be. It is recorded in the Bible that there were about six-hundred thousand men, plus women and children, along with many non-Israelites. This would have numbered some two million people in total! Compare this to the entire Egyptian population at the time of around three to three and a half million. If these numbers were true, then those fleeing would have been better to stand and fight, rather than run.' Then wagging her finger added, 'Also we must know, that if they were walking, let us say ten abreast, and without accounting for any livestock, they would have formed a line one hundred and fifty miles long. Need I say more?'

'Now here's a good point,' said Bob, interrupting, 'With so many numbers wandering for so many years, they would certainly have left some evidence behind for archaeologists to find.' Bob paused, then pursed his lips, 'Well they have been searching now for over one-hundred years for that evidence and none has ever been found. It just did not happen on that scale, or evidence of it would have been found by now.'

As Bob was speaking a dust devil of spinning sand suddenly appeared, blasting hot air into their faces and scattering a few papers around, prompting Bob to thrust his iPad back into his bag for protection. As the miniature whirlwind passed the three dusted the sand out of their hair and sat down again.

'Damn these dust-devils,' shouted Bob. 'They get sand everywhere.'

Jacques was fascinated with the revelations he had been hearing, 'So what we have is a moderate number of religious extremists, some were Hebrews but mostly they were Egyptians; a group of people who were led by an Egyptian prince, being expelled from Egypt for their beliefs.'

'That's about it Jacques, the majority of those leaving were Egyptians,' acknowledged Bob, then added, 'and we are rapidly getting the proof of that.'

'So what did the worshipers of Aten actually believe in?' asked Jacques.

Bob was happy to answer, 'That the Aten was the only true god, and all other forms of worship must be renounced, denounced or destroyed. The very existence of any other gods was denied. Some of their beliefs are still with us today. There was to be no image of Aten, or no graven image as it is said in the Bible. There were strong punishments for any failure to carry out worship in the manner as set out for the followers of both Aten and Yahweh. Let's also take a look at Muslims and their insistence on public prayers. Akhenaten insisted prayer must be public and offered up three times a day: as the sun rose, at mid-day and as the sun set. Muslims still do this and have added two more to that list, making public prayer five times a day. I say public, because if they are seen going to the mosque then that is public, and it becomes a peer-pressure requirement. Often such prayers are performed out on the streets for all to see, either that they are obeying God's law, or to show to others how righteous they are. Islam has relied heavily on such peer-pressure with each member attempting to conform to the expectations of the group. The fact is, religion flourishes where individual critical thinking is absent or stifled.'

'So you see how important our work is,' said Mary. 'Especially as these events of so long ago are still affecting the world we live in today. Once Bob's work on the origins of Israel is published it will have political consequences all over the Middle East, and beyond to America. We are close to proving there was never a divine promise for the Hebrews to take over the Promised Land; they were simply fleeing religious persecution. We can prove this because something was discovered in King Tut's tomb...' she did not finish her sentence.

'Not now Mary. We are not ready for that yet,' Bob was abrupt, hurting Mary unintentionally.

'I'm sorry Bob, I thought…'

'No, I'm sorry Mary. I didn't mean to bark at you.' Then turning to Jacques by way of explanation, 'You see Jacques this is so sensitive it cannot be made public until we have all the facts, and there are people who do not want this to be even spoken about.'

Jacques felt embarrassed, 'Well, I won't say I'm not curious, but I do understand your concern. It does seem to have political consequences.'

The three got up to leave and started to walk slowly back down the slope to where their Land Cruiser was parked.

'You didn't finish telling me about the beliefs of the Aten worshipers,' said Jacques in an effort to break the embarrassed silence that had descended upon them.

Bob took up the story, 'The Hebrews never had a temple, nor even the concept of a temple, until they left Egypt. However, Aten worship did required a temple and Moses was the first to introduce the need for one for the worship of their one-god Yahweh He did this initially when he created a tabernacle in Sinai. There was no Israelite priesthood before the time of Moses. It was Moses who arranged for the first priesthood, structured in two main levels, the high priest and the ordinary priests. The rituals of this newly established priesthood were similar to those introduced by Akhenaten. Instructions were issued to them about what specific garments to wear, also how purification should be carried out, the need for anointment and how to go about fulfilling the duties of their offices. None of which was known to the Hebrews before the time of Moses and the influence from Aten worship.'

'We have evidence that the priests who were appointed by Moses were some of the same men who had officiated as priests under Akhenaten,' added Mary.

'That will have to be for some other time Mary,' said Bob. 'It's getting late and we have a long journey on bad roads back to Khartoum.'

After their early start and their long journey they all felt rather tired as they climbed back in to their vehicle ready to head back to Khartoum. It had been an enlightening day for Jacques.

'There are many such sites in Sudan as this one at Merowe,' said Mary as they started to drive off. 'All of them are full of great archaeological interest and all of them almost unknown to the rest of the world.'

After they had been driving for a short while Bob mischievously said to Jacques, 'Did you know there is a tomb in Egypt on which is written *"The Great Hymn of Aten"*? It is a beautiful piece of work. So beautiful it has been called one of the most significant and splendid pieces of poetry to survive from the pre-Grecian world.' Bob gave a broad mischievous grin, which puzzled Jacques a little. He looked more like a little boy about to play a trick. 'This hymn to Aten is very similar to, or almost the same as, Psalm 104 in the Bible.'

'What?' expressed Jacques in genuine surprise.

'I thought that would astonish you,' laughed Bob. '*"The Great Hymn of Aten"* reads, concept for concept, just like Psalms 104. Many think that Akhenaten himself wrote this psalm; now just think of that for a moment; this was nearly three and a half thousand years ago. Both this hymn and the psalm depict creation and the giving of life by God and it is also reminiscent of the Genesis creation account. I do not think there is any doubt that Akhenaten either wrote this psalm, or inspired it to be written. It is too similar to be otherwise.'

'Is there no end to the surprises you have for me,' laughed Jacques, delighted at the things he had learnt this day. 'So now we have an Egyptian pharaoh inspiring, or even writing, a passage in the Bible. What a day this has been.'

'Well there is one more I could add,' Bob had a cheeky grin as he said this.

'Go on then, surprise me,' retorted Jacques.

'Some of the texts written by Akhenaten have him saying:'

> *I will build the House of Aten, for the Aten my father. In this place shall I make the Mansion of Aten for the Aten, my father.*

'In other words he was saying the Aten god was his father, so on that basis Akhenaten would be The Son of God!'

Jacques opened his mouth to speak, but nothing came out.

****

Derby - England

'Do you believe?' asked Adnan peering intently into the eyes of Ali Farouk. 'I must be certain of your faith in Allah.'

'Yes I do believe in him and I wish to serve him to the best of my ability,' Ali replied with an intensity reserved for those whose belief is unwavering. Ali was a heavy set young man, very well educated with a high degree of intelligence. He had worked hard to become a helicopter pilot for a large construction company, specialising in high-rise construction projects. Well liked and respected, he had a simple uncomplicated belief in the teachings of Islam. Yet beneath his calm exterior hid a fanatical passion for revenge: revenge fed by what he saw as the attacks on his faith by Western society. He threw himself wholeheartedly into the religious activities within the Islamic community of Derby, to such an extent that he proudly sported a permanent bruise on his forehead, which had been obtained by repeatedly striking his forehead hard against the floor during prayer times, in the mosque and elsewhere. He felt, and many agreed, this would demonstrate to all who saw this, his commitment and devotion to Allah. For Ali, this permanent bruise was the mark of Allah. He was intensely proud of his devotion to the one true God. Adnan was now seeking to use this man's unquestioned skills.

Both men sat close together, cross-legged on the large red and gold Arabic carpet which covered most of this Derby mosque. They sat quietly in one corner of the large open space, Adnan resting his back against one of the many pillars. His assistant Nasser Mohammed stood some way off from the pair, but frequently glanced in the direction of Adnan, concerned that Ali would go along with their plans. He knew how much they needed Ali.

The reason Adnan and Nasser had recently driven north from London was because the planning application to change that old church in Derby to a mosque, had been rejected. Now he was determined this rejection would come at a cost.

'Do you believe that Islam is the one true faith which will dominate the world, and that all Muslims must live by Sharia Law?' Adnan was almost making Ali take an oath.

'God knows I do,' was the earnest reply.

'What is the just punishment for homosexuals?' asked Adnan, enlarging upon this verbal test.

'They should be stoned to death. They should not be allowed to live,' was the unequivocal answer.

'What justice should be dealt out to thieves?' Adnan's eyes grew wide as he spoke.

'The hand that stole should be cut off; and if they try to run away then they will forfeit a foot.'

Adnan pulled a folded sheet of newspaper out of his pocket. 'Here is a British man who has insulted Islam. He says his book will show Islam was not the cause of the great Arabic invasions and that the holy city of Mecca did not exist at the time of Mohammed. How should we deal with this Doctor Robert Boucher?'

'All who insult Islam must be beheaded,' was the uncompromising reply.

Nodding in agreement, Adnan was content he had found the right man. 'Allah has said anyone who kills or is killed for the sake of Islam will receive rich rewards, even the fair maidens of heaven, with their lovely eyes. It says so in Surah 44:54. Do you agree with the Koran that the punishment of those who wage war against Allah and His messenger is death?' (Koran 5:33) He opened a copy of the Koran at and read aloud:

> *'When you encounter the unbelievers, strike off their heads, until ye have made a great slaughter among them. (Sura 47:4)*

Ali gave an instant response, 'If I can serve Allah, show me how and I will do as he says.'

'You are willing to take part in God's holy war, the Jihad?' asked Adnan.

'Indeed I am. It is my life's dream.'

'Know then what our Jihad is about.' Adnan took a book and read from its pages. 'These are the words of the great Osama Bin Laden, they state clearly why we are on a holy war. This is a copy of an open letter sent by him to all who would listen in

America. But they would not listen and they murdered him. When you strike your blow for Allah, this will be posted to the authorities. It will let them see the spirit of Bin Laden is still alive.'

Adnan began to read:

> *'We call you to be a people of manners, principles, honour, and purity; to reject the immoral acts of fornication, homosexuality, intoxicants, gambling and trading with interest. You must not separate religion from your policies. You are the nation that permits usury, which has been forbidden by all the religions. You are a nation that permits the production, trading and usage of intoxicants. You are a nation that permits acts of immorality, and allow your women to be uncovered. You are a nation that permits gambling in its all forms. You elevate women and use them to serve passengers, visitors, and strangers to increase your profit*

Adnan closed the book with an action which could be heard at the far end of the prayer room. 'And then I will add to this a final sentence:'

> *Cease your persecution of Islam, otherwise God will punish you further.*

Adnan closed the book and stood up to take his leave, 'Note this well Ali, Allah's apostle was once asked, "What is the best deed?" He replied, "To believe in Allah and his Apostle." The questioner then asked, "What is the next?" He replied, "To participate in Jihad in Allah's cause." Therefore being on a Jihad is the second most important deed in Islam. If you are caught they will not kill you, but you will then serve Allah in their prisons, where many now gather. Many can be, and are being, converted from within their prisons. If God calls you to sacrifice your life in this act, you will become a martyred hero of Islam and God will reward you well in paradise.'

Both men stood up and faced each other. Adnan reached out and embraced Ali in both arms. 'There will be one other who will assist you. When the time is right you will receive your instructions. Allah Akbar.'

'Allah Akbar', responded Ali.

****

Khartoum - Sudan

Two days after their journey to Merowe, something made Jacques hurry back to the Hilton Hotel where Bob and Mary were still staying.

Ashen faced sat down with Bob and Mary in the coffee lounge. 'You should see this Bob,' gasped Jacques opening up his laptop, still a little out of breath.

Looking at the laptop's screen, Bob's face went pail as the blood drained from it, 'They've done what?' Bob's jaw dropped from the shock of what he was looking at, he was almost speechless. 'I don't believe it. How could they do this?'

'I didn't think you knew about this,' Jacques was concerned, and by the look on the faces of Bob and Mary, so were they. Bob began to read some of the text before him on the screen, he could hardly believe what he was reading.

When Bob had seen enough, Jacques set out what had transpired, 'This pre-publication publicity campaign had gone out worldwide, advertising Doctor Robert Boucher's amazing new book, *"The Origins of Islam"*. It says the associated documentary TV programme on this subject, was broadcast two days ago in

Canada and Britain,' Jacques emphasised this latter statement. 'It has received rave reviews by some and anger by others. Already there are demonstrations taking place.' Jacques looked into the solemn faces of Bob and Mary, 'If this goes viral there will be demonstrations all over the Muslim world.'

'Not just the Muslim world,' said Mary looking at her own opened laptop. 'Look at these images here, hundreds are on the streets with placards and burning effigies; and this is in London! London is becoming the capital of the Third World,' said Mary with unbridled contempt in her voice.

'Holy shit!' lamented Bob. 'Now what do we do?'

'This was not supposed to happen until we were in secure accommodation in the heart of England,' added Mary. 'What went wrong?'

Bob pressed his mobile phone tightly to his ear and made a frantic call to his publishers. Agitated and enraged he explained their situation. The conversation went on for some time. 'Well that's a lot of help,' commented Bob when he finally came off the phone. 'It would appear a new, young executive, did not know of our agreement and decided by himself, that now was a good time to go public. For what it's worth they have apologised.'

'We have so much more research to do here in Sudan,' stated Mary. We had intended to scour the area looking for hieroglyphs which may refer to Israel. Similar to those found on the Merneptak Stele, in the Cairo museum. Bob tells me he told you about that.'

'Yes he did,' replied Jacques, 'it was truly fascinating. So you expect to find such references here?' he asked.

Bob looked depressed, 'We really don't know. There are so many sites in this country, many of them still largely covered in sand; as you saw at Merowe. It could well be that there are hidden keys here which could unlock the origins of the Jews for us. Look at what that Swiss archaeological team found; stone slabs at Pnubs in Kerma, in northern Sudan, stones which had been turned upside down and used for flooring hiding their artwork. Stones which revealed that Aten worship came to Sudan, there may well be hundreds more, equally well hidden, which could tell us about the origins of the Jews.' He shook his head sadly. 'I had hoped to be able to carry out a lot more research here.'

'You can't think of that now. We must get you out of this place as soon as possible,' said Jacques. 'I can get you on a private flight to Cairo using my Company's aircraft, but after that you will have to get a scheduled flight to London.'

Bob shook his head, 'No not London, they will be expecting that. London has become a headquarters for Muslim extremists, as has Birmingham and Manchester. No; I will fly to the continent then to East Midlands Airport, which is a lot quieter than London. I'm an Honorary Research Fellow of the University of York; I have an office in York, so I'll head there. I have to go to Cairo first anyway to get our research material together. There is too much work we have done to leave it behind.' Bob was wringing his hands together. 'Years of work,' he repeated.

'I can look after that for you,' said Mary. 'They have kept my name out of it and you should not delay in Cairo. The place is still in turmoil anyway since the revolutions there. It will not be safe for you to hang around.'

'Yes, but, so much work...' Bob did not finish.

'No buts,' said Jacques. 'You are leaving first thing in the morning. Your work on the origins of the Jews is too important to risk losing all you have done. It seems to me that this work is more important than the work you have already completed for the *"Origins of Islam"*. This is the greater of your two books to my mind, because *"Origins of Israel"* is about the origins of the world's three main religions.'

'Thank you Jacques, I will be forever grateful to you,' said Bob, struggling to raise a smile.

With glum faces the three ordered more coffee. Their flight would not be until the next morning so they had some nervous time on their hands.

'If only they had listened to Lawrence-of-Arabia', mumbled Bob, 'the world would not be in this state today.'

Jacques sipped his coffee, 'The Imam I visited in Calgary spoke to me about that period of time, although he didn't mention Lawrence.'

'Well it's too late now anyway; but Lawrence warned them of the need to pay attention to Arab sensitivities. He said, "You cannot be heavy- handed with them. Their pride has to be respected." To our cost they ignored him. He even accompanied the Arab delegation to the Versailles Peace Conference at the end of the First World War. Lawrence and the Arabs were fully expecting their reward for helping the Allies in the war, namely full independent Arab states. Instead Britain and France carved up the Middle East between them, into their own zones of influence. The French even ejected King Faisal, the leader of the Arabs from Damascus.'

'And today the world is still paying for their mistakes,' added Mary.

While they were talking, a TV screen situated toward one end of the lounge, with its sound turned down, started to broadcast a series of images depicting riots taking place around the world. Bob and Jacques followed Mary's gaze as she looked transfixed at those silent images of enraged, wild eyed religious fanatics on the streets, burning effigies and flags and demanding the death of Doctor Robert Boucher.

****

South London - England

Nasser was nervous as he approached his home in South London. There was so much about to happen, and the training for the big event was going on at a fast pace in and around Derby. He was not the brightest man in the group, far from it, so his mind was in a turmoil of anguish. Adnan was good, but things could so easily go wrong he thought, and he was not so calm and collected as Adnan, when under such pressure. Sexual contact with local girls had been forbidden by Adnan, in case it compromised their plan, so he had decided to return to his home in London for one night, to take his sexual gratification from his wife Salma.

He was shocked, and just a little afraid, when he entered his house to find his timid wife not there. What should he do? He could not tell anyone where he had been, nor could he lose face by going to the mosque and saying his wife had gone missing. What should he do? What could he do? He was perplexed.

Moving his car to hide it in another street adjacent to his own, he now sat alone for several hours by his upstairs bedroom window, uneasily glancing out from behind the curtains. An hour went by, then two; finally after nearly three hours he saw Salma approaching the house and she was dressed in Western style!

He rushed downstairs, and as the door opened he reached out, grabbed Salma's arm and pulled her in, sending her sprawling onto the floor. 'Whore, bitch, worthless scum,' he yelled as his fists thumped into her face.

With blood pouring from her nose and mouth, she spluttered, 'It was only a cup of coffee, I only went for a cup of coffee.'

But it was no use, Nasser continued to beat and kick her tearing at her clothes as he did.

Hours later Nasser drove the bloody mess of his wife to a friend's house. Salma was curled up on the back seat, dressed in a black Burka and only half conscious. 'It is all your fault,' he chided. 'Your place is in the home, not on the streets. You are a wife not a whore.' He had been ranting like this since she had returned home. 'You will stay with my cousin Yousif, he will keep an eye on you while I'm away. You have brought shame to me. I will not let you do this again.'

****

Cairo - Egypt

'I'll just lay low for a while, this will soon pass,' Bob felt a little more relaxed now he was back in the relative safety of his office in Cairo.

'No Bob, you must get out while you can,' insisted Mary. 'You know it's not safe here.'

'If it comes to that it's not safe anywhere for you at the moment. Look at the awful, inhuman things Muslims do to people who disagree with them, or are perceived, rightly or wrongly to insult their religion. Look how Jacques has suffered, you cannot reason with the sub-human tactics they employ.' Mary was being carried away with her fears. In her short life she had become aware of many Muslim atrocities, both in Egypt and elsewhere.

'Are you trying to cheer me up Mary? If so you are making a very poor job of it.' Bob said this as a joke, but she did not laugh! 'I may as well I just lay low here for a while until this frenzy passes over. It will be alright, I'm sure.' Bob was trying to convince himself, as well as Mary, it was safe to stay.

'No Bob, you have to leave, you have to,' screeched Mary sounding almost hysterical.

'I can't leave all this,' Bob waved his arm across two trestle tables piled high with photographs. 'There are all these, and dozens of other boxes all full of photographs and documents, all waiting to be analysed and recorded.'

Mary looked around the room, which looked more like a rubbish tip than an office. Papers were stacked everywhere, with boxes full of papers and photos. So many boxes, they were stacked almost up to the ceiling. For years Bob had been assembling this stockpile of material, but his filing system was chaotic. His desk was so covered in papers that no part of the actual desk could be seen. Mary found it ironic that, even with all this chaos and disorder, Bob could still, somehow, put his hands on most of the items he wanted. Even so, she had been hired to help him get a semblance of order with his work, but he was always taking her away to visit one site or another and so she was never given the time to get the order they both craved for into his work.

Bob looked downcast, 'We are on the verge of something big here. I can't just walk away from it all. All these photos have to be digitised so we can computerise them all. Only then can we begin to read and understand what we have here.'

'You go back to England and I'll start work on all this,' Mary was insistent.

'Yes, but we could actually have here those missing parts to the origins of the Jews. Information I have pursued for years.'

'And it will still be here when its safe for you to return,' then looking him straight in the eyes said, 'I insist you return to England Bob.'

Bob laughed, 'Now I know why I hired you. I guess I needed someone like you to keep me in order.'

'It's no joke Bob, you have to leave. Let me get you a taxi,' she insisted.

'Not today, maybe tomorrow.'

'Today Bob, today.' Mary was not giving up on the man she had come to admire and respect so much. Never before had she worked on such an exciting project and she desperately wanted to look after the man responsible for it. She was determined to protect their work and the man who headed it.

'Oh alright,' conceded Bob. 'I'll take tonight's flight to Frankfurt or Paris; whatever is available. You had better book me a ticket and a taxi.'

'You must call me when you get into the departure lounge, so I know that you are all right, insisted Mary.

'Yes, OK, I'll do that. Don't worry so much, I'll be alright,' said Bob, as he pointlessly moved one box to another place, lovingly fingering the contents.

Bob felt dejected and rather aimlessly began to look through one group of the photographs piled high on his desk. Photographs of ancient images and hieroglyphics, some of stone carved images, some from the painted walls of tombs and some from ancient papyrus. 'One day all this will come together,' he said to Mary.

****

Derby - England

The rain fell heavily as Ali Farouk, trembling with pent up tension, drove a truck belonging to his company along a newly built road, which led to a little used industrial estate. This estate had been built with the hope it would bring new work to a relatively deprived area, but it had not been successful and many of the units there still remained empty. It was the middle of the night and heavy cloud layers made it even darker and harder to see than normal. It was difficult for Ali to decipher which of the many prefabricated buildings was his intended destination. A biting cold wind blew outside, but Ali was sweating with tension at the prospect of the task ahead of him. He drove down several small roads, each one branching off from the other. Keen to drive with care, not wanting his dangerous cargo dislodged or broken in anyway. Arriving at a small cul-de-sac he stopped, flashed his lights and waited. It was not long before Adnan and several men emerged from their rented unit; one of them driving a fork-lift truck.

Adnan, with rain running down his face, came up to the cab of the vehicle to speak to Ali, 'Once we have unloaded your vehicle, you must return this truck immediately before anyone becomes suspicious.' Ali nodded his head. 'Then at two o'clock this afternoon the package will be ready for you. It will be left in a net in the middle of the field behind this unit; it will be clearly marked. Our engineer has everything ready, we now need to work quickly and assemble it in time.'

Another man came out of the shadows, equally as wet as Adnan. 'This is Abdu Kamal who will be travelling with you. He has been fully briefed and knows what to do, but talk things through as you travel together.' Abdu reached into the cab to shake hands with Ali.

Ali looked at Abdu and realised here was someone not to be messed with. His lean hard face bore a scar across his lips and part of his cheek; his cold eyes had a glazed look about them. Without saying a word he climbed into the cab alongside Ali.

Ali had been tense for some time and was beginning to feel apprehensive, 'You are sure this will work?' he asked Adnan.

'Yes, just as long as you follow my instructions,' snapped Adnan, indignant that such a question should even be asked. Adnan then swung around and glared at Nasser who had been hanging sheepishly back. 'All of you, no matter who you are will obey my instructions at all time. Anyone who disobeys me again will reap the consequences of his actions.' They knew he was referring directly to Nasser who had left the group without permission and had come back babbling and in a dishevelled state. 'I will not tolerate anyone who threatens the success of our mission.'

Adnan thrust a small package into Ali's hand. 'Here are your tickets to Pakistan on tonight's flight from Birmingham. There is money and passports for you and Abdu inside, look after this well. All is ready. You will be away from here before they know what, or who, has hit them. That godless Council, who refused us the right to pray in a new mosque, will be meeting at half past two. We can't fail.'

'I feel good that at last I can hit back at the Crusaders,' said Ali, in an act of bravado, while watching his precious cargo being carefully unloaded.

'Allah will reward your actions; this you can be sure of,' Adnan reassured them.

One of the men unloading the vehicle signalled all was now complete. 'Go back as quick as you can, and return here at two o' clock,' ordered Adnan.

As they drove off Adnan beckoned to Nasser to come over to him, 'You nearly ruined this whole project by your foolishness,' he said angrily.

'Yes, I am sorry,' replied Nasser. 'I will make it up to you.'

'If your wife had gone to the police, or if you had killed her, we would have police everywhere.' Adnan was not letting Nasser forget this. 'You say you are going to divorce her for the disgrace she brought to you?' he asked.

'Yes, just as soon as I can,' was the sullen reply.

'There is one way to redeem yourself,' said Adnan, who was still keeping Nasser standing with him in the heavy rain of the night.

'Anything,' responded Nasser.

'Tonight I will be heading out of this country, but you, you will stay here and go into hiding at this address,' he handed a paper to Nasser, who opened it to look at it. 'Not here you idiot, it will get wet. Once the deed is done you will head there. I have arranged for your wife to join you.'

Nasser looked shocked, and was about to voice his objection; but quickly thought better of it.

'They will keep you both well hidden while they train her to redeem your name. One way or another she *will* redeem your name.' Adnan turned and walk briskly away, leaving Nasser looking stunned.

That afternoon it was still overcast but the rain had stopped, when a construction company's helicopter, piloted by Ali Farouk, hovered over the field to the rear of the rented industrial unit. Clear markings had been laid to denote the area and a large box surrounded by a heavy net was close by. As the helicopter landed the large side door slid open and the lifeless body of a man was pushed out onto the grass, followed by a perfuse amount of blood. His throat had been cut deeply. Ali and Abdu jumped out onto the grass.

'They would not let me fly without a co-pilot,' said Ali, by way of explaining the situation. 'Abdu hid in the back and as soon as we were airborne…' he did not complete his sentence. Then simply added, '…he moved so fast!' Abdu just stood there impassively, cold faced.

Adnan snapped out an order, 'Take this body away and bury it where it will take some finding: and do it quickly.'

The engineer, dressed in workman's overalls, walked over to where they stood by the helicopter, 'Within that net is five-thousand pounds of ammonium nitrate, mixed with one-thousand two-hundred pounds of liquid nitro-methane, along with three hundred and fifty pounds of tovex. It has been packed in that crate very carefully; one mistake and it could go off before you reach your target.'

The blood drained from Ali's face.

'Before you detonate make sure you are well clear, it will make quite a bang.' The engineer laughed as he spoke this last comment. He handed a mobile phone to Abdu, 'This is your detonator. You know what to do.'

Within the next minute, the helicopter lifted off the ground, slowly taking the strain of the extra weight slung beneath it. The net tightened around the crate and the lethal cargo became airborne.

Immediately that Adnan and his group had observed the helicopter clearing the nearby trees they all jumped into several cars and headed away in different directions. Unbeknown to the rest, Adnan had a large commercial truck waiting to take him out of England. Security was tight for such vehicles upon entering England, and inspections more thorough than they used to be, but not so for vehicles leaving the country. He guessed that the police would soon catch Ali and Abdu, and doubted they would be able to use their tickets to Pakistan that night, nor any other night. Security would drop tight around all airports and seaports that evening. 'If they survive they will serve Allah well in prison,' Adnan reasoned as he climbed into the rear of the waiting truck, settling down for the long journey ahead of him.

Only moments later Ali and Abdu were looking down on the city of Derby. As they came close to the river they quickly located the local government offices of the Council House. It was an old building recently refurbished, the modernised roof being semi-covered in glass, allowing light to permeate within. The front of the building had a three story glass front; it was this which was Abdu's target. The voice of the air-traffic controller came frequently over the radio, urging information from Ali, which he consistently ignored.

Hovering over the government offices, with the net holding the crate slung beneath them, Abdu slid open a side door. 'Steady,' he shouted over the noise of the engine. When he deemed the positioning right he quickly lowered the crate down to the pavement below, scattering people as he did so. Two angry and concerned police officers appeared on the scene, waving their arms and gesticulating for the helicopter to leave. Many others came to windows and doors to look outside of their offices to see what all the noise was about. Once satisfied the crate had settled down on to its pre-planned position, adjacent to the large glass frontage of the building, Abdu released the rope, letting it fall to the ground. Rushing forward to the cockpit he waved Ali to fly away. A few seconds later Abdu dialled the required number into his phone in order to detonate the huge explosive device. The shockwave from the explosion rocked the helicopter violently as it sped away.

****

Khartoum - Sudan

The morning after Bob had been due to depart from Cairo, Jacques had just finished yet another meeting in Khartoum, discussing ways in which to bring stability to the oilfields, when his phone rang. It was Mary. He knew immediately something was wrong, her voice was trembling and he thought she was crying. 'Say that again Mary.'

'Bob has disappeared,' she repeated. 'I think they have him.'

'Oh no! Tell me what happened,' he said hesitantly, not wishing to really hear the answer.

'He should have flown to England last night. Everything was booked alright I had him on a flight to Frankfurt and then on to England. We had an arrangement for him to call me when he got through to the departure lounge. He didn't call,' her voice trembled. 'When he didn't call I knew something was wrong, and his phone was switched off. So I checked with the airline this morning and they told me he had never got on the flight. I am so worried for him,' a sob came from her lips.

'We were afraid this might happen. I take it you are sure he did not get on that flight?' Jacques voice betrayed his own feelings, for he had come to like Bob, not only for his work, but also for the kind hearted person he was.

'Yes I am sure,' she repeated. 'I just don't know what to do. The taxi came for him as we arranged, and then nothing. It is so unfair, he is a great man.'

'Did you know the taxi driver?' he asked.

'No, we just phoned,' she replied.

'What name did you give?'

'I didn't I just asked for a taxi from this address.'

Jacques gave a sigh, knowing Bob's whereabouts could have reached the taxi driver prior to his departure. 'I am about finished with my work here. We have made what progress there is to be made, and things are a little quieter now. I'll come over to Cairo tomorrow to see if I can help in any way. Although I am not sure what I can do.'

'If you would,' said Mary. 'I don't know what to do and I know you have some good contacts with people in high places; we may need their help.'

'Yes, there is one man here I know, Omar Al Mahdi, I can trust him. He is a religious and political leader here in Sudan. A fine gentleman, he may be able to help us.' He thought for a moment then added, 'In fact I'll go round and see him before I come to Cairo, so I may have to wait a couple of days before I can get to you.'

'Thank you Jacques, I knew you would help. I just did not know who else to call. Please come as quickly as you can. I have great fear for Bob's safety.'

After Mary put the phone down, Jacques had a feeling of anguish come over him.

The next day, Jacques pulled into the entrance gateway of a large white villa overlooking the River Nile in Khartoum. White robe guards checked out his car and bag, before allowing him to be shown into a large room, the floor of which was covered with a series of traditional handmade Arabic carpets. Around the room were a series of pictures depicting past family members, including one of the most famous of all, 'The Mahdi', who had been the Osama Bin Laden of late Victorian times. It was The

Mahdi's forces who had fought and lost against the British, in a different age.

After a short while of waiting, a friendly man ushered Jacques into the private quarters of Omar Al Mahdi. Before him stood an elderly gentleman dressed in traditional white robes, with a white silk scarf around his neck. He wore the distinctive white headdress of the Sudanese consisting of a long cloth intricately woven around his head. Omar had been educated to a high level in England, and so spoke English fluently.

'Welcome to my home,' he said, 'please have some tea.' He beckoned to a servant to come over and serve them.

'Thank you for taking time to see me,' said Jacques, 'I have need of your advice.'

'And I also have need of your advice,' was his gentle and smiling response. 'First though I want to thank you for all the hard work you and your Company are doing to help Sudan with their oil production. This conflict between the North and the South is a thorn in our side. Your work is greatly appreciated.'

The servant poured the tea into small classes; a tea which had been brewed in the Arabic way, a method so different to the European methods and yet distinctively refreshing.

Jacques was surprise to hear Omar also required his help, so asked, 'How may I help you?' curious as to what would be the answer.

'I was horrified at seeing the images of the bomb outrages carried out yesterday in the city of Derby in England. These people claim to be Muslims, yet they are not, for they are bringing the name of Mohammed - peace be upon him - into disrepute.' As he spoke he pulled out several sheets of paper from a computer printer. 'I intend to go to England and speak in the Mosques there to condemn those who purport to speak for Islam and yet do not. I would like your opinion on this.'

'I am honoured you seek my opinion for such a weighty matter. You realise my wife was killed in one of these bombings?' Jacques was unsure where this was going.

'Yes I am, and I am sorry this has happened to you. I really just wanted you to know that not all Muslims agree with such actions.'

Is he trying to make some sort of apology, thought Jacques to himself? His mind was flying back to his meeting with the Imam in Calgary. He did not want this to become a similar confrontation; that would be of no help to Bob at all.

'Let me read you a small section,' Omar pulled out one of the sheets of printed paper.

> *'The hospitality of Great Britain afforded to Muslims is received with great appreciation, and is highly treasured in our country. And therefore we are both sad and sorry that this country, a citadel of freedom, justice and law, a great example to the entire world, should have been subjected to the terrorism and destruction which it has recently experienced in London and Derby. I would like to assure everyone that we firmly, absolutely and categorically condemn such incidents and behaviour. Is this our reward for people who have harboured us?'*
>
> *'Is this our attitude toward those who have accepted us, our mosques and allowed our religion to practice in freedom? No – that is unbecoming and that is not Islamic.'*

Jacques, was emotionally moved upon hearing these words, 'If the whole world felt like this, there would be no terrorism,' he thought to himself; not wishing at this stage to express an opinion.

Omar continued, 'I will take this to London and read it in the mosques there for the Festival of the Eid Prayers of Sacrifice.' The gentle voice of Omar was soothing and sincere. 'I hope in some small way, it will also help you.' Suddenly he stood up and walked across the room toward the double glass doors, 'Let me show you the river.'

Jacques followed. Both men walked out through the large class doors onto the wide balcony overlooking the River Nile. 'A beautiful sight is it not?' said Omar looking out across the water.

'It certainly is,' responded Jacques.

As both gazed out looking across the expanse of the River Nile, Omar turned to Jacques, 'Now how may I help you?'

Jacques did his best to explain that his friend appeared to have been kidnapped in Cairo. Jacques took some comfort on seeing that Omar seemed keen to help; until that is, he realised who the man was who had been taken.

'My friend, you must understand I cannot be seen helping someone who is accused of insulting Islam, even if that accusation is not true. In the mind of the people they would not understand.'

'Yes I understand.' Jacques despondency was clear to see.

Omar saw Jacques disappointment, 'What I can do though, I can pass on to you any information comes my way; I can do no more.'

'It is something,' replied Jacques. 'I wish you well in reading your sermon to the mosques in London. They are wise words. I only wish there were more who felt like you.'

****

Cairo - Egypt

Two days After Jacques visit to Omar Al Mahdi, Mary showed Jacques into the Cairo office she shared with Bob.

'Good god, what a mess,' declared Jacques in sudden shock at the unkempt state of the dingy room Bob and Mary called an office; papers, books and boxes were everywhere. Boxes were stacked so high it was almost impossible to see the walls of the room, and what furniture there was contained piles of papers and books upon it. It was clear which area was a work area, for that contained a computer and a table light, but the screen was dwarfed by the stacks of materials around it.

'Yes I know, it is embarrassing,' she said sheepishly, 'it is how Bob worked. He was never well organised so he hired me to help him; but no sooner had I started on something than he would take me away from it and we would head out to somewhere else, returning with even more material. We were supposed to be helping on a dig in Sudan right now! That was our plan after we had left you.' She struggled to hold back a sob, 'Before all this happened.'

In a vain effort to try and reassure Mary, Jacques said, 'I went to the British Embassy in Khartoum before I left. I have a lot of good contacts there and they are doing all they can to help. They have dealt with this type of thing before; they know what they are doing; so they should find out something very soon. Bob's disappearance is also getting a lot of coverage from the news media, which will help. It would have been no good you going to the police here on your own; they will just shrug their shoulders and maybe even accuse you of being involved. They are less than useless and can be more of a hindrance than a help.'

Mary agreed, 'You are right about the police here, I know them better than you do; don't forget I am half Egyptian.'

'Yes of course, I'm sorry; what am I saying. You obviously know them a lot better that I do,' Jacques was annoyed with himself for missing the obvious.

Mary smiled, 'If I had gone to them by myself, they would probably have arrested me and accused be of hiding him for a ransom, or something equally as stupid.' As she spoke she had started to move a pile of papers on one of the chairs so Jacques would have somewhere to sit.

'Come to my hotel, where we will have more space and comfort to talk,' said Jacques without thinking.

Mary didn't answer, but raised her eyebrows at Jacques.

Realising the implication of what he had just said, Jacques quickly sought to untangle himself. 'No! I didn't mean *that*, or anything,' he was struggling to get his words out. 'I just...'

'It's alright Jacques, but as a woman in this culture I have to be very careful,' she grinned at his boyish embarrassment.

'Yes, of course you do.' He lifted a handful of papers off a chair and put them on top of another pile elsewhere. 'As I was saying, I have contacted the British Embassy and also my colleague in Khartoum, Omar Al Mahdi. At first he said he wanted to help, that is until he knew Bob was the reason for all the riots going on at the moment. Then he realised he could not be seen to help a man who was being accused of insulting Islam. Which I understand; but he did say he would let me know if any whispers came his way.'

'Not much, but better than nothing I suppose,' was Mary's sullen response.

'I understand why you cannot go to the police, so I have decided I will go by myself tomorrow. I am a Canadian citizen and the missing man is British, so they will have to at least do something.'

'You really think they will?' mocked Mary, with a sad laugh.

Jacques began to look around the office. 'What are all these papers anyway,' he asked. It irritated Jacques tidy and methodical mind to think that anyone could work in such a chaotic place.

'You remember when Bob showed you the Merneptak Stele in Cairo's museum?'

'Yes indeed. The first recorded mention of Israel.'

'Well Bob has been on a quest, photographing and compiling as many records from ancient Egypt as he can, to try and find if there are any other recorded artefacts which mention Israel. It's a bit like some slabs which were found in the temple of Karnack in Luxor, Egypt. Those stones were from older buildings which had been pulled down and then those stones were used as infill rubble inside newer structures.'

'You will have to explain that Mary,' said Jacques, finally finding somewhere more comfortable to sit.

'They are called Talatat slabs, which are stone blocks cut so that one man could just about carry one. It means "two hands width" and was therefore much easier to handle than dragging huge heavy blocks of stone around when building.' Mary had also now made a space for herself to sit in a little more comfort. 'And most importantly, many of those discarded stones had fragments of writing or illustrations on them.'

'You see, when the old religions were restored after the death of Akhenaten, many of the Aten monuments were defaced or destroyed. So when they built the Temple of Karnack, most of those smaller Talatat blocks came from the earlier Temple of Aten, but were used as rubble, or filler blocks within the pylons of that wonderful temple, dedicated to Amun or Amen. The Great Hypostyle Hall at Karnack is built using thousands of these blocks. In total there were over forty-thousand stone blocks recovered when archaeologists investigated this rubble within the body of the pylons. Of these, only those found in the Ninth Pylon of the Temple of Amun were sufficiently ordered, and carefully removed, to enable a reconstruction of the earlier Aten temple wall. This wall has now been reconstructed and is on show in the Luxor Museum. The left half of the wall is dominated by scenes of Akhenaten worshiping the Aten.'

Mary searched among one of the piles of papers and produced a photograph of this reconstructed wall. The wall had been reassembled by using these previously hidden slabs. 'This is one of the most impressive exhibits in the Luxor Museum; it is a renewal of that section of wall from a temple of Amenhoteb IV, or Akhenaten.'

'It is like a giant jigsaw,' commented Jacques full of admiration for all the work which had obviously been put into this.

'Indeed it is. They took photographs of each stone, and then with the help of computers they sought to match them up. It was a very long and difficult job. It would have taken years by hand, but by putting them into computers these computers were able to search for a match to a particular block.'

'So now I am beginning to understand why Bob has all these photographs. He wants to do the same thing with them.'

'It was Talatat slabs of this nature which were found by the Swiss archaeological team when excavating near the ancient city of Pnubs in Kerma Sudan. You remember Bob telling you while we were at Merowe about the ones which had been turned upside down and used for flooring, which told of Aten worship arriving in Nubia, north Sudan.'

'Yes I remember you telling me about this,' acknowledged Jacques.

'Well there are many stones like that, thousands of them.' Mary handed Jacques another group of photographs. 'There are Talatat blocks in collections scattered all over the world, but to date the Luxor example is the only comprehensive reassembly which has so far been completed. You would not believe it, but in Luxor there are still blocks piled upon blocks standing stacked waist high, and unguarded, waiting for the archaeologists' attention.'

The realisation of the enormity of Bob's work now dawned on Jacques. 'And Bob has been collecting photographs of these artefacts, some from collections which were distributed all around the world.'

'Exactly Jacques, so you see it certainly is a big job,' she sighed. 'Bob had hoped to be able to collect a lot more evidence, especially from the thousands of Talatat stones which are now in private collections, or in little known museums all over the world.'

'Have you found mention of Israel among those you have collected yet?' Jacques was curious to know.

'Until we can compile them into recognisable pictures we won't know. It is like holding one piece from a jigsaw puzzle and expecting to understand the full picture. Many of them are just fragments, so first we photograph them and then with the help of computers from the university we can try and match them up together.'

'And you say there were forty-thousand of these in just one temple in Luxor!' exclaimed Jacques. 'Wow!'

'Yes we could do with a big team, but as always funding will not stretch to that. There are some tantalising clues as to what they may reveal, such as possible references to Israel, but no more than that as yet.'

'So who was it that destroyed the Aten temples after the death of Akhenaten, and used that stone as rubble?'

Mary went across the room and pulled out a picture of a pharaoh, a stone carving depicting a young looking, strong and muscular man. 'This is the pharaoh Horemheb, it was he who ordered the destruction of the temples which had been built by Akhenaten. Horemheb rose from an obscure background while serving up to four pharaohs of Egypt, including Akhenaten and Tutankhamen, before finally he become the pharaoh of Egypt in his own right. He must have really hated the worship of Aten, for he set about removing, not only all reference Aten, but also to any of his predecessors who had any connection at all with Aten worship; he made a determined effort to remove them completely from the historical record. Given his advanced powerful position when Tutankhamen became pharaoh it is most likely that he was an official during the reign of Akhenaten.'

'Hmm!' said Jacques, seems he could have been an unpleasant fellow.'

'Possibly', she agreed, 'but more likely he was a firm believer in the old ways and their original gods, so he sought to rid the country of those who thought otherwise. Although there are many who have put forth a strong argument to say he murdered the young King Tut.'

'Another religious fanatic, but this time for the old gods,' Jacques was trying to make a joke, but it didn't work.

By now Jacques was hooked on this subject, he spent the next several hours looking through many examples from the material Bob had assembled over the years in that room. Jacques was mesmerised.

****

Derby – England

Les Forrester looked at the total devastation covering the ground in front of him. The local government offices were utterly destroyed, with no glass left in place in any of the windows. A huge gaping hole yawned where once had been an attractive glass frontage. As the bombers had intended, much of the glass had acted as missiles under the force of the explosion, causing even greater damage. Half of the roof hung precariously at an acute angle and unsupported, ready to collapse in any minute. Most of the human body parts had been carefully collected and removed, but blood still stained large areas. He rubbed the grey stubble on his chin; he had had little sleep and his brain was becoming addled by the pressure he was under.

'Those bastards,' he mumbled to himself. 'You won't get away with this.'

He took some comfort from the knowledge that most of the terrorist gang, who had committed this outrage, had already been caught. Three were still on the run. The helicopter had been easy to track, but the pilot Ali Farouk, as well as Abdu Kamal and Nasser Mohammed had not yet been caught. A quick scan of the many CCTV systems had revealed who these suspects were and which vehicles they had tried to make their getaways in. Those already apprehended had been locked up within hours of committing this atrocity. Similarly those who had fled to various airports had likewise been systematically arrested. It was 'Mister Big', Adnan Al Saqqaff who had eluded the law so far; he was the man believed to be responsible for planning all this; along with the air crew and Nasser Mohammed. As he looked at the scene of devastation Les vowed he would use all the powers he had as a Superintendent for the National Counter Terrorism Security Office. He would find them; no matter where he was. NaCTSO had many tools that he could use, and use them he would.

Turning to Patrick, one of the detectives assigned this case, 'Is it confirmed? Is this the work of the same man? Is this the same one responsible for the suicide bombers at Tottenham?' Les already had his suspicions, he just needed it confirming.

'Yes sir, it is.' The detective was in a state of disbelief at what he had found so far. 'Some of the young girls…' He hesitated before continuing, 'they were using as forced sex slaves.' He shook his head in an action of incredulity. 'We have interviewed them and they confirmed it.' Patrick grimaced as he spoke, 'Several of them were so young they were still at school. This gang had been abusing them for years. I don't think some will ever get over their ordeals at the hands of these monsters.'

'Are you sure we have all of the rest of them under lock and key? It's just those three on the loose?' Les was struggling to contain the explosive outrage he felt boiling within himself, but knew he must be professional at all times and not let his emotions get in the way; even in times like this. 'The aim of CT Command is to protect Britain from the threat of terrorism,' He said bending down to pick up a piece of twisted metal and holding it without purpose; turning it over and over in his hand. Then looking at Patrick said, 'We can succeed ninety-nine times, but we only have to fail once, and they win.' His temper flared as he threw the piece of metal onto the floor with a crash. Striding away with gritted teeth, he marched from the scene.

****

Cairo - Egypt

The day after his arrival in Cairo, Jacques made his way down to the El-Khalifa Police Station. It was a modern sprawling building covering several city blocks, constructed in a large triangular shape. Just approaching it made Jacques feel intimidated. Several unfriendly faces stared at him as he entered. Wondering where he should go, he turned to an older man sitting on a broken chair smoking a cigarette. 'I need to see someone in charge,' he requested. 'Someone who can speak English,' he added. The man did not move, but just looked at him, as though to say, 'What are you doing here.'

Without a verbal reply the old man pointed to a grubby door. 'Thank you,' said Jacques, who then proceeded to knock on the door. No answer. So he knocked again. Again there was no answer. By then the old man had stood up and as he came over opened the door for him. The door opened up into a long corridor with several other doors leading off.

'There,' was all the gruff voice of the old man could muster, pointing to another door.

'Thank you,' said Jacques again, as he walked over to the door. Then before he could knock on this second door, the old man pushed in front and thrust it open for him.

'A fat unshaven man in a dishevelled police uniform sat in a plush leather chair; he was also smoking a cigarette. Jacques found the cigarette smoke permeated the whole room, making it difficult for him to breathe.

'I want to report a missing person,' said Jacques.

'Come in and sit down,' was the reply in heavily accented English. 'What is your problem?'

Jacques knew this was going to be an uphill battle.

'I want to report a missing person,' he repeated.

'Passport,' said the officer, without waiting for Jacques to state the details of his visit.

'What? No, I want to report a missing person.' Jacques was already feeling frustrated.

'Passport,' was the only reply.

'Oh very well,' Jacques reached into his briefcase and pulled out his passport and handed it over.

'Canadian?' was the wasted statement from the officer.

'Yes,' Jacques was beginning to realise this was a big mistake.

'Holiday?'

'No. Look, are we going to continue with a one word conversation?' Jacques irritation was plain to see.

The man looked either hurt or angry; Jacques could not be sure which.

'Somebody missing you say,' was the more conciliatory response.

'Yes. My British friend was taken in a taxi and we have not heard from him since.' Now maybe we are getting somewhere thought Jacques.

'British?' again the monosyllabic question.

'How long is he missing?' asked the officer.

'Three maybe four days,' Jacques replied.

'Name?'

Oh no, not back to the one word questions again, protested Jacques in his inner thoughts. 'His name is Doctor Robert Boucher,' blurted out Jacques.

A dawn of realisation came over the face of the police officer. 'He is bad man,' was the ill considered reply. 'He is on the TV news. Bad man.' The officer thrust Jacques passport back into his hand.

'Bad man, you go British Embassy,' was all Jacques heard as he walked out of the door.

Jacques trudged wearily up the dark stairs leading back to Bob and Mary's office. Mary looked at him expectantly as he entered the room. 'We are getting nowhere,' said Jacques. 'After three days of trying to track down what has happened to Bob, we are no further advanced.'

'It has been on the news here, and on BBC, CNN and Sky.' Mary turned on the TV set, which had previously been hidden by yet another pile of boxes. 'They are all saying he has been kidnapped.'

'The embassy must have started things rolling,' suggested Jacques. 'It was certainly a waste of time going to the police.'

'Well I did try and tell you that.' Mary smiled.

'I just felt so helpless I needed to do something,' there was a note of despair creeping into Jacques voice.

'I have been in contact with my relatives and the Coptic Church, as well as my university colleagues, but they are nervous about getting involved. Bob is perceived to have insulted Islam and that makes it very difficult for them.' Mary tried to sound reassuring, but was failing. 'If they hear anything they will let us know.'

Jacques was silent. He paced up and down the room, even stepping on papers without thinking. His wasted experience with the Egyptian police had made him angry. He mind was in turmoil. Something snapped in Jacques mind. His jaw set in a determined manner. For the first time since his wife died he felt his old inner strength returning. Standing up he stretched his arms, 'Mary, we must not let them get the better of us.' For most of his working life Jacques had relied on his innermost hard and determined character. It had been this which had served him so well in handling many of the problems he had been required to face in the oil and gas industry. He was not a man to back down from a challenge. 'I am not going to let these bastards win.'

Mary looked a little startled at this sudden change in tone.

'I did not lose my wife to fanatics, only to let them take my friend as well. Bob is doing important work here, which could have an effect on world affairs; or at the least explode the origins of the Jews and monotheistic religions. Whether they hurt Bob or not, his work must not stop.'

Mary did not answer; she just looked at him with a new feeling of admiration for this man who had somehow stepped into her life.

'I think Bob may have been taken as a hostage somewhere, it's quite possible and the signs all point to that. If we can confirm this, I will help you get through all this mess. His work needs compiling and I am good at that type of thing.' For the first time since the bomb in London, Jacques had a feeling of purpose in his life again rising within him.

'How can you,' asked Mary with a puzzled expression on her face. 'You already have a job; you could not possibly have the time.'

'Yes I can,' said Jacques confidently. 'I am owed two months leave, and due to the intense nature of my work, my Company is very generous with the leave periods they offer and I am also due a month's sick leave due to my injuries anyway, which I didn't take. By that time I am hoping Bob should be back with us again. If he is then fine, I will go back to my work; but if not, and something goes wrong…!' Jacques saw the look on Mary's face and cut short what he was going to say.

'It will take more than three months to sort this lot out,' she said.

'Let us hope before then, Bob is back here, if not, and we can't do all this work in that time, then I'll hire someone to help us.'

'I don't know what to say,' said Mary. 'Bob will be so pleased to hear you say this.'

****

Cairo - Egypt

The next day, in the conference room of the El Borg Hotel, on Zamalek River Island near the centre of Cairo, Jacques sat in front of an array of cameras and a bank of microphones. He had organised a press conference to send out an appeal for information concerning Bob's whereabouts and to try and seek his safe return. He also realised he would have to defend Bob's book, *'The Origins of Islam'*, which had caused all this trouble. The room was full as Jacques and Mary entered. Jacques had been hesitant about Mary being with him in case it brought undue attention to her; but she had insisted. All the main media channels were there, including BBC, Sky, Al Jazeera and CNN; all were eager to hear what Jacques had to say.

Jacques started by reading from a prepared statement:

> *'Doctor Robert Boucher is a kind, just and hardworking academic. His main interest is in the recorded history of religions outside that of any holy texts. He has spent many years researching this subject seeking only to find archaeological connections to the main religions, if it is at all possible to do so. His research is for academia purposes only and not to undermine any religion. His book merely points out the actual historical records and nothing more. It is important for all mankind to know the origins of their beliefs, and if possible to give them a factual basis rather than a mythical or faith only basis. Doctor Boucher never set out to hurt nor insult the followers of Islam, only to seek a historical basis for their beliefs. I appeal to*

> *those who are holding Doctor Boucher to release him unharmed. Such an action will show to all that Islam is truly a religion of peace.'*

A host of hands shot up each person seeking an answer to a question which would appeal most to their subscribers.

'Many people are saying this book insults Islam. What do you say to that?' asked the correspondent from Al Jazeera.

'No, it does not insult Islam. It merely seeks to look at the historical record of Islam from sources outside of that of the Koran,' answered Jacques.

'Why do you think so many Muslims are offended by this book?' asked this same man again.

'It should not offend any educated mind. Anyone who thinks he would be offended by it should not buy it or read it,' was Jacques more flippant reply.

'Why does this book question the need for the pilgrimage to Mecca; the Hadj?' asked another delegate.

'It does not question the requirement of the Hadj to Mecca. If you think that, then you haven't read it correctly. It just says that many modern scholars, and Doctor Boucher lists them all by name, have questioned whether Mecca truly existed at the time of Mohammed. You are free to disagree with that if you wish.'

The British journalist raised his hand, 'Do you have any idea what happened to Doctor Boucher and what do you say to those who hold him?'

'We have no idea where he is, which is why we called this press conference today in an attempt to ask those who have him to get in touch with us or the British Embassy.' This question had been pre-arranged before the start of the meeting. 'We ask those who know where he is to release him. I say to them, read his book and do not take wild accusations against him as facts. Read it and you will see it is a study of facts and events of the time, evidence which has been gathered together outside that of the Islamic holy texts. It looks at what is known of those early years from sources other than the holy Koran. It's a historical record, no more than that.'

'Do you think Al-Qaeda is holding him?' asked the American reporter from CNN.

'I don't know why they should,' was Jacques evasive answer.

A Muslim gentlemen dressed in traditional Middle Eastern garb, stood up, 'Don't you think that books such as this and Salmon Rushdie's "Satanic Verses" do more harm than good to the West's relationship with Islam? Why don't Western governments ban this book?'

Jacques wondered whether this questioner was a 'plant' and if so where from. He took care when answering his question. 'God made man with an enquiring mind; surely he would want us to use our minds in the way he created it? If you find such books offensive then I invite your intellectuals to write an equally considered response to them. In this way open debate can be used to discern these matters more clearly. The West will not take offence if you do; better if we can work together on such matters and bring our relationships closer together. As regards your second question, Western governments do not, and cannot control what is published. Our laws would not allow them to curtail freedom of speech.'

A female journalist dressed in a black 'burka ' her face completely covered stood up, 'Do you see any other books being produced by Doctor Boucher?' she asked.

Jacques nodded to Mary to answer this one.

Mary was a little nervous looking into a sea of cameras and reporters, 'When Doctor Boucher was taken he was working on a book looking at the historical accuracy of the origins of the Jews.' The room suddenly went quiet, as Mary continued. 'This research will show what historical evidence there is regarding the origins of the Jewish people. This will be material which is not from any religious sources, and it will seek to shed light on whether a promise made to the Jews by God, will stand up to modern scrutiny.'

There was a clear delight from some of the delegates upon hearing this answer.

'You mean the Jews may not have had a divine promise to inherit the land of Israel?' shouted the American from CNN.

'It is not my book and it is not yet written,' stated Mary firmly, 'but it will have implications toward that.'

A sudden uproar ensured. Questions were being thrown by many; all at the same time. The flashing of cameras dazzled Jacques and Mary. Still the questions flowed. In the midst of the pandemonium Jacques tried to answer some of the shouted points but was soon drowned out by others. The meeting had become too chaotic to continue. Jacques and Mary left the room together, still with questions being bombarded at them.

'Maybe you should not have said that Mary,' said Jacques as he shut the door behind them.

'Oh dear, what have I done?' Mary was clearly distressed at her unguarded statement.

'I think it is called, "opening Pandora's box"', he joked, trying to put a brave face in things. 'I can just see the headlines in tomorrow's papers now.'

'Oh no,' responded Mary wishing the ground would swallow her up.

For almost a minute Jacques stood where he was, blinking, disorientated as if he was in some kind of confused dream. Then propelled by an imperative he could neither explain nor resist, he shouted a taxi outside the hotel and almost pushed Mary into it.

'You are coming to my hotel tonight to rest and escape this mayhem,' he ordered. 'I can't let those news hounds get to you. I know now what we must do.'

****

Cairo - Egypt

In the quiet of the hotel early the next morning Jacques sat opposite Mary outside in the coolness of the garden, situated to the rear of the hotel's concourse. Shaded by palm trees, listening to the gentle sound of water from a fountain, it was a pleasant place to be. A place where normally they could relax and unwind, but not so today.

A waiter came over to their table, so they ordered breakfast.

Jacques had predicted it last night and sure enough, the main news on TV was not so much about Bob, but more about the Jews not having God's promise to inherit Israel. Jacques unfolded two of the newspapers he had. Their headlines blazed with banner headlines, '*Suspected Al-Qaeda Hostage May Have Secret to Jewish Origins*', '*Is This Doomsday for Israel?*' and '*Does Israel Have a Right to Exist?*' Without bothering to read them he simply folded them up and placed them on an empty chair by their side.

'We can't stay here,' Jacques said concerned at the stressful look on Mary's face.

'I can't say how sorry…' Mary was about to apologise but Jacques cut her off, guessing what she was about to say.

'Don't attempt to apologise Mary, you were not used to such settings. I should never have put you in that position. We have to look at what we are going to do now, not what we should or should not have done.'

Mary tried to smile, but still felt awkward about her insensitive statement the night before. 'So what do you want to do then?' she asked.

'Firstly we must not let the world forget about Bob's predicament. We must keep his name to the fore in the news media.' Jacques stopped talking while the waiter severed breakfast to them. He gave them a curious and stern look; both of them knowing he must have seen them both on the repeated news broadcasts throughout the previous night.

'We will give it a couple more days and then if we still have not heard from Bob, we will take all his work to Canada.'

The look of shock and horror on Mary's face spoke a thousand words. 'You can't do that,' she said indignantly. 'This is not your work, its Bob's and mine. You have no right to do that.' She glared at him with her beautiful eyes displaying a fierce resentment Jacques had not seen in her before.

'No Mary, I didn't say *I* will take this work, I said *we* will take this work.' Jacques tried to give her a reassuring smile.

A frown spread across Mary's forehead, not fully understanding what had been said. 'What do you mean?' she asked slowly.

'Think about it Mary.' Jacques spoke calmly in a reassuring manner. 'Bob has set out on a work of world importance. He has so many papers, photographs and documents you could fill a ships container with them,' he said with only an element of exaggeration. 'With Bob out of the way, and the instability within Egypt at the moment, all sorts of fanatics could break in and set fire to it all. There are many Christians, Jews and Muslims who would like to burn that office down. We have plenty of historical precedents for that. You must know there have been numerous times in history when poorly educated people, often driven by religious fanatics, have burnt extremely valuable documents and books, simply because they lacked the understanding to know what they were doing. This has happened only recently in Mali when retreating Al-Qaeda insurgents burnt hundreds of valuable African documents.'

For the first time Mary realised just how vulnerable Bob's work was. 'Yes of course, you are right; I'd never thought of it that way before.' Then she gave a girlish cock of the head to one side, 'You said, *we*.'

'Yes Mary; *we*. You know far more about all this than I do, more than anyone except for Bob. So you will be in charge *and I* will be your assistant. Together we will compile his work, then when Bob is found, his materials will be safe, you can carry on with Bob in charge, and I'll go back to the oil business.' For a brief moment Jacques wanted to reach out and grasp her hand reassuringly, but held back this urge.

'Will they let me go to Canada?' she said without really thinking clearly. 'I have both British and Egyptian passports, so it should be alright.'

'Of course they will. You are on a research project which any university will justify, and besides I have contacts in high places; not that we will need them for this.'

'It sounds good,' she said, 'but Bob's work is part of a grant for the position he holds as an Honorary Research Fellow of the University of York. All this material really belongs to them. They will not allow this to be moved to Canada. They will want it back in England.' she protested.

'If they want it they can have it, but I have better contacts in Canada than I do in England. I am sure the University of Calgary can come to an agreement with York, especially due to these estranged circumstances.' Jacques was not going to let a technicality like this get in his way. 'If it comes to it I can possibly get my company to buy the grant from York. The important thing is we look after this stockpile of material and do not let it get destroyed by some fanatical, raving nut cases.'

'There is so much to pack,' she said rubbing her hand on her forehead.

'Yes there is,' agreed Jacques. 'So let's spend the next two days boxing it all up.'

'I don't know where to start,' she moaned.

'Let's start by ordering some good strong packing cases.' Jacques was beginning to feel excited, just as he did in the oil business when he was about to face a new and difficult challenge.

'The police may give you a hard time,' she cautioned. 'There has been so much stolen from this country over the years, they are keen to check any packing cases leaving Egypt.'

'Let them! What is there to see, except papers and photographs; there is nothing of national importance to them.'

'Thank God you came along when you did,' said Mary with genuine earnest feelings.

'Tell your family you will be heading for Canada for a while,' said Jacques as he poured another cup of coffee.

Mary suddenly looked crestfallen, 'What's the matter?' he asked.

'You won't know this of course, but I do not have much of a family left,' she confessed. 'My father died of cancer while I was studying at the University of York. My older Brother and sister got married a while back, and when they did my mother was on her own so she returned to her family in Egypt. Tensions have always been high between Muslims and Coptic Christians, but things are getting a lot worse over the last few years. The fact is conditions have become terrible for Christians here in Egypt. In the village where my family lived a Muslim customer in a Coptic Christian shoe shop got into an argument with the Christian owner, and three days of rioting and street fighting erupted. Gangs of Muslim youths raided the houses of the Christians,' tears came to her eyes as she spoke. 'They left my mother and twenty other Christians dead. No one has ever brought to justice for it, even to this day. And they never will, not in this country.'

'Oh! I'm so sorry,' said Jacques. 'So you too have known personal tragedy from religious extremists, just the same as I have. It must have been terrible for you.'

'Yes it was; I still find it hard; which is why I immersed myself in this work with Bob.' Mary had a faraway look on her face, a look which remembered happier times. 'It was a great escape for me. A way to ease my grief.'

'So I guess you met Bob at York?' questioned Jacques.

'Yes, he has been so good to me and I love his work. It has given me a reason to live, something special to aim for. I owe him a great deal. He is such a kind man by nature, kindness comes naturally to him.'

Jacques was moved, when he saw her distress. He was now more determined than ever to get Bob's work, and his materials, protected.

****

Gaza Strip - Palestine

'Is this true?' Taha asked with a look of genuine puzzlement on his face. Taha was a tall thin man with a skeletal face; his deeply sunken eyes and high cheekbones emphasised this uncomplimentary feature. Taha looked like a man who had suffered for much of his life; a man who knew pain and hardship. He threw two newspapers on the floor, which landed by the knees of the chained prisoner. Then, realising the prisoner could not respond to his question, he took a key from his pocket and unlocked the three padlocks holding several chains in place. The chains had been wrapped around an old cast-iron radiator securing the prisoner's wrists; his ankles were still firmly fastened to the radiator.

'What?' Bob was dazed, sweat soaked his body, and all his muscles ached and throbbed with cramp. Being confined in such tight restraints for so long had made his body cry out in pain. As the upper chains were released it was a relief to lower his arms back to his side again, and feel the tingle of blood rushing through his veins; which had previously been so constrained. He tried to stretch his legs, but they would only move a little.

'Is this true?' Taha asked again, as he pointed with his calloused hand, to the headlines of the two English language newspapers laid out on the dust strewn floor.

Bob looked without comprehending what he was looking at. He saw two banner headlines which made no sense to him at all, '*Suspected Al-Qaeda Hostage May Have Secret to Jewish Origins*' and '*Is This Doomsday for Israel?*'

'I don't understand,' said Bob. Then with a start, as he looked more closely, he saw a photograph of himself on the front page. This was a photo of him as he was, not as he looked now. The photo was of a well groomed, clean-shaven middle-aged, slightly podgy man; now though his beard was rough, ragged and itched like mad. His eyes were sunken, bloodshot, with heavy bags underneath each eye.

'You read, I will be back,' Taha climbed the dirty concrete steps and unlocked the steel door to this cellar, and then carefully locked it behind him.

Bob had lost all track of time; he guessed it must be somewhere around two weeks since he had climbed into that taxi to take him to the airport in Cairo. It may only have been two weeks but it seemed more like a year to his worried mind. Driving to the airport that night, he had not really been paying much attention to where the taxi was heading. It was only when the driver left the main thoroughfare and started to twist and turn around the back-streets of the 'City of the Dead', that Bob realised he was not going in the right direction. Bob anxiously looked behind and saw there was another car behind. 'You are going the wrong way,' he said in a feeble shaking voice. There was no response, as the taxi drove onto a small dirt road. The vehicle stopped and the door of the taxi was flung open. Strong arms grabbed him and something was roughly wrapped around his head.

He did not know whether he had been beaten or some drug placed in the head covering, whatever it was he went unconscious. Dazed and confused, he slowly regained his senses to find he was tied up in the back of a truck. Judging by the number of potholes they kept on hitting, it must have been either back-roads they were taking or the open desert, for the vehicle bounced around all the time. Bob began to feel sick as well as disoriented. He kept trying to ask what was happening but no one spoke, except for once, when they stopped in the middle of the night in a desert area. He had been allowed to relive himself, so taking the opportunity he asked, 'Why are you doing this?'

The reply had been frightening, 'You will learn what it means to insult Islam,' was their only reply. After that he did not ask again.

Since the various revolutions in Egypt there had been a marked deterioration in the security of Sinai. During the short period of Muslim Brotherhood's rule over Egypt, they had seen no reason to keep the security imposed in Sinai by the former Egyptian President, Mubarak, along their northern border in place. The Egyptian military had initially become paralysed in their efforts to chase extremists because of the Brotherhood's alliance with the radical Islamists. With the subsequent military coup and subsequent instability things had improved very little, leaving much of Sinai in the hands of religious extremists.

For Bob, after what seemed like an eternity of a journey, the border with Gaza had been reached: of which Bob saw nothing, for an old dirty sack had been kept over his head for almost the entire journey. All he heard were lots of voices and shouts, and he had been pushed heavily into another vehicle. At one stage he had been carried bodily by several men, through what seemed to be like a tunnel.

Fear spread through every fibre of Bob's body. Everyone seemed to be threatening him. Eventually he had finally ended up in this cellar, chained to an unused radiator. Taha was the man who appeared to be in charge of his captivity, but the whole thing was chaotic. No one seemed to know what to do with him.

As he read, Bob did not understand these newspapers which Taha had given him. 'What on earth is all this about,' he asked himself. The article was vague, in typical journalistic fashion; where the headline said more than the content. As he read he saw that Mary and Jacques had called a press conference, 'God bless them,' he thought. Then smiled at these subconscious thoughts, 'Would that God be Yahweh, Allah or Aten?' and chuckled at the thought. He quickly saw that Mary had let slip the dogs of war, when he read, what the American reporter from CNN had asked her, *'You mean the Jews may not have had a divine promise to inherit the land of Israel?'* And her naive response, *'It is not my book and it is not yet written, but it will have implications toward that.'*

'Mary my dear, you must learn to be more circumspect with your comments,' thought Bob. Bob was looking wistfully at the photograph in the newspaper of Mary, his mind dreaming of better times; when all too quickly the door was unlocked again and Taha descended down the steps.

'Well?' was his one word question. 'Is this true?'

Bob had been thinking carefully what would be the best way to answer Taha. Should he deny it, or should he elaborate it? He knew he had to choose his words carefully, 'I have been engaged in a study of this; that is true.'

'What have you found?' was the unequivocal response.

'The study is not yet finished,' Bob replied truthfully.

'So you have found nothing,' responded Taha as he gathered the chains together to refasten Bobs arms.

'I didn't say that,' a feeling of panic came over Bob at the thought of his arms being chained once again. 'I need more freedom,' he implored his captor. 'I can't think straight.'

Taha hesitated for a moment, 'Then tell me what you have found.'

'If I do you will simply chain me up again, and I can't stand much more of this. I can't escape. Where can I go?' Bob had nothing left to bargain with.

Taha, pulled up a rickety old wooden chair, placed it a few feet from the prone position of Bob, sat down and asked, 'Tell me enough, and you will have more freedom.'

Unsure whether he could trust Taha he said the only thing he could, under the circumstances, 'Swear to God, you will release these chains.'

'I swear to God,' was the uncompromising response.

Bob decided he had to take a gamble, 'We have found enough evidence to show Israel does not have, and never did have a divine promise from God to inherit the land of Palestine.'

Taha leapt to his feet, 'Yes!' he yelled. Then, looking up to heaven and holding the palms of his hands upwards he repeated over and over, 'Al-ham del-Allah, (Thanks be to Allah), Al-ham del-Allah, Al-ham del-Allah.' Taha run round in circles, lifting his open hands to heaven and tilting his head back. 'Allah Akbar, Allah Akbar.' (God is great)

'But I can't prove it from here,' interjected Bob.

Taha suddenly stopped his rejoicing, 'Where is your proof?', he snapped. Taha was now in a confused state. He was looking down on the prone figure of a man, who clearly had been named as an enemy of Islam, yet was he really an enemy or a friend? Taha was perplexed. 'Where is your proof?' he repeated.

'Once my research is published, then you will have your proof,' Bob was getting concerned, unsure which way this was going to take him.

Taha bent down and unfastened the chains holding Bob's feet, then without saying a word, he turned and left the room. Bob stretched his aching bones and tried to stand, but with considerable difficulty.

As Taha opened the steel door to the cellar he turned looking back down on Bob, 'I need the proof,' he said, then slammed the door behind him with an ear splitting crash.

****

Tirana, Albania

It had been a long and tiring journey. For several days Adnan had been required to keep himself concealed within the special compartment of the haulage truck, designed for that purpose. There had been only a cursory check of the vehicle upon leaving England and they had met with few problems as it traversed across France and on into Italy. After arriving in Turin,

Adnan had taken on the guise of a tourist using his Pakistani passport displaying only his little used middle names. In keeping with most Muslims, his full name consisted of several names some of which were seldom used. These silent names could be recalled if and when required. Adnan Abdul-Aziz Salim Al Saqqaff, had become Abdul-Aziz Salim for the purpose of this passport. He was sure the required visa for Europe had cost his Saudi benefactor quite a lot of money; but Adnan felt he had earned this. A car had been provided for him in Turin, by his sponsor. Driving down the east coast of Italy, almost the full length of the country, he headed for the port of Bari, on the south east coast; from where he had taken a ferry across the Adriatic Sea to Albania.

Every law enforcement body in Europe had been on the lookout for this known terrorist, Adnan Al Saqqaff. However, he had chosen this tortuous route for that very reason; avoiding all airports.

As he travelled he read the newspapers with relish, absorbing how his two main attacks in England had now made him notorious; or infamous as many called him. He took a great deal of satisfaction from the knowledge that his work against the evil forces of Satan was bearing fruit. Many had urged him to go to his parent's family in Pakistan, but he had wisely resisted this, knowing full well his family could be monitored for any such rash action. Adnan had a long held desire which was eating into his very soul. There was one more thing he wanted to do before he would even consider fleeing to Pakistan and the clandestine hero's welcome which he knew awaited him there. Adnan had a grander vision, he wanted with all his heart to make a strike against the most hated enemy of all; Israel. 'If I can do this, he reasoned, my life's work will be fulfilled, and I will reap rich rewards from God in heaven. If God wills it, I must help my brothers to strike against Israel. It is what my life is for.'

Still exhausted from his confined journey, he spent some time looking around at the beautiful art-work decorations within the grand Et'hem Bey Mosque, in the capital city of Tirana. The intricate Islamic patterns were second to none; they seemed to relax him as he let his gaze traverse them one by one. His contact had told him this mosque is considered one of the most beautiful in the whole of Albania; and Adnan found it restful after his long retreat from England. Upon learning it had been closed down when Albania had been under communist rule, Adnan writhed at the thought that anyone dare to take such action.

Things had not gone too well for Adnan after his arrival in Albania. He rapidly became frustrated by the people there, for although the majority of the people were nominally Muslim, which was the main reason he had decided to head there; to his irritation he found them to be more atheist than religious. This was a secular nation, something he just could not understand. Very few seemed to have a strong commitment to Islam, which perturbed him greatly.

'How could this be?' he asked Suleiman his aged mentor, whom his benefactor had arranged to aid Adnan in his quest. 'This place is full of contradictions.'

Suleiman did not like Adnan finding his extremism distasteful, still he needed the money and so agreed to act as his mentor while he was in Albania. 'What do you mean, by contradictions?' he asked.

'In Albania the people are mostly Muslims but not really Islamic, you have unpaved streets, yet with many brand new expensive cars, you have youngsters carrying iPhones who are rubbing shoulders with poor street vendors and you have gleaming glass towers which are looking down on abandoned buildings. So many contradictions.'

Suleiman did not really understand Adnan's criticisms. He gruffly responded to Adnan with a scowl, 'You are young,' he said, as though that was an excuse for all things. 'For a long time people hated religion here. The memory of what the Turks did to us under the Ottoman Empire is still very strong, they committed many massacres here. Then we had communism rule us for a long time, they drove religion out of the people. In fact for a long time Albania was classed as an atheistic country. The result of all this is that now the people have turned their backs on religion.'

'How could anyone turn their back on God, he will surely punish them,' stated Adnan indignantly.

'He already has punished us, our history will tell you so,' was the factual reply. 'At one time under communism we did not have much of a choice. The government conducted a violent campaign to extinguish all religious practice in Albania. They claimed that religion had divided the Albanian nation and kept it mired in backwardness. The government sent out student agitators who repeatedly combed the countryside looking for any form of practiced religion, then forcing any Albanians caught to quit practicing their faith.' Seeing Adnan's look of horror, he quickly added, 'But now Islam is getting stronger.'

'Now is the time to show God that you believe. If you truly believe in God then help me get to Egypt.' This was more of a command from Adnan than a request. He wondered why it was that he had found more faith in Britain than in this country, especially as this was a country that had once been ruled over by the Islamic Empire of the Ottoman Turks. This apparent contradiction was beyond Adnan's comprehension.

****

Gaza Strip, Palestine

Taha opened the door of cellar and walked into the room. He was quickly followed by two armed men. Bob felt apprehensive at their presence.

'You come with us,' ordered Taha, gesturing Bob to rise from the mattress he lay on. Bob was only too glad to be no longer shackled to that iron radiator, so he jumped up as ordered.

'Why? Where are we going?' Bob did not like the look of these other two men.

'Move,' was the uncompromising reply.

Bob was blindfolded, taken up the cellar stairs and bundled into a waiting car. After a few minutes drive he could hear steel gates being opened and then they moved forward with the steel gates being slammed shut behind them, the sound reverberated all around. Still blindfolded he was made to climb a long flight of stone steps; at the top of which they all entered into a room. Bob was led to a chair and pushed down into it, where he waited for several minutes, his heart thumping. Suddenly his blindfold was removed.

In the room there were several men, all reclining on cushions laid out around the perimeter of the heavily carpeted floor, each man was lying sideways, resting on a bolster under his armpit.

Bob's heart began to race. 'This looks bad,' he thought, as he looked around at those stern uncompromising faces, all looking at him intently.

Taha reclined with the rest, while two armed guards stood by the door. 'You will be making a video for us soon,' said Taha. So saying he turned to look toward the far end of the room. Bob turned to look in the direction Taha had indicated. There the whole area was draped in black flags with Arabic writing on them, a chair had been placed in front of the banners and a large camera was pointing at that chair. Some sort of lighting apparatus stood to one side of this arrangement.

Bob said nothing, but simply bowed his head.

Darwesh, was a man who exuded sinister aggression. A podgy faced man with a double chin and facial stubble which he only occasionally shaved. A cigarette dangled from his mouth as he pushed himself up from his reclining position and spoke, 'First you will tell us about your so-called studies.' Standing up he walked over toward Bob and bent slightly forward so his face became close to that of Bob's. The strong smell of tobacco smoke on his breath, mixed with that of unwashed sweat, made Bob feel like retching. 'What have you been saying to Mister Taha?' he asked scornfully. 'He tells us that he almost believes you.'

Bob's voice trembled, 'What is it you want to know?'

'Well, Doctor Boucher, we know how you like to insult Islam; of that there is no doubt. What we want to know is about Israel. You have evidence that God did not promise our land to those cursed Jews?'

'It is not that simple,' said Bob. His heart was nearly jumping out of his chest.

'Hmm! I thought not,' he mocked. 'Because you are a liar, trying to buy time and maybe save your miserable life for a little longer.' Darwesh turned to the others. 'See Taha, I told you there was no substance to this wretch. We should kill him now, in full view of the camera, so others may learn what happens to blasphemers.'

Bob's heart nearly stopped beating. 'There is evidence. I have evidence. It just needs compiling.'

'What evidence? Where is your proof?' retorted Darwesh.

'Something was found in the tomb of Tutankhamen,' he spluttered.

'What was?' demanded Darwesh.

'A document. It was taken away and hidden, soon after it had been discovered.'

'Now that's convenient,' mocked Darwesh again.

'There is a written record which refers to that document.'

A silence fell over all the men there, wondering how they should take all this.

'Where is that record?' asked Darwesh.

'In my office, in Cairo,' he blurted out before he realised it was not a wise thing to do in giving away the location of his work. But all he could think of right now, was how to save his life.

Darwesh looked slowly around the reclining men. Then turning back to Bob asked, 'Is this all your evidence then?'

'No there is a lot more.' Bob suddenly checked himself. These men would not understand any of his evidence which would seem to undermine their faith in the Koran and in particular the teachings of Moses. He could not say Moses was an Egyptian priest who worshiped the Aten, or that the Exodus was embroidered folklore. Instead he stood up.

'Sit down,' demanded Darwesh. The armed men levelled their assault rifles at him.

'Let me go over to that wall,' he asked. 'It will help me give you an answer.'

Unsure of what to do, Darwesh beckoned to one of the armed men to follow Bob as he walked to the wall. The wall was typical of the area with cement rendering. Ceramic tiles were stuck to the wall partly covering it up to three or four feet from the floor, many of the tiles were broken. Bob reached for one of the broken pieces and pulled it off the wall. It did not come away easy, but come away it did. He then tuned and made his way back to the chair.

The tile had part of a pattern on it. Holding it up he said, 'Imagine this was writing or part of an Ancient Egyptian image. If all I had was this, I would not be able to read it. If tiles like this were scattered all over the world, I could not possibly collect them all; for let us say, many are in museums or in private collections. Even though I could not collect them all, I could however photograph them. Then I could collect the photographs together and bit by bit, match them up so I could read them.'

They could see the logic in this, but not where it was leading.

'Some of these scattered remains refer to the *time* when the Jews left Egypt, and more importantly *why* they left Egypt. I have photographs of some of these pieces. My work will show they did not leave Egypt because of a promise made by God; no, they left because they were driven out and some references describe them as no better than lepers, driven out because they were not fit to live with the Egyptians.'

Bob did not know what to expect by these revelations to these men, but he had not expected raucous laughter. Their laughter was not at him, but with him.

'Lepers! By Almighty God that at least is true,' stated Darwesh whilst laughing. 'Driven out because they were not fit to live with Egyptians you say,' Darwesh gave out a deep laugh then turned to the rest, ' Some things do not change my brothers, do they?'

Hysterical laughter filled the room.

'All this is in your office in Cairo?' asked Darwesh.

'Yes, it is,' said Bob.

'Then we must bring it all here so you can work on it with us,' Darwesh was not now laughing. Bob was overcome by a feeling of deep despair. Had he said the right thing, had he said too much, or not enough? He could not be sure. 'You give us proof the Jews are lepers, and maybe we will let you live.'

'Now for the video,' said Taha, as he and Darwesh marched Bob over to the seat in front of the camera and lighting and sat him down.

'You will read this while looking straight into the camera,' commanded Darwesh. he held up a large white card with writing on it. 'Read it first so you know it, and then we will run the cameras. This will then go out onto the Internet. Say nothing other than what is written here.'

****

Calgary - Canada

'Welcome to your new home,' said Jacques as Mary entered the large room he had rented in downtown Calgary. 'What do you think?'

Mary was a little overwhelmed. The room had so much more space than the office in Cairo she had shared with Bob; it was cleaner, light and airy. All sorts of cupboards, shelving and tables were in place and ready to use; as were several computers, scanners and printers.

'This is wonderful,' she said. 'Thank you so much for all you have done for us. I can never thank you enough really. How did you manage to get your Company to refund the grant the University of York had paid out for this work?'

Jacques was wandering around the room, opening cupboards and numerous empty draws and peering into them, 'I have worked for them most of my life. I knew they could find funds for such things, especially if it could be in their interest. Once I had explained what was happening here they realised there may be a knock-on effect toward their own benefit. They have so many outlets in Middle Eastern and Islamic countries, that to finance this may just curry favour in those volatile regions where the oil is.

Then Mary looked a more serious. 'I am still not convinced whether Bob would rather his materials be here or back in England at York.'

Jacques tried to give a reassuring smile, but failed, 'If Bob gets out of there alright and he wants to return to England, then no problem, he can return. In the meantime all his work is now well protected.'

'You said *if*', said a despondent Mary.

'I'm sorry, I meant *when*,' replied Jacques, crest fallen.

'That video,' she said with a deep look of sadness in her face, 'It was so awful. Bob looked terrible. I almost did not recognise him. What must he be going through? What anguish of mind he must be in.' A tear fell onto her cheek.

Jacques reached over and put his arm around her, as further sobs ensued. Burying her face in his chest she continued, 'Do you think we will ever see him again? This is so awful.'

He wanted to say, 'Of course we will,' but deep in his heart he knew the odds were stacked against Bob now. 'It is not looking good,' he confessed. 'The demands they set out will simply not happen. Their demand for the freeing of prisoners is a regular ploy, as is their demand to make Palestine into an independent state; no government will concede to such things. That final demand of theirs to destroy all copies of *'The Origins of Islam'* shows they do not understand things at all. No government in the West can exert such a power over a free press.' He needed to lift her spirits, so added, 'I am sure Bob will be happy when he finds out we have all of his materials safe and sound.'

'We so nearly didn't,' replied Mary wiping the tears from her eyes. 'My family told me just six hours after we left, the old office had been raided and trashed.'

'So it will still look the same then!' Jacques endeavoured to make a lame joke.

A mixture of laughter and tears, from Mary, helped to drive away her cares a little.

Jacques crossed the room, walking toward closed double doors at the end of the room. Pulling both open simultaneously he revealed dozens of cardboard and wooden boxes stacked high. 'We have all these to sort out, so we have no time to be feeling sorry for ourselves. I suggest we get to work.'

A period of feverous activity ensued over the next week, as Jacques and Mary began to sort out all the materials assembled by Bob. It fell into three main categories: *Circumstantial, Archaeological and Documentary*. With more space and time for the enterprise, rapid progress was made gathering these materials together into these three main groupings. Jacques soon realised though they would certainly require more help in the subsequent registering and recording of each individual piece of work within those main group headings.

It was while they were unpacking a box labelled 'Documentary' that Jacques came across a large sealed package marked, *'Osarsiph-Moses'*. 'What's this?' he asked.

'This is to go under the *Documentation* section,' was her somewhat evasive reply.

'Maybe, but what is it?' repeated Jacques.

'References to the Expulsion are not only found in the Bible and the Koran you know. There were several early historians who also referred to it.' As she spoke she began to open up the package, and spread out on the table. They consisted of a number of photocopies from books old and new, along with copies from ancient documents. 'You see there were several ancient writers who wrote about this period of the Expulsion.'

Jacques was amazed. 'I never knew that. Why isn't that more widely known?'

'Because religious doctrine and beliefs get in the way; so it is not widely taught. Also, as with all early attempts at recording written history, there are some inconsistencies in those stories and sometimes you cannot be sure what is fact and what is mythical legend.'

'Bit like the Bible then,' he chuckled. 'Who were these writers?'

'They go as far back as the third century B.C.,' said Mary looking a little smug.

'What!' Jacques shock his head in disbelief. 'That is incredible. Now you just *have* to tell me more about this,' he insisted.

'OK. Let's sit down first though.' Mary pulled up a chair and started to search through some of the papers in front of her. 'As I said, the oldest record of these events is from the third century B.C., it comes from a man called Manetho. Manetho worked under the Greek Ptolemaic pharaohs and he recorded the history of Egypt, in which he writes about the upheaval of the Aten period. Unfortunately his original work was lost and no known copies survive.'

Jacques looked puzzled, 'So how can that help us then?'

'Fortunately in the first century A.D. the Jewish historian, Flavius Josephus, quotes extensively from Manetho and we do have Josephus's works which are still in print to this day. There were also several other early historians, including Tacitus, who either quote from Manetho or referred to it.'

'Now I am really curious, so tell me what do they have to say?' Jacques was now getting excited to know.

Mary was happy to see Jacques' genuine enthusiasm for a subject which had played such an important part of her own life. 'Manetho was an Egyptian priest,' she began. 'He claimed that the founder of monotheism, whom he called Osarsiph, later assumed the name Moses. He tells how Osarsiph led his followers out of Egypt during Akhenaten's reign. Bob's research however, has shown this took place a little later than that, during the reign of Akhenaten's son, namely King Tut. Interestingly this story depicts Osarsiph as a renegade Egyptian priest who led an army of lepers, and other unclean people out of Egypt, saying they had been accused of ravaging Egypt by committing many sacrileges against the gods.'

'Well this is exactly the story of the Exodus, sorry the Expulsion,' Jacques corrected himself, 'as recorded in the Bible and yet this is from a source other than that of the Bible. I had no idea that these events were recorded by any other source outside of religious scriptures.'

'Well they were,' said Mary. 'So you see how all this fits together.'

'It certainly does; it certainly does,' he repeated.

'Josephus also goes on to say, that Osarsiph instituted many new laws and customs, which were quite the opposite to those associated with the original gods of Egypt. He told his people that they should never worship the Egyptian gods, and that they were not to join themselves to anyone who did not believe as they did.' Mary found the look on Jacques face amusing. 'You looked shocked,' she teased.

'I am. I don't know what to say,' Jacques was struggling for words. 'So, let me get this straight: here we have an Egyptian priest, a historian, who records the Expulsion of the worshipers of the Aten, and it is clearly documented.'

'Yes, that's about it,' Mary started to put the papers back into the box they had come from. 'Manetho tells us that Moses belonged to an elite religious group known as the as the Priests of Heliopolis. We are also told in this account that Moses directed them to turn toward the sun as it rose, in order to pray, and all Christian churches have been built with their alters in the east.' Mary turned to Jacques with a knowing look in her eyes as she said, 'In other words to turn to pray toward the east.

Mary picked up the package and walked over to a cupboard. 'Now look, even we can talk all day about these things, or we can continue trying to get some sort of order out of this lot.'

'Yes, you're right,' agreed Jacques as he prized open yet another of the boxes.

****

Sinai - Egypt

Adnan had been an embarrassment to the Muslims in Albania. They could not understand his fanatical desire to strike at all who were non-Muslims. His radicalisation was not only strange to them, but they found it dangerous as well; so they were glad when he left them, heading toward his intended destination of Egypt. At seven o'clock in the morning Adnan exited Cairo airport and headed for a taxi.

'You want me to take you where?' The taxi driver stared up at Adnan suspiciously, 'Across Sinai Desert to the Gaza border!' The driver shook his head, fingers drumming nervously on the steering wheel. He then fell silent.

'Are you for hire or not?' growled Adnan. He was in no mood for discussion. 'Either you take me or I'll find someone who will.'

The driver bit his lip, torn between a desire for the fare and the thought of a long journey in a car which was not too road-worthy. Besides which he was apprehensive knowing there were many extremists around the north of Sinai. 'It's a long ride,' he grumbled. 'The Bedouin's are running wild out there. It's dangerous. It will cost a lot.'

Adnan pulled out of his briefcase a wad of Egyptian pound notes. 'Here!' he said almost throwing them at the driver.

The driver's eyes opened wide. Economics had won the day. With a grudging nod he leant across and opened the passenger door.

'For that I would even take you to Israel,' he muttered.

Adnan climbed in and they set off, driving in silence. Adnan knew that since the revolutions in Egypt which had first toppled Mubarak and then the Muslim Brotherhood, Sinai had become a no-man's land due to the security vacuum in the peninsula. Well armed Islamists were making the area into a major resistance base. Prior to his journey he had contacted the Jihadists in the north of Sinai telling them of his training, but no more than that. It was not they who worried Adnan, but the Egyptian security forces along the way.

After an hour or so driving, 'Checkpoint,' said the driver, with a hint of concern in his voice.

Adnan handed over his British passport for inspection. 'Why you come here?' asked the guard.

'To attend a wedding in Al Arish,' he lied.

'What is the name of the family?' asked the guard, while he passed the passport to another, who looked at it closely.

'Bin Hariz,' was the name he'd been told to say.

The taxi driver sat there nonchalantly, with a look which almost said, 'I told you so!'

'Fifty pounds.' The guard looked directly at Adnan, with an expression which said, 'Pay up, or go back.'

'Because I'm British does not mean I am rich,' protested Adnan.

'One hundred pounds,' was the uncompromising reply. 'There are many people in Britain looking for you!' The guard glared at him.

Adnan felt a wave of panic flow over him. Thrusting Egyptian pound notes into the guards hand brought a sickly smile to the guard as the passport was returned. Adnan's mood turned panicky now. He had been unsure whether to use his British or his Pakistani passport. There must have been a large hue and cry over him. 'Maybe I should have used my Pakistani one, he thought.' He knew the Egyptian police would be a possible problem, but his confidence in being able to buy them off had been confirmed.

Hours passed, the drive becoming even more tedious and boring. Brief rests were taken with the diver insisting on eating at a rundown refreshment house; for which Adnan had to pay. Eventually they arrived at Rafah, near the border with Gaza. It was now dark and the address Adnan was looking for was difficult to find. With each wrong turning the diver became more irritable.

'Shut your whining,' snapped Adnan. 'I have to find my friend who will get me permission to cross into Gaza.' He used the word 'friend' in its broadest form, for he had never met the man as yet.

'Gaza!' exclaimed the driver. 'Why Gaza?'

'Not your business,' he barked. The look in Adnan's eyes persuaded the driver not to pursue this.

The taxi's engine had been over heating for a while, now it burst forth in a cloud of steam. Adnan's anger erupted, he thrust open the door and walked off, leaving the driver cursing his luck. Finally, he managed to find his contact, a man from Hamas. He greeted him and entered into his house. Inside, Adnan looked up on the wall, in the dim light of a single bulb he read an Arabic text framed and displayed in a prominent position:

> *And slay them wherever you catch them, and turn them out; For persecution is worse than slaughter; But fight them not at the Sacred Mosque, unless they first fight you there. But if they fight you, slay them. Such is the reward of those who reject the faith. (Q.2-191)*

Adnan embraced Darwesh, 'Greetings brother, I am a Student of Ayyash, come to help with your struggle against Israel. I have been well trained.'

'You are most welcome; student of Ayyash,' said Darwesh. 'Come and rest and take some food, after your long journey.'

****

London - England

Several parts of London had become, in recent years, the centres of radical Islamic extremists, making those places almost no-go areas for non-Muslims. It was into such an area that Salma had been taken. Confined to a basement flat, she was no longer being beaten, instead she was being cajoled by militant men-folk to help them in their cause. Day after day, hour after hour, they spoke to her strongly, denying her food and sleep, until she agreed with some particular point of their radical views.

It was only when they brought her twelve-year-old sister to see her that she finally cracked and agreed to go along with their plans.

'She will soon go on a holiday to Pakistan,' said one of her guardians who constantly read to her from the Koran. 'Unless that is, you are prepared to redeem your family's name.'

Salma knew very well what was meant by this and could not bear to think of her little sister going through what she had endured.

Finally she gave a weak nod to agree to their wishes. The change with her captors was immediate. Now she was a wonderful person, a daughter of God, a credit to her family. As if to underline this new found status, her husband Nasser Mohammed was brought to see her.

His fat lips still slavered when he spoke to her, 'Salma you have done me proud. Your name will live forever. You are a wonderful wife. God will reward you.'

Was this the same man who had bullied and ill treated her so much, she wondered? But she no longer cared. All she wanted was to be free of all this.

It was some days later when her husband entered her small room, with another man she had not seen before. 'This is Abdu Kamal,' he said with an element of pride. 'He will instruct you on the path you have chosen to follow.'

Salma looked at him and a chill ran down her back. His black bearded face was lean and hard with a scar across his lips and part of his cheek; his sunken cold black eyes had a glazed look about them. He just stood there and looked without saying a word of greeting.

'He will train you on what must be done,' repeated Nasser. 'He has a lot of experience in...'

It was Abdu's sudden turn to look at Nasser which stopped him from completing his sentence.

'You must do what he says,' gabbled Nasser; failing to tell her of Abdu's bloody actions in the helicopter attack on Derby city.

****

Calgary – Canada

The room hired by Jacques was a hive of activity. Six students from the Department of Archaeology, within the University of Calgary, had volunteered to help tabulate, scan and record as many of Bob's document and photographs as they could. After years of frustration trying to work within the confines of Bob's untidiness, Mary's spirits were lifted to see how quickly willing hands could move such a mountain of work. The students had all been briefed regarding this work; and knew what it had cost Bob so far. They all knew of the tense hostage situation and the reasons for it. Nevertheless, the ultimate aim of this project inspired the students, so they were now helping out, each one eagerly working upon this special project.

It was a Sunday afternoon, and the students had all offered to work through their weekend, so keen were they to help out. As a result Jacques had sent for copious amounts of take-away food for their mid-day lunch. Now they were all sitting down enjoying the food, happy with the rapid progress they were making on this project.

Pulling another slice of pizza from the box, Jacques turned to Mary and asked quizzically, 'Mary, once or twice Bob has hinted that he has more information about the origins of the Jews than he was prepared to talk about. I remember when we were at Merowe you were about to tell me something about this, when he shut you up. What was it you were going to say?'

Intrigued by this, all eyes in the room now turned intently toward Mary, each student excited to be part of a project which could soon be going worldwide. Reaching into her briefcase she brought out a hand-made manual. 'There is no reason to keep this quiet any longer,' she said. 'It is part of a work Bob had written on this subject. Other people have also pursued this theme for a long time now, which is why Bob did not want to tread on their toes, or to give others per-conceived ideas about his work.'

Mary went over to the large cupboard at the end of the room and retrieved a box. Bringing it to the table where they all sat, she opened it up. 'This subject is key to our studies on the origins of the Jews. Bob has underlined some of the key points here.'

Mary looked tense and began reading from Bob's notes:

'There are many documented accounts to show that Howard Carter and Lord Carnarvon did find

> *something of world importance within the tomb of Tutankhamen when they were in the early stages of opening up that tomb in 1922. What they failed to disclose to the world, was that after finding the sealed tomb Carter enlarged the spy hole and Lord Carnarvon, his wife Lady Evelyn, Arthur Callender and Carter all went inside, without waiting for official permission. That this did happen was recorded later by Lord Carnarvon himself and by Mervyn Herbert, (Carnarvon's half brother) who were present at the official opening of the burial chamber.'*

Jacques handed out a number of deep fried chicken legs to the students who were now all huddled around carefully listening to Mary, as though she was telling children a bedtime story.

'This sounds like it will be very interesting Mary, please carry on,' Jacques requested.

Mary continued:

> *'There is now indisputable evidence that the four of them, three months before the official opening of the tomb, breached the sealed doorway and explored the inner rooms of that tomb. While they were in there they helped themselves to a few selected items and removed them from the tomb. All of which were not known about until recent revelations by noted academics on the subject, in the book by Collins and Ogilvie-Herald, called "Tutankhamun - The Exodus Conspiracy".'*

> *'Eight days after the official opening of the tomb, Carter was forbidden to enter the tomb by the Egyptian Antiquities Department, who had it locked and bared against him. Carter was furious at*

this. He felt there was only one course of action left open to him; to seek the assistance of the British Consulate in Cairo. He wanted the Consulate's support against what he saw as unjust and unlawful official interference. However, the Consulate informed him this was beyond British jurisdiction and they could not, or would not help him.'

'Carter flew into a rage and stormed into the offices of the British Consul in Cairo. Angry words were exchanged and then he delivered his bombshell. Quote: "Unless I received complete satisfaction and justice, I will publish for the whole world to read the documents that I found in the tomb giving the true account, according to the Ancient Egyptian Government, of the Exodus of the Jews from Egypt." Unquote.'

'The Consulate realised that such a revelation would expose the deal the British government had made a few years before with the Jews. Namely: if the prominent Jews in America would help to get America to enter the First World War, the Jews were promised they would get their own state of Israel in Palestine. Also the Jews had made the claim, which had been sold to the general public, that the return of the Jews to Palestine was based on Moses and the Exodus and the promise that God gave to give the land of Palestine to them. And now, at the time of Carter's outburst, there was a growing Arab hostility towards the establishment of a Jewish homeland in Palestine a serious fermenting problem was developing.'

'Knowing this background and what depended upon it, the British official also lost his temper and flung a bottle of ink at Carter. So it was clearly taken as a serious threat by that British official. Carter's threat must have worked for the revelation was not carried out and Carter was allowed to return to his work. This serious event has come down to us from "The Memoirs of Lee Keedick", who was President of the Keedick Lecture Bureau and Carter's lecture agent in America. Someone who clearly knew Carter well and what transpired within that tomb.'

'That a hidden number of papyri were actually found inside the tomb was openly discussed later by Lord Carnarvon himself; which he did several times. Also on his return to England he was interviewed by the London Times when he openly admitted; "One of the boxes contains rolls of papyri which may be expected to shed much light on the history of the period, and other papyri may be discovered in other of the boxes which have yet to be examined." These papyri have never been released to the public.'

'This incident illustrates clearly, the Jews left Egypt because they were expelled and not because of some divine promise. As Carter said, those documents were able to; "give the true account according to the Ancient Egyptian Government of the Exodus of the Jews from Egypt". It was the Expulsion which, those Ancient Egyptian papyri would have exposed: it could not have been anything other. So by denying the historical validity of the Biblical account of the Exodus, modern Arabs

would have a good reason to call into question Jewish claims over the land of Israel.'

'With this in mind we must now ask, was this threat by Carter to expose all this, connected to the untimely and unexpected early death of Lord Carnarvon; Carter's friend and sponsor?'

'Also, Carter's threat shows us quite clearly that the Expulsion occurred either before Tutankhamen died, or at the time of his death. Otherwise this record would not have been within that tomb, and Carter would not have had a viable threat to expose this, unless he got his way and was allowed to re-enter the tomb.'

'That there must have been informative papyri within this tomb was illustrated in 1985 by the Department of Egyptian Antiquities of the British Museum, when they wrote, "The discovery of the tomb of Tutankhamun in November 1922, at the time believed to be a virtually unmolested royal burial, raised for some Egyptologists the prospect of a rich harvest of papyri .... however, no papyri were found in the tomb of Tutankhamun, this particular class of inscriptional material was notable only by its absence. The reason for this absence...- has never been satisfactorily explained."'

'So when Lord Carnarvon said, "One of the boxes contains rolls of papyri which may be expected to shed much light on the history of the period, and other papyri may be discovered in other of the boxes

> *which have yet to be examined," he was clearly telling the truth, a truth which was quickly suppressed by interested parties,'*

Those in the room were now tense from hearing these amazing revelations. Mary folded up the document, and pulled out a photocopy of a letter. 'This is a copy of a letter written on 2nd November 1917, during the First World War. It was written by Balfour, the man responsible for the Balfour Treaty which was the foundation for the British agreement for the Jews to return to Palestine. It was written to the most powerful Jew in Britain at the time, namely Lord Rothschild: this document is referred to as "The Balfour Declaration".'

Mary read the letter:

> *'Dear Lord Rothschild,*
>
> *I have much pleasure in conveying to you, on behalf of His Majesty's Government, the following declaration of sympathy with Jewish Zionist aspirations which has been submitted to, and approved by, the Cabinet.*
>
> *His Majesty's Government view with favour the establishment in Palestine of a national home for the Jewish people, and will use their best endeavours to facilitate the achievement of this object, it being clearly understood that nothing shall be done which may prejudice the civil and religious rights of existing non-Jewish communities in Palestine, or the rights and political status enjoyed by Jews in any other country.*
>
> *I should be grateful if you would bring this declaration to the knowledge of the Zionist Federation.*

Yours sincerely, Arthur James Balfour'

Mary drew a deep breath, 'What also needs to be pointed out here is that Lord Rothschild was a cousin of Lord Carnarvon's wife. So now we can see that those who were there at the opening the tomb, were related to a leading advocate of Zionism, people who were seeking to establish the state of Israel. Obviously any discovered papyri which would threaten the establishment of Israel, would not see the light of day. Such a cover-up suggests that this information would have put into question the establishment of a modern Jewish state.'

'This is heavy stuff Mary,' said Jacques, his mind deep in thought.

Mary concluded, 'Bob's document goes on to say:'

> *'Thomas Hoving, a former head of New York's Metropolitan Museum, using material he found relating to Carter and the opening of the tomb, wrote in this book, "Tutankhamun - The Untold Story" the following: "...documents contained in unrevealed papyri he (Carter) had found in the tomb, documents presenting the true and scandalous account of the exodus of the Jews from Egypt."*

There followed a stunned silence for a moment until Emma one of the students asked, 'Has anyone written a theist on all this?'

'Yes indeed,' concurred Robin, another of the students, 'what a great subject this would make.'

'As far as I know no one has taken this up from you intake year. Speak to your professor about it, but it will have to be on the archaeological side and not the modern, to comply with your studies, if he agrees we will be glad to help you if you wish to do so.' Mary was delighted to find so much enthusiasm from these young students. Not wishing to let this moment pass, she reached again into her briefcase. 'Let me explain the British thinking behind that letter from Balfour. Bob has a copy of it here,' she opened up another paper from Bob's folder.

> *'In Luke 21:24 it reads "… and Jerusalem shall be trodden down by the Gentiles, until the Times of the Gentiles be fulfilled." And verse 27 goes on to say, "And then shall they see the Son of Man coming in a cloud with great power and great glory." To Christian fundamentalists in the early part of the twentieth century, it was only when the "Times of the Gentiles" had been fulfilled and the Jews returned to Jerusalem that the Son of Man (Jesus) could return to earth.'*

> *Therefore according to this fundamental belief, it was their duty to see the Jews return to Jerusalem to facilitate the return of Jesus Christ and establishing the Kingdom of Heaven here on earth.'*

'So there you have it everyone,' stated Jacques. 'Combine this with all the evidence we have already, along with that which Doctor Bob Boucher is compiling, and we have all the evidence we need to write this up as a book and/or a thesis.'

'Just to add to this,' said Mary as she opened up another of Bob's photo copied documents, 'here is an item of modern evidence on Britain's attempt to manipulate history. Let me read this to you:'

> *'In November 2002 in an interview with the New Statesman Magazine, the British Foreign Secretary, Jack Straw said, "The Balfour Declaration and the contradictory assurances which were being given to Palestinians in private, at the same time as they were being given to the Israelis*

again, is an interesting history for us, but not an honourable one,"

Clearly here a member of the British government is blaming Britain's imperial past for many of the modern political problems, including the Arab-Israeli conflict.'

'There is a final footnote here; it is a quote from T. E. Lawrence, or Lawrence of Arabia as he is better known, when he wrote:'

'The dreamers of the day are dangerous men for they may act out their dreams with open eyes to make it possible. This I did. I meant to make a new nation.'

Mary eulogised Bob's notes by saying, 'And today we now live with the results from the actions of those "dangerous men". Finally, Bob concludes these notes by saying:'

'This is exactly what the British did, with their conniving twists and turns to facilitate the birth of the state of Israel, thereby hastening the return of Jesus Christ.'

The feeling of elation permeated everyone in the room. They feverously commenced the scanning and documenting more of the many items from Bob's collection. All thinking deeply on what they had heard.

****

Gaza Strip – Palestine

Darwesh was pleased to escort Adnan to where Taha and a small group of men were guarding the house in which Bob was being held hostage. These armed men looked on as Taha stood to embrace Darwesh, then, standing to one side Darwesh addressed them all, 'This is our brother Adnan Al Saqqaff, he has come to join us and help in out fight. He is a Student of Ayyash.'

'Ah! Ayyash,' said Taha as he embraced Adnan. 'Ayyash, "The Engineer", our engineer; he was our great bomb maker; sadly murdered by Israel. If you are a student of him, and have his skills and ways, then you are one of us and are most welcome my brother.' The three sat down on the stone steps to the villa, shaded away from the sun.

'Thank you my brothers,' said Adnan responding to the warmth of his welcome. 'I have long yearned to be able to strike against Israel. Allah has been good to me to bring me this far.'

Darwesh spoke up so that even the guards could hear, 'Adnan has delivered a great blow for Allah in the heart of the Great Satan's brother. He has twice struck hard at the unbelievers in Britain; we are proud to have him here with us.'

The guards slung their weapons over their shoulders and came across to embrace Adnan, beaming smiles on each of their faces.

'I can help you build and assemble rockets to strike against Israel,' said a jubilant Adnan.

The smiles on the faces of the men remained in place, they knew the implications for those in Gaza in the past, when such actions had been carried out. Frequently Israel had struck back hard by incessant bombing and sometimes even by entering their land and ruthlessly targeting the enemies known to be plotting against them.

'This you will do brother,' agreed Darwesh, 'This you will do.' The greetings now over, the three sat down on the steps again, out of the sun and in the shade afforded by the building. After a while tea was made by Taha boiling water on an open gas ring, with the gas canister close by. He filled several small glasses with the strong liquid, added copious amounts of sugar and handed the glasses out to each one there.

'Maybe Adnan can help us with a small problem we have?' said Darwesh with sinister intent. Taha looked a little annoyed, for he had been locked in repeated arguments with Darwesh for several days now and he guessed Darwesh was seeking support for his stance.

'It is not his decision,' retorted Taha without knowing for sure what Darwesh was about to say.

'That maybe so,' agreed Darwesh, knowing any such decision could be taken out of Taha's hands if he so wished.

Adnan could see and feel the tension between these two men, and realised this could be a delicate situation. 'Brothers, I do not know what you are talking about, but I do not want to get involved in an argument between the two of you.'

'It is not an argument, just an honest discussion,' was the smarmy response from Darwesh. 'It will not hurt to hear your opinion.' Darwesh just glared at Taha as he spoke, knowing full well what he was trying to do. 'Taha has done a great deed, a great service for Islam, and we honour him for that.'

Adnan wondered where all this was going, so he just smiled in acknowledgement of these vague statements.

'Taha has captured an infidel, who has insulted Islam,' Darwesh looked directly into the eyes of Taha as he spoke.

'Then he should die,' interrupted Adnan without any hesitation.

'Exactly,' said Darwesh, sipping his tea. 'This is my thought also.'

'Then what is the problem?' asked Adnan.

'Taha wants to keep him alive,' Darwesh made his last words sound as though this was a ridicules thing to even comprehend, that such a man should be allowed to live.

Taha saw he had no choice but to put forth his reasons for this. Without speaking he went into the villa. Adnan and Darwesh looked at each other, wondering why Taha had not replied to them, but simply walked away.

After a brief moment Taha reappeared, carrying two newspapers. 'It is said this man can hurt Israel and I believe he can. I think we should give him the chance to do this.' He opened up the two papers displaying the emotive headlines, *"Suspected Al-Qaeda Hostage May Have Secret to Jewish Origins"* and *"Is This Doomsday for Israel?"*

'This is just newspaper talk,' scoffed Darwesh. 'It is not true.'

'But what if it is true?' responded Taha. 'Are you prepared to take the risk and lose this valuable information?' Taha's irritation with Darwesh was clearly displayed in his voice. 'You have spoken with him, surely you can see, he has something we could use.'

'If he did have such information, he does not have it now.' Darwesh was beginning to raise his voice. 'When you sent men to his office all his so-called materials had vanished.' Darwesh threw both arms in the air in an arc, to mimic a magician's vanishing trick. 'Whatever he had, it has all now gone to Canada of all places! Are you now going to send our infidel over to Canada, where he could carry on for years, and let him escape Islamic justice?'

Adnan could see a furious argument could be developing here soon, 'Have you questioned him?' he asked in an attempt to defuse the situation.

'Many times,' confirmed Taha. 'And the more I speak with him the more I believe him. He can show that Israel stole our land, and that Allah did not give them any promise.'

'Who is this man?' asked Adnan.

'Doctor Robert Boucher,' sneered Darwesh with his lip curled.

'Al-ham dell-Allah (Allah be praised),' replied Adnan in genuine surprise. 'You have this man? The very man the whole Muslim world justly hates? This is wonderful news. Surely he has to die. We should show the world what happens to those who insult Islam.'

****

Calgary – Canada

They had not intended their day to end this way. It had been a celebration Indian meal at one of Calgary's best restaurants. The restaurant had been cosy and charming, with dim lighting giving a romantic feel. They were celebrating because in less than two weeks all of Bob's materials had been filed and recorded. The students had worked wonders, their willing hands had now managed to get everything into its given place, and all documentation had been registered and allocated to a topic. Even some of the scanning of the hundreds of photographs had actually been started. It was a time for celebration. For the first time since those awful events before last Christmas, Jacques felt a lot better. Yet somehow, in a way he could not understand, he also felt a little guilty. Should he feel guilty for feeling happy? How could he possibly feel happy, with a dead wife and his friend still held as hostage; God knows where?

It was a paradox, but he knew *his* Mary would understand, as he looked into the eyes of a new Mary, who now lay beside him, naked in his bed. *His* Mary had had clear blue eyes and light blond hair, now he was looking into eyes which were much darker, almost black; beautifully framed by her long dark hair. Jacques lay on one arm gazing at her beauty. It must be that Middle Eastern perfume she wore, he mused to himself. It certainly worked. If it was not an aphrodisiac, then it should be. The mere whiff of it had aroused his inner masculine feelings.

How sweet her breasts were. He delighted to pull gently on each nipple with his lips, a pleasure equally shared by Mary. He rolled over to lay on top of her, pecking and nibbling at her face and lips as he did so, feeling skin to skin. Her legs splayed out ready to receive him in eager anticipation. His manhood erect, he held himself above her, supported on his elbows. For a moment he was transfixed with her beauty; but as he looked intently at her he saw *his* Mary for a moment; and his manhood went limp.

Mary sensed the change. Jacques looked despondent. 'I'm sorry. Maybe it's too soon after I lost my wife?' he lamented.

This was not what Mary wanted to hear. Reaching below the sheets her hands began to work his sensitive areas, gently, but persistently until soon his full arousal was again obtained. Both groaned with pleasure as he entered her. Jacques had thought he would never be able to feel this happy again; utter contentment flooded his very soul.

He whispered in her ear, 'From the moment I first saw you, I wanted you.'

Her smile was enchanting. 'I felt the same for you,' she confided. 'I can't say why I felt that way; I think it was love at first sight. I never knew such things really happened.' For a long time they lay in a state of bliss in each other's arms, until sleep over took them.

The next day Jacques walked hand-in-hand with Mary as he showed her the sights of his city; the city of Calgary. He felt elated just walking with her, just being with her. Jacques was proud of his Canadian heritage, and wanted to show her how his home town had developed so quickly from such small beginnings the a great city it now was, and how it had been built so quickly. He decided first he would take her to see the rebuilt wooden fort on the banks of the Bow River. It had been the first main structure to be built in Calgary, less than one-hundred and fifty years ago, and now it was a historic appendix to a thoroughly modern city.

Looking together around the inside the wooden enclosure of the fort, he said, 'Just a couple of generations ago this was the wild west of Canada and now look at how my city has grown,' he bragged, pointing across to the tower bocks of the modern city.

Mary could understand his pride, and began to feel Jacques' sense of awe also.

They had lunch at the top of the Calgary Observation Tower, whilst admiring the stunning views from the top. The dizzying height of this structure made Mary feel a little nervous at first, which was soon over come. Just being together like this, for them both; it was a day to remember.

'We must go for a weekend to Lake Louise,' suggested Jacques; the sadness he felt on his last lonely visit there quickly fading. 'You will love it, it is so beautiful. I think it is the most beautiful place on earth.' He looked into her eyes and added, 'But not as beautiful as you.'

Mary liked the suggestion, and snuggled up to him. But then she cautioned, 'We have too much work to do to go off on holiday at the moment. Once your leave is over your Company could be sending you away anywhere, and I want to get as much of Bob's work ready for him as we can. I want him to start to get ready for publishing all this. The more we can do now the sooner will come that day.'

Jacques nodded his head, 'Yes you are right Mary.' Then he gently mocked her, 'Do you mind if first we enjoy today though, and our new found love?' He squeezed her hand in his, 'We can continue with all that tomorrow.'

Both had never felt so happy for a long time, neither wanted this moment to pass. 'There is one event we must see together this summer,' said Jacques. 'We will make time to go to the Calgary Stampede you will love it. They call it the greatest outdoor show in Canada, it's a wonderful time for everyone, but especially for those in love.'

'That will be wonderful,' she said. She pulled him toward her as she spoke and kissed him tenderly on the lips, then teasingly added, 'As long as we do all we can to get that book ready.' They both laughed.

****

Calgary – Canada

Two students were already at work when Jacques and Mary arrived for work the next morning. Emma and Robin greeted them as they walked in. 'We have something to tell you,' they said almost in unison.

It was Emma who continued. 'Our professor has agreed we can take subjects linked to, *"The Origin of the Jews"* for our dissertation.'

Jacques shook their hands, 'This is good news; it will help both you and us. What are the subject details?'

Emma answered first, 'Mine is the *"Archaeological and Documentary Evidence for Religion in the New Kingdom Period of Egypt"*, which will cover the time of Aten worship.'

'And for me,' added Robin, 'my subject is, *"Akhenaten: the World's First Monotheist or the World's First Machiavellian Politician? Or Both?"* which I think you will agree, is intriguing.'

'Indeed it is,' replied Mary. 'This is great news for us all.'

Emma opened up her note book, 'Our Professor said in our dissertation we must look at archaeology's ability to recover hidden information about the past and how it can create many new thoughts for today's historians.'

'Both of us can include,' said Robin reading from his notes, '*evidence, or lack of it, for the authenticity of the Exodus tradition.*'

'Well this must be compiled from your own research,' commented Jacques. 'You cannot simply use what we are finding here. It must be original and come from your own conclusions. But of course we will be glad to help you wherever and whenever we can.'

'The professor has already told us that.' Emma was a little affronted that they would even have considered anything else. 'I have a question for you though, if it won't take too long.'

'Fire away,' said Jacques, knowing it would not be him who answered the question.

Emma was ready, 'We saw the information from Doctor Boucher, which you read out to us about the papyri, which was presumed to have been found in King Tut's tomb, and we see how this gives a lead to the date of the Expulsion,' Emma was already up to the mark with her terminology, 'but what other evidence is there for this date or period?'

Mary knew there were long and a short answers to this, so she chose the short one. 'I will give you the bullet points but you must research the details. First we know the Expulsion was before the Merneptak Stele, which names Israel as a people or tribe rather than a kingdom, who were living in the land of Canaan. So it had to be before that date. Then there is what you have just referred to, evidence of the Expulsion in King Tut's tomb.'

The two students took notes as Mary continued, 'The most important evidence though are the beliefs they took with them upon leaving Egypt, which were so similar to, or the same as, the teachings which came from the worship of the god Aten. For example; Akhenaten didn't allow any graven images of the god Aten. As the unseen God, Aten could not be represented in animal or human form, as the old gods had been depicted. Then there was the introduction for the need of a temple in their worship, which early Hebrews never had. All this is so similar to what Moses taught that it had to be from the same source, and at a time when Aten worship was being practiced by some of the people.'

Mary went to the far end of the room looking for something; returning with yet another photocopy. 'This also helps to set the time of these events. It is called "The Restoration Stele", a stone upon which are recorded the events of the Expulsion, written or rather carved, during the time of King Tut.'

Mary handed out the photograph of a flat stone with a carved rounded top, 'Although this stele is dated to the reign of Tutankhamen, it was later usurped by his eventual successor Horemheb. It was obviously Horemheb who was pulling all the strings here, for King Tut was just a boy at the time, so he would never have usurped his father's religion without some powerful individual ordering him to do so; and Horemheb was the chief general of the Egyptian army at the time. Horemheb later even became pharaoh himself. And remember it was Horemheb who ordered the destruction of all the temples that had been built by Akhenaten. It is clear this man really hated the worship of Aten, for he set about removing all reference to his predecessors who had any connection at all with Aten worship; he made a determined effort to remove them completely from the historical records. And this was the man who was then in control of, or the guardian of King Tut when he was a boy, so he was determined to use this boy to stamp out Aten worship.'

'This round-topped stele is a very important historical stone document commemorating the end of the Aten worship and the official return to the traditional Egyptian religious system under King Tut. So it clearly dates these events precisely for us. I will read part of this translation to you:'

> *"The good ruler, performing benefactions for his father (Amen-Ra) and all the gods…,"*

'The "good ruler" is King Tut. Notice here that they do not name his real father Akhenaten, but simply say his father was the god, Amen-Ra. So the boy is not even allowed to name who his real father was. Kings usually bragged about who their father was; but not so in this case, as you see his real father was not mentioned. '

Mary smiled at Jacques as she saw the rapt attention on his face. 'It goes on,' she said.

> *"...for he has made what was ruined to endure as a monument for the ages of eternity and he has expelled deceit throughout the Two Lands,"*

'The Two Lands are Upper and Lower Egypt, but note that it says, *"...he has expelled deceit..."* the deceit was the heretical worship of the Aten, that was the "deceit" and it says he has "expelled" them. It could not be clearer than this that an expulsion took place. Here is you evidence of the Expulsion,' Mary was almost gloating.

Jacques was clearly enthralled. 'That's it,' he said jubilantly, 'so here we have a clear reference to an expulsion taking place. It is obvious from this that the Aten worshipers were indeed expelled.' Jacques put his hand to his chin in deep thought, 'The Bible says that God performed miracles or plagues which came to Egypt in order to force pharaoh to let them leave; but according to this, they left because they were driven out.'

'Now you are getting the picture,' said Mary quietly.

'I have not finished yet,' she said, nodding towards the picture of the stele. 'There is more:

> *"...and justice was set up so that it might make lying to be an abomination of the land, as in its first time."*

'The word "lying" was referring to the teaching of one god, or monotheism. The monotheists were here plainly called the liars or deceivers. This was the abomination they are referring to here, so now it says, they are returning to the *"first time"* which means returning to how things were before.'

'It then goes on to say how bad things had become under Aten worship. They really paint a vivid picture here.'

> *"Now when his majesty appeared as king, the temples of the gods and goddesses from*

> *Elephantine down to the marshes of the Delta had gone to pieces (or fallen into neglect). Their shrines had become desolate, had become mounds overgrown with weeds. Their sanctuaries were as if they had never been. Their halls were a footpath (or trodden roads). The land was topsy-turvy and the gods turned their backs upon this land."*

'There must have been some bad things happening to Egypt for this to be written, and there were; which we will not deal with now but at another time. Suffice to say whatever it was that was bad, it had all been blamed on the worship of Aten. Those who held to the old beliefs were blaming their current misfortune fortune on the anger of those old gods. They reasoned their bad fortune was because they had been negligent in looking after their temples, priests and the required sacrifices. They even go on to say the gods had turned their backs on Egypt.'

> *"If the army was sent to Djahi to extend the frontiers of Egypt, no success of theirs came at all. If one prayed to a god to seek counsel from him, he would never come at all. If one made supplication (or petition) to a goddess similarly, she would never come at all."*

'It is clear from this stele that the worship of Aten had so disrupted the land that the temples had begun to collapse, the religious sanctuaries were falling into ruins and covered in piles of rubble or weeds.' Mary could see the message Bob and herself had worked so hard to uncover, was getting through to the other three.

'There is one more thing which helps us to fix the time of the Expulsion.' Mary did not want this to become a lecture, so she added, 'This is a subject in itself, so all I will do is to point you in the right direction. It is for you to gather the evidence.'

She opened up her laptop and pointed to a page she had been working on. 'This helps us to see that many who left Egypt at this time were not Hebrews at all, but were Egyptians. You see,' she said pointing to the screen, 'there were many of those who left Egypt who had traditional Egyptian names. Let me show you how this helps us in locating the period of the Expulsion. For example: Akhenaten's two highest priestly officials of the worship of Aten were Meryre and Pinehesy. In the Bible we find a priest called Merari is described in Genesis 46:11, as one of the sons of Levi, who were the priestly tribe of Israel. Then again at Exodus 6:25 we are told that Phinehas was the son of the high priest. Now the Egyptian equivalent to Phinehas is Pinehesy and the Egyptian equivalent to Merari is Meryre. This is simply too much of a coincidence. So with these names alone we have evidence we are dealing with the very same high priests who had officiated and served Akhenaten who were now among those being expelled.'

Mary chuckled for it reminded her of her own time as a student discovering new things. 'There are other names like these, but that is for you to find out.' So saying, she closed her laptop.

'Thank you Mary,' said Emma, 'I am so glad we decided to come along to help you. It really is a fascinating subject.'

All this time Jacques had been sitting there, silent. In his mind many thoughts were racing through, not the least of which were the implications of all this for Israel today. Then, shaking himself away from these deeper thoughts he said, 'Let me see if I have got this straight? There was a profusion of Egyptian personal names amongst all those leaving Egypt, but especially among the tribe of Levi, the priestly tribe. Now Bob once told me, there were no such names among other countries and nations around the area, so either they were using Egyptian names because of their long association with Egypt; or,' and he paused, 'they really were Egyptians.'

'That about sums it up Jacques,' agreed Mary. 'We find from the Bible, concerning that priestly tribe of Levi, that it was they who were particularly zealous in demanding that no one strayed from worship of Yahweh, or Aten; for on one occasion when the Israelites returned to the worship of the golden calf, the Levites rounded up three thousand individuals and put them all to death.'

'Hmm!' grimaced Jacques. 'And that act is supposed to have found favour with God!'

Mary now added a key point, 'If the Israelites were truly a foreign people dwelling within Egypt they would have been mentioned as such in the many Egyptian texts which have survived; but none exists. Other national groups were mentioned, such as the Hyksos, but never the Israelites. So some have argued that they were all Egyptians who left Egypt in the Expulsion.'

'Look,' said Jacques, if we continue to talk all day we will not achieve much work.' Still it was clear his mind was elsewhere for he looked a little concerned with his innermost thoughts. 'I think it is time we continued to do some more scanning.'

****

Gaza Strip - Palestine

Bob had overheard several heated arguments being carried on, somewhere above him. He had no choice but to listen, for there was nothing else he could do. At least now he was not chained to that old iron radiator; but for how long that would last he was not sure. He frequently could hear the voice of Darwesh, a man who made his skin crawl, he also heard the voice of Taha, but there was another voice in the mêlée, a voice he did not know. Occasionally when he heard this strange voice they sometimes spoke in English, and it seemed to Bob that this new voice had an English accent. 'Should I be troubled about this?' he thought, 'Or is this someone gaining their confidence, someone who has really come here to rescue me?' Not knowing what was happening was the hardest thing Bob found to deal within his mind. The days just seemed to drag on and on, he was beginning to lose all track of time. How long had he been here now in this god forsaken cellar? Was anyone trying to find him? There were no answers to these questions which constantly ran through his mind.

The steel door was unlocked and thrown open with a crash. Darwesh and two armed guards descended the steps menacingly. The two armed men walked briskly over to Bob, grabbed his arms and roughly pulled them behind his back. Handcuffs were then snapped into place. Bob knew it was no good even asking where they were going, he doubted very much if they would have told him anyway. It was only when Bob stepped outside he realised it was night time. In his cell he had no way of knowing whether it was night, or day. Within seconds of this realisation a sack was placed over his head and he found himself bundled into a vehicle. The drive only lasted for about ten minutes, then, when the car stopped unseen hands propelled him along. He heard steel gates being opened and slammed hard behind him. Pulled roughly along, he stood still, as his head covering was removed.

In the dim light Bob saw he was standing outside in some kind of inner courtyard of a large house. Numerous men lounged around all looking intently toward him, most appeared to be armed. Nervous tension was high in Bob's whole body as he looked around at his three escorts; Darwesh, Taha and a man he did not know. The man he did not know studied him intently, looking him up and down with a look of pure hate in his face, but did not speak.

Darwesh moved to stand in front of Bob face to face, then raising his arm upward he pointed to something behind Bob's head. 'This man was an Israeli spy,' he said whilst spitting toward the object of his attention.

Bob turned around slowly. Looking upward to where Darwesh pointed his finger. Bob's heart missed a beat at the vision of terror before him. The shear horror of what he was looking at did not register at first. A man, naked except for a pair of ragged shorts, hung from an old wooden telegraph pole, large spikes had been driven through each of his hands which were stretched directly above his head. His legs were splayed either side of the pole with a four inch nail driven through the inner arch of each foot. A knife, which had been stuck into the pole, protruded from his genitals, blood pouring from around the blade. Bob could not tell if the man was still alive, but he hoped that he wasn't.

'Oh my God!' Bob's voice trembled as he muttered his words.

'This is the will of Allah,' declared Darwesh. 'This is what happens to the enemies of God.'

'And this will happen to you if we so wish,' declared the man he did not know.

Bob looked at him with equal feelings of disgust, fear and loathing.

'This is Adnan, our brother, he has come from your own country to help us, all the way from England,' Darwesh was almost bragging in his uncalled for introduction. 'He has done many fine deeds for Allah, even blowing up the football game in London, as well as the bombing in Derby. He has struck a hard blow against those unbelievers.' The assembled men nodded their agreement.

Bob's brain was racing, 'So this was the English voice I had heard from my cellar,' he thought. Then, a sudden realisation, there would be no rescue from him. The little thread of hope he had clung to now vanished. The possibility of rescue was something he had clung to, a dream which helped him to somehow keep going. Now that had been taken away from him.

Bob looked at the man who had killed so many and was now threatening his own life. 'You k-k-killed my friend's wife,' stuttered Bob. A bitter bile of hatred rose into Bob's mouth, as he spit a ball of hard phlegm into Adnan's face.

'Bastard!' screeched Adnan, as he swung his fist in an arc straight into Bob's face. Bob's hands were still handcuffed behind him so he could do nothing to protect himself. The first blow sent him spinning, the second knocked him to the ground; whereupon a rain of thunderous kicks and blows pummelled into his face. Blow after blow.

Darwesh just sat there enjoying the spectacle for a while. 'Enough!' cried Taha, reaching up and grabbing hold of Adnan's flailing arms. 'Enough.' Taha pushed Adnan away and stood between him and the bloody figure of Bob, who was gasping for air on the sandy ground.

'Now he will look nice and pretty for us on the TV tonight,' laughed Darwesh. 'When he sits in front of the camera, they will know we mean business.' He walked over to where Bob lay, then bending forward he spit into his face. 'They paid no attention to the first video we sent. For your sake they had better listen now.'

Merciless hands dragged Bob up and plonked him roughly onto an old wooden, straight backed, chair. Blood and sand hurt his swollen eyes, forcing him to squint. He could still see the figure of the man impaled on the pole. Then for the first time he saw another man, cowering with fear at the foot of that pole. Two men held a shoulder each, keeping the victim down on his crossed legs.

'You have seen what we do to Israeli spies,' snorted Darwesh. 'Now you can see what we do to thieves, who steal from their own people.' He looked at the trembling figure of the man. He nodded to the two men holding the whimpering figure. 'Bring him here,' commanded Darwesh.

The man was now dragged forward and placed onto a table, set out in the middle of the courtyard and laid on his back upon it. Darwesh held up a large knife as he turned to the armed men viewing this spectacle, 'This man has been found guilty under Sharia Law, the law of God; he is guilty of stealing from his own people. For this he will lose his right hand.' Darwesh allowed his words to sink in for a moment. Darwesh continued, 'Then he tried to run away, and for that he will lose his left foot.'

'No!' screamed the man in helpless terror. 'Mercy, mercy,' he pleaded.

'This is the law of Allah and you have been found guilty. There is no mercy for you.' Darwesh walked over to the table as six men held the victim down. A quick deep incision was made around the wrist of the man, until the bones were exposed and prised apart from the arm. Darwesh held up the severed hand above his head in an act of triumph. Walking around the group he held it high for all to behold, waving it around as though it was a trophy. He now strode across to the telegraph pole and nailed the severed hand below the impaled figure of the tortured man's splayed legs.

The foot took much longer to amputate, the bones being particularly difficult to sever. No one seemed to mind, or care, about the screams piercing the night sky coming from this victim of Sharia Law; for to their primitively conditioned minds they were convinced they were doing God's will.

Bob's mind convulsed at these unspeakable horrors he was being forced to witness. He was a kind and gentle man by nature and never imagined to see such hellish things. The horrors permitted and commanded by Moses came to his mind. 'This is how it must have been for them,' he thought, 'when Moses told his followers to show no pity. Back then they did similar unspeakable horrors believing they were carrying out God's will.' Bob's bloodied and swollen eyes took in this sight of unbelievable gratuitous violence. The mutilated man was eventually carried away in a large blanket, held together by four men, blood gushing from it.

'Now it is your turn,' said Darwesh.

Bob thought his end had come. 'Oh no! What are they going to do to me?' whirled through his mind.

'You will perform better for us this time I think,' Darwesh pointed toward a corner where black Islamic flags were draped. As he looked on a bright flood light was switched on and he realised they were going to force him to make another video recording.

This time as he sat facing the camera his beaten face would tell its own story. Sitting there several men, their heads completely covered with Arabic head gear, held knives to his throat; in fact they even drew a little blood, so hard did the push their sharp blades into his neck.

'Israel must release the captives they hold,' he read from the painted cards held up in front of him. He then read out a list the names whose release was now demanded. *'Palestine must become an independent state,'* he read. 'As it used to be, before it was taken from them,' he added as an unscripted extra.

'Keep to the script,' ordered Darwesh, unsure as to why he had added this.

'I can nite help it. I want to go home,' continued Bob, completely disregarding Darwesh's order.

Darwesh was about to come over and stop Bob from saying any more, but was restrained by Taha holding his arm. 'This may be useful to us,' argued Taha.

Darwesh snatched his arm away from Taha aggressively, but allowed Bob to continue.

'I can nite help it. I want to go home,' he repeated. 'Please do all you can to help me; listen to their demands, I want to get back to my home in Epsom; Epsom where I was born. Please help me.'

****

Calgary – Canada

Mary looked up from her work as Jacques entered the room. 'My office just called me,' Jacques eyes were wide and his jaw clenched tight.

Mary saw this look on Jacques face and knew immediately something was wrong. Her heart sank, 'What is it Jacques?' she asked.

Jacques walked over to her and held her hand tightly. 'It's Bob. They have released another visual recording of him on the Internet, and it does not look good. They are not showing the video on TV, it's too graphic for that; but the release of this clip is all over the British news media, Sky and BBC, it has also got on to the CNN channel.'

Mary gave a gasp and put her hand to her mouth, 'Have you seen the video?' she asked.

'Yes,' he confirmed. 'It is on the internet. My Company were informed of it and they told me immediately.' He shook his head, 'He is in a bad way Mary. It looks like they have beaten him up terribly. The bruises on his face are simply awful.'

'I want to see it,' she said as she fought back the tears.

'No, I don't think you should,' said Jacques trying to protect her.

'I want to see it Jacques, I have a right to, no matter what they have done to him.'

Mary was insistent and Jacques knew it would be no use arguing with her. 'It is on this website,' he said handing her the web address.

Mary typed in to her laptop the given address and waited a moment. The sight of Bob, bloodied, bruised and dishevelled, with knives pressed into his neck was something she never wanted to see. 'Oh Bob, what have they done to you?' She stood up abruptly and turned to Jacques, 'We have to get him out of there. Who is trying to find him? Is anyone?' Floods of tears now burst forth as she cried uncontrollably.

Although her reaction was very understandable, seeing Mary so upset hurt Jacques as well. 'I will get on to the British Embassy right away and see what they are doing about this.' Not only did he want to console Mary, he wanted to see his friend Bob, back home safely. 'I will go to my office and see what my contacts can do. I'll be as quick as I can.'

It was more than three hours later before Jacques returned. Mary looked numb her eyes were red and glazed. 'The British Embassy have got all their resources onto this, they have given me the name of a man from the Foreign Office who is heading this case in London. It is still the middle of the night back in England so I'll call him later. The problem is they do not know which country he is being held in.' Jacques saw no reaction in Mary to what he was saying, she just looked into open space. He continued slowly, 'I have put feelers out to many of my contacts in the Middle East, as many as I can, but it's still night time there as well.' Still he saw no reaction from her, 'Mary, are you listening?'

'There's something wrong,' she whispered, barely audible.

'Yes of course there is,' Jacques felt he was somehow not connecting with her.

'There's something wrong,' her face was glued to the laptop screen. 'There's something wrong,' she kept repeating as though in a daze. 'I think he is trying to send us a message,' she feebly whispered.

'Why! How! What do you mean?' This was not what he had expected to hear her say.

'It's in the video. It's there for us. Look at what he says. He wants to go home to Epsom where he was born,' Mary's distant eyes looked up at Jacques.

'Yes, of cause he does, he will…'

Mary did not let him finish, 'He was born in York, not Epsom!'

Jacques mouth remained open but no words came. He tried to work his jaw to say something, but all that came out was, 'York?'

'Yes, York,' she repeated a little more forcefully. 'He is trying to tell us something, but what is it?'

'I don't know,' Jacques thought he had better try and go along with her, and humour her in this time of distress. He feared she was in shock; 'as well she might be he thought.' He pulled up a chair and sat by her side, 'Well why would he say he was born in Epsom, if he was born in York? It does not make sense.' Jacques was struggling to gather his thoughts, but he was unable to think clearly.

'Why Epsom?' responded Mary, her frustration and strain was beginning to show. 'Why Epsom? Why Epsom?' she repeated. 'What's at Epsom? What is he trying to say to us?'

'I've no idea?' admitted Jacques. 'I've never heard of the place before.' He leaned over Mary's shoulder and typed the word *Epsom* into her laptop. He read from the screen:

> *'Epsom is a town in the borough of Epsom and Ewell in Surrey, England. Some parts of Epsom are in the Borough of Reigate and Banstead and Mole Valley District.'*

Jacques looked puzzled. 'Well, that's not much help.'

'They have a racecourse there,' said Mary as she opened up another website. 'Oh yes, it's where The Derby horse race is held.' She looked up at Jacques, 'Isn't that where the recent helicopter bomb was?'

'No Mary that was in the *city* of Derby, but that is not where The Derby horse race is held.'

'Then why tell us he was born in Epsom?' she again questioned. 'What *is* he saying?'

'I don't know, Mary. And to be honest I can't think straight at the moment. Derby horse race, Derby bomb, Derby horse race, Derby bomb,' Jacques repeated the phrase over and over. 'I don't get it, I don't.....' He did not finish. There was a silence as the two looked at each other, a sudden realisation dawning on them both simultaneously.

Mary stood up, turned looking at Jacques, 'That's it Jacques. We know that the man who was behind the murder of your wife was the same man responsible for the Derby helicopter bomb.'

'My god!' said Jacques. 'Could he be telling us that that man is out there with him? Could it be? Is that what he is really saying? That bastard Adnan Al Saqqaff?' A look of horror spread across their faces. 'My god!' repeated Jacques. 'If he is then he is in the hands of a callous killer.'

'I must phone this information through to the British Embassy,' Jacques lurched to his feet. 'Trouble is we may know who has him, but we still don't know where Bob is being held.'

'The Gaza Strip, Palestine,' asserted Mary confidently.

Jacques stopped dead in his tracks as he was about to leave the room. 'How the hell do you know that?' quizzed Jacques.

'Bob told us,' Mary had a look of assured authority on her face.

'How?' asked Jacques.

'It was a play on words in his video. I have played it over and over again, a dozen or more times. When he was told to keep to the script, he said "I can nite help it." They would think he was saying "I can not help it", but he wasn't. "Can nite" sounds a bit like "Canaanite". He was telling us he is in the land of Canaan, or what's left of it; it has to be The Gaza Strip.'

****

Gaza – Palestine

The voice of the Imam filled the mosque, shrill and impassioned, it echoed around the whitewashed walls. It was Friday midday prayer time and the mosque was full of men, young mostly, each eager to be seen by his brothers as a true Muslim. They were kneeling on the carpet covered floor gazing up at the rousing speaker in the pulpit, their eyes bright with anger and indignation.

'It is our duty as Muslims to oppose the hated Israelis,' the Imam pointed his finger in the direction of Israel. 'They are an unholy race, greedy, unjust, a murdering race: they are the enemies of Islam. Did not the Jews reject the holy prophet Mohammed? Does not the Holy Koran curse them for their wickedness? Look what they have done to this, our land of

Palestine. This land, inhabited by your people for thousands of years, and they stole it from you.' A wide acclaim from the congregation could be heard.

Adnan immediately took up the call of the Imam, for all to hear, 'There can be no peace with these people, for still to this day they continue to steal your land. They are a cursed race and should be wiped from the face of the earth, like the disease they are.' Adnan raised a clenched fist, 'They will burn in hell, every last one of them.' Cheers now arose from those gathered there. 'They will not be allowed to sleep peacefully in their beds, No!' he yelled, 'Hamas will see to that.'

A teenage boy stood up and raised his fist, 'Death to the Jews. Death to Israel.'

'Death, death, death,' began the chant.

Adnan headed for the main entrance, leading them outside, the congregation still reciting the chant 'Death, death, death. Allah Akbar.'

At night, later that day, Adnan was crawling through a tunnel trundling a number of steel pipes on a trolley behind him. This was the fulfilment of his dream; at last a chance to make a strike against Israel. He felt a sense of pride, for he was eager to strike his blow against the hated enemy of Islam. At the end of the tunnel a lifting device was hauling up several crates of heavy equipment. Adnan pulled his own load into place; after which he continued on toward the shaft, while others handled the lifting equipment. He was impatient, waiting for his turn to climb the wooden ladders to the surface.

Finally he emerged out of the shaft leading up from the tunnel, where a military officer of the Palestinian army met him. Reaching out they shook hands warmly with each other.

'Welcome, I am Captain Abdul-Salem. You are welcome to join us.' Abdul-Salem was a middle aged man, of heavy muscular build, but with a pronounced pot belly. His khaki coloured uniform shirt was well worn giving him an untidy appearance. 'I have been told to show you around, and from what they tell me I understand why they are so happy to have you with us. Those pipes you have brought are for our own Qassam missiles. We make these ourselves.' It was with some considerable pride he said this.

'Come with me,' he beckoned to Adnan as he walked off into the dark.

They soon arrived at where there was a complex of ruined houses; dwellings which had been reduced to rubble by Israeli air strikes two years before. Abdul-Salem led Adnan up several flights of broken concrete stairs until they came into a room containing the rockets. The room was open to the sky, the ruined walls hiding the missiles. A steel frame held a number of these missiles in place ready for launching.

Abdul-Salem stood by the side of them, 'These are the Qassam rockets of Hamas. We have manufactured them ourselves,' although he had said this before, he wanted to repeat it. 'This is the work you will be set to do for us. We have three models in regular use, with a fourth still in the developmental stage.' He smiled at Adnan, 'So you will have quite a lot to do for us in the coming weeks.'

One of the missiles lay in bits on the floor. Crouching down beside it he pointed things out to Adnan; as an instructor would. 'As a matter of construction, there's not much to a Qassam rocket. It is just a two metre long pipe; the same as you brought along with you tonight. These pipes are packed with fuel, which we make from fertilizer and melted sugar, and a warhead screwed onto the front. Their ranges vary from just under two miles to just over nine. They are unguided, so precision strikes aren't really part of the equation. But because they cost less than one thousand dollars to make, what we lack for in quality we make up for with quantity.'

'So you cannot strike deep into Israel with these,' observed Adnan correctly.

'True, we cannot,' confirmed Abdul-Salem. 'However we do have some Katyusha rockets, which are made in China. They have a far greater reach and larger warheads. But because we have to smuggle them in by way of the tunnels from Egypt, they lack the vehicle mounts they really need. So once again we improvise, but they are still pretty unreliable with regard to where they land. However, their increased blast radius compensates greatly for this shortcoming.'

Adnan was in a dream of pleasurable excitement. He could not believe this was really happening. 'You have to smuggle all this equipment in from Egypt?' he asked.

'Yes, but that's not such a problem my friend,' Abdul-Salem was clearly pleased with the recent events, as he laid out the details to Adnan, 'When the revolution came against Mubarak wonderful things started happening for us. With Mubarak kicked out and the Muslim Brotherhood in power, President Morsi relaxed the border for us. Even when the army removed Morsi, the rightful and legitimate President, the border was still relaxed; so there are now thousands of Hamas and foreign freedom fighters who have been given the citizenship of Egypt. I am told that seven-thousand members of Hamas from the Gaza Strip have arrived in Egypt so far. As you saw, you had no trouble getting through from Egypt,' so saying he slapped Adnan on the back. 'Even to this day it is not surprising that the rightful government, the Moslem Brotherhood, relies upon their Hamas brothers, for Egypt cannot trust their own security services,' he burst out laughing at this. 'Even though the army is in control their illegal Egyptian government no longer controls northern Sinai anymore; it is open country for our Hamas fighters as well as for men like yourself, who support us. Now that the border between Gaza and Egypt is virtually open, many other kinds of armaments have been smuggled in from Libya. After the fall of Gaddafi in Libya, our freedom fighters have utilized the chaotic situation there to raid the weapon stores of the military and to sell it to anyone who will pay.' Abdul-Salem held up his Chinese assault rifle and grinned. 'And many of those arms found their way here into Gaza.'

Adnan was almost speechless, 'It would seem things are moving well for our brothers,' said Adnan. 'If this is the case then we need to get better missiles into Gaza.'

'We are well underway with that my brother.' While he was talking Abdul-Salem started to prepare the rockets for launching. 'In November 2012 we fired Iranian Fajr-5 artillery rockets into Israel. These are much better. They have a range of around fifty miles and Tel Aviv is only forty miles away.'

'Wonderful,' declared Adnan. 'So now we can really hit them where it hurts.'

'We can and we will. Not only can we hit Tel Aviv we can also hit Jerusalem with these weapons.'

Adnan looked a little concerned at this information, 'You must be careful of the holy site there brother.'

'Yes of course,' Abdul-Salem felt a little insulted by this remark, but quickly passed it off. 'Now come with me, out of the way, for these are ready for firing.'

Retreating to a safe hideaway Adnan waited while Abdul-Salem went away to launch the missiles. It seemed an eternity until; 'wooosh, wooosh, wooosh,' could be heard.

Abdul-Salem with a look of gleeful satisfaction on his face, returned to Adnan, 'Now get out of here as fast as we can. Quickly, back the way we came, before Israel has time to launch any air strikes against us.'

****

Calgary – Canada

They were hurting her mother again and she could do nothing about it. She started screaming calling for her mummy and daddy. She was frightened, lost and afraid. Hold me daddy. Evil men were all around her preventing her from helping her parents. They were taking her mother away, as she called out her name. Her mother was leaving her. Don't go mother. She mustn't let them take her away. She must help her, she must help her, she must; but she couldn't. Hold me! She wanted the tender loving caress of her parents, but she could not reach them, they were just too far away, slipping away, out of her reach. Then suddenly there was Bob, his face all covered in blood, his hand reaching up toward her.

'No!' she screamed, snapping wide awake, arms thrashing wildly. 'Please, God, no!'

'Mary!'

She opened her eyes and looked up. There was Jacques by the side of her; holding her. 'You have been dreaming,' he said in a voice so calm after the mayhem of her dream.

'Oh Jacques, it was awful. I was with my parents again. I couldn't help them.' Mary was sweating.

'It's all right my love. I know how you feel. I have had similar dreams about my wife. Let me hold you.' He put his arm around her and pulled her tight. 'It's over now, I have you.'

'Oh Jacques hold me tight. Don't ever let me go. I love you so much.' The warmth of Jacques caress made her feel better, but sleep was a long time in returning to her.

'You had a bad night,' stated Jacques in the morning as he prepared their breakfasts.

'I don't feel we are doing enough to help Bob,' she said quietly.

'Well I told the British Embassy what you said about Bob's clues. They were a little sceptical, but they put me in touch with the British Foreign Office.' In his own mind Jacques agreed with Mary and felt they should be doing more, but was unsure what more they could do.

'I'm going to write an Email to Hamas, they have a website address,' she said.

'They will only deny having any knowledge of Bob or those videos,' stated Jacques, knowing full well this is what they would do.

'Well I have to try. I will say we have information about Bob and we know he is in Gaza. I will also tell them we know they are harbouring an international terrorist, Al Saqqaff.' Mary sipped her coffee as she started to look for the Hamas website on her iPad.

'They will still deny it my love; but if it makes you feel any better, then go ahead and do so.'

'Well I have to do something Jacques,' she insisted.

'Yes, OK. I'll tell you what my sweet, while you do that I will contact the London police to see if they have any leads on Al Saqqaff. He is the one who was behind the death of my wife. So I will say the same thing to them. Then we can see what response we get.' It wasn't much, but they both felt they were doing something to help Bob.

****

Birmingham – England

The tall gaunt figure of Les Forrester stood looking at the rain beating against the windows of his office. His office was situated high above the city of Birmingham, looking down on the city below, where he could see a canal built more than two-hundred years ago, yet still in regular use, with many brightly painted boats moored along its length. He saw two people in full rainwear, apparently oblivious to the weather, struggling to open up one of the many canal locks, which his city was famous for. In spite of the rain he wished he could forget everything and go down and join them. There and then he vowed to himself, 'I must try that one day soon.' They looked so free, yet he was tied up with many dreadful things; things which troubled his mind. Events, which in spite of his professional approach; had disturbed him greatly.

It had been a tough day. It had been a successful day, yet Janet Monroe, Head of the Special Crime and Counter Terrorism Division had given them all a hard time. 'I guess she did not like reporting back to the Home Office,' he mused.

'Intelligence has let us down, it needs tightening up,' she had bellowed at him in that high pitched voice of hers. Monroe had not been happy with their progress, or rather lack of progress, as she put it, in finding the terrorist leader, Adnan Al Saqqaff.

'I suppose congratulations should be in order,' she had reluctantly conceded, 'now that we have Ali Farouk the pilot of the helicopter bombing behind bars. But God damn it Superintendent, he was right under our very noses. If CCTV had not monitored him going to the mosque, he could still be free. As it is we still have to get hold of Nasser Mohammed, Abdu Kamal and the ring leader Al Saqqaff.'

Les had gone through things repeatedly in his mind. He had made sure all of the properties of those involved in the Derby terrorist atrocity had been torn apart in their search for evidence; any evidence. Forensic experts had virtually lived in the houses of those charged with these crimes. Since most of the assailants had been apprehended, his teams of experts had ripped out everything from the floorboards to the lawn in their gardens. There was plenty of evidence to implicate those British Asians, yet nothing had been found concerning the whereabouts of the Al Saqqaff, the man he was most keen to get behind bars, and his two cohorts.

What made things worse was that before all this happened, some of those recently arrested had been under surveillance for several months prior. Now Monroe was blaming him for not acting sooner. 'If I had have acted too soon,' he said in a vain attempt to justify his lack of action, 'we could have driven them further underground and lost touch with them altogether.' It was a lame excuse and he knew it; but he had to say something. However, he knew he should have acted sooner.

Les opened his mobile phone and pressed the button for his assistant, 'Pam, I'm calling another meeting with TAM (Terrorism and Allied Matters) we will have to go over things again. This is getting crazy. We have to check all options. We have to find him.'

His internal phone was buzzing; it registered 'Monroe' on the screen.

'Shit, now what does she want,' he whispered beneath his breath.

He picked up the phone and waited, 'Les,' she snapped, 'I have just had an urgent call from the Foreign Office. They want to see us both in London, immediately.'

'What about?' he asked, but did not really need to.

'Al Saqqaff,' was all she said before hanging up.

Les looked weary at the thought of a dash from Birmingham to London. 'I hope they've found the bastard, he mumbled.' However, it did not sound good. 'Why on earth would the Foreign Office be calling and not the Home Office?' he mused.

****

London - England

It was difficult to watch where he was walking, while his eyes were constantly wanting to look upwards and take it all in. Les could only wish that his own office was something on a par with this place. High ornate ceilings with huge windows, allowing light to flood in to the interior, expensive oil paintings hanging on silk covered walls. Here was an extravagant richness of a former glory, which declared this was where the fate of half the world's population were once decided; here within these walls. The grandeur of the Foreign and Commonwealth Office, to give it its full name, or the Foreign Office as most people called it, was lavish by anyone's standards. The entrance alone from King Charles Street almost took his breath away, but once inside he literary held his breath. Looking around Les thought to himself, 'This place is seldom seen by Joe public. I wonder how many decisions of world importance, were made, and are still made here, even today.'

Together with Janet Monroe, they followed the young woman who had greeted them. They were walking briskly, too quickly for Les to absorb it all. He wanted to take is time, as he would have done wandering around a museum; but this was no jolly, it was work. They were shown in to a modest meeting room, modest by the standards of this place, but still rather grandiose.

'Wait here they will join you in a minute,' said this pretty young lady dressed in an expensive two-piece suit, with a pencil thin skirt.

Les thought she looked too young and was hardly old enough to be in such a job, 'She should still be at university', he thought. 'Who are "they"'? he asked.

'It's the Director General who has arranged the meeting,' was the reply. 'That's all I know.'

Les looked at Janet and raised his eyebrows, but said nothing, as they both sat down at a large table in the centre of the room. After a few moments the door opened and several people walked in, taking their seats around the table, giving Les and Janet just a nod of acknowledgement by way of a greeting.

A well dressed, late middle aged gentleman took his place at the head of the table, 'I'm Sir Gordon Harcourt, Director General; thank you for coming.' He turned to look at Janet and Les, 'You must be Janet Monroe, Head of the Special Crime and Counter Terrorism Division, and Les Forrester, Superintendent for the National Counter Terrorism Security Office.' Without waiting for a response he carried on. 'We are joined by Alison Rhodes, Director for Middle East and North Africa; John Tye, Director for International Security and Fatimah Salim, Digital Research Analysis for the FCO.' (Foreign and Commonwealth Office)

Addressing Janet and Les he said, 'You have been involved with apprehending the culprits of the recent terrorist attacks in Derby. Fortunately I understand you now have the majority of that gang awaiting trial.'

'Yes sir, that is correct,' replied Janet.

'You are to be congratulated on this most excellent work. Well done. However, I understand there are two or three still at large, including the ringleader of this group,' the Director raised his eyebrows. 'A Mister Adnan Al Saqqaff: and that has eluded you so far I understand?'

'Yes sir,' she repeated.

Sir Gordon clasped his hands together on top of the table, 'Well, we have reason to believe Al Saqqaff is no longer in this country and that he has fled to the Middle East; the Gaza Strip to be exact. This is why the FCO has become involved.'

'So how can we help?' asked Janet.

'We will need your involvement in the developing events which are evolving around this character.' Then looking at Alison he said, 'I'll let Alison explain to you what has led up to this information.'

'Thank you Sir Gordon,' responded Alison. 'Our British Consulate, in Calgary, Canada has had several visits and Emails from friends and colleagues of Doctor Robert Boucher. Doctor Boucher is the British subject who is being held hostage by Islamic extremists. He disappeared while in Cairo, where he was on a research project for the University of York. He is particularly vulnerable due to his latest book, entitled, "*The Origins of Islam*". This is a book researching the archaeological and documentary records concerning that period. As you will know he has been widely condemned for producing this work, especially within Islamic countries; even though scholars say it is an academic book and not a populist one.'

'This is all common knowledge,' said Les, rudely breaking into Alison's flow of words.

Clearly irritated, Alison continued, 'As though this was not enough of a problem, Boucher's colleagues told the Calgary Consulate about a second book he is writing concerning the legality of the state of Israel.' Several around the table shook their heads in disbelief. 'However, what is of particular interest to us is that his colleagues said they knew where Doctor Boucher was being held.' Les pricked his ears upon hearing this information. 'We thought their claims were, how shall I say, a bit eccentric, so we did not take them too seriously. We gave them the standard reply and informed them that we were pulling out all the stops to find Doctor Boucher. We had an idea he would be somewhere around north Sinai, but we had no proof. Since the Arab Spring uprisings the north of Sinai has become uncontrolled and full of Islamic extremists.'

Alison now turned to look at Fatimah, 'Then an Email was intercepted due to some good work being carried out by Fatimah here. Please tell us what you found Fatimah.'

Fatimah looked a little nervous. She was used to looking into a screen all day and not into the faces of so many important people. 'It was an Email from Doctor Boucher's work colleague, Mary McIntire; she is a British national, from a British father and Coptic Egyptian mother. She had written to Hamas in Gaza saying they had information giving them reason to believe that Bob Boucher is in Gaza. The Email also said that they know that Hamas, is harbouring the international terrorist, Al Saqqaff.'

'How did they find that out?' asked a surprised Les.

'I don't know that, but I think Alison does,' replied Fatimah.

'Yes. There were seemingly obscure clues in the video put out by the captives of Doctor Boucher,' responded Alison. 'Clues that we had either missed, or they had not been treated seriously enough. Doctor Boucher's colleagues told our Consulate in Calgary about these clues, but we thought it was just wishful thinking on their part, and dismissed this idea.'

'Then Hamas responded,' interjected Sir Gordon. 'They flatly denied knowing anything about it. However, it was not their denial so much as the way they vehemently denied it. We would normally have expected no such response at all, treating such an Email as nothing more than a spam, or something similar. Yet it was the strength of their denial which was strange.'

John Tye interjected, 'We have now carefully analysed that video of Doctor Boucher at the hands of his captors and concur with the suggestion that he was trying to tell us something. It was crude, but effective.'

'So crude that you missed it,' Les's sarcasm brought a brief but embarrassed silence to the room.

Offended, but showing it only in his eyes, John Tye continued, 'Given the circumstances the poor man could hardly have done anything else. He did well to say what he did.'

'So now,' said Sir Gordon forcefully, 'we have informed the government of Israel of these findings. And you will not be surprised to learn, they were not exactly startled to know this international terrorist was hiding there in Gaza. Apparently they have been on the receiving end of a fresh barrage of rockets and missiles coming from Gaza on a daily basis. Satellites have been monitoring suspicious movements and activities, helping us and the Israelis to locate the centre of these activities. There does seem to be a ground swell around one specific place.'

All eyes looked intently toward Sir Gordon, wondering where all this was leading. Sir Gordon continued, 'It is this second book which Doctor Boucher wants to publish which could be a problem for us.' He paused, as though seeking to find the right words, 'You see Israel, sooner or later are going to strike at that area we have located. It would usually be in the form of an air strike, but they have informed us they would be prepared to send in assault troops in order to try and get Doctor Boucher out.' He clicked his tongue. 'It's risky of course, but we feel it is worth the risk.' He looked around the table at them all, 'Unfortunately Israel does not think it would be in their interests to free a man who wants to undermine their legitimate right to the land they hold.' Sir Gordon gave a knowing look toward Alison.

Alison took the hint, 'As you will know, we did not cover ourselves in glory over the establishment of Israel. There is nothing new about this, it is generally known about, especially among the educated classes, if not the common man. Even so, we feel such a book could become a tool for Muslim extremists to use. It could inflame the Middle East even more, as well as many people in our own country, they could all use it to increase their opposition to Israel and maybe Iran could use it as an excuse for a pre-emptive strike against Israel.'

'You are saying this book could become a cross between Mao Tse-tung 's *"Little Red Book"* and Hitler's *"Mein Kampf",'* said Les, with visions of the damage such books can cause.

'Please don't be so flippant Superintendent,' said Sir Gordon. Then he added as an afterthought, 'However there may be an element of truth in that. Please continue Alison.'

'Thank you Sir Gordon. This book could not only inflame the Muslim extremists around the world, but it could also be used by the Right Wing elements here. People, who will only be too glad to use such disturbances to their own political advantages.'

'I understand how it could bring Muslim extremists onto the streets,' said Janet, with a sidelong look toward Les, 'but I don't understand how it would affect the Right Wing parties.'

'Because one feeds off the other,' interjected Sir Gordon. 'If Muslim cities around the world erupt, because of a book which inflames their cherished belief, that Israel should not exist, it will spill over into the streets of Europe and especially here in London, where many such extremists reside. Then we could find that groups such as the British National Party, the English Defence League, the National Front, even so-called anti-fascists groups, to name but a few, they could all use this a book in different ways; each group pursuing their own political objectives. These Right Wing groups hate the immigration policies of British governments, both past and present. But they especially hate the Muslim extremists who seem to have a vocal and violent vendetta against this country. It is true these Islamists have not done themselves any favours in the eyes of the general public, unfortunately many have never settled well into our culture, as former politicians had hoped they would. Now the recent bombings in England, carried out by these Islamic extremists, have turned the silent hatred of the general public into an increasingly vocal one. There is an intense anger from the British people against those who seek to perpetuate their hatred through bombings. The Right Wing will latch onto this for all they are worth, which could result in, not only demonstrations, but full scale attacks against any Islamic centres and individuals.' Silence descended at the forceful strength of Sir Gordon's argument as he turned his gaze toward Alison, 'Carry on Alison.'

Alison swallowed hard, 'The FCO feel it is in the interests of both Israel and this country, to keep this book under wraps, at least for a while. As Sir Gordon has said it is a very sensitive time right now, not only for our own country, but also for the whole of the Middle East. We are sitting on a tinder-box which should not be ignited.'

'So you see,' interjected Sir Gordon once again, 'it is in no one's interest to let such a book be published. Therefore, we have made an agreement with Israel that we will do all we can to hold back on that book and delay its publication for as long as we can. Outside of this room it will be stated that it is purely on a humanitarian basis that Israel has agreed to make a rescue attempt on Doctor Boucher.'

Les was puzzled, 'Forgive me Sir Gordon, but I don't understand what we are doing here and why you are involving us in this meeting?'

All eyes looked to Sir Gordon, 'Good point Superintendent. Then let me explain. Janet; as I said before, your department has taken the lead in hunting down the terrorists responsible for the Derby outrage. And of course you want to find and apprehend the ringleader.'

'Yes sir,' replied Janet, unsure where this was going.

'Then it would not be out of place for senior personnel from the Counter Terrorism Division to pursue their enquiries by going over to Canada in order to interview Doctor Boucher's colleague, Mary McIntire and at the same time a victim of the London bombing, Jacques Gendron.' Sir Gordon sat back in his chair waiting for this to sink in.

'That is correct sir, I could send a member of our CTD team,' acknowledged Janet. 'But Gendron was interviewed while he was in hospital here in London, so I don't see why one of my staff needs to go there.'

'I think you are missing the point, Ms Monroe,' Sir Gordon looked intently toward her.

Janet looked blank.

'You want one of us to go over there and tell them not to publish that book,' said Les, suddenly beginning to realise what this meeting was all about.

'That's a yes and a no, Superintendent,' was the double edged response. 'Yes I want one of CTD to go over there, but not to tell them to refrain from printing that book. There is no way to communicate with the author anyway whilst he is being held as hostage. So such a request would be pointless,' Sir Gordon loved to score points over others like this, 'but of course you will be well aware of that.'

His cynical note hit home, as Sir Gordon continued, 'However, apparently there is a large amount of materials amassed by Doctor Boucher which could become a propaganda tool in the wrong hands. Such material could then be used against Israel, and thereby strengthen the hands of the terrorists.' Sir Gordon was now looking a little smug. 'Israel has agreed to attempt this rescue, but only as long as any material Boucher may have; material which could be used to try to undermine the state of Israel, is confiscated under the Anti Terrorism Act and classed as terrorist material, likely to harm a friendly nation. Only on that basis will any sort of rescue attempt be undertaken. However this could never be seen to be the purpose of your visit. I hope you understand that.' Sir Gordon waited to make sure they had heard him correctly. 'Ms Monroe, you will merely send over someone to speak of a possible rescue attempt, sounding out what information you can to legitimise such a visit. That person can then observe how and where this material is stored. Once that information is in place, we will arrange for those materials to be transferred into a secure location. When, or rather *if*, Doctor Boucher is released, he will be strongly requested not to pursue his declared aim to undermine the state of Israel; after all they are the people who, it will be said, risked all to rescue him: and we will have to emphasise that. Also, it will be pointed out that if he wants to see his materials returned, and not be prosecuted under the ant-terrorism laws, then he should rethink his stated aims.'

Janet was a little dazed by the impact of this information. Not wishing to be seen lagging behind her Superintendent, she made her contribution, 'There are several team members, any one of whom I could send over to Canada carry this out.'

'No, Ms Monroe, what has been said here must remain in this office,' Sir Gordon was adamant.

'Then who…?' she did not have to finish her sentence, she just turned and saw all eyes were looking towards her Superintendent, Les Forrester.

****

Calgary – Canada

Spring was in full swing in Calgary. The long hard winter was just a memory and the countryside had taken on its best hue. Students Emma and Robin were getting on well on with their studies, only occasionally frequenting the workshop of Jacques and Mary. Today was one of those occasions.

'Hello you two,' Jacques greeted them as they walked through the door. 'Have you come to help?'

'Well,' Robin hesitated. 'We can help, but we have come to you with a couple of questions.'

'He's only kidding,' said Mary. 'We said we would be happy to help you whenever you needed it.'

A coffee area had been set up at one end of the large room, situated by a large window. 'Come on, let's have a coffee and see what it is you want,' said Jacques.

Both Jacques and Mary were still very worried about their colleague Bob, and the vague news that there may be some developments with regard to Bob. Yet the work they had set themselves was now more than half way through.

Emma spoke first, 'The first question is for the pair of us, because we are both looking at a certain aspect of these events for our studies.'

'OK, well fire away,' said Jacques as he poured the coffees, and relaxed back in an easy chair.

Emma put the first question to Mary, 'The reason for the Expulsion of the Israelites was clearly based on religious differences; but where did the stories of the plagues come from? And is there any factual evidence for these tales? If you remember, when you told us about the "The Restoration Stele" and Horemheb, you said there were some bad things which had happened to Egypt around the time of the Expulsion, were these bad things the plagues?'

'Well as you know,' said Mary, 'I will give you the outline, but it is for you to find the detail. Most historian scholars agree that the plague stories as set out in religious texts are mythical folk-law and inspired by passed-down accounts of earlier natural disasters. Some have speculated on a possible series of such natural disasters behind the story of the succession of plagues.' Mary opened up her laptop. 'There is historical evidence of at least one plague, and that things were not going too well during the latter part of Akhenaten's reign.' She brought up a translation of a text from this period. 'This is a text written by the Hittites, not the Egyptians, around this time:'

> *'The Egyptian prisoners which they (The Hittites) had taken, a plague broke out among the prisoners and these began to die. When they moved the prisoners to the Hittite land, these prisoners carried the plague into the Hittite land. From that day on people have been dying in the Hittite land.'*

Mary continued with her explanation, 'This text implies that some form of plague was ravaging the Middle East at this time. The existence of a plague is mentioned in many other texts written in the Middle East around the same period. Given the scale of this epidemic, it is possible that the sudden deaths of several members of Akhenaten's own family could be linked to this plague. Within a two or three year period, Akhenaten lost his mother, three daughters and maybe one of his wives. Scholars believe that because there were so many deaths in such a short period of time it must have been the result of a plague or epidemic.'

Jacques raised his eyebrows, 'So this plague would have been felt by the people and priests to be a punishment from their old neglected gods,' he suggested. 'So, no doubt they would have blamed such things on the cult religion of the Aten. Thus when a plague like this began sweeping across Egypt towards the end of Akhenaten's reign it would be seen as a just punishment for Egypt having not supplicated the gods for some thirteen years.'

'You have picked things up well Jacques,' said Mary with a broad smile. 'It was possibly a pandemic, or perhaps the world's first recorded outbreak of influenza. What we do know is that it also killed the Hittite king during this time. Interestingly, influenza is a disease associated with the close proximity of fowls, pigs and humans, and its origin as a pandemic disease may be due to the development of agricultural systems which allowed for the mixing of these animals and their wastes. Some of the first archaeological evidence for this type of agricultural system is found to be in operation during this period. I suggest you both look into this as a possible cause.'

'Well that fits,' agreed Emma. 'There are some who say the ten plagues of the Bible were the result of a volcanic eruption elsewhere. What do you say about that?'

'Yes, there are many who are now saying that. And it could well have had an effect,' agreed Mary. 'One of the biggest volcanic eruptions ever in human history occurred when Thera, a volcano that was part of the Mediterranean islands of Santorini, just north of Crete, exploded around three-thousand five hundred years ago, spewing billions of tons of volcanic ash into the atmosphere.'

'That amount of ash would have certainly darkened the sun, at least,' said Jacques.

'Exactly. It certainly would have done that,' continued Mary. 'But this occurred around two-hundred years before King Tut came to the throne. So my own feeling is that these terrible events were already in their folk-law memory when the time came to leave Egypt, and as such these stories had been repeated to younger family members on a regular basis. Later generations would blend these events in with their own experiences of the expulsion; either that or they were deliberately added after the

Expulsion, as a fearsome example of God being on their side.' Turning to Emma, she added, 'I suggest you draw your own conclusions in your studies about this particular element of the Expulsion.'

'Thank you Mary, I will,' agreed Emma.

'Now I have a question,' said Robin. 'Besides monotheism is there anything else which still lingers on from the worship of Aten?'

'A very profound question,' stated Mary. 'I think the answer to that must be yes, there is; namely intolerance. Which Jacques and myself have both been victims of. We have shown you how intolerant the worshipers of Aten were towards all other forms of worship; how all the religious practices of the old gods were banned under Akhenaten, resulting in the temples of those gods being pulled down or abandoned. Well it is that kind of intolerance which was carried on when the monotheistic Jews first entered Palestine and killed all around them, simply because those people had different beliefs.'

Jacques butted in to add his point, 'One only has to think of the Inquisition, the Crusades and the Protestant Reformation to see how such intolerance was carried on.'

'Yes Jacques, but it goes back much earlier than that.' Mary wanted to make her point clear. 'Early Christians were also very intolerant toward other religions. Under the Roman Christian Emperor Theodosius in the 380's, he reiterated Constantine's ban on pagan sacrifice, and prohibited all other forms of worship, on pain of death. He destroyed pagan temples, and even any visits to such temples were forbidden. He then went so far as to persecute other Christians who did not follow the Roman dictates, classing them as heretics and pagans. One of the edicts of Theodosius prohibited Christians from holding public discussions of any religious questions. So you either followed their idea of worship, or you were killed. That is how intolerant they were.'

'A bit like the Taliban today,' commented Jacques. 'It was because such beliefs were enforced, or held onto so strongly, that the religious wars during the Reformation were so bloody and gruesome. It was this type of monotheistic intolerance which was taken up by the Muslims, producing a clash of cultures which is still being fought out today. The fact is they all babble on about how God will condemn the others for not believing exactly as they do.'

'That's right,' agreed Mary. 'Islam today is the most intolerant religion on earth; but they are only following what Jews and Christians have done in the past, before they became more enlightened. As Christians have warred between themselves; because each thought they were right and God was on their side, so too have Muslims. The fractions between Sunni and Shea are just as violent and intolerant as it once was between Protestant and Catholic Christians. Intolerance is something Jews, Muslims and pre-twentieth century Christians all had in common with the worshipers of Aten.'

Emma and Robin were furiously making notes, taking all this down.

Jacques became sombre, 'As Mary said, it is because of this intolerance they killed my wife and Mary's mother. Many are still dying today because of such primitive beliefs. They think this is what God wants, for them to carry out such intolerance according to the monotheistic way. They follow teachings in the Koran which say, "And slay them wherever you catch them. Such is the reward of those who reject the faith". It is something the West has largely grown away from, but these Islamist have not. Maybe one day there will be an Islamic Reformation which will bring them away from such intolerant beliefs; but I fear that will be a long way off.'

'There is one more thing,' said Mary, 'which still lingers on from the worship of Aten. In ancient times the gods of Egypt, Babylon, Greece and Rome all depicted their gods with faults or human traits. Such gods were depicted with all the failings and frailties that humans have. For example: they were said to have lusted sexually after the women of earth, they fought among themselves, even killed each other, committed murders and were vengeful and jealous; those ancient mythical stories are full of such things. But it was not that way with the Aten. The Aten was depicted with no such frailties; this god was perfect, faultless. Although Aten in many ways was a god of the sun, official Egyptian language avoided calling the Aten a god, giving this solar deity a status above that of mere gods. Aten was *the* god, being above all others in every way. In other words he was an invisible force for good, which is how modern worship depicts God to this day.'

The two students finished taking their notes. 'Thank you for that,' said Robin. 'We do have time to help you for a short while. Do you want any scanning doing?' Robin's offer was genuine.

'No, that's alright Robin,' responded Jacques. 'We are making really good progress, so you go and get your notes and studies finished. Besides we have a visitor coming later, to talk to us about Doctor Boucher. He is coming all the way from England to see us, so it must be important. The fact is we are both just a little bit worried about what it is he wants to see us for.'

The two students left the room, with both Mary and Jacques feeling contented with the way things were going for them personally, in spite of their shared tension over Bob they were more than happy in each other's company.

****

Calgary – Canada

A car pulled up outside the office and research workshop of Mary and Jacques. They both saw him coming at the same time. Jacques noticed that Mary had a look of apprehension on her face, so he tried to lighten things up a little. 'What is it about cops?' he said. 'Even when they are in plain clothes you can spot them a mile away.'

Mary just managed to raise a smile, as the tall thin faced man, in an expensive long dark dress coat walked in.

'How do you do,' he said with a refined English accent. 'My name is Les Forrester; I'm the Superintendent for the National Counter Terrorism Security Office in England.'

'Come in and sit down,' Jacques shook his hand. 'Let me take your coat and hang it up. This is Mary McIntire, my partner and Bob Boucher's assistant.'

'You have news about Bob?' asked Mary immediately, impatient to know.

Les did not answer, but just gave a slight smile and handed his top coat to Jacques.

'Would you like a coffee?' asked Jacques. 'It's a long way for you to come to see us.'

'It certainly is,' replied Les, settling down into a soft easy chair.

'What's this all about then?' Mary feared there may be bad news about Bob.

The niceties out of the way and the coffee poured, the three of them sat down together. An air of tension seemed to be with the Superintendent, as though he did not know quite where to begin.

'You did well to decipher the hidden message in Doctor Boucher's last video.' Les was tired from travelling and jet lag had made his mind a little duller than normal. 'As a result of your information the Israelis and Britain have used satellites to scrutinise certain areas in Gaza where Hamas terrorists, or freedom fighters, depending on your point of view, are most active.'

Jacques leaned forward in his chair, 'And what have you found?'

'We are now fairly sure Doctor Boucher is in Gaza, as is also Al-Saqqaff.' Les grimaced when he said that terrorist's name, recalling the horrors he had seen in Derby. 'And we have a good idea where they are in Gaza.'

'That's the bastard who killed my wife,' said Jacques, clenching his teeth.

'Yes I know. It must have been terrible for you to go through all that. I had personal experience of his actions when I saw the terrible things he did in Derby,' Les slowly shook his head. 'I can assure you; I will do all I can to bring him to justice.'

'It's been very hard for Mary as well,' Jacques gently took hold of her hand. 'She has worked with Bob, since her student days.'

'Can you do anything to help Bob?' asked Mary, still a little unsure as to why this man was here.

'Possibly,' Les scowled as he said this. Then he sat back in the chair and looked her straight in the eye, 'Israel may be able to help.'

Mary's attention was now focused, 'How?' she asked.

'It's a long shot, and not one I am too confident with,' Les fought to find his words. 'Through the satellites they have located an area of activity and have observed certain comings and goings which would indicate the area where their hostage is being held.' Les felt a little embarrassed at having to give such an evasive answer.

'Are you suggesting Israel will send in a rescue mission?' asked Jacques knowing the implications of such an action.

'It would not be a rescue mission as such,' responded Les. 'Hamas has been firing missiles into Israel again, so a rescue could become an off-shoot of any possible reprisal actions which Israel may undertake.'

'That could be too dangerous for Bob.' Jacques was shocked at the mere suggestion of such an action.

Les tried to reassure them both, 'The Israeli forces are some of the best trained in the world. They know their targets well and could be in and out of there before most people who live there even knew they had been.'

'That's not what I understand,' refuted Jacques. 'They usually go in very hard with all the power they can muster.'

'Yes, when they wish to draw attention to their actions, they will do so. But that is not always the case. They have people on the ground there,' Les let that statement sink in. 'Very brave people, who sometimes get caught and pay a very heavy price.'

'Do we have a say in this matter?' asked Mary.

Les raised his eyebrows, 'Well no, not really.' Les was looking even more serious. He was finding this difficult. 'We are sure Israel will go hard into Gaza soon, all the signs are there. It is just,' Les hesitated again before continuing, 'just a risky operation, which could result in the hostages' death.'

Mary put her hand to her mouth and gulped.

'What are the alternatives?' asked Jacques.

'As you know, Israel is surrounded by enemies. People who have openly stated, they want to wipe Israel off the face of the world. Israel's position is tenuous. It has been since the founding of that country.' Les was speaking slowly, but carefully. There was another along pause before he continued. 'There are many people who will seek to use such an action to further their own political and religious grounds. Israel has to decide; do they want to risk an attempted rescue mission, with possible Israeli fatalities, for someone who has stated he intends to publish a book which may undermine the legality of the state of Israel.'

'Jesus fucking Christ,' yelled Jacques.

'Jacques!' Mary looked at Jacques with startled eyes.

'I'm sorry: but what a thing to say,' Jacques's face was flushed with anger. 'Are you saying if he does not publish his book, they then may attempt a rescue?'

'No, of course not. I am sorry if I gave you that impression. I am not saying that at all,' Les lied, 'I must choose my words more carefully. How could we even think of such a thing anyway, because it's impossible to get in contact with the author to make any such arrangement.' This is going to plan thought Les.

'So what are you saying?' Jacques's face had now gone red with embarrassment.

Les waited and sipped on his coffee, 'I am saying that Israel were initially not overly keen to attempt a rescue. So appeals were made through diplomatic channels as a request to their humanitarian side for any such action. Even though this is a man who could possibly hurt them later on. And I have to tell you they have responded well. You see it is possible that Doctor Boucher could be held there for years, while the politicians talk about ways to get him out. Only Israel has the wherewithal to actually do something, within what is a very sensitive area. However, even though they have agreed to help there are political and religious elements within Israel itself who would rather leave him where he is. You see, there are religious fanatics within Israel who are just as extreme as those within Islam.'

Jacques put both arms behind his head, subconsciously gesticulating his thoughtful mood, 'This reference about the religious and political elements who would rather leave him there; it would seem,' said Jacques in a thoughtful mode, 'that there are much bigger forces than us at play here. From what I have learnt from Bob and Mary, there are those who are fearful of the ancient and recent past becoming common knowledge, and they fear anything that might shake the established order and institutions they serve.'

'Indeed there is,' replied Les.

'You must understand, it is Bob's lifetime work,' said Mary with a calmer appearance, but equally as angry as Jacques.

Les sympathised with this, 'I came over here to tell you of this current situation only, and I do not want to raise your hopes too high. It is only a brief visit, to let you know of possible actions being considered to free Doctor Boucher. It is not something which could be written, and I am sure you will respect this confidentiality.'

Jacques was puzzled, he said nothing, but he thought to himself, 'Why didn't they just send someone from the British Consulate here in Calgary to tell us this? Why send this man over from England?'

'I do not understand much about the book Doctor Boucher intends to write, it sounds interesting though. Can you tell me more about it please?' Les was fishing. 'Is there a synopsis for the book?'

'No, it is not written yet,' was Mary's reply. 'There are hundreds of notes and prepared materials, and an overview, but Bob was to write it. I only work as his assistant.'

'I see,' smiled Les, wishing to explore more about the materials they had which could be so sensitive.

'Regarding the book,' said Jacques as he stood up and gazed out of the window, 'I will tell you a little about it.' Jacques could not hold back his inner thoughts, 'First though tell me why you had to come all this way to tell us what the British Consulate could not?'

Les answered calmly, but lied, 'Of course they could have told you this, but being as I had to come over to Canada to give a lecture on counter terrorism, I thought the personal touch would be better for you. Also, I knew you had suffered at the hands of Al Saqqaff, and I was heading the hunt for him in Britain, until he left our shores, but I want to reassure you I will not rest until he is captured or dead.'

'Well thank you for that,' said Jacques, his anger flaring at the mere mention of Al Saqqaff's name. 'I hope you soon can find him. That monster has the morals of an insect.'

Jacques tried to compose himself, still unsure of the reason this superintendent was here. 'Let me tell you about Bob's book; Bob himself told me these things,' Jacques topped up the coffee cups. 'His book will set out to show how Christianity, Judaism and Islam, the three major monotheistic religions, which are extant in the world today, are all based essentially on a single religion, Judaism. It is Judaism which is at the root of all three religions, and in many ways all three are inherently indistinguishable. This book will clearly show that the original religion, namely Judaism, came from a religious cult in ancient Egypt and not from some divine revelations as portrayed in the Torah, Bible and Koran.' Jacques sighed. 'Just think about that for a moment Superintendent. The Jewish claim on Palestine is the basis of their whole religion. Their belief in Moses and the Exodus states that this was all a great miracle from God Almighty who promised the land of Palestine to them. A promise which was later used by the Zionists, the British and Americans in the early twentieth century to justify establishing the modern state of Israel. Bob's book will show that no such promised was ever made to ancient Israel. It will also show how twentieth century Christian Fundamentalists worked to establish the nation of modern Israel, believing, as those Christians did, that the establishment of Israel would hasten the return of Jesus Christ. The actions of these Christians was supported by, Jewish Zionists who united with the Christians toward this one aim of establishing the modern state of Israel.'

Les knew clearly now why he was here, and what action he had to take. 'This is fascinating stuff, can you tell me more about it and show me how it can be proved. I understand you have gathered together a lot of material on this subject.'

'We will be delighted to show you and explain things,' Mary walked around the workshop side of their complex and began to eagerly open up cupboards and draws, exposing some of their precious materials, for Les to see.

'The story starts with an Egyptian pharaoh called Akhenaten,' she began.

It was more than two hours later before Les left their company, with a clear understanding that here was a potential for world disorder.

****

Gaza – Palestine

For several nights Adnan had been helping to launch rockets into Israel. Night after night he busied himself, engrossed in an operation which he saw as the fulfilment of his life's ambition: to be able to strike at Israel. He was taking only a few hours sleep a time during the night, then during the day he worked feverously constructing yet more of these devices now striking within Israel. The adrenalin rush he received from all this work spurred him ever onward. Most of the rockets fell short of their intended targets or wandered well off course; landing aimlessly in a farmer's field, but one or two did get through. It was when they fired the Iranian Fajr-5 artillery rockets toward Tel Aviv that Israel decided to take action.

The sound of sirens going off in Tel Aviv had sparked panic in the streets, prompting once again the Israeli Prime Minister to declare, 'We will not accept a situation in which Israeli citizens are threatened by the terror of rockets. No country would accept this. We know where the foreign terrorists are hiding in Gaza they had better not show their face to the sky again, or they will never see another day. To the people of Gaza we say, for your safety, you should stay away from Hamas infrastructure and personnel.'

A sudden loud explosion rocked the cellar where Bob lay. Sleep had never come easy since his capture, but this night somehow he had been in a deep sleep. Startled, and in the total blackness of his cellar nights, he could not orientate himself and wondered what was happening outside of his prison. Before Bob could gather his thoughts together, another explosion sounded, quickly followed by another, then another. Machine gun fire rattled across the night in between these explosions. Bob had never before heard such loud explosions. 'This must be an attack,' he reasoned. Muffled shouts and screams rent the air, resounding through his head. He was shaking.

Bob lay there, unable to do anything but listen to this unparalleled noise, which instilled a deep fear within him. 'They will be too busy to bother with me,' was a thought which gave him a modicum of comfort. Every so often the very ground seemed to bounce with vibrations radiating from the bombs being dropped by the Israeli air force. Some shells were also being fired from Israeli warships, positioned close to the Gaza shore. Pieces of plaster and cement fell off the walls and ceiling each time a bomb fell close by. 'This is what it must have been like for my grandfather during the blitz in London,' he thought.

After what seemed like hours, the explosions began to gradually ease a little, until eventually they stopped altogether. The silence felt strange after the incessant noise; almost unreal. Bob wanted some water to drink, it was hot in his cellar; but in the confusion and darkness he had knocked over the open plastic bottle spilling it all. The heat of the cellar seemed to intensify as a result, drying his throat.

Strangely it was the silence which he now found unnerving. Suddenly, another noise made every sinew of his body tense up. The bolts on the door were being unfastened. The light went on dazzling Bob, before the steel door was thrown open with a crash against the wall. Adnan, Darwesh and Abdul-Salem hurried down the steps of the cellar, with several other armed men remaining standing on the concrete stairs.

'You bastard!' screeched Adnan as he almost ran down the stairs. 'You bastard, you told them.'

Bob did not know what they were talking about, but rational fear filled his very being.

Darwesh pulled Bob to his feet, and then struck him such a hard blow it knocked him down again, crashing him onto the cement floor.

With his uniform looking more dishevelled than ever Abdul-Salem, then grabbed hold of Bob's dirty and stained shirt, pulling him upward, 'How did you do it?' he asked.

'Do what?' said Bob spitting blood from his mouth.

'You son of a pig,' barked Adnan as he spit into Bob's face. 'Israel has said they know I am here. How do they know?' Adnan pushed Bob to the floor again. 'How do they know?' he repeated kicking Bob in the ribs. 'How do they know?' he repeated, while he continued to kick out at the prone figure of Bob.

Bob got surreal satisfaction from this information; for Adnan's outburst informed him that his little message had somehow gotten through. A thought rushed through Bob's mind, 'Well done Mary, well done.' He did not respond to the repeated questions being thrown at him.

'You think Israel will win against us,' barked Darwesh. 'Allah will soon destroy all the nations except Islamic ones,' he began to yell at the top of his voice, 'All nations will be destroyed by Allah, but especially Israel. The day is coming when God will wipe Israel off the face of the Earth. Only Islam will stand before God. Only Islam! You will not win. You cannot win,' Darwesh threw another kick at the crumpled figure of Bob.

'You think Israel will come and rescue you?' Adnan started to drag Bob across the floor. 'Just let them try.'

Many people in Gaza had died, or were dying that night, due to the heavy Israeli attack. In typical fashion Hamas had deliberately put families within close proximity of their military activities. As a result many civilians had been killed or injured, inflaming the passions of those men there in that room with Bob even more. It was only through Bob that they could somehow hit back at their enemy and unleash their intense hatred of the West; a hatred which knew no bounds.

All there now realised what was about to happen, so they moved in closer toward Bob. He was forcefully sat upon a wooden chair, whilst more men came rapidly down the steps. Many hands held Bob, while another stood in front with a camera. Plastic ties were placed around Bob's legs and his arms pulled tight. Bob was securely bound to the chair. Adnan, with his head covering pulled tightly over all of his face, save for his eyes, which were ablaze with hatred, approached Bob. Adnan's pulled out a sharpened bread-knife, grabbed hold of Bob's hair and began a sawing action.

****

Calgary – Canada

Jacques saw the car pull up outside their office. He turned to Mary, 'I thought he said he was going back to England today?' he said, with a sound of unease in his voice, wondering why the Superintendent had returned.

'He did,' she replied. 'Maybe he has come to say goodbye,' but she was equally unsure of the purpose for this visit.

As soon as Les opened the door and walked in, both Mary and Jacques knew something was wrong. Les looked ashen. His long face was drawn, with bags under his eyes as though he had not slept for a long time. He just stood there. No greeting was exchanged they just looked at each other, in a moment's silence. Mary put her hand to her mouth to hold back her fear.

'I'm sorry,' was all Les said.

'No!' yelled Mary. 'Don't tell. Don't tell me he's dead.'

Jacques put his arm around Mary as she went weak at the knees, and led her to a chair where he sat her down. 'What's happened Superintendent?' asked Jacques fearing to hear the answer.

'I'm afraid it is bad news. Your friend and colleague has been killed last night,' was the unwelcome reply.

'No – no – no; not Bob. Oh Bob what have they done to you?' Mary's grief exploded within her.

'Good god. How did this happen?' asked Jacques with his arm held tightly around Mary.

'He was murdered, I'm sorry to say.' Les took off his long overcoat and sat down in front of the grieving pair.

'How? Did the Israelis try and free him? How did he die?' Jacques was feeling frantic now.

'He was killed before Israel could get to him.'

'How was he killed?' he repeated. 'How do you know about this?' demanded Jacques.

'I'd rather not say how he died, but,' he waited, 'they put a video out on the internet of his death.'

'Oh! How cruel, how evil. Those people do such unspeakable horrors,' Mary was raising her voice until she yelled at Les, 'Tell me! How! How did they kill him?'

'I don't believe this,' said Jacques, feeling dazed at the shock.

'I demand to know how he died,' shouted Mary, tears streaming down her face.

Les just stared, not really wanting to say what he must, 'There is no easy way to say this,' he admitted. Then he braced himself, 'They cut his head off, in a most brutal manner.'

A piercing scream came from Mary as she collapsed into Jacques arms, sobbing uncontrollably. Jacques was speechless, unwilling to comprehend his friend's terrible fate. He just held on to Mary. The three sat there in stunned silence for an age.

'I am so sorry,' repeated Les. 'There was nothing we could do. It was just a slim chance Doctor Boucher had. It was a terrible end. There will be reprisals. Already attacks are underway. It is sad his work will now never be finished.' Les genuinely felt this sad loss himself, even though his professionalism told him not to get too involved with the emotions of the moment. He had seen such grief so many times during his career, but these last few months had been the worst of his life.

Jacques looked up from his settee, with Mary curled up laying on his lap, holding him tightly, whilst her sobs rang out, 'Superintendent,' he began slowly, 'the French philosopher Voltaire once wrote: *"Those who can make you believe in absurdities can make you commit atrocities."* This is so true. The violence of that religion has taken my wife, Mary's mother and now our good friend. I am now determined if it is the last thing I do I will make sure Bob's work is published. His findings may well undermine some the stories of the Old Testament, the Torah and the Koran. It may well show that God did not promised the land of Palestine to the Jews, but it will be written and,' he spoke slowly and determinedly with a tear in his eyes, 'it will be published and Mary will write it. This I swear this, on the life of our dear friend. His life and his work will not be wasted.'

Much later, after the departure of Les Forrester, Mary approached Jacques, 'How can you say I will publish the book when you know it will take years, if not a lifetime, to gather photos of the lost materials Bob was seeking?'

Jacques took her in his arms as they sat together on their settee, 'My love, this is a terrible day for us, and now is not the time to dwell on this. I will just say that sometimes we cannot see wood for all the trees?'

'What does that mean?' she asked; her red eyes looking up to him from her prone position curled up on the settee.

'It is so obvious, and yet we have both overlooked the obvious,' He sat by her side holding her hand tight, 'Bob was seeking to record all the bits and pieces from Egyptian images and hieroglyphics, some which are still hidden, some which are stacked and waiting for interpretation and some which are scattered around the world in museums and private collections. He was seeking any early references to Israel; and as you say, that could take a lifetime.'

'Yes, so we will not be ready to publish for a long time,' she reiterated.

'Just look at what you know already. You have more than enough to write your book already. People will love to read about the real reasons for the Expulsion, and the reasons for the establishment of modern Israel. This in itself is more than enough material; all this can be written from the material you already have. After that you can continue with Bob's greater search.'

'Bob's work was an academic research, we do not have enough material to publish in that genre.'

'So don't write for the academic genre, write for the general public, make it a popular genre. That way we can get Bob's message out to a wider audience and much more quickly,' Jacques was almost insistent.

'Maybe Jacques, but not now, I can't think straight just now.' Mary was in no mood to pursue Jacques thoughts clearly after hearing the sad news, so she just let his idea drift away, for the time being.

****

York - England

The grandeur of York Minster was a wonder to behold. Jacques sat with Mary holding her hand, just after the conclusion of the memorial service. Earlier in the day they had taken time to absorb fully the magnificence of their surroundings, a favourite haunt of Bob, when he was alive. It was Jacques' first visit, and he quickly came to realise this edifice was truly a mediaeval masterpiece. The intricacy of the giant stain glass windows, the many stately pillars and the sweeping arched roof, made him feel in awe toward those master builders who created this majestic structure to the glory of God, so many years ago.

The first few days after Bob's death had passed by as an unreal dream for both of them. The news media had been filled with information concerning Bob's terrible death, repeating it over and over again, until they could no longer bear to watch the TV news channels any more. Neither of them had been able to sleep and so they had sought medical assistance to help them through that restless time. There could be no funeral for Bob because his body was lost, his captors refusing to release the body, or say where it was. Even so, this memorial service to Bob in York Minster had been conducted to commemorate his life and had truly been a fitting tribute to him. It had been the university who had arranged for this service to take place and also who had invited Mary to take on Bob's role as Honorary Research Fellow at the University of York, thereby pursuing his work.

The pair now moved together around the magnificent displays of flowers sent by people from all over the world in respect for the person, his work and the achievements of Doctor Robert Boucher. Reading one such label, which was tied to a wreath of white lilies, a tear ran down Mary's face, 'I still can't believe I will never see him again,' she lamented with a tremble in her voice. As she was speaking she tightened her grip around

Jacques' hand, for she had just seen Les Forrester approaching them.

'Glad you were able to get over for the Memorial Service,' said Les.

'We would not have missed this for anything,' replied Mary. 'He was our dear friend and colleague.'

'Yes, of course. I hope this service was of some comfort to you. There was a lot of good things said about him,' Les looked up at the immensely high arched roof, 'and it is a fitting setting for such a tribute to him.'

'Thank you for that,' acknowledged Jacques. Jacques looked at yet another flower display as they spoke, 'There is violence within Islam which greatly exceeds the violence of other religions, and we know all religions have been violent enough throughout their history. Bob's death was such a sad loss.'

'You can't really say Islam is more violent than Christianity, both have been very violent,' retorted Les.

Jacques stopped their little walk around the church and looked at Les face to face, 'You know when I first met Bob, whilst I was in hospital in London and recovering from my wounds and I was still very distressed over my wife's death; he said something to me I will never forget.'

'What was that?' asked Les.

'He said, "The Koran says: *those who follow Mohammad are merciful to believers but harsh to unbelievers,* (Sura 48 v. 29) which is a stark contrast to Jesus' injunction during the Sermon on the Mount, when he said, *Love your enemies and pray for those who persecute you.* (Matthew 5:44) This is the fundamental difference between these two religions."'

Les arched his eyebrows, 'That is very true, I must admit.'

Not content with that, Jacques continued to make his point, 'So if a Muslim kills unbelievers he is doing the will of his God.

If a Christian kills unbelievers, or anyone else for that matter; he is breaking God's law. This is *the* prima-facie difference between these two cultures.'

'Impressive, Mister Gendron, but I am not here to discuss theological matters; I am here just to pay my respects and to inform you of two recent developments. The death of Doctor Boucher has created a lot of tension here in England; especially as people began to discover the manner of his death.'

This hit a raw nerve with Jacques, 'Well it would not do for the news media to report the actual brutal manner of his death; would it? Far better to disguise such things, which is why people had to find this out for themselves via the internet,' Jacques let his bitterness sound forth. 'Not for the media to say anything which might upset multiculturalism.'

Les ignored this last remark, understanding how upset Jacques still was. 'All I can say is that it is a good job that book is not out on the streets right now, or that could have been the straw which broke the camel's back. After the two bombings here in England and Doctor Boucher's death, we already have had to put extra lookouts and CCTV cameras around mosques and Muslim Centres. There is a great deal of tension here.'

'Hardly surprising is it?' mocked Jacques. 'What else do you expect?'

Les did not like the way this conversation was going, so he said, 'I do have some news for you. Israel went in hard last night to attack the rocket and missile sites. They also sent in shock troops to seek out Al Saqqaff. Those bases were destroyed, but unfortunately, it looks like Al Saqqaff had already been spirited away. They must have guessed this was coming.'

'The devil looks after his own,' was Jacques flippant comment.

Les looked solemn as he spoke, 'You may be able to help locate him, if you are willing.'

'Willing?' responded Jacques, 'I am more than willing. I will willingly give you all the support I can to get that evil bastard,' was Jacques forthright reply.

'Jacques! This is a church. Watch your language.' Mary was offended by the use of such a word in a holy place and on such an occasion.

'I am sorry,' responded Jacques. 'All this is a bit much to take in.' He swallowed hard in an attempt to control himself, 'How can I help you Superintendent?'

'Mister Gendron, we are aware of your extremely good contacts within the Muslim world. We have an idea, and at this stage it is only an idea, that Al Saqqaff may be heading for Pakistan. It is not thought by our intelligence office that he will head for his grandparents home there; he would not be that stupid. We know your Company have some outlets in Pakistan, so we hoped you could use your contacts there to help us locate him.' Les was anxious this would be acceptable to Jacques.

'Consider it done,' responded Jacques. Then, with a big beaming smile he reached out to shake the hand of Les. 'It is time I got back to work for my Company again. I have been away rather a long time.'

'No Jacques, I can't lose you as well. Don't put me through all that again. This is not fair Superintendent,' Mary's real fears engulfed her.

Jacques threw his arms around his distressed Mary, 'Darling, I will not put myself in danger. I promise you that. I will just use my contacts to locate him, if I can.'

'Then I'll go with you,' she demanded.

Jacques went silent for a moment; then he gave a broad smile, 'So if I say it's too dangerous for you to go, you will say I should not go either.'

She gave a girlish smile in return, 'I don't want to lose you,' she repeated.

Jacques quickly gave in, 'OK, you can come, but only as long as you start writing the book as we travel, and in the idiom of the common man.'

'It is already started,' she said. 'And you know that.'

'Indeed. But it is important you get this written now as quickly as you can.' His forehead wrinkled, 'However, you realise there will be some areas I will visit that you will not be allowed to go simply because you are a woman.'

'As long as I am close to you, that will be all I ask for,' she said squeezing his hand.

'Good to hear you accept,' said Les. 'This will be out of my hands from now on. Either the FCO or MI6 will deal with any further communications with you. All I can say is good hunting, and I wish you well.'

Les turned and was about to go, when he stopped, 'There is something I will warn you about.' Les was about to step out of character.

Jacques and Mary listened intently.

'You have a great deal of sensitive material, collected by Doctor Boucher and yourself. Can I ask what you hope to do with it all?'

'We told you this when you visited us,' Mary was surprised by this question, but continued, slightly irritated. 'Bob was looking for any ancient references to the Hebrews and Israel especially around the time of the Exodus and the reasons for that event. We know they exist and we have references to them; also know some written records were found in King Tut's tomb, but then they were hidden away. Many of these references are in fragments so Bob was collecting all the photographs he could of those fragments, using computers to match them up together.

This would mean what has been hidden for so long could then be read.'

Jacques added, 'That was to be the academic study for scholars, but I inform you now, Mary will first make a popular, easy to read book of these findings, with the academic study following on at a later date.'

'Tell me; those documents you refer to which were found in King Tut's tomb, why were they hidden away?' asked Les, with a seemingly innocent demeanour.

Mary hesitated, 'Because they would upset certain groups of people,' she admitted.

Les gave a knowing smile, 'You surely realise those people have not gone away. I suggest you take more care of Doctor Boucher's materials. Either lock them away better than they were when I visited you in your office, or make lots of copies,' Les paused for a moment. 'I suggest the latter will be the better option.'

This statement startled Jacques as he realised what Les was actually saying to the two of them, 'Thank you for that Superintendent. Thanks for the warning.'

'If you help find Al Saqqaff, it will be a fair deal. I think you understand what I am saying.'

They all shook hands as Les departed, leaving Mary and Jacques to continue looking around the displays of flowers. Jacques felt elated at the prospect helping hunt down Al Saqqaff. Once more he could return to the Middle East and be back in the job he loved, a job he felt he was born for.

They walked around the church hand in hand. Jacques gently increased the grip he had on her hand, 'We must draft a synopsis for your book and begin writing immediately. We can start as we travel if we have to.'

'*We*!' she laughed.

'Well, no. It will be *you*, you will be the rightful author, but I'll help all I can. I will want an acknowledgement in the book though,' he teased.

Mary shook her head, 'Look Jacques, I am not convinced I should leave all the scanning of Bob's photos just yet so that we can get a popular version of his work out. There are still dozens of places to visit to get more photos of long forgotten inscriptions. I don't feel like stopping all that just yet.'

'No, Mary. You must leave all that for now. Leave all this searching for hidden and lost inscriptions. You have a mountain of information already to hand, work on what you already have. You may never find all you are looking for anyway. You know you have more than enough material which will show that Israel does not have a divine right to the land of Palestine. Work on that for now. This is the book which could change things.'

Jacques knew that Bob's vision was a task which could possibly never end. He needed Mary to concentrate her thoughts on what they already had, and bring that to fruition now. Then, and only then, pursue the hidden artefacts trail.

'Fancy a return to Sudan?' asked Jacques, changing the subject.

The look of puzzlement on her face made him chuckle. 'I have a good contact there who said he would help, unofficially, if I wanted.'

'But that's not Pakistan,' she said.

'No, it's not,' he smiled with a knowing look into her eyes. He pulled her toward him and hugged her, as they stood under the sweeping arches of the west wing of the cathedral. 'Why don't we go and try out that nice big mattress in our lovely hotel?'

She put her head on his shoulder as they left the church arm in arm together.

Khartoum – Sudan

Flying in from London, it was obvious things had not improved in Khartoum. It was still as chaotic, dusty and dirty as the last time they had seen it. Areas of construction were going on, but some buildings never seemed to get finished. The Hilton hotel was a quiet refuge away from the hurly burly of the city centre. Jacques paid for the taxi and headed with Mary to the hotel's check-in desk. 'I have a room reserved,' he said as he handed over their passports, as required in Third World hotels.

The smile on the booking clerk's face faded as he looked at their passports. 'I am sorry sir, you cannot have one room. It will have to be two.'

'Why?' asked Jacques.

He looked surprised that Jacques should even ask such a question. 'You are not married sir, and it is against our law for you to have one room.'

A look of disbelief came over Jacques. 'OK, so can we have two adjacent rooms?'

'No sir. Your lady will have to be on a different floor to you. It's the law.' He looked down his nose at Mary as though she was a common prostitute, brazenly accompanying a man she was not married to. Mary caught his eye and her anger flared; but she decided to contain it.

Jacques turned to Mary, 'My Company has a transit flat here for senior executives, we will go there. We may have to get someone in to cook for us, but it will be better than here.' Turning to the clerk he retrieved their passports and said, 'Thank you; we will not be staying.' And they strode out of the hotel, in a fit of anger.

The transit accommodation on the fifth floor of a block of flats was pleasant enough, but fairly basic. This simple accommodation had been intended only for people, usually men, who would not be staying in Khartoum for more than a couple of consecutive nights.

Jacques made preparations to travel to the oilfields early the next morning, 'It is time I had a check on how things are going with the oil production and security there. Things have been quiet for a while, but trouble could always flare up at anytime.'

'Well I have plenty of work here. I will start writing my book.' Mary hesitated for a moment, 'You know it seems strange for me to say *my* book, when it was always Bob's book before.' Mary felt a little wistful.

Not wanting Mary to dwell on these sad things again, Jacques laid out his plan of action, 'Let's spend the time we have left today getting the synopsis ready, then, while I travel to the oil fields you can start writing. I'll be away for three or four days and when I return, I will go along and see the contact I have here. I will make an appointment with him for five days from now.'

Mary opened up her laptop, 'I have already got the ancient part of the synopsis written. Let me read it, then tell me how it sounds?'

Mary began to read from the screen:

> *'The rise of the Aten cult: The religious leadership of Akhenaten: The monotheistic beliefs of that cult: Akhenaten's banning of all other forms of worship, and the subsequent resentment or hatred from traditional believers and resident priests: How*

his son King Tut initially carried on with that belief, but was forced by a powerful military leader to abandon his father's beliefs and return to the ancient ways: How those who continued to worship the Aten were referred to as lepers, or outcasts, a people not wanted.'

Jacques was opening up his own laptop as Mary continued. 'Then we come to the Exodus,' and she continued to read:

'No archaeological evidence, for such a number of people as mentioned in the Bible and Torah has ever been found, even after a century or more of looking: The records from other countries which show there was an epidemic of some kind at the end of Akhenaten's reign; which was blamed on the Aten worshipers for abandoning their ancient gods: How the worshipers of Aten were also blamed for the country's misfortune, because the temples of the gods had been abandoned or neglected: How the evidence is that the Aten worshipers were driven out of Egypt, in an expulsion of unwanted people: How the records show most who left were Egyptians, with Egyptian names: How the high priests of Akhenaten were the same men who became the high priests of Israel. All of which will show there was no divine promise to Israel to take over the land of Canaan or Palestine.'

Mary paused for breath.

'The cruel and inhuman actions of the Israelites as they invaded all the territories around: The unbelievable cruelties carried out by these escaping Aten worshipers, now called Israelites, which by our standards would be classed as war crimes, or ethnic cleansing or both: How similar cruelty would continue for much of Christendom's

evangelical conquests, and is still continuing today within Islamic fundamentalism. '

'Then I'll come to the big one,' she said as she opened another page.

'The overwhelming evidence that manuscripts were found in the tomb of King Tut. Manuscripts which were hidden because they would have exposed the real reason for the Expulsion: How if they had become public knowledge it would have upset the political and religious drive of the British and Americans to oversee the formation of modern Israel: How a cache of papyri was openly discussed when the tomb was first opened.'

'That will lead nicely into the modern side of the story,' said Jacques.

'Yes,' she replied looking a little more puzzled now. 'It is this second part I'd like your input to. In fact I'm thinking of making the book into two parts. I need to toss some ideas around with you for this second part.'

'Fine; now is as good an opportunity as ever. Have you decided what to call the book yet?' asked Jacques.

'Not really,' but I think it will be called, *"The Expulsion"*.'

'Now that sounds great,' replied Jacques. 'That title alone will get people to read it. So let's look at a suitable synopsis for the second part of the book.'

Jacques made comments from the notes from Mary's screen, 'You must show that the current nation of Israel is a completely artificial and arbitrary construction, which came about as the result of political and religious manoeuvrings leading to the Balfour Declaration in the early part of the twentieth century. You must quote the letter from British Foreign Secretary Arthur James Balfour, to Lord Rothschild, who was the most powerful British Jew at the time, and leader of the British Jewish community. Show how the letter was for transmission to the Zionist Federation, a private Zionist organization, whose sole aim was for the Jews to take over Palestine. You must show that Walter de Rothschild, or Lord Rothschild, was a cousin of Lord Carnarvon's wife. So if documents were found within the tomb, which exposed the real reason for the expulsion, both of those men had the reason and the power to hide such information. Zionism and Christianity would make little sense if the entire foundation of Judaism could be shown to be based on a lie and that lie has been covered up by those with Imperialist agendas.'

'Wait a minute let me get all that down,' said Mary busily typing on her laptop.

Jacques waited and then continued, 'You must show that at the time of that "Declaration" letter most of Palestine was still under the control of the Ottoman Empire, and the borders of the modern Middle East had been outlined as part of the Sykes-Picot Agreement between Britain and France, set out in 1916.'

Mary now added her own points, 'Here I will make it clear that this Sykes-Picot Agreement was a secret understanding between the governments of Britain and France defining their respective spheres of post-World War 1 influence and their subsequent control in the Middle East. Because of the changing progress during the war, the British switched their earlier arrangement from needing Arab help to subsequently trying to enlist the help of Jews in the United States, in order to get America to join the First World War. At this time they all but promised the American Jews a homeland in Palestine if they would help by bringing America into the war.'

Mary looked up, 'This was one of the reasons the Germans hated the Jews so much.'

'Don't let's go into that just now,' Commented Jacques not wishing to get their thoughts distracted. 'It is enough to say that this of course was the turning point in Western and Arab relations, as it negated the promises made earlier to the Arabs through Lawrence-of-Arabia for the Arabs to have their own national homeland in exchange for them siding with British forces against the Ottoman Empire.'

Jacques shook his head, 'Talk about twisting and turning. As a result of all this, I lost my wife, you lost your mother, we both lost a good friend and thousands of others have died.' Jacques shook his head in a display of utter disgust.

Saddened by these thoughts, Jacques went over to the kitchen unit, 'It's time we had a cup of coffee,' he said. 'Didn't these people have any idea of the troubles they were stirring up for future generations?' he asked, clearly despondent. 'The root of the present global crises has Israel at the centre. And it was all based on a promise from God which never existed in the first place, yet written about after the event to justify the ruthless actions of those ancient invaders.'

Mary needed to concentrate their thoughts again, 'I will mention here what Howard Carter said in detail,' Mary read again from her electronic notes. 'In relating to the missing papyri, Carter said:

> *"Unless he received complete satisfaction and justice, he would publish for the whole world to read the documents that he found in the tomb giving the true account, according to the Ancient Egyptian Government, of the exodus of the Jews from Egypt."*

This is a very important part of the story,' she concluded.

'Yes,' said Jacques. 'There must have been some tremendous political pressure behind the suppression of this document. It's hard to imagine Carter being persuaded to suppress such information and to go away quietly. I wonder if the sudden and mysterious death of Lord Carnarvon, might have been part of the persuasion to silence him?'

'That we will never know, and anyway it's beyond the scope of our work right now,' stated Mary 'Let's look at what we do know. I need to show how it was the beliefs of the Christian fundamentalists which played a key role in the establishment of modern Israel.'

'Indeed,' agreed Jacques. 'Maybe you could show how the British have had a long-term fascination with the idea of Israel and its central role in biblical prophecy, which dates back to their earliest recorded literature. I have quotes here which show that both Gildas in the sixth century and the Venerable Bede in the eighth century saw the British as "the new Israel", God's chosen people. There are many cases where the British perception of being an elect of God can be shown, such as how many of their early battles were understood in the context of Israel's battles against the Philistines, Babylonians and others.'

'I have something here on that,' responded Mary searching through her electronic documents. 'An Anglican clergyman, Thomas Brightman in 1585, urged the British people to support the return of the Jews to Palestine in order to hasten a series of prophetic events that would culminate in the return of Jesus. In fact I have a whole list of British people stating this same thing. It was a common theme and was a basic idea imbued into the British people, that if the Jews returned to Israel this would be the "*End of the Times of the Gentiles*" and the return of Christ.'

'Make it clear Mary what that expression means. The average reader might not understand the "*Times of the Gentiles*" refers to the period when the Jews did not control Jerusalem.'

'Good point,' replied Mary.

Jacques clarified his point, 'Set this out carefully Mary. In 1917 when General Allenby's army took Jerusalem, it was two days after the actual conquest, before the British entered Jerusalem. The general's arrival was meticulously planned, because they recognised that Christian armies were once again returning to the holy city for the first time since the First Crusade had done so in 1099. Allenby arrived at Jaffa Gate riding a white horse, with all the pomp of a king. Then, before he entered the old city, he dismounted and walked in on foot. The reason being his Saviour, Jesus had entered this city on foot, and so would he. Allenby's action makes sense of the Balfour Declaration: Conquering Jerusalem had not only to be militarily strategy, but also it had to be accomplished according to prophecy of the Bible. You see they really believed the "*End of the Times of the Gentiles*" *would be when they would see the Son of Man coming in a cloud with great power and great glory.'* (Luke 21:24, 27)

'Was that entry into Jerusalem by Allenby the End of the Gentile Times then?' asked Mary.

'No, that could not be; because the British were themselves Gentiles. However the British wanted to do all they could to bring about the End of the Gentile Times. And they felt that by being in control of Jerusalem they could speed that day on. The Jews did not get to control Jerusalem until they took it by force during the "Six Day War" in 1967. That was the End of the Gentile Times; bringing the Temple Mount under Jewish rule for the first time in almost two-thousand years. But of course nothing happened.'

'What do you mean nothing happened?' inquired Mary.

'Jesus did not return, as these fundamentalists had expected him to.' Jacques contemplated possible interpretations of this, 'So nowadays we have some Americans and Israelis who interpret this to mean it will be the rebuilding of the Jewish temple on the holy mount which will be the true *End of the Times of the Gentiles.* Which is really an emotive thought, for any such attempt to rebuild a Jewish temple would have to be over the removal of the existing Haram Ash Sharif Mosque, the Dome of the Rock. Such an action would certainly result in a major conflict, if not a total world war.'

'All of this will show Israel did not have a divine right to the land of Palestine. That it was a completely artificial and arbitrary construction, which came about as the result of political manoeuvrings,' Mary was tired, it had been a long day. She closed her laptop, 'The fight was not an equal one,' she said. 'The desire among the Christian West for the Jews to re-create Israel and to fulfil that prophecy was behind the West's support in establishing modern Israel. The Palestinians didn't have a chance from the beginning, they were out gunned.'

'Have you thought about a conclusion yet?' asked Jacques.

'No not yet, but I have more than enough here to be getting on with. Let's get to bed, I'm tired and you are off early in the morning anyway.'

Four days later, Jacques returned from the oilfields to Khartoum. After a brief reunion with Mary, he was soon off out again being driven in one of his Company's cars. The driver soon pulled the vehicle into the familiar grand entrance to the home of Omar Al Mahdi. This benevolent religious and political leader of Sudan, and descendent of the famous 'Mahdi' of Victorian times, had said he would be willing to help locate the whereabouts of Bob, when he had been held captive. The fact that he had been unable to do this, did not mean he would not be able to help now. Due to Mary not being married to Jacques, respect for Omar's culture required Jacques not to take her along. She would have been received, but not welcome, so in order to avoid any embarrassment, on both sides, they decided she should stay in the transit quarters.

Jacques had been a little apprehensive, wondering if Omar, would, or could, really help him. It was a long shot, but Jacques knew Omar had powerful influences and there was not much he could not find out, if he so wished. The question was; would he wish to help? Of the many people Jacques had met and knew in the Muslim world, it was Omar he had the most respect for. A genuine believer in the peaceful path of Islam, Jacques had been impressed by the pamphlet of peace Omar had shown to him during his first visit. A pamphlet Omar had said he intended to read in the London mosques during the festival of the Eid.

Shown into the large elaborate reception room, Jacques had no sooner sat down than he was ushered up again to follow a servant into the private quarters of Omar Al Mahdi.

The tall, but frail looking gentleman stood up immediately upon seeing Jacques entering into the room. 'Welcome to my home again Mister Jacques,' said Omer, holding out his right hand while his left hand visibly trembled holding onto an elaborately carved ebony walking stick, inlaid with intricate silver patterns. Omar had a refined elegance which his advanced age did not diminish. He was dressed as always in the traditional vivid white robes of the Sudan, with an expensive white silk scarf around his neck, and a distinctive large white headdress.

'Please sit down and have some tea,' he beckoned the servant over, who almost ran to do his master's deed. 'I was sorry to hear of the death of your friend, I offer you my condolences.'

'Thank you Omar. It has been a hard time for us,' acknowledged Jacques as he sat down onto an easy chair.

'To lose your wife and good friend within a few months of each other is really hard. But I now hear you have another companion,' Omar wished to reassure Jacques of his genuine concern.

'Thank you,' said Jacques. 'Tell me did you go over to London to read that pamphlet during the Eid celebrations? I was impressed by the words it contained.'

Omar looked pleased that Jacques had remembered this, 'Yes I did. I read it to the people of Ansar, the Mahdists, in several mosques in that fine city. I told them they must work selflessly, without ulterior motive and with farsightedness, in order to bring together the Sudanese in Britain, to socialise more and intermix without prejudice. I told them to honour and represent their new country which is known for its courage, honour, morality and good manners.'

'That is very impressive,' acknowledged Jacques. 'If they all were like you, the world would be a much happier place.'

'Thank you Mister Jacques. God tells me this is my duty in life and I am happy with that.' Both sipped their strong tea for a moment; then Omar continued, 'Whilst I was in London, I told them, as I said I would, how wrong were the terrible bombings carried out in England. I spoke out strongly to say how, not only were such things anti Muslim, but they also cause unbelievers to ridicule the name of Allah and his prophet Mohammed: Peace be upon him. Any Muslim who is responsible for such things will be condemned by God.' He gave a determine look at Jacques, 'And we must root them out.'

'Which is why I am here,' said Jacques.

'Quite,' smiled Omar, 'I guessed as much. Tell me, the work of Doctor Boucher, is it still continuing?'

This sudden switch in topics threw Jacques a little. 'Well yes,' was his reply.

'The lady, Mary, is she carrying on with this work?' asked Omar.

'Yes, she has taken on where Bob left off.'

'Good,' was the unexpected response, 'When will it be finished?'

'Mary is confident she will have it completed after three or four months of hard work.' Jacques was unsure where this was leading.

'Good,' repeated Omar. 'And I understand this book will show Israel has no right to the land they stole?'

'It will,' confirmed Jacques.

No one spoke while both finished their tea. Then, almost as a matter-of-fact Omar revealed, 'Adnan Al Saqqaff is heading for Pakistan. If he gets to North Waziristan you will never find him. I suggest you move quickly Mister Jacques.' Omar then immediately stood up to indicate this meeting was over. Jacques jaw had opened with a look of total surprise, as the servant escorted him to show the way out.

Jacques gazed out of the window of his transit quarters, situated only the fifth floor this still seemed high in a city where there are very few tall buildings.

He looked over the enclosed walled garden below, beyond toward the international airport of Khartoum. Flights were not frequent into this city and very few were from Europe; mostly they came from Africa, the Middle East or the Far East; and never any from North America. Jacques was deep in thought. It was the strange sight of a Ferris wheel adjacent to the runway, which gave the view a surreal feeling. There were very few cities in the world which had their major airport in the centre of the city, as Khartoum did; it all seemed rather bizarre to him.

Mary was paying no attention to Jacques, while she typed rapidly on her laptop. She had been hard at work for several days now, working up to twelve hours a day on her book. There was a growing sense of tension about her. After a while she paused, 'If you are going to Pakistan I may as well go back to Calgary and continue with this there. I want to get it finished now as soon as I can.'

Jacques knew she was angry with him, but this was what he wanted to hear. 'I know you want to go with me, but...'

She did not allow him to finish, before she snapped back, 'Not much point', she said begrudgingly. 'It would only be the same as here; no shared hotel room because we are not married.'

Jacques walked away from the window over to the table where she was concentrating on her work. 'We will have to work on that then; won't we?' he said with a smile.

Mary stopped typing and looked up a little startled. 'Was that a proposal?' she questioned, suddenly softening her former anger.

'Not really. When I propose it will be more romantic that that,' he laughed.

Mary stood up pulled him close to her and kissed him lovingly on the lips. 'I will be very happy to be married to you Jacques. You are a wonderful man.'

'Yes, I know I am,' he teased.

She punched his chest, affectionately. 'Well I hope you can find a more romantic place than this place. Once you decide to ask me,' she chided. Then looking more serious added, 'How long will you be away in Pakistan?'

'No more than a week,' he said. 'I feel ill at ease in Pakistan; the people make me nervous.'

'What do you mean?' she asked.

'They have an unpleasant habit of staring at strangers, even to the point of rudeness. It is most off-putting. They can make women feel really uncomfortable. So I'm glad you have agreed not to go with me. Since the Afghan war, the whole of the north-western border is Taliban country; a no-go area for Westerners.' Jacques walked over returning to gazing out of the window again.

'Don't tell me you are going there,' she asked a little frightened at the thought.

'No, I'll stay in Islamabad if I can,' he tried to reassure her, but was failing.

'And what will you do if you find that monster?' she asked, not really wanting to know the answer.

'I'll just pass the information on to Les Forrester and let him inform the Foreign Office or MI6 or whoever it is that deals with these things. I just want to nail that bastard if I can.' Jacques understood her concern and wondered if he was really doing the right thing. Maybe he should just leave it to others. But Jacques never left anything unfinished.

'Does you company have a big operation there?' she asked.

'No; far from it. It is far too dangerous for Western people to go there away from the cities. We have geologists surveying large areas and they have made some promising discoveries, but getting people to invest in such an unstable country is not easy. Sudan is a lot safer,' he joked.

Still looking out of the window, he watched as an aircraft from the United Arab Emirates landed. He became wistful, 'I pity poor England allowing so many people from Pakistan and Bangladesh into their small country. They will never blend in with the British way of life. Those short sighted politicians, who allowed that to happen, were creating a time-bomb for the future, but they didn't seem to care at the time. I can see big trouble developing in England soon. I'm glad we will not be there to see it.'

'That's not a nice thought though Jacques.' Mary was concerned at this train of thoughts. 'Things may not turn out like that.'

Jacques moved to the table and opened up his laptop. He shook his head slowly, 'I would like to agree with that; but I can't. Al Saqqaff is from that British Pakistani stock. Look at this, this is his family's background.' Jacques opened up a website and read the following:

> *'North Waziristan in Pakistan's federally administered tribal areas has been described variously as "the epicentre of global terrorism" and "the most dangerous place on earth." It is home to*

> *some of the world's most virulent insurgent and terrorist networks, including Al-Qaeda, the Haqqani Network, the Tehrik-e-Taliban of Pakistan, Lashkar-e-Taiba, Lashkar-e-Jhangvi and others. Recent reports indicate that Pakistan government may be gearing up to launch a long-awaited military operation in those troublesome areas.'*

Jacques clicked his lips, 'Not exactly a hive of peace and tranquillity is it? And it is those people with that type of background who were allowed uncontrolled and free entry into England over many years; which is why I fear for England's future.'

'You have good contacts over there I hope,' Mary was now clearly worried.

'I have one,' he declared. 'A man I promoted a long time ago. He is a geologist; by the name of Badreldeen. I never did know his other names,' he confessed. 'He has done some good work for us. His team have found massive reserves of oil and natural gas in North and South Waziristan and Peshawar. Trouble is they are all highly unstable war-torn areas, where one right move could make all the difference, and one wrong move could ignite a conflict with irreversible consequences.'

'OK, I'll head for Calgary via London, and you go on your little jaunt to Pakistan.' Mary was clearly not happy at this prospect. 'Promise me though to keep in touch and out of trouble. I could not bear it if something was to happen to you as well.'

'I promise my love; I want to get home as much as you do.' They gave each other a nervous embrace.

****

Islamabad – Pakistan

Jacques had been to Pakistan before, but he was still surprised to see how green the city of Islamabad is; especially after the drabness of Khartoum. The Marriot Hotel was one of the better up-market hotels in the city, situated at the footsteps of Margalla hills, close to Rawal Lake. It was in a district which also contained the President and Prime Minister's houses, along with foreign missions, the World Bank, and many government offices. It was a far cry from the wild, terrorist hideouts of the northwest; along the border with Afghanistan. Even so, the hotel still found it necessary to brag in its adverts that this location was bomb proof and shockproof with a double security wall; and that it had bomb proof and shockproof pass-through gates at the hotel entrance.

Jacques found such a statement nothing short of weird; hardly encouraging to the foreign tourist he thought, yet here it seemed to be accepted as normal. He should not have been surprised by such a statement, for in September 2008 a dump truck filled with explosives detonated in front of this hotel, killing at least fifty-four people, injuring more than two hundred and sixty and leaving a huge crater outside the hotel. The blaze which followed quickly engulfed the entire structure. No, he should not have been surprise by the hotel's need for assurances; yet somehow he was.

The hotel was certainly lavish in its decoration, yet the bar, where Jacques sipped his cool beer, was in a windowless basement with very few other people in there, and those who were, were all men. Looking at his watch it was early evening, so he finished his beer and made his way to the hotel lobby to order a taxi.

Badreldeen would not meet with Jacques in the hotel, said he would be too exposed there. 'No one trusts anyone,' thought Jacques. Instead Badreldeen had directed him to meet in a café; the Café Lazeez. It was almost ten years since he last met with Badreldeen, when he was a young man just starting out on his career as a student geologist in Yemen. His mother had been Somali and his father white British. Badreldeen's father had been a friend and colleague of Jacques, and although his father had converted to Islam in order to be allowed to marry Badreldeen's mother, the family had never been trusted by the Yemenis. His father had died as the result of a hit-and-run traffic incident in the city of Sana'a, which no one really believed to be a true accident. After this, his mother had been hounded by the Immigration authorities, throwing her into the hellish jails of Yemen several times, simply because she was a Somalian woman, with no means of support other than her only son, who was desperately trying to study his way out of poverty. Jacques had taken Badreldeen under his care, and saw to it that he had regular employment with his Company, training him in an English university, where his mother had been allowed to reside as a refugee close by. Badreldeen was good at his work and had been instrumental in finding many new oil and gas fields for Jacques' Company. His current explorations in Pakistan, being no exception, were also proving fruitful.

Jacques entered through the door of the Café Lazeez, which was more like a restaurant than a café. He was immediately shown through the main eating area to the side of the building and into a beautiful spacious outdoor terrace garden. Truly a lovely space in which to dine, he thought when he saw the garden full of lush greenery, lemon trees, and a cobble-stone walkway, carefully positioned around a fountain. In the centre of the garden was a traditional wood-burning pizza oven, with pizzas being cooked on the open fire. Tables with overhead umbrellas made for the perfect alfresco dining experience, 'I should have brought Mary along,' he thought to himself.

Following the waiter, he walked past the open fire toward a shaded section behind a lemon tree. Immediately Badreldeen stood up to greet him and threw his arms around Jacques almost lifting him off the floor. 'Mister Jacques,' he beamed, 'It is wonderful to see you again. It has been too long.'

Badreldeen was a big man, at least six foot six inches tall. Dressed in traditional Pakistani clothes of white baggy trousers, mainly covered by a long over shirt which came down to his knees. He wore an open black waist-coat and a brown, pudding like hat on his head.

'You have grown your beard long,' said Jacques, looking at his full-faced black beard.

'It helps me blend in,' he said. They don't take kindly to strangers in Waziristan you know.'

'Yes, I've heard. You have done some great work over there. Will we ever be able to produce oil in that region?'

'Well it's true there is a lot of oil and gas there,' he said and then shrugged his shoulders, 'but with the Taliban and Al-Qaeda being there and with the on-going conflicts in Afghanistan, it will be a long time before those fields will be producing anything.'

Jacques shook his head slowly, 'That's what I feared,' he said. 'It's so sad. 'It could become a prosperous area, if it was not for those extremists.'

'Is that why you are here?' asked Badreldeen, keen to know why he had been asked to meet with Jacques.

Jacques smiled. 'No,' he said, then hesitated. 'of course I do wish to know all about your discoveries over here, but there is another reason for my visit. Have you heard what happened to me in London?' he asked.

'I had not, until I saw an article about you in our Company's magazine. I was so sorry to read about the death of your wife. How are your injuries? You look OK now?' Badreldeen was truly glad to see Jacques again, but unsure why this executive of the Company should be here in Pakistan.

'Those wild places where you have been working; they understand there about blood feuds don't they?' There was a sting in Jacques question.

Badreldeen looked surprised at this question. 'You bet they do Mister Jacques. Some families have been at war with each other for centuries. On-going feuds; and no one is quite sure how they started. Sometimes feuding local Waziri leaders have enlisted outsiders in the Pakistani government, and even American forces who are hunting Al-Qaeda fugitives, in attempts at score-settling.' Badreldeen stopped himself from being carried away. Turning serious he said, 'Why do you ask me this?'

'If someone killed your wife and your best friend what would you do?' was Jacques barbed question.

'I would kill them Mister Jacques, I would kill them.' Badreldeen was smiling as he said this, until that is, he saw the look on Jacques face. 'Oh! No Mister Jacques.' A dawning realisation spread over Badreldeen's face. 'The man who killed your wife: He is here?'

'Shall we order a meal?' asked Jacques.

'Suddenly I don't feel like eating, Mister Jacques.'

'I am just looking for information Badreldeen, nothing more.'

'Information like that can get a man killed, or worse. They have terrible ways of handing out reprisals here you know.' Badreldeen was visibly afraid.

'I have no wish to put you in danger. Forget I even came here, and we will leave it at that. Now let's order our meal.' Jacques had in effect appealed to the testosterone instincts within Badreldeen.

Badreldeen went quiet for a moment. 'I owe you a great deal Mister Jacques, as did my mother before she died.'

'You owe me nothing Badreldeen. I did what I did to help you, because your father was my good friend, and you as his son needed my help.' Then wishing to change the subject he asked, 'What is life like in Waziristan?'

'Not easy Mister Jacques. My work there is nearly done, and I will be happy to return to less extreme areas of Pakistan,' replied Badreldeen.

'Will you return to England?' Jacques asked.

'No Mister Jacques, I am promised to a wife here in Pakistan. I will make a family here. Now my mother is dead I have no reason to return to England.' Badreldeen went quiet for a moment again, he was obviously troubled. 'Who is this man who killed your wife?' he asked with concern.

'A British man of Pakistani origin, name of Adnan Al Saqqaff. He has done a lot of damage in England. Not only killing my wife.' Jacques began to wonder if he had done the right thing in coming here. Maybe he should just leave and let the authorities deal with this?

Badreldeen brushed his fingers through his long beard. 'I hate those people who have done so much damage to the name of Islam,' he said thoughtfully. 'You would not believe some of the things they have done. Although that area is in Pakistan they all support the Taliban and Al-Qaeda. Pakistan is a big supporter of the Taliban today, if not the government then the people are. I can't understand it. The Taliban are no friends of Muslims, they hurt more Muslims than they do unbelievers. It is just that there is so much corruption here the people think the Taliban will remove it. But they won't; they'll make things worse; a lot worse.'

'Tell me how that is Badreldeen?' Jacques asked.

'Well for one thing, their treatment of women is appalling. They frequently target women for human trafficking. I am told that during one Taliban and Al-Qaeda offensive in 2009 in the Shomali Plains alone, more than six-hundred women were kidnapped. The women were from ethnic groups in Afghanistan. Taliban, as well as Arab and Pakistani Al-Qaeda militants forced them into trucks and buses. There, the women were penned up inside a camp in the desert. The more desirable among them were selected and taken away. Some were trucked to Peshawar with the apparent complicity of Pakistani border guards. Others were taken to Khost, where Al-Qaeda has several training camps. These Afghan women were forced into Pakistan where they were sold into brothels or into private households to be kept as sex slaves.' Badreldeen had a look of intense sadness about him as he related this.

'That is awful,' responded Jacques, 'those poor women.'

'I dread to think what they will do again once they return to power in Afghanistan, for everyone says they will certainly return. When they took control of Afghanistan the first time, religious police forced all women off the streets of Kabul, and issued new regulations ordering people to blacken their windows, so that women would not be visible from the outside. You know they even banned music, television, playing of chess, dancing and artistic painting. Have you ever heard of such bad people?'

'No I haven't,' acknowledged Jacques. 'This is wild extremism.'

'Yes it is,' Badreldeen agreed. 'By doing these things the rest of the world thinks all of Islam is like this, and so condemn Islam because of them. They bring disrespect on Islam because of their extreme actions.' Badreldeen shook his head again, 'Yet the West does not help itself. Everywhere I go I hear stories of how America treated its prisoners. The only thing America has won is the bitter enmity of Islam, rightly or wrongly they all believe the whole world is turning away from America and coming to see the justice of the Islamic cause. Many Muslims who fell into American hands during the wars which followed the September

11th attack on America were treated barbarically. They were stripped naked, beaten, interrogated endlessly to no purpose, and always kept isolated and ignorant of their situation. They were made to endure years of physical and mental torture. Now these people go around the country warning everyone how bad America is. So the people will once again easily fall into the hands of the Taliban.' Badreldeen was now in obvious distress. 'I see no way out,' he concluded.

Such a barrage had shocked Jacques. 'I will move you away from Waziristan it has obviously become a strain on you. You have done more than enough there, it would seem.'

'I have to go back one more time, Mister Jacques,' Badreldeen looked impassioned.

'Why is that?' asked Jacques.

Badreldeen looked straight into Jacques eyes, 'Your enemy is my enemy, Mister Jacques. I will see what I can find for you. I will not communicate words with you. Words can be intercepted. All I will send you will be grid references; nothing more; after all I am a geologist. If you get such a reference, what you do with it is up to you.'

Jacques felt humbled, and at the same time guilty, in that he could have put this man at risk of his life.

****

South Waziristan – Pakistan

The Land Rover trundled out of the Swat Valley, climbing steadily as it went along the dusty, twisting endless roads.

Badreldeen had all his equipment, as well as the required permits for the long drive ahead of him. Following behind were two trucks, filled with Pakistani soldiers, sent by the government to protect the surveying work Badreldeen was to carry out. This work was in the national interests of the country, so an armed guard was considered to be essential. Badreldeen was glad to have their protection, although he found that sometimes they could be more of a hindrance than a help. Pakistan's tribal area of South Waziristan appeared relatively peaceful after the military operations against the Taliban some years before. For Badreldeen it felt a singularly unreal experience of temporally displaced violence. Whenever they stopped for a rest, residents were keen to point out a seemingly innocent looking shop, or an intersection of streets or a police station, to tell him of an atrocity the Taliban had once carried out there. One told of a barber who was executed by hanging for continuing to carry out his 'un-Islamic' business of cutting men's hair; another told of a journalist stoned to death for not writing enough praise of Allah in his newspaper.

It was difficult to communicate with the locals because Pashto was their main language, and whereas Badreldeen was fluent in Urdu and Arabic, he knew very little of Pashto. South Waziristan is the most southerly agency of the seven that constitute Pakistan's federally administered tribal areas bordering Afghanistan, tribal areas which had been given a large degree of autonomy; that is until they sided with the Taliban. Badreldeen well knew that North Waziristan was correctly known to be wild and uncontrolled by the governments national Pakistani forces. Most of the locals from that area readily said the time will soon come when those northern tribes will soon have to face a Pakistani led military operation; similar to the one which had been carried out here in the south.

Badreldeen had heard that over two-thousand foreigners were being held by Pakistani troops on suspicion of having links to the Taliban. Men who were mostly from, Yemen, Saudi

Arabia, Somalia and yes, some were even British Pakistanis. Badreldeen well knew that Britain had become a haven for Islamist extremists; something he found hard to understand. He wondered if Al Saqqaff could be one of those currently being held by Pakistani troops, but simply to ask such a question would bring suspicion down upon him hard. He would just have to bide his time, to watch and wait. he dare not ask such a forthright question.

The convoy was heading for the town of Sararogha, just south of the North Waziristan boarder. One thing which struck Badreldeen was the contradiction between the hard fought peace and the rugged tribal environment. This area had long been considered to be an area outside the jurisdiction of law and authority, yet over recent years all that had changed. As they travelled Badreldeen thought, 'If only this peace will last then maybe Mister Jacques will be able to send the drillers up here to start work. After all it is not long ago that this was a no-go area, until the local Taliban leader was killed by an American drone strike, and now it is peaceful.' On the other hand he knew Waziristan to be one of the least developed and least educated sections of Pakistan. Literacy rates for women in some areas were only in the single digits.

The breathtaking mountainous terrain stretched away on all sides beyond the valley as the convoy trundled to a halt at an army encampment, atop of a high advantaged position. An immaculately dressed military officer approached Badreldeen's Landrover. The officer saluted Badreldeen, at the same time as another soldier was opening the door of Badreldeen's vehicle for him.

'Welcome,' smiled the officer. 'I am Brigadier Husain Mayat the commander of the Sararogha side for the Fortieth Division. I am in command of this area.' Husain spoke in fluent English; his large moustache seemed to fit in well with his dark berry, tilted to just the correct degrees, emphasising his smart uniform.

'Thank you Brigadier,' said Badreldeen while grasping Husain's outstretched hand. 'I have come to carry out a survey for the exploration of oil or gas in this region. I am hopeful it will be successful.' Badreldeen felt a little nervous when he saw so many soldiers looking at him with stern looks on their faces.

'Yes, of course, which is why I am delighted to provide you with this escort.'

Badreldeen felt a little embarrassed at having stated the obvious. 'I thank you for that. This can be a troublesome area.'

Husain raised his eyebrows, 'At one time, yes it was, but not anymore; those days have passed.' He gave a sweeping gesture with his arm, 'Look around you. On every mountain you can see from here, we have a military lookout post. We have driven the terrorists away from this land.' He spoke with an obvious amount of pride. 'Peak after peak has been wrested back from insurgent control and now each has one of our military posts upon it. Your work is of national importance and if it is successful it will make a big difference to South Waziristan. Which is why I will do all I can to help you succeed.' He started to walk toward some temporary cabins, the type often used by construction workers. 'This will be your quarters for the next few days while you carry out your work.'

As he advanced toward these temporary quarters, Badreldeen looked to one side where two men, heavily manacled to each other, were sitting on the ground. Brigadier Husain saw Badreldeen look toward them, 'Yemenis,' he said with a casual air. 'They were caught trying to get across to the North to fight for Al-Qaeda or the Taliban, or both. It will be prison for them,' he spat on the ground, 'if they live that long.'

Badreldeen thought he saw his chance, and rashly spoke up, 'Have you caught any from Britain here?' The look on Husain's face made him immediately wish he had not spoken so rashly.

'One or two, but nothing lately,' Husain turned and strode quickly away without saying another word.

Badreldeen's heart sank; fearing he had he said too much?

A few hours later Badreldeen drove with his convoy into the small town of Sararogha. Marks of the former conflict were everywhere, it was obvious there had been some fierce fighting here, but rebuilding was rapidly taking place. Badreldeen looked with pleasure on seeing a new shopping complex on the edge of Sararogha as they entered the town. A large group of men had gathered at the market place and there was a lot of excited talk going on.

'Find out what is happening,' he asked one of his armed escorts. Badreldeen could not risk any kind of confrontation.

The soldier walked briskly into the crowd, and stood talking for around fifteen minutes. Then he returned, 'There are many men from North Waziristan; they are with their children. There is no problem,' he reassured Badreldeen. 'Everything is OK. They are fathers bringing their children for vaccinations.'

Badreldeen smiled, relived it was no more than that. 'Why bring them here?' he asked.

'The crazy Taliban in the north would not let them have the polio vaccination, so they have come here to get it. The Taliban have killed the women who were carrying out the vaccinations there?' He shrugged his shoulders in an act of despair when he said this.

'Why on earth would they do such a thing?' asked a puzzled Badreldeen.

'Those militants in North say such vaccines are harmful for their children in some way, and that it will make them infertile. They say the Pakistani government is trying to sterilise their tribes. They are uneducated illiterates, soon we must wage war against those in the North, just as we did here in the South. Look how much better it is here now.' He walked away shaking his head sadly.

Looking around at the mountains Badreldeen tried to comprehend the challenge faced by the security forces just to keep those insurgents at bay in this extremely difficult terrain. Then he thought to himself about the real reason he was here. 'How on earth am I going to find Al Saqqaff in this wild area?'

****

Calgary – Canada

It felt good for Jacques to be back home again. Mary had made such good progress with her book, that it was now nearing completion. Sometimes she had spent up to twelve hours a day, studying texts and writing it all up. Their special office and storage room was a hive of activity. Emma and Robin still occasionally came along whenever they could, to continue with the scanning work which they had found so exciting. Today was one of those days. The two students were concentrating on finding the documentation for Mary, whilst Mary herself was resolute on her computer, typing up the script which she hoped, and expected, would become a best seller.

Jacques felt at a lose end, for the three were all so busy they hardly knew he was there. He had offered to help the students, but they didn't really need any help, they were so efficient.

'Fancy a bacon sandwich?' asked Jacques, in an attempt to find something to do.

'Love one,' said Robin.

'And me,' said Emma.

Mary looked up and smiled, 'Now that sounds like a good idea,' she agreed.

Shortly after, all four were tucking in to a plateful of delicious bacon sandwiches on fresh bread.

'I always think,' said Jacques, 'that Jews and Muslims miss out on such delightful food.'

'Why is it,' asked Emma, 'that Christians eat pork, yet Jews and Muslims do not? Especially, as we have seen, they all stem from the same roots.'

'Well I know why Christians eat pork,' bragged Jacques.

Mary looked quizzically toward Jacques, wondering if he really did know why. 'So why is it?' she asked.

'Well according to the Bible book of Acts, the Apostles Peter was shown animals in a vision deemed unclean to the Jews; which would include pigs, and he was told to eat their meat. He replied that he could not eat unclean meat. Whereupon God told him to, "stop calling unclean what God has cleansed". Saint Paul also said similar things about it being OK to eat former unclean meat, so pork became acceptable food for Christians.'

'Well done Jacques,' said Mary in a mildly mocking way. 'What we should be asking though is why it was banned in the first place.'

'I would have thought it was because in hot countries pork meat would go bad quickly,' offered Robin.

'There is an element of truth in that;' agreed Mary, 'but that would not explain why other ancient Middle Eastern countries ate pork, when the Israelites did not. Pork bones have been found in excavations of non-Jewish tribes, such as the Philistines, Moabites and Ammonites. So it was not just for climatic reasons this food was banned.'

'Now that *is* interesting,' said Jacques. 'Tell us more.'

Mary grinned, 'Well, like so many other things, the banning of pork came originally from Egypt. I have found that both Jews and Muslims abstain from eating pork without knowing why; other than their law forbids it, but no reasons for this ban are given. In fact most just accept the ban, without ever asking why their God wanted such a ban in the first place.'

'OK, so how did this ban come about?' asked Robin. 'You will have to tell us now.'

'I'll keep this short because I want to get on with my writing,' said Mary. 'There is evidence to show Egyptian distaste for the pig in the many mud-brick alters for animal sacrifice in and around ancient Egypt. You see, among the numerous charred remains of sacrificed animals little or no pig bones have been found; this shows that in their offerings to the gods, pigs were not acceptable and considered taboo. Herodotus, the Greek historian of the fifth century B.C., noted that Egyptians considered the pig to be an unclean animal, so much so that if a man accidently touched a pig, he instantly ran into the river with all his clothes on, in order to clean himself. Also, the Roman historian Aelian, in the first century A.D., recounted how Egyptians detested the pig saying it was an abomination to the sun and the moon.'

Mary searched through her computer until she found her notes on this subject, 'The pig in ancient Egypt was associated with the god Set, who is also called Seth; he was the god of chaos, disorder and the ruler of the burning desert, he was associated with storms and bad weather. In general he was a nasty god all round, and people were frightened of him for he was portrayed as the evil enemy of the god Horus. Some have said it was Set who was the origin for belief in the devil. The worship of Set was associated with the hippopotamus, the pig and the donkey. To eat the pig was a taboo in Set's cult because the pig was connected directly with the rituals surrounding Set, due to Set being said to transform himself into a pig. When the Expulsion occurred, those fleeing took with them this deeply entrenched Egyptian aversion toward the pig and so wrote it into Jewish law. The Islamic faith later took up this Jewish aversion to the pig and incorporated it into their own Islamic law.'

'So this is something else which came from the ancient religion of Egypt,' said Jacques. 'Truly amazing.'

Mary reached to the plate, 'Now can I have that last bacon sandwich please?' They all found this rather amusing.

After their fried bacon sandwich break, Mary began to type her script again while the two students moved to carry on with their scanning.

'Do you have much more writing to do?' asked Jacques in a casual fashion.

Mary returned the question with a loving smile across her beautiful face, 'I'm about to finish,' she declared. 'I hope to finish by next Sunday; Aten's Day!'

'What? Wonderful!' said Jacques equally puzzled and please. 'That's great. What do you mean by saying Aten's Day?'

'Aten was the sun deity and the first day of the week was dedicated to the sun; so Sunday is the Sun Day, Aten's Day.'

'Of course,' acknowledged Jacques as he walked over to her and kissed her forehead. 'This is truly wonderful,' he repeated. 'How have you managed to complete it so quickly?'

'Well large portions of this work were already written, by Bob and myself before he was captured. It was mainly a matter of compiling it all together,' Mary almost bragged, she was so pleased with the outcome of her determined efforts. 'Without the support of you three, I would not be able to have completed so quickly. I do appreciate your help.'

Emma and Robin smiled, 'It has been a pleasure said Emma,' we have both leant a lot from this.'

'That's true,' agreed Robin.

Jacques now asked, 'You once told me, you were not sure how to conclude this book. So what will be your conclusion?' Jacques was curious as to what would be the answer.

'I am now quite happy with this, although I thought long and hard on this for a while. I will conclude by summing up the contrived attempts from Britain to establish a homeland for the Jews in the early twentieth century; an attempt spurred on by the strong Christian fundamentalist belief, in both Britain and America, that Christ would return once the Jews controlled Jerusalem. You remember the Bible called it the, "*End of the Times of the Gentiles*".'

'Yes, we have spoke of this enough times', said Jacques.

'Then,' she continued, 'I'll reiterate that it was during World War I, when British forces were at the gates of Jerusalem, in November, 1917, that the British Foreign Secretary, Arthur Balfour, who was exceedingly anxious for Jewish support in the war against Germany, issued his epic yet ambiguous Balfour Declaration. Wherein he said, the British government, *"viewed with favour the establishment in Palestine of a national home for the Jewish people,"* and that he will use Britain's best endeavours to facilitate the achievement of this objective. The Arabs of Palestine were not even referred to by name in Balfour's document. So, I'll conclude by showing how Arabs were therefore increasingly angry at what they feared would be their eventual replacement and domination by an alien, and technologically superior people of different religion, namely the West; as we all now know this led to continued Arab resentment.

The penultimate section will recall how Britain promised American Jews a homeland in Palestine if the Jews used their considerable influence within that country to bring America into the First World War. Which they did; and this was one of the reasons Hitler hated the Jews so much, for without America joining that war, when they did, Germany would have won the First World War.'

'That's something not generally spoken or written about,' observed Jacques.

Mary looked at them all intently, 'Just look at the timing of all this; in April of 1917 America entered the First World War on the side of Britain. Then, as a reward, and to keep their half of the bargain, Britain issued the Balfour Declaration stating they would establish a homeland in Palestine for the Jews, and that was on the 2nd of November 1917. The result was one hundred and seventy-five thousand American troops attacked the Germans in France. No wonder the Germans under Hitler did not like the Jews. But the victors chose not to highlight that!'

'Finally I will show that as a result of strong Arabic resentment to these plans, the British had to later seriously restricted Jewish immigration at that very crucial moment, in 1939-40, when Hitler was at his most dangerous in his persecution of the Jews, resulting in the Jews taking matters into their own hands and forming their own independent state of Israel, in 1948.'

There was a pause while they all tried to absorb what Mary had said. 'Then my final sentence will be: *"This study shows that Israel does not have, and never did have, a divine right to the land of Palestine"*. I think that should do it,' she concluded with conviction in her voice. 'This is what Bob would have wanted to see and the book will be dedicated to him.'

'We will both want a signed copy of it,' said Emma, referring to herself and Robin.

'Yes of course,' agreed Mary. 'You have done more than enough to deserve that.'

'It will be ready for proof reading by next week. My agent is already jumping up and down with excitement. He can't wait to get it out there.' Mary looked satisfied, but strained after all the hard work she had gone through to get this book ready for her publishers.

****

North Waziristan – Pakistan

A large group of men had gathered in the market place of Miran Sharh. Over the last several years fourteen American drones, had targeted and killed numerous militant leaders in this isolated, estranged town, giving the inhabitants an air of nervous persecution. No one could be sure where and when sudden death would fall upon them from out of a clear blue sky. Tensions were high. These wild eyed men were all shouting and chanting, incensed, shaking their fists, with many holding guns in the air. 'He is an atheist he does not deserve to live,' they bellowed.

A considerable number of them wore the black turbans of the Taliban. All had long black beards, some of which hung down to their chests. They surrounded a cowering figure, kneeling on the hard, stone strewn ground, head bowed with his turban removed and hands tied behind his back. Some, eager to show their active participation, were taking it in turns to kick the prone figure; the object of so much verbal aggression.

'He has been judged and found guilty by a Sharia Court,' yelled Adnan in broken Pashto. 'The order of the court must be carried out.'

The victim looked up at Adnan, with hatred in his blood shot eyes.

Those all around Adnan now took up the cry, 'Stone him! Stone him, stone him.'

Adnan did not know what the man's crime really was. All he knew was the victim had been found guilty of Atheism by a Sharia court and that was enough for all who were there, no more justification was needed, for either Adnan or the crowd.

Less than an hour before this the man had been taken before a court of thirty Taliban men, who had quickly found him guilty of his perceived crime. There was no appeal under Sharia Law; therefore once found guilty the sentence upon this man had to be carried out immediately. Men were busy collecting stones, making small pyramid piles, strategically placed around an imagined circle; in the centre of which two men were struggling to dig a hole. The ground was so hard and stony it was slow going. The sun was already low in the sky, but still the heat of the day lingered on. The two men wielding the shovels were sweating profusely.

'Those stones are too big.' This statement came as an order from a Taliban leader to Adnan. 'Too big,' he repeated kicking Adnan's pile of stones. 'The stones must be no larger than the palm of a man's hand. It is the law of God,' he yelled. So saying he scattered Adnan's the stones in disgust. 'If you want to take part, you must start again, otherwise you cannot be a participant. We will only allow you to watch.'

Adnan gritted his teeth, but did not attempt to disagree; instead he started to look around for smaller stones, as he had been ordered.

One hour later, the hole was deemed to be large and deep enough to carry out the prescribed proceedings. The victim was dragged toward the hole; he was then carefully placed into it; his hands still tied tightly behind his back. The look of abject fear on the man's face brought satisfaction to the crowd. There were no words, nor actions, he could have said or done to change his fate. Those who had dug the hole now started to shovel the dry earth back from where it had been taken, pinning the man down into the hole, up to his waste. Around fifty men stood around him, each with his own pile of stones. Adnan looked down to his own new pile, with an air of expectancy.

The bellicose noise of the crowd suddenly fell silent as a Taliban leader stepped into the centre of the circle. Sweat streamed from the victim, even though the sun was setting quickly. The black turbaned man addressed the crowd, 'The law of God has found this man guilty of Atheism, and under Sharia Law he has been sentenced to death; as befits all who deny Allah the worship and service he rightly demands. Allah is the most merciful: therefore this man has only been buried up to his waste, as is correctly laid out under Sharia Law. Allah in his mercy allows a chance for this man to escape. If he can reach the circle of men who condemn him, then he shall live. God will decide. Allah Akbar.'

The mob chanted in unison, 'Allah Akbar.'

As they were chanting their praise to God, the evening call to prayer came across shrill and piercing from the loud speakers situated high on the minarets of the local mosque. Immediately all the men walked away from their stones to wash themselves at nearby public water taps, before the ritual of evening prayer. They washed their feet, head and hands, they then slowly gathered to stand in straight lines behind their Mullah. Prayer mats were laid out in front of each man while they fell to their knees, foreheads touching the ground and proceeded to pray for several minutes. All this time the victim remained with his own thoughts and prayers, bound and half buried up to his waste.

By the time they had finished it was dark; when once again they took up their stance around the victim. 'If Allah wills it you will live,' cried the Taliban leader, who then hurled the first stone, missing its mark. Suddenly they all reached to gather handfuls of stones and began throwing them hard at the man in the pit. Many hit their mark. Adnan's cold and self righteous heartfelt no pity, no remorse, no humanity for his actions; he just hurled stone after stone. The man frantically struggled to free himself from the restraints of earth around his legs and waste. He pulled at every sinew in his body to try and break free from this pit of death. It was hopeless. Blood poured from his many head wounds, until he ceased to try and free himself any more. The cruel chance of escape had eluded him; as it always did in such cases.

Even when no further movement could be detected from the victim, Adnan along with the rest continued to hurl his stones until his personal pyramid pile had become exhausted.

Ehab Obeid had not been idle whilst sitting in his temporary cell in Miran Sharh, awaiting the court's decision tomorrow. Although some distance away, he could not help but hear the shouts and chanting from the mob rule execution drawing to its inevitable conclusion in the town's market place. He was determined not to let this happen to him. He had been charged with blasphemy and apostasy and tomorrow this same Sharia court, who were now carrying out an execution, would be sitting in judgement on him as well.

'A head that doesn't control its body is useless,' had been the dower threat from Adnan when he had earlier accompanied Mustafa Zahed the Field Commander of the Taliban into the small two roomed block where Ehab was being held captive.

Mustafa nodded his head in agreement and added, 'The law of Islam is just, the provisions of the law will be followed.'

Ehab had been born and brought up as a Sufi, a very different form of Islam. Ehab truly believed he was practicing "ihsan", perfection in worship. He had argued that Sufism was a way of Islamic truth, through which one can know how to travel into the presence of the Divine. But they would not listen and he feared they would not listen tomorrow when they were to sit in judgment of him. No matter how many times he asserted his life was totally dedicated to Allah the most High, and that he had complete disregard for finery, ornament and pleasures of this world, it had no effect. All they could see was that his form of worship involved dancing as a branch of the Whirling Dervishes. Such was the Sufi tradition, this type of dancing was a way of becoming closer to God. But not for the Taliban and Adnan. Dancing, any form of dancing was an anathema to them both.

Traditionally Sufis were travelling preachers and mystics spreading their message through poetry, devotional song and of course their famous dance. The followers of Sufism prided themselves to be the inner, mystical, and psycho-spiritual dimension of Islam. Yet here in Miran Sharh many accused Sufism of being outside the sphere of Islam. If he used song and dance, then he must be from the devil. This had been their wild accusations when they came to arrest him.

Ehab was an intelligent Islamic scholar, who had lived by his wits here in the North for almost one year. He was determined to try an open the closed minds of the Taliban and as a result he had friends on the outside of his hot and dusty cell, friends who did not want to see him suffer. While the mob was distracted by the public execution, Ehab had been busily removing a breeze-block stone from this rough single story prison. He used tools provided by his friends. It had been easy to remove the crumbling cement, and soon he was squeezing through the cobbled gap in the outside wall of his temporary cell. An old motorbike had been left for him, which he eagerly took hold of and quietly wheeled it away from the noise and commotion still carrying on around the market place. He was more than a mile away before he dared to fire the engine to life and sped away as fast as he could; heading south.

****

South Waziristan – Pakistan

Badreldeen vaguely heard the motor bike rider enter the camp during the night, but paid no attention to it. It was only when he opened his cabin door early in the morning and saw Brigadier Husain, talking to a man who was not in uniform, that his unease returned.

Husain looked up and upon seeing Badreldeen beckoned for him to come over. 'This is Ehab Obeid,' he said by way of introduction. They both shook hands. 'He has had a lucky escape,' added Husain, and then proceeded to relate the story of Ehab's escape from custody in the town of Miran Sharh.

Badreldeen listened with quiet intensity, until Husain said, 'Tell him about the British man.'

Badreldeen broke out in a cold sweat, every sense in his body shouted out to him to beware.

'One of the ringleaders,' related Ehab, 'he is British. His parents are from Pakistan, but he was born in Britain. He is a British national.'

'What of him?' asked Badreldeen trying to appear casual and hoping Husain would not hear his racing heart.

'He is a dangerous man,' said Ehab. 'He brags about many of his conquests against the West and Israel. Others have told me while I was being held in jail, that he actually helped with attacks against Israel from Gaza and that he has bombed the infidels in England. I don't know how true this is. All I know was that he wanted to sit in judgement of me, because I am a Sufi.' Ehab looked tired and nervous, the exertions of the last day was beginning to tell on him.

'You look like you need some rest,' said Husain to Ehab. Then turning to Badreldeen he snapped, 'Are you ready to go? My men are waiting for you.' This was not a polite request, but an order.

'Yes sir I am ready. I intend to continue from where I left off yesterday.' Badreldeen was glad to be able to leave Husain behind. He was not sure why, but he always felt uneasy in Husain's presence; was it the forceful look in his eyes or just his over bearing manner? Maybe it was just his imagination? He could not be sure. Whatever it was, he was glad to be away from there.

The convoy set off to continue with the surveying work Badreldeen had set himself to do.

It was dark when the convoy returned. The food cooking on the charcoal smelt good and all there were hungry. Husain was not in the camp, so Badreldeen settled himself down to eat beside Ehab.

'That Englishman seems to have frightened you,' said Badreldeen, referring to Al Saqqaff in as casual a manner as he could.

'His eyes are cold, and thirsting for blood,' was Ehab's reply. 'He talks of his love for God, but I saw no love for man in him. He more or less told me he wanted my head. If it had not been for my friends he would have had it too.'

'Then I am glad you are safe,' said Badreldeen to reassure Ehab. 'It seems that man must have good connections.'

'Indeed he does. They treat him as a hero. He is even staying in the home of the Taliban Field Commander. They go everywhere together; Mustafa will not stop talking of Al Saqqaff's many wonderful Jihadist deeds. He seems proud to be in the presence of a man who has struck at Israel.' Ehab drank a copious amount of water from his plastic bottle.

Badreldeen needed to find out where this Mustafa lived; but how could he do that without drawing attention to the fact? He decided to risk a question. 'I expect the Field Commander will live like a king in a fine house?' he ventured.

'No not really,' grinned Ehab, 'he lives in Darpa Khel fifteen miles west of Miran Sharh near the Omar mosque. If you think the Taliban live in fine houses then you don't know the Taliban. It is a modest house,' he added.

Badreldeen held his breath. Had he got it? He could not be sure, but maybe this was as good as he could expect. He decided not to pursue this any further. After eating his meal he withdrew to his cabin to check his many maps of the area and to Google, Darpa Khel into his computer.

****

Birmingham - England

It had taken some time, but this day had finally arrived. Salma saw no other way out; in fact she felt a strange sense of relief knowing it would all soon be over. No more bullying and sexual cruelty from her older overpowering husband, Nasser Mohammed. Ever since the age of fourteen, when her father had taken her on a so called 'holiday' to Pakistan, all she had ever known was unhappiness. Forced to marry a brute of a man, a man as old as her father, a man of revolting habits and a religious extremist, had depressed her very being. She still carried the physical scars from the frequent beatings she had received at the hands of her husband, but it was the mental scars that hurt her the most. Her childhood innocence had been ripped away from her; prevented from having contact with anyone, other than her husband, whom she hated; she had not even been allowed to see her younger sister. They had threatened to send her twelve year-old sister Nina to Pakistan to get married, if she did not follow their wishes. And she knew they would do this. She did not trust Nasser's word, nor that of his friends; she could not believe them, no matter what she did, she believed they would still force her delicate sister to marry. Only when they brought a sworn statement from the Mullah, to say they would honour this agreement, did she acquiesce to their demands.

In his own mind Nasser had been convinced Salma had had an affair. He had convinced himself of this as a fact, even though there was no evidence of such, nor could there be. Her walks to the coffee shop had been no more than to find company and to get out of that house, nothing more than this. No matter what she had said or done, Nasser would never listen to any explanation from her. As far as he was concerned she had brought disgrace onto him and his distant family. Her life had been miserable before, but since her trips to the coffee shop her life had become impossible. She hated living.

The cold hearted Abdu Kamal had been training her, or so they said; and he simply would not let up. Frequently he would tell her the details of his brave, but callous acts for God. He was never physical aggressive toward her, but always verbally so. Constantly shouting, allowing her only limited food and limited sleep; sometimes she was so tired she could hardly stand. Different men took it in turns to keep her awake, day after day. She was ready to agree to anything, just to be free of the mental pain she felt.

These men constantly told her of their brave deeds for God. How God had used them to carry out his aims. How Abdu had been on the helicopter which had bombed Derby and how Nasser had assisted Al Saqqaff many times. They were proud of their deeds and spoke of the brave pilot Ali Farouk, who even though he was now behind bars would still spread their beliefs for them within those walls. They constantly liked to brag of those events in Derby and also the bombings in the football ground of Tottenham Hotspurs in London. Now, they had another source of pride; herself.

Salma was dress as she always was on the few occasions she was allowed outside. She was in her full black burka, with just her eyes showing. It would be more than enough to hide the suicide bomb strapped around her body.

'God will be with you my dear wife,' said Nasser, as the car they were in drove into the multi-story car-park of the Bull-Ring shopping centre in Birmingham. 'Today you will see God and be rewarded as a martyr to his cause. We are so very proud of you.'

They had chosen their venue well. The Bull-Ring is a major commercial area in the centre of England's second city, Birmingham. They well knew that this shopping centre is one of the busiest in the country and always packed with shoppers and tourists alike.

Salma looked out of the window, in a dream like state.

'Remember', instructed Abdu, 'you must go to the most crowded part of the Bull-Ring. Then pray to Allah to strengthen you. Shout his praise, Allah Akbar, before you detonate, so all may know why they are dying.'

Abdu sat with her on the back seat while Nasser drove. All were very tense. Under normal circumstances it would not be Islamic for a man to sit with a woman he was not married to; but this was different. Abdu knew how to arm the bomb and did not want any mistakes. So Nasser had reluctantly agreed to drive while Abdu prepared her special belt full of explosives.

Salma lifted her outer garment so Abdu could arm the bomb; while Nasser continued to drive into the car park.

'There it is ready,' said Abdu. 'Go to those lifts they will take you to the shops. Once you are among the crowds select wherever you want. '

There was silence for a moment. 'There are the lifts,' repeated Abdu, pointing in the direction of the lifts.

Salma looked around carefully. She waited a moment while an old couple parked their car and headed for the lifts.

'Don't wait,' said Nasser, concerned as to why it was she just sat there. 'You know what to do. God will be with you.'

Salma did not reply. She was just glad it was all over as she detonated the device.

****

Birmingham – England

'What the hell are they playing at?' thought Les to himself. 'If this carries on we will soon be having to give twenty-four hour protection to Muslim communities and Islamic centres.'

Yet another bomb had exploded in England, further infuriating the populace; this time it was close to home, too damn close. The Bull-Ring, the main shopping precinct of Birmingham had been struck just two days ago. Once again Les Forrester had witnessed the carnage, such a bomb could cause, only this time, he reasoned, it must have gone off accidently, because it only killed the perpetrators within the vehicle in which they had travelled. There was nothing left of them; they could not even be sure as yet, how many were in the car. As yet he did not know who they were; it would take some time to find this out. The car had been stolen two days before. Yet whoever they were, their remains were just a mash of pulped meat, bone and blood. Even though they had only succeeded in hurting themselves, Les knew the sheer anger and resentment such incidents were causing within the general population, and he was getting concerned, very concerned.

He was glad their bomb had gone off prematurely, because when his mind went back to the Derby atrocity, when he had walked through the hospital to interview casualties there, he dreaded to see such horrors again. He had seen children who were suffering terrible wounds, some with their young legs blown off, and others now permanently blinded. It was heart wrenching to recall.

As though he did not have enough to do with these terror incidents, he had now received this weird Email which told him to await an urgent phone call from Canada. He did not know what to make of it. If it had not been from someone he knew and respected, he would have binned it and carried on with his priority work; which was the tracking down and the apprehending of the support team behind this latest outrage.

The public's angry and restless was fast becoming the country's priority. The media were doing all they could to keep the word Islam out of their headlines, but they could not control Twitter, Facebook and other social media outlets. Cyberspace was alive with accusations, so much so, an internet communication frenzy was developing within the British population as a whole, most of which was directed against Islam and the Muslim community. People who had never been radical or political were now going on-line to vent their fury against radical Islam; many were whipping up the wrath of the common man. Government departments were working overtime to address this tense situation; but no matter how many times they called the culprits 'Asian' or 'unknown assailants' or 'British nationals', the public still referred to them correctly as Islamic terrorists. 'And now,' Les contemplated, 'to add to these troubles there was that inflammatory book which was beginning to add fuel to this fire.'

Les was in a black mood, brooding on these things when his phone rang. Looking at the display screen he saw it was an international call. 'Les Forrester,' he snapped.

'Jacques Gendron here, calling from Canada.'

'What can I do for you Jacques?' he said with a note of tired irritation in his voice.

'I have the location of Adnan Saqqaff.'

'Well for God's sake don't tell me over this phone,' barked Les, almost shouting down the phone.

'Understood; but I'm not sure for how long this information will remain accurate,' replied Jacques.

'I'll call you back. I have a secure military grade encryption phone, I can use that. Then you can tell me what you have,' and with that he immediately hung up; took out his encryption phone and called back. 'Now make your information clear and tell me precisely what you have.'

'I have the grid references for you of his location in Pakistan, along with that of a senior Taliban Field Commander, Mustafa Zahed.' Jacques sounded nervous as he spoke, a little taken aback by the sharp tones of Les.

'How the hell did you get that?' asked Les. Then quickly added, 'No, don't tell me. What am I supposed to do with this information?' he asked.

'Inform the Americans,' was the reply. 'They will know what to do. I suggest you ask them to monitor these coordinates very carefully. As I'm sure they will.'

'Why are you telling me this? My authority does not stretch beyond the borders of this country. Why not go straight to the

Americans yourself?' asked Les. 'This is not in my job description.'

'I do not have a contact with the Americans, not one I could trust with this anyway, and I understood your job description was to get Al Saqqaff, no matter what.' Jacques now snapped back at Les in equal measure. 'I also know how much you want to get that bastard. Here are the grid references. How you deal with this is up to you.' Now it was Jacques turn to have anger in his voice, 'Just remember Superintendent, a man has risked his life to get this information to you, please use it well. Are you ready for these coordinates?'

'Yes, fire away.'

After receiving them Les was a little more conciliatory. 'You are right. Sorry if I snapped at you. We have had another terrorist attack here, I guess I'm a little up tight. Thank you Mister Gendron for this information. I will see to it right away.' Les hung up and waited for a moment or two, looking at the figures he had just written in front of him, he felt an elation he had not felt for a long time. 'This should go through Monroe,' he thought. However things had been strained between him and his boss. He thought for a moment and then picked up the internal phone, 'Pam, get me a car ready to go to the American Embassy. I'll be in London for a few days.'

****

Calgary - Canada

It was now over a year since Jacques had lost his wife in the London bombings. Christmas in Calgary had been a mixed blessings with conflicting feelings for Jacques over the happiness he now felt with Mary, intermingled with the sorrow he went through on the anniversary of his wife's death. Mary's book *'The Expulsion'* had been selling well over the Christmas holiday and now the last few weeks had been frantic for both of them. As soon as the book had been published it sold better than Mary, or her publishers had dared to hope for. Sales in the Muslim world in particular were fast outstripping production. Thousands of copies were selling by the hour. Demand for the book was exceeding the printer's ability to keep the supply flowing.

Now everyone wanted to talk to her. She was in constant demand for interviews, photo shoots, TV appearances, newspapers and magazine articles: these were now daily happenings for Mary. So many from the world's media wished to talk to her that it was difficult to find time to fit them all in. Her agent did his best, but, there was hardly enough time in the day to cover all the venues which were required of her. Political shows on TV debated her findings; questions were raised in the parliaments of Canada and Britain, as well as in the White House of America. It seemed everyone was talking about her book.

Tonight Mary was to be interviewed on the CBC (Canadian Broadcasting Corporation) and Jacques saw how nervous she was, because this was going to go nationwide. Jacques held her hand and gave it a gentle squeeze. 'You will be all right my darling. Just think how proud Bob would be of you.'

'Yes I know,' she said. 'I just hope I don't let him down. This is primetime TV.'

'You won't let Bob down, nor yourself my love. That sharp brain of yours has all the answers you will need.'

'I hope so,' she replied. 'I do hope so.'

Knowing the unforgiving cameras would focus on her appearance she had taken considerable time to get herself ready.

They left together in a chauffeur driven car, provided by the TV network.

Her makeup had been applied, the interviewer had given her a rough programme outline; now she sat on the set waiting for him while he informed the viewers of the background to her book and the effect her book was having worldwide, especially within Muslim cities where demonstrations in support of the book had been taking place on a daily basis.

Finally the presenter turned to her, and after a welcome he asked, 'Are you concerned about the affect your book is having worldwide?' His face was bland and expressionless.

It was not the question she had been told he would start with and was taken aback, 'I haven't had time to think about that too much.' It was not a good answer and she knew it.

'So you are not bothered that your book is causing riots in city after city and people are dying as a result of these demonstrations, or should we call them riots?' It was cutting, and it hurt.

'That is not what I said,' she replied. 'I am not responsible for such reactions to my book.'

'Did you, or did you not write that book?' was the barbed question.

'Yes I did. It took years of research.' Mary was surprised why he seemed to be attacking her, for he had been so friendly before the programme had started.

'So you are therefore responsible for the riots and deaths your book is already causing,' then he raised his voice, 'and is likely to cause many more such deaths.' He did not wait for a reply, but went straight on into the next question without a pause, 'Did you inform, or consult with Israel, before you decided to publish your book; to tell them they have no right to live in their country?'

That was too much; Mary snapped, 'I did not say Israel has no right to live in their country. What I did say was that Israel does not have a *Divine* right to live in their country.'

'Oh that makes a difference does it? Well I put this to you...'

He was not allowed to finish before Mary butted in, 'Israel and most Christians have perpetuated the myth that God led Israel out of captivity in Egypt. Well please examine the facts and not the myth. If you take the time to do this you will see the documentary and archaeological evidence shows the Jews were driven out of Egypt because of their faith. They had a faith in one God, which Egypt found offensive, they even equated them to lepers, and so drove them out. It was not an Exodus, it was as my book shows, an Expulsion. They were hated and not wanted in that country.' Mary was flushed with anger.

'So the story of the Exodus in the Bible is not true?' he sneered.

Mary's very being instinctively told her to beware how she answered this question. 'All my research, along with that of my late colleague, has been to find evidence for these events outside of that of any holy writings. We both researched archaeological and proven historical evidence outside of holy writ, all of which agrees with the Bible in that the Israelites did leave Egypt, but strongly disagrees with the reason they left.'

The interviewer decided to changed tack, 'Is modern Israel the fulfilment of Biblical prophecy; when it says that the Jews will return to Palestine?'

'No, definitely not,' she took a deep breath, 'Christian fundamentalists, in the early 1900's, thought they could speed up Christ's return by manoeuvring events to establish a modern state of Israel. This idea was seized on by Zionists and their supporters, who were more than happy to go along with this idea. Modern Israel is an artificial state concocted by Britain and America. Britain even made an agreement with American Jews that if they would help to bring America into the First World War, then in return Britain would do all it could to give the Jews a homeland in Palestine. This was done and America entered the war; resulting in the defeat of Germany.' Mary was getting carried away, and not thinking too clearly; which is what the interviewer had intended to happen. 'This was one of the reasons that Hitler hated the Jews so much, but you don't read that in your history books!' She saw the look of triumph on the interviewer's face realising she had fallen into his trap; so she added, 'Israel does have a right to exist, but not as a *Divine* right, it is purely a political state and not a religious state. Israel is the result of political decisions taken over one-hundred years ago, and we are still reeling under the affects of those short sighted decisions.'

'Well, thank you Mary, your book sounds fascinating. I am sure our viewers will go out and buy a copy.' The TV programme now showed some of the many demonstrations taking place around the world and slowly superimposed Mary's book over these images.

With that the programme concluded. The interviewer came over and shook her trembling hand. She could not understand why he had such a broad grin on his face. 'I think we can safely say you have sold a lot of copies tonight from this programme. I wish you well.' Still laughing at the startled look on her face, he quickly withdrew leaving her trembling.

'You must expect that my love,' said Jacques, rather proud at the way she had handled herself.

"Was it alright?' she asked, still in a state of nervous exhaustion and unsure of her own ability.

Jacques put his arm around her, 'The presses will be running hot tonight my dear. They tell me this has also gone out on CNN, BBC, Al Jazeera and Sky as well as CDC.'

Mary gripped Jacques hand as they headed out of the building, 'Well we knew it would be controversial, and it's proving to be just that.'

Once outside they climbed into a chauffeur driven Limousine and headed for the airport, 'Next stop London,' said Jacques.

****

London – England

The London Borough of Tower Hamlets, had been allowed to become the home of Muslim extremists over recent years; ever since the British government failed to keep a track on immigration, and deliberately allowed masses of uncontrolled numbers to flow into their land.

Two former Labour party government ministers Jack Straw and David Blunket belatedly both admitted that letting so many people settle in Britain was a 'spectacular mistake' and also that immigration under their government had changed the face of Britain. As a result of such policies many cities and suburbs, like Tower Hamlets, became a haven for extremists. Sometimes these new immigrants were people who had even been driven out of their own homelands because of their radical views. Successive British governments had not only failed to even record who had entered into their country, but later openly admitted they had no idea how many illegal immigrants were now living in Britain. Tower Hamlets was one such place to benefit from this gross negligence, or incompetence or deliberate social engineering of successive poor British governments. It had become a hotbed, a ghetto, for radical Islam.

Former residents of Tower Hamlets lamented how it had become a far cry from its traditional background. Now it had the highest ethnic population in the capital, so that a stranger going there more often than not felt like he was like entering into a city of the Third World. Very few of the indigenous English population now remained there, the native English had left by their thousands, leaving behind a majority of the residents who originate mostly from Bangladesh and Somalia. The reluctance of these new immigrants to integrate, and their self imposed isolation from the rest of Britain, made these alien residents feel they could set up their own laws independently of the British government, and frequently did so. So-much-so, that those same residents openly referred to where they lived as, *'The Islamic Republic of Tower Hamlets'.* They ignored British laws on female equality, female circumcision, homosexuality, animal rights - insisting on meat being killed in a primitive inhumane fashion; and freedom of speech. They frequently took up very un-British stance by threatening to kill any who dared to criticise Islam. They even had posters stuck on lampposts saying *'This area is under Sharia law, women must dress modestly',* and *'This is a Gay free zone. Verily Allah is severe in punishment',* as well as *'No alcohol allowed on these streets.'* Even though the authorities chose to ignore these anti-British statements, the public did not, biting their lips in frustration. This resulted in growing resentment by the native British, which had been festering away for years.

Unable to express their real concerns on this unwanted transformation of their beloved country, seething anger was getting close to the surface. For too long the native British had been unable to speak how they truly felt, for the word 'racialist' would be thrown toward anyone who dared to say this 'alien' invasion was wrong.

Now immigrant residents in areas such as Tower Hamlets regularly and openly shouted and displayed their aims and goals; namely, to bring England under Sharia Law where, stoning for adultery, amputations for theft, death for apostates and second-class status for Christians and Jews, would become the law. Within the public libraries of Tower Hamlets, books which contained a large amount of extremist Islamist literature were common place, yet still the authorities did nothing. Even British councillors in local government offices had been told they should observe the Muslim fast of Ramadan during meetings, a request which had greatly angered several of indigenous councillors.

In perusing such actions these new residents undervalued and underestimated the English people; who had said nothing while their politicians undermined the very nature of their English culture. These immigrants made little or no attempt to integrate with their indigenous host nation. Instead they congregated together, to such an extent that in Tower Hamlets forty seven percent of schools were now exclusively non-English, with seventy-eight percent of primary-school pupils having English as a second language.

It was this mix of disaffected immigrants who now spilled out onto the streets of London. For several days large crowds had gathered as an open display of their support for Mary's book. Today was the day when they burst out of Tower Hamlets, waving placards and shouting their support for this book, *'The Expulsion'*. Several thousand Muslims began a long march across the heart of London, spurred on by their avowed aim to head for the Israeli Embassy, waving their copies of this book which had so inflamed their passion. They were vociferous in their loud denunciations of Israel, America and Britain combined; there was no appeasement, no reasoned argument and no curtailing their pent up aggression toward the country who had taken them in.

Police, hopelessly outnumbered, sent for emergency reinforcements from all over the country. They had at first tried, in vain, to contain this mob, but it was too large. The military was put on standby.

London was not the only city experiencing this, similar actions were occurring throughout Britain and simultaneously all over the world, but especially in those Arab nations who had recently gone through the so-called Arab Spring.

Mary and Jacques had arrived in England to do a lecture tour promoting her book, and to partake in numerous book signings across the country. Now however, they were glued to their television screen in the bedroom of their London hotel. Both agreed it was ironical they should be on such a promotional tour, when the book was selling itself without their help and demand was fast outstripping supply. The scenes they now watched coming in from all the twenty-four hour news channels were disturbing. The common theme of all these demonstrations was for Israel to give up the West Bank, which they had taken from Jordon, along with the Golan Heights they had taken from Syria and Jerusalem itself conquered during the Six Day War of 1967. All of these demonstrations were using Mary's book, as an inciting agent to see Israel vacate the territory she had once taken by force.

'What have I done?' Mary said to Jacques as they gazed out of their hotel window onto the heaving mass of people in the streets below. She saw banners displaying her book, even placards displaying her face, all were being carried aloft. 'I never thought it would come to this,' she said with due concern.

'You are a very popular woman,' said Jacques in an effort to try and cheer her up. 'It is not often Muslims will sing the praise of a woman, let alone a Christian woman. You are making history my love. This has never been seen before. This is something new.'

The chant below became louder, 'Expulsion - Expulsion,' they shouted. 'Jews must be expelled.'

Jacques in an effort to calm Mary's obvious fears said, 'You know it's funny in its own way.'

'What do you mean?' she asked a little annoyed by such a statement.

'Well it must have been a similar kind of hatred which led to the original Expulsion, all those years ago.'

'That's not funny Jacques,' she was transfixed by what they beheld below them. 'Jacques I think we should go home.'

'Can't do that my love. We are contracted to carry this out. If we stop now there would be court cases which could cost us millions and even bankrupt us. We can't risk that. I'm afraid we have to carry on.'

Mary knew Jacques was right of course, but it still did not make it any easier.

As they continued to look down at the throng below them she let out a cry, 'Oh! No! Look at that.' She grabbed hold of Jacques arm tightly. A group of three English youths carrying the national flag of England, waved the blood red cross in the air and shouted their opposition to the rampant mob. Like a coiled spring the mob pounced on them. They quickly ran after the fleeing young men, pulling them to the ground and ripping their national flag apart. Instantly they began punching, kicking and beating them without let up; trampling upon the remains of the English flag. Suddenly knives and meat-cleavers were seen as the frenzied attack reached its awful conclusion.

Mary could not watch. 'It's awful Jacques, they are killing them! Why don't the police do something?'

Jacques looked down as the police tried in vain to reach the youths, but to no avail, the crowd was too strong.

Police reinforcements eventually arrived running toward this incident; as they did so the crowd stepped slowly back revealing the blood soaked lifeless bodies of the three young men. Even though clearly dead their mutilated bodies were still being kicked and further disfigured, until the strong police unit managed to break through. The crowd now began to fragment, not wishing to become caught up in a murder charge. They knew that CCTV cameras would be recording this attack, therefore many of the mob began to run down the back streets away from the mangled bodies.

Mary sobbed uncontrollably; and Jacques was in a state of shock himself. They both retreated from the window and sat down in the chairs of their hotel bedroom. They had difficulty in comprehending what they had just witnessed.

Outside more police had come onto the scene, succeeding in containing various groups as they did. Slowly but surely the police gained strength in numbers, preventing further advancement through the city of London's banking sector.

Mary and Jacques were now holed up in their hotel for the rest of the day. It was twelve more hours before finally the last of the rioters were removed, still protesting, from the streets.

The streets had been cleared; but a tinder-box had been lit!

****

Darpa Khel - Pakistan

Evening prayer time was over and night had fallen. The Taliban Field Commander, Mustafa Zahed and Adnan sat cross legged on the carpeted floor together, in Mustafa's modest house. Two other officers had been invited to join them for dinner and to discuss events elsewhere, during this meal time. Mustafa was pleased to have someone of Adnan's international standing within the world of Jihad, to share his home with him. They had many things in common and spoke at length how Islam would one day soon rule the whole world. It had to happen, they reasoned, for it was God's will. They spoke of a world in which Allah would kill all unbelievers and consign them to the fires of hell. All four men spoke with glowing pride when imagining such a day dawning.

Adnan rapaciously devoured this situation, 'Only true believers will survive God's wrath and that includes many who profess to be Muslim; but we all know they are not really zealous enough to be classed as true believers,' he said with forthright evangelical zeal.

Between the two men they spoke as to how they would clean up their own area; make it free of any who had shown un-Islamic tendencies. Mustafa was still angry at the escape of the villain Ehab Obeid, whose evasion of justice he reflected on with deep regret. He had chastised and disciplined those he held responsible for such a dereliction of duty. Still there were others like Ehab who would soon be facing justice.

When Mustafa and Adnan had walked out together earlier that day, both had enjoyed seeing women scurrying out of their way when they saw them coming toward them. 'These women know their place,' Mustafa had proudly bragged to Adnan. 'It was not always so. Some had to feel the kiss of the whip first, and others were stoned or shot, but we hear little from them nowadays.'

Inside Mustafa's house the four men now waited to be fed their evening meal. It was early night time and two faceless women worked feverously away in the kitchen. Hidden away, for no man other than Mustafa, was allowed to see his heavily clothed women. Let them dare serve a dish of food he was not pleased with and they knew they would feel his wrath.

'Women,' shouted Mustafa across the room toward the kitchen, 'Do not keep my friends waiting any longer.'

There was a shuffle in the kitchen and a wooden serving hatch slid open. A pile of plates stood on the shelf. No one spoke. Mustafa simply looked toward his eleven year-old son who sat by himself crouched up in the corner. The boy jumped up and went across to gather the plates handing one out to each man. The serving hatch slid open again revealing a hot cauldron of food, displayed upon a large metal plate. The hatch quickly was closed again leaving the food on a wooden shelf. The boy rushed over to collect it, but it was too heavy for the boy to lift, so Mustafa lifted it to the centre of the floor around which they all sat on cushions. Mustafa served Adnan himself; an act of respect for an honoured guest. Then each man in turn reached in to the pile of food, with his religiously 'clean' right hand. Only the right hand could be used this way, as the left hand was considered unclean and used only for the toilet. A reason why the right hand was sometimes cut off, as this would prevent the victim from eating in such company. The boy was about to serve himself as the last and lowest of the group, when Mustafa held up his hand, 'No, you must serve our guest first with his water and juice,' he ordered.

The boy moved over towards Adnan to serve him a liquid refreshment, as their honoured guest.

No one heard what happened next.

****

South Waziristan – Pakistan

It was time for Badreldeen to leave Waziristan. He had carried out all of his planned surveys so he intended to return to Islamabad early the next morning. It had been a tiring and stressful time for him, he would not be sorry to leave these wild hills behind; yet he took satisfaction in knowing that he had done what he had set out to do. The seismic tests indicated there may well be oil in this region. He would tell this to Jacques as soon as he returned and had written up his report about his findings.

All his equipment was packed and ready for him to leave. Strolling round the camp site he said goodbye to the soldiers who had escorted him every day. They had been helpful, although most were of limited education, but they had been keen to help wherever they could. The sun had set and the evening payers had been said, when Badreldeen saw Brigadier Husain standing in the doorway of his cabin. He was looking across the compound directly toward him, but did not smile nor offer a greeting. This unnerved Badreldeen a little.

Husain beckoned over two officers who approached him and all three spoke together for some time. This group were constantly looking in Badreldeen's direction. The other soldiers who Badreldeen had been speaking to moments before also saw this and visibly began to back away from him, until soon he realised he was standing on his own. Turning away he headed for his cabin, but before he reached it, the two offices grabbed him firmly by each arm. They pulled him around to face Husain, who glared at him.

'You are under arrest,' declared Husain.

'Why? What for?' demanded Badreldeen, his heart pounding.

Husain did not reply, but just nodded to the others who frog-marched Badreldeen behind Husain, as he strode out ahead of them. They entered the only stone built building in the compound and shut the door behind them.

'What is all this about?' asked Badreldeen, as he was thrust onto a wicker chair in the centre of the room.

'You are under arrest for passing information to the enemy,' barked Husain.

'What! That's crazy,' replied Badreldeen. 'I have been with your men all the time. How could I pass information to those in the North?'

'I did not say you passed information to men in the north. I said you passed information to the enemy,' sneered Husain.

'I don't know what you mean,' he protested; but now realised in Husain's eyes the enemy were not the insurgents in the North, but the West!

Husain stood over Badreldeen looking down on him, 'There was a drone strike last night in the town of Darpa Khel.'

Badreldeen's blood ran cold, as he caught his breath. 'W-what does that have to do with me?' he stammered, feeling the bottom drop out of his stomach.

'Four men were killed, two woman and three children,' hissed Husain. 'American drone strikes have killed many in these hills. We curse the infidels to hell for this. Do you know what it is like to have death suddenly to fall on your friends, with no warning. These were good men who were killed. Men who fight for Allah.'

'That has nothing to do with me,' he protested again.

'Did you not ask me if there were any insurgents from Britain which we had caught?' he pushed his face close to Badreldeen. 'Why did you want to know that?'

Badreldeen gave no answer.

'And did you not ask Ehab where Mustafa Zahed lived, the Taliban Field Commander?' Husain handcuffed Badreldeen's hands behind the wicker chair, and slowly unfastened the leather cover over his field pistol.

'You have this all wrong,' insisted Badreldeen. 'I have done no wrong. I am here to help you.'

'I don't know how you did it,' Husain paused, 'but you did. Now thanks to you Mustafa is dead along with his good friend, the British man, Adnan Al Saqqaff. Well now you can go to hell and account for your sins.'

Husain walked around the back of Badreldeen, pulled his pistol out of its holster and fired one shot into the back of his head.

****

Sheffield - England

The fuse having been lit, now exploded. The British public, incensed by the repeated bombings within their homeland, flowed onto the streets in their thousands. Anti-Muslim protesters surged for a showdown throughout the land. Squadrons of officers in helmets and carrying shields converged on the rioters, but the huge numbers of protesters put up fierce resistance for hours, shoving back at police lines to keep them away from key sites. Protesters had been gathering around the clock to demand the government restrict and ban the many centres, known to be housing radical Islamists.

In better times the earlier Islamic demonstrations, which had accompanied the release of Mary's book, would have been tolerated, even the repeated bombings would not have caused a violent reaction; but the senseless killing of three unarmed English protesters had been the final straw that the public were prepared to tolerate. In city after city, town after town angry crowds swarmed into the city centres. Understandably affronted by repeated events of anti-humanitarian activities from Muslims, the enraged population of Britain had boiled over. Their anger toward the perpetrators of those witnessed violent activities had become the main topic of conversation, both verbally and electronically; wherever people gathered together this was the eminent topic of conversation.

The list of grievances was long and entrenched in the minds of the indigenous British; people felt they were no longer prepared to tolerate such observed violence manifest within the Islamic religious minority. Unofficial leaks had shown how there had been countless numbers of radical Islamic extremists whose earlier deadly plans had been repeatedly foiled by the police before they were able to come to fruition. Within the minds of the public they consciously listed the bombings, the attacks on non-Muslim individuals, the numerous Muslim rape gangs who had hunted and abused English under aged girls for a dozen or more years, the insults to the British soldiers and the symbol of their sacrifice - the poppy. Now they had witnessed the murder, via CCTV cameras, of the three English youths in London, added to which was the recent repeated loud aggression from British Muslims who had earlier been demonstrating on the streets: a violent reaction to all this had now become inevitable.

One of the many planned demonstrations was due to take place two days from now on Saturday, in the city of Sheffield. This was a city which had taken in thousands of Yemeni immigrants over recent years, and the city in which Mary and Jacques now found themselves, whilst endeavouring to carry out their obligation toward the contract which Mary had with her publishers; an obligation to tour Britain. Such a march had been carried out before, but not against this background of rising genuine hatred toward the Muslim population. A feeling of utter revulsion toward these alien immigrants, who had shown so little respect for the culture which had taken them in, was fast becoming rampant amongst the once silent population.

The authorities were understandably uneasy as to whether Mary's lecture should therefore go ahead. Mary and Jacques temporarily found themselves in a state of limbo, reduced to hanging around in their hotel, while awaiting a decision from the police and local government council concerning the planned lectured that night.

Jacques had been idly searching his laptop to see what he could find out about the English Defence League, or EDL as it was often referred to.

'It says here Mary that the English Defence League, or EDL, was formed some years ago, when banner waving Muslims had spat on British soldiers parading through the streets of their own home town as they returned from Afghanistan: and similar protesters had publically burnt the symbol of the British war dead, the red poppy. This was why the EDL had been formed.'

'Not now Jacques,' she rebuked. 'I just want to go home and get out of this dark and dismal city.'

There was a knock at the door, which Jacques opened. Framed in the doorway stood a smart, but rather obese man in a three-piece suit and carrying a briefcase.

'I am sorry to inform you,' he said, making no attempt to enter the room, 'but the local Council and police have found it necessary to cancel your planned lecture here.' He was assertive and not open to any discussion.

'I understand,' said Mary. 'We will make our way back to London tomorrow.'

He gave a thin smile, 'Before you leave, I have been asked to invite you to a press conference in this hotel at midday Friday tomorrow. We do hope you will accept.'

Neither Jacques nor Mary were sure if he really meant what he said.

'Well I don't know about that,' responded Jacques, letting his annoyance show. 'I think we should leave as soon as possible.'

The official looked downcast. 'Please reconsider as I have arranged for the press to be there to hopefully try and bring some calm to this volatile situation.'

Jacques and Mary looked at each other, both knew they had no choice really. 'If we can help, then I suppose we must,' agreed Jacques reluctantly.

'Thank you,' he said still standing at the door. 'We must do something to try and stop this Islamaphobia.'

'Getting them to obey the law of the land might be a help,' mocked Jacques, still peeved with the man.

'Jacques that's not helpful,' scorned Mary. 'I will do this press conference, then leave afterward Friday evening, even if that means travelling to London overnight.'

'I don't want you to do that Mary, you will be too tired. This tour has taken a lot out of you. Let's have restful morning and then leave here on Saturday afternoon.'

The official looked on whimsically and the two had this debate in front of him. 'I'll see you tomorrow then.' He turned and walked away.

It was a setup to which both Mary and Jacques had become familiar with. Both sat side by side in front of around twenty journalists and reporters, some of whom had been following her around the country, reporting on her controversial lecture tour. Mary read her prepared written statement expressing her regret over the cancellation of her planned lecture in Sheffield, and her regrets over the disturbances, some of which had been attributed to her book: she then invited questions from the floor. She knew the questions would be the same as last night's and the night before that; questions such as, 'Was the book written to help the Arabs reclaim Palestine? Will Israel hand back the West Bank? What does Israel have to say about all this?' It was this last frequented question which Mary found the most difficult to answer. In fact Israel had written to her publishers, demanding the book be withdrawn; but it was selling too many copies for that to be considered. It was obvious to them both that Mary was getting very weary of this merry-go-round, and Jacques had become understandably concerned for her, as the strain of all this was beginning to tell on them both.

One man, who Mary had seen before at other lectures but had not spoken, now stood up to ask a question, 'I am Massoud Kalifa, correspondent for the Yemen Times newspaper. I have followed your tour with keen interest. Please tell me if the Jews were not all Hebrews, but mostly Egyptians and therefore had no God-given promise to claim the land of Israel, will you join with the Arabs to demand Israel evacuates the West Bank and return to the borders agreed to by the UN?'

It was yet another barbed question, which Mary had met so many times before. 'My book is historical, looking at historical origins both ancient and modern. I will not take sides, and have no intension to do so. All I seek to do is lay down the historical facts. There is no room for myths, when carrying out historical research. That is what my book is, simply historical research, nothing more. What others seek to make of this is up to them.'

The man had not finished, 'So you are saying the Koran and the Bible are myths and not holy facts, as many believe them to be?'

Jacques, who had been sitting quietly, grabbed hold of the microphone, almost shouting into it, 'That is for the reader to decide, once they have read this work. Now if you will excuse us it has been a long tour.'

Jacques bustled Mary out of the room. Returning to their hotel room, were Jacques took hold of Mary in his arms, she was shaking, 'We need to get you to rest my darling as soon as possible. I am looking forward to returning home to Canada tomorrow. I have told your publisher this strain is too much for you and you need a rest.'

'You are right,' she said, I'm so tired. We were told there are demonstrations planned here in Sheffield tomorrow, we don't want to get caught up in all that so let's just have a full day's rest here, then set off home on Sunday, the day after.'

Jacques smiled, 'Agreed. OK one day's rest and then we head home.'

Later that Friday night the police announced they would not allow the planned march by the EDL to go ahead, but agreed they could hold a public assembly. This restriction added to the already inflamed state within the city; the fact that this march was banned; when many former marches by Muslims had been allowed to carry on, even when one of those marches resulted in the deaths of three young Englishmen. This further added to the anger of the public.

Saturday morning, the day after Mary's latest press conference Mary and Jacques were resting and taking things steady, looking forward to setting off home at last for Canada. A late rise had been enjoyed, after which they had indulged in a full

English breakfast, which both had found to be very filling. Now they could begin to unwind, ready for their long return journey back home. By mid afternoon they decided they should go for a walk. Jacques thought Sheffield was a dower unattractive city but at least they could take some time outside and stretch their legs; both felt they needed some fresh air.

As they approached the outer door of the hotel a man rushed in from outside; he was dishevelled, red faced and panting, 'I'd advise ye not tu go out there mate,' he said looking worried and concerned.

'Why not?' asked Jacques.

'There's trouble on streets. Ant ye seen the news on the TV?' he asked.

'No! Why what is happening?' Jacques then noticed the man's eyes were only half on him and half were fixed to the TV screen situated discreetly to one side of the reception counter, displaying scenes of riots throughout the country.

'It's those bloody mozzies again,' he said barely lifting up his head.

'Mozzies?' questioned Jacques. 'What are mozzies?'

'Muslims,' he replied. 'Always cozing bloody trouble they are; folk have ad enough on em. Now those bastard mozzies have got that bloody book to shout and rave about, look what damage they are cozing. That lot are not happy unless they ave something to shout and rave about. Well it looks like the tables are turning at last. And not before time, I might add.'

'What was the book you were referring to?' asked Mary. Jacques did not speak but squeezed her hand tightly, indicating to Mary not to pursue this.

The man looked her up and down, 'You're not from round ear are you?' he observed with a quizzical look.

'No we're from Canada,' replied Mary.

'Oh!' he said, 'that explains it then. You probably dunna know about that damn book all those mozzies are shouting about. They recon it says the Jews have got to leave Israel.'

Mary and Jacques had an incredulous look on their faces as they turned toward each other. Mary whispered 'Shush', to Jacques and put her finger to her lips.

'Why do you say it is not safe to go outside?' asked Jacques.

'Like I said, yon streets are full of people, tis getting a bit rough ye no. They're attacking the mozzie mosques all ova. We have them here ye no.'

'Yes I did know,' replied Jacques trying to patronise him.

'Some mozzie mosques are only in back street terrace houses, converted from private houses; well they have targeted those first. The talk is they will soon be heading off for the big un, that bleedin big mosque we av ere. I hope they'll burn the bloody thing down if they can. Bloody coppers will try and protect it though. Let it burn if you ask me. Burn the bloody lot down.' He was now in full swing with his belligerence.

'How did all this start?' asked Jacques.

'Oh, it's been brewing for a long time,' he suggested, 'eva since they beheaded that soldier in London, raped our children, butchered those three young lads, then those bleeding bombings. Bloody mozzie child rapists deserve all they are goin tu get. Bloody inhuman they are. I tell you English folk ave ad enough on em. They ill-treat their women shockin, want us to ave their primitive Dark Age laws and won't eva have a drink. I say good luck tu those in London who are also demonstrating now. I'd planned tu catch a train tu go and join em me sen, in Tower Hamlets, but it's got too violent by the look on it. I waz hoping we cud sweep through that place,' he started to walk over to the bar in an adjacent room. 'Fancy a beer?' he asked.

'No thank you, I think we will go to our room and catch up with what is happening on TV.'

'Yeh: you do that pal,' he was just about to walk away when he turned and said, 'I'll tell you another thing they let those bloody mozzies ger away with. Not content with raping our children; ye no they even let em bring ere that drug they all chew. Bring it freely they do into this weak bloody country on ours. I think they call it Khat, or summert like that. It's banned in all of Europe and America, they say it's banned in most counties, but they let those bloody mozzies from Yemen and Somalia sell it in the shops round ere yu no. Openly selling drugs they do and no one bloody bothers. Disgusting! Bloody disgusting, allowing em to sell drugs openly in my own bleeding town. Bloody disgusting; that's what I say. Well they've gor it cuming to em, and not before time,' and with that he disappeared into the hotel bar, still chuntering to himself.

'I think we had better go back to our room and put the TV on,' said Mary.

It did not take long for them to see the picture of what was happening all over Britain. Years of pent up anger and emotion were now being released onto the streets of a dozen British towns and cities. It was no longer simply the Right Wing youth of the country who were protesting, it was all kinds of people, both young and old alike, thousands of them were on the march. Mary and Jacques sat glued to their TV screen. As they watched they saw many old people who had joined the marches, some even walking with the aid of sticks, all were now letting their voices be heard. Voices that for so long had been silenced, due to the imposed stigma of racialism; when the media, almost as one had set out to castigate anyone who voiced opposition to the uncontrolled influx of people: people whose culture was often alien to, and at odds with that of Britain.

Britain had a long history of taking in the oppressed and persecuted from many nations, and they were justly proud of this tradition. Usually though, such refugees had in the main been thankful to be taken in and integrated well into British society;

contributing in a positive way toward British society. However, this was not the case with many of the Muslims who had chosen to live in Britain. It was against these ungrateful and violent immigrants that people now flowed onto the streets, to let their voices be heard.

Starting with the demonstration in Tower Hamlets, all major towns and cities in Britain, including Sheffield, had tens of thousands on the streets attacking anything and anyone connected with Islam. London, Bradford, Birmingham, Leeds, Derby, Halifax, Cardiff and many other towns and cities all had people simultaneously on the streets protesting against Islamic radicalism. This huge backlash had been successfully held back for a long time, but now it had erupted as a reaction to those earlier demonstrations by Muslims in support of Mary's book. Now, in response, the people were telling their politician's enough was enough. Unmitigated violence flared throughout the land.

Jacques and Mary sat dumfounded watching these scenes unfold before them, through their TV screen. One of the many interviews taking place as part of this intensive twenty-four-hour news coverage was of one elderly retired man. They were replaying this interview over and over on several news channels. What he said was poignant and touched a raw nerve with the presenters and viewers alike. The trembling voice of the old man seemed to speak out for many, 'Our British identity is under threat by mass Muslim immigration. Parts of East London such as Tower Hamlets already have an Islamic-fascist mayor with the council giving priority to their fellow Muslim's interests. It's only a matter of time before more cities become full of lawless Muslim ghettos where police and non-Muslims are not welcome.'

Lifting his glasses to wipe his aged running eyes he continued, 'We are sick of being forced to witness things allowed in this country which are against our Christian based culture. The Muslim's insist on eating halal meat, which we all know requires the torture of animals. Their primitive Sharia Law dates back to the Dark Ages. Then there is the child rape and prostitution, female genital mutilation, honour killings, daily bullying and attacks by gangs of Muslims on women and men. It has to stop. It has to stop. When will our Politian's listen to the people who elected them?'

This interview seemed to sum up the mood of the nation.

The riots in Tower Hamlets and the subsequent riots in most major cities were being put out on all major TV channels to the point of saturation.

CNN had run an interview with a Muslim man, who when being questioned about a woman's position in Islamic society and was caught out saying, 'A woman's witness value is half that of a man,' he bragged to the reporter.

To which the reported retorted, 'So the courts will tend, therefore, to take the man's position in a divorce or rape case?'

These interviews added to the popular revulsion now sweeping the nation.

The violence coming across from their TV screen disturbed them both. 'I should never have written that book,' said Mary. 'Instead of writing a book for the masses I should have waited, as Bob was intending to do, and make it a purely an academic research; material for students and professors, but not this.' Mary was quite sad.

'Then it would have been hidden away and the public would be unaware of your findings,' Jacques flailed around to find a way to consol her.

'Would that be such a bad thing?' she asked.

'Mary, remember this; religious deception flourishes where critical thinking is absent. If your book will bring thinking people to discuss these topics, like that old man being interviewed on TV, then it will surely be a good thing.'

Mary's phone rang before she could reply, 'Hello, this is the BBC,' said the caller. 'We would like to interview you about the riots your book is causing throughout the world.'

'You already have interviewed me. I have nothing more to add to what I have already said,' and she hung up.

As soon as she pressed the cancel button on her phone it rang again. 'Hello, this is Sky News,' said the unknown voice. 'Do you have any comments about today's events?'

Jacques took the phone away from Mary and answered it himself, 'Mary is not well and will not be taking any more calls,' and with that he disconnected the caller.

Jacques own mobile phone then rang, by which time Jacques was getting rather annoyed. 'Yes,' he snapped.

'Is that Jacques Gendron?'

'Yes,' he repeated wondering if they should switch both their phones off.

'Les Forrester here.'

Jacques went stony faced. 'What can I do for you Superintendent?'

'I thought you should here this from me, rather than the media,' said Les ominously.

'What is it Superintendent?' said Jacques as Mary's eyes opened wide.

'Adnan Al Saqqaff is dead.'

'Great!' shouted Jacques, with an obvious note of triumph. 'Are you sure?'

There was a moments silence. 'Yes we are sure,' answered Les. 'There have been demonstrations in Pakistan as a result.' There was a prolong silence while Les looked for words. ' also, I am not sure if this is connected, but the body of a man has been left at the entrance to your Company's office in Islamabad. He was wearing your Company logo on his clothes. I can only assume this was one of your people, but I may be wrong.'

'Oh no!' sighed Jacques. 'I think I know who that will be. Do you have a name?' asked Jacques through clenched teeth.

'Nothing definite as yet, but I will keep you informed,' responded Les.

' Thank you superintendent,' and with that he hung up.

With his face drawn and sadness in his eyes, he turned to look at Mary. 'It's bitter sweet news I'm afraid,' seeing her concern. 'The sweet news is that bastard Al Saqqaff is dead; but I fear it may have cost the life of Badreldeen, my contact.'

'Oh Jacques, I'm so sorry,' Mary embraced him in her arms.

'I have been trying to Email Badreldeen several times, and unlike him there has been no answer.'

Mary's phone rang immediately again, Jacques snatched the phone, 'No more calls,' he yelled. 'Mary will not be having any more lectures and no more interviews.'

'This is Jake, Mary's agent. Let me speak to her please.' Jacques put the phone on hands-free so both could hear the conversation.

'Oh! I'm sorry Jake. We have been getting too many calls, and some are very distressing' said Jacques apologetically.

'That's understandable,' replied Jake. 'I suggest you leave Europe immediately and get back here to Calgary as soon as you can.'

'We are both more than ready to get home Jake, but why are you saying this?' said Mary.

'There are threats to your life from Israel. You may have won over the Arabs, with all those street demonstrations, but the "Haredi" the ultra-orthodox Jews are incensed. The Jewish Defence League has threatened to take action against both you and Jacques: better if you get out of there now, and do so quickly.'

Jacques looked at Mary, 'We are on our way Jake, we will be in London later tonight,' and closed the phone, switching it off completely. 'So much for our day of rest,' said Jacques.

****

London - England

It was not long after Jacques and Mary had arrived at their hotel in London, near midnight Saturday, that Jake called again. Mary set her phone to hands-free so Jacques could listen.

Jake was obviously troubled, 'Mary I thought you should know this. The Ha'aretz is an Israeli daily newspaper which has printed your findings, that the Jews were not just Hebrews, but mostly Egyptians and therefore they have no God-given promise to claim the land of Israel. 'Jake's voice trembled, 'As I told you the ultra-orthodox Jews are incensed about all this and now they are demonstrating against you right now. Also the JDL, Jewish Defence League, has said they will take action against you!'

'Now I am frightened,' Mary said nervously.

Jake hesitated for a moment, 'The JDL has stated through this newspaper that, they are an organisation whose stated goal is to protect Jews from anti-Semitism by whatever means necessary and that they will target all enemies of the Jewish people. They could not make this any clearer.'

'We have to do something about this,' said Jacques, startled by this information.

'First you need to get back to Calgary as soon as you can. There is possibly one thing you could do to help ease the situation,' he sounded unsure.

'What's that?' asked Mary.

'Sunday mornings on British TV they have popular current affairs and political programmes, I can get you on one of these, which will be a good opportunity for you to appeal for calm,' was Jake's unconvincing reply.

Mary was silent.

'I have a better idea,' said Jacques. 'I'll do it. You have just said the Jews are now targeting Mary. I don't want to have her further exposed to such extremism. So I'll take it. Get me a TV slot on one of these channels, either here in England or back in Canada.'

'Well, they really want Mary; but I'm glad you said that Jacques because I've already booked a slot on tomorrow morning's show. I rather took the liberty, but I knew you'd want to help if you could. Afraid you won't get much sleep though, you have to be there very early.'

'Thanks for that Jake,' said Jacques sarcastically. 'I don't know who said it, but someone once said, "To have news value is to have a tin can tied to ones tail".'

'That was Lawrence of Arabia,' said Jake.

There was a slight pause and then they all chuckled at the thought; more as a release from the tension, than anything else.

Very early Sunday morning Jacques and Mary readied themselves; both were blurry eyed having only had a couple of hours sleep. In their room the TV was showing the aftermath of the riots, which was still evident from the many scenes of clean-up and extensive damage being regularly reported by the news media.

Jake was good at his job. To get a slot like this at such notice was amazing and the possibility of Mary's appearance of this programme had been announced on Saturday whilst Mary and Jacques were travelling down from Sheffield, and this was even before Jake had told them about the programme. This was a live prime-time TV programme, a popular show which usually concentrated on politics, religion and lifestyle; but the recent riots and discord over Mary's book had made her a sought after participant as the author of *'that'* book. The producers had tried desperately to get Mary to take to this slot herself, but Jacques insisted this was not an option, and that he, as her partner, would stand in for her.

Jacques now sat on the set of the programme awaiting his introduction. There was a small audience already in the studio. He was sweating and tense, feeling correctly that a lot depended on this. Mary sat at the back away from the view of the cameras. The secret intension of the programme's producers, was to ignore the wish of Jacques to carry out this interview on his own; so knowing where Mary sat they would, at the appropriate time, swing the questions and cameras suddenly toward her direction.

The TV presenter started his introduction, 'We have all seen the mayhem around the world caused by the book *The Expulsion*. It has been the cause of demonstrations within the Muslim community here in Britain and throughout the Muslim world; which unfortunately has resulted, not only in many deaths during these demonstrations, but has also resulted in what can only be described as a backlash within our own cities. This book was written by Mary McIntire and we are pleased to welcome her partner Jacques Gendron to our studio this morning. Mister Gendron before we start, I understand there is something you want to say to the nation.'

The tension built up in Jacques. Would he be able to do this? For Mary's sake he had to. 'Thank you for this opportunity,' he began. 'I am here to appeal for calm over what has been a distressing time for us. I ask you all to stand back for a moment, and take stock of the situation. Every nation has its own myths and legends, from Robin Hood to Billy-the-Kid. These are stories which have been told and retold over the years; each time with a new twist, or a new adventure. It has always been this way. However many will say that the stories of Moses and the Exodus were different, they were stories involving God and his divine will. Many accept these stories as just that, of divine origin and therefore unchallengeable. Mary McIntire does not accept that, and neither do I. In her book she set out to show there may be more to this story than we have been led to believe. But what she has found does not change our modern world. Israel exists as a modern democratic independent country. No amount of demonstrations can change that. How it came into being, may not always be a pretty story, but the evolution of every country has periods within its history they would rather not remember. Every country has had periods of hate, violence and war, and ill-treatment of individuals or entire groups, which to the modern mind we would consider disgraceful or even appalling; but nevertheless they took place.'

The interviewer did not attempt to interrupt Jacques or to ask a question, as he continued, 'I appeal to you all to let those who want to live in peace, do so, and those who want violence let them feel the full force of the law. You cannot let your children and families suffer in the way we have seen recently on the streets. Israel has a right to exist, just as do the Palestinians, the British, the French and the Americans. Each has a right to their own established country.'

The presenter could not let this go on, he had been impatient to ask a question, and now did so, 'This is all very well Mister Gendron. However, this book has succeeded in simultaneously upsetting half of the world and yet being heaped with praise by the other half: which in itself is a truly remarkable achievement. Is it not true that the findings in Mary McIntire's book undermine the teachings of the Old Testament and the Torah in that God promised the land of Canaan, or Israel to the Jews?'

'This book shows how the origin of the Jews came after the death of the pharaoh Akhenaten and his son Tutankhamen. At that time those who still believed in the one-god teachings of those pharaohs were hounded and driven out of Egypt, by either the new pharaoh Tutankhamen, or more likely by the then military leaders and the priests. Those fleeing Egypt were led by an Egyptian prince called Moses, taking with them their teachings of one god, which are still with us to this day.'

'All very well Mister Gendron, but why is the author of this book hiding at the back of this room? Why don't we ask her to answer these very important questions for us?'

The lights and cameras suddenly concentrated on a startled Mary. Jacques sought to distract the attention of the presenter, 'Mary's book allows for free thinking individuals to reason for themselves the origins of these stories, and ...'

Jacques did not finish his sentence. There was a crash, shouting and loud noises. Something whistled passed his ear with a thump, hitting the back-drop just behind him. Shouts continued and the presenter looked shocked and decidedly nervous, unsure what he should do. The live coverage of the programme went dead and an earlier pre-recorded programme was hurriedly transmitted instead.

'What the hell,' cried the presenter, as several men tumbled over each other in a brawl in front of him.

Jacques saw someone lunge at Mary. Upon seeing this he leaped from his chair to try and protect her. Everything moved so fast, he had trouble trying to comprehend what was happening. On reaching Mary he saw another man was grappling with Mary's would be assailant. Both were on the floor. People screamed as pandemonium broke loose. Several men were now fighting in two different places within the studio. He could see some were police, striving to contain two or three others who were intent on either escaping or finishing what they had set out to do.

Jacques held Mary tightly in his arms. He looked to the side of her and saw a large dart sticking out of the wooden panel behind her head. He tried to get her away from the men who were still fighting on the floor in front of them. The TV presenter ran off the set, as others now entered the fray. Arm in arm Jacques and Mary just stood back, watching as heavily armed police held three assailants to the ground while others handcuffed them; as they did so they forcefully removed strange looking objects in the assailants hands.

After what seemed like an eternity, securely restrained the three male assailants were bundled out of the studio, away from the numerous staff involved with the programme's delivery. Jacques and Mary just stood there locked in each other's arms and looking around at the scene and the considerable damage sustained to the equipment, computers and cameras.

'That was a close one,' said a familiar voice behind the two of them, who were still in a fearful embrace.

Jacques turned around to see who it was who spoke. 'Superintendent,' he uttered almost inaudibly.

'You had better come with us Miss McIntire and Mister Gendron,' Les Forrester's lean face was expressionless. 'That was a close run thing. They wanted to execute you, live, if you pardon the pun, on national television.' He did not smile at his poor joke.

'Who did?' asked Jacques in shocked reaction.

'That is something we have to find out. But I think we may find they are the Jewish Defence League. Mind you,' he said raising his eyebrows, 'there are plenty of others out there who could be possible culprits.'

Jacques reached out toward the dart behind Mary, 'don't touch that,' snapped Les, 'we will need that as evidence.'

Jacques quickly withdrew his hand from the offending article.

'Now follow me please,' said Les as he strode out of the room carefully avoiding the broken seating, backdrops and cameras.

Later that evening, Superintendent Les Forrester, dressed immaculately in a three-piece suit, held up a plastic bag to Jacques as the two men and Mary sat in the interviewing room. 'This is the dart,' he said. 'Vicious looking thing, is it not.'

Jacques looked intently at the object within this plastic bag. He saw a barbed plastic dart about six inches long, with a broad jagged point and barbs reversing away from the point along the length of the shaft.

'Our labs will have to analyse this to make sure; but I am informed there is also a poison on this nasty thing. They were certainly keen to get you.' Les had little sensitivity about such things.

'How did they fire it,' asked Jacques, 'and how did they get it passed Security?'

Les pulled out another plastic bag holding what looked to be like a miniature cross-bow. 'Everything is made of plastic, so no alarms would be sounded. It was dismantled and the parts were carried in separately, so if found they would not look dangerous. They then surreptitiously assembled the object into what you see here.'

'God! That looks horrible,' exclaimed Mary.

'And just to make sure, it was poisoned. Or so they tell me,' observed Les.

'Who were those men?' asked Jacques, staring in awe at the object which could so easily have killed either, or both of them.

'They worked here as part of the television crew,' Les shrugged his shoulders, 'just happened to be Jewish. We knew you would be a target for someone, so when we heard you were to appear on this programme we closed in. In fact we have kept a close visual on you for some time. I was concerned for your welfare so I've had you followed everywhere, and it's paid off.' Les put away both plastic bags. 'I suggest you go home now back to Canada, where I hope you will be safer.'

'You saved my life,' said Mary. 'You have done your job well.'

'Not only have you saved Mary and myself you have removed that bastard Al Saqqaff,' commented Jacques.

Les opened his eyes wide arching his eyebrows, 'Don't know what you are talking about Mister Gendron. Al Saqqaff is nothing to do with me, I just passed on the information.' Then for the first time that day, Les smiled. 'I suggest you to keep a low profile for a while.' He shook the hands of both of them. 'Time for you to go home, we have all we need from you here.'

'Oh! And,' Les went into a whisper, 'don't forget to look after all that material you are still working on. Make plenty of copies of all that stuff, so that if some are stolen or destroyed you will still have it all in intact.'

Mary stood on tiptoe and embraced him cheek to cheek.

'Thank you we will, said Jacques as they departed.

****

Lake Louise - Canada

In the full bloom of a summer's day the green water of the Lake Louise looked as magnificent as ever. Set against the towering snow capped mountains, conifer forests and blue-white glacier this was an ideal place for a honeymoon. Jacques and Mary walked hand-in-hand together along the pathways climbing above the main lake to take in the lesser, well hidden lakes high above.

'I told you, you would love this place,' said Jacques.

'Yes, it's magnificent,' she agreed. 'I love you so much. I am so happy we met.'

After walking a little further, it was obvious something was on Mary's mind, 'We must follow the advice of the Superintendent and lay low for a year or more. It's important.'

'Yes of course we will my love. I have promised you that.' They stopped to admire the view again, then decided to sit down on a well placed rock to eat their lunch, whilst looking down on the beautiful scenery below them.

'It really is exciting though isn't it my love,' said Mary, with a cheeky grin on her face.

Jacques knew what she was referring to, but only responded by saying, 'Indeed it is.'

But Mary simply could not contain herself, 'I knew references to Israel would be in there somewhere, we just needed that computer which helped us to locate them.'

Mary was referring to how some of the many fragments of stone work, photographed and copied onto their computers had finally been successful in matching some of those many fragmented pieces together. Now they had found parts of tablets and stones, which, when pieced together, could now be read. Years of hard work by Bob and herself had finally managed to identify another source of genuine historical references to Israel; inscriptions which told how those people had indeed been driven out of ancient Egypt because of their faith in one God, and their refusal to worship the many gods of ancient Egypt.

'It was a mammoth jigsaw,' she acknowledged. 'We would never have been able to see the full picture until we found those matching pieces. It confirmed what Bob had said all along,' Mary was visibly excited by her thoughts.

'I must say,' added Jacques, 'I did have my doubts that you would ever find what you were looking for; but it was amazing to see just how those damaged stones could be pieced together electronically with the aid of those powerful university computers. It has certainly revealed long lost references to ancient Israel. And it has silenced those who criticised your book.'

'I am sure we have more of them as well, we just need to continue our search more,' Mary could not leave her work behind. Her mind was ever active on this project.

'Mary we are on honeymoon. Let that wait for now.' Jacques pulled her toward him in an embrace.

****

AUTHOR'S NOTE

The reader may be interested to note that there are many elements within Christianity today, the origins of which can be traced with relative ease to the religion of ancient Egypt. I hope this novel has whetted your appetite and shown to you how monotheism was first followed in ancient Egypt; even the possible origins of the word *'Amen'*; the depictions of 'mother and child' as a form of worship and the cruel death and resurrection of a 'god'. This may, or may not surprise you, but the evidence is there, if only you will look for it.

With a little research you will also find the following acts of devotion or beliefs can all be traced back to the same source in ancient Egypt. Such as: - the cross as a religious symbol - Winged angels - The Last Judgement - Resurrection to a better life - The priesthood - The impregnation of a woman by a god or divine being, with the child therefore becoming a 'son-of-god' - The shepherd's crook as a religious symbol - The secret and unspoken name of god - Holy water - Mother of God, or Mother of Heaven - The halo and Tithing. Added to which are the stories of creation in Genesis, and Cane and Able. Sadly though, the inherent violence, which has been endemic within monotheist religions is still with us to this day.

So, enjoy your research and remember this old Egyptian text, which said:-

'There is no God but Aten and Akhenaten is his prophet.'

Now read Mike Kelley's other books.

'My Shadow on the Clouds'

Order from Lulu - http://www.lulu.com/

This is an amazing account by Mike Kelley's of his life as a British expatriate for more than twenty-seven years.

He lived and worked in Libya, Bahrain, The Emirates, Yemen and Sudan. Got caught up in the First Gulf War and the civil wars of both Yemen and Sudan. He was at a gas plant when it exploded, held captive by Al Qaeda in Yemen. Was evacuated by the French Foreign Legion. He saw beauty and horror and met with Radical Islamists as well as Imam preachers of peace.

Here you will find tears and laughter and a first-hand account of world events.

ALSO:

'The Fall of Saxon England'.

England was never to be the same again after this eventful year.

Here is a powerful story, where you can feel the tension, live the actions and be amazed at the intrigue. This story covers just one tumultuous year, from Christmas Day 1065 to Christmas Day 1066. You will meet the heroes who stood against overwhelming odds to protect their families, and the traitors who sold their country for a price.

What was it like to stand behind an English shield-wall on foot, against charging cavalry?

What was it like to see 10,000 Vikings sack Scarborough?

What was it like to be at the battles of Fulford, Stamford Bridge and Hastings?

What was it like to see the rape of your beloved country?

This is a book you will never forget; all based on real events

Write to the author of these books at - mgkelley@hotmail.com